"Altogether a satisfying book...provocative and engaging..."
~ THE NEW TIMES, Seattle, Washington

"A new window on the much neglected invisible dimensions
of our humanity. Great reading!"
~ Wayne W. Dyer

"Invites us to look beyond the surface...to find the mystical
connection among us all."
~ AHP PERSPECTIVE

"You'll like the people, you'll enjoy the journey, and most
of all you'll want to find a place just like it for yourself."
~ NAPRA REVIEW

"Shows power of meditation...spiritual and
ethical beliefs provide a vision of oneness with nature."
~ THE DALLAS MORNING NEWS

"Fascinating account of how we each
create our own experience of life."
~ Shakti Gawain

"...realizes Earth as a finite, living thing with a spirit..."
~ SAN FRANCISCO CHRONICLE

"...helps capture the spirit of a particular animal in your
mind and gives you a new way of looking at things."
~ THE WALL STREET JOURNAL

"...compassion and wisdom born of experience and humility."
~ Julia Cameron

"Practical and spiritual information woven together
in an easy flow...a pleasure to read."
~ MAGICAL BLEND Magazine

"...communicates with experience, honesty, and a genuine concern
for the reader..you'll find this book both helpful and appealing."
~ INTUITION Magazine

Other Books by The Author

White Mountain Blues*

Write From the Heart: Unleashing the Power
of Your Creativity

Follow Your Bliss,* with Susan J. Sparrow

Zuni Fetishes: Using Native American Objects
For Meditation, Reflection & Insight

Invitation to Success: An Allegory About Creativity*

Spirit Guides: What They Are, How to Meet Them,
and How to Use Them In Every Area of Your Life*

The Lens of Perception

Mind Jogger (Divination System)

The Well Body Book (out of print)

* All starred titles published by TENACITY PRESS

Spirit Circle

a story of adventure & shamanic revelation

by

Hal Zina Bennett

TENACITY PRESS

Copyright © 1998 by Hal Zina Bennett

TENACITY PRESS
1-800-738-6721

ISBN 0-9656056-3-9
CIP 98-67603

Cover photo by Susan J. Sparrow
Cover design by Angela Werneke
Prepress for cover by ChromaGraphics
Interior design by Patchwork Press

Special Editorial Support by
THE BOOKWORKS
Del Mar, California
(619)481-6048

Printed by GILLILAND PRINTING
215 North Summit
Arkansas City, Kansas 67005
1-800-332-8200

1 2 3 4 5 6 7 8 9

ACKNOWLEDGEMENTS

No book is possible without the help of many unsung heros and heroines.

Thanks to Susan, my loving soul-mate and partner in life, whose quiet genius births so much but takes so little credit. She stuck with me through rewrite after rewrite, ten in all, reading every word and providing the constant support that makes it all possible. In addition, she provided the wonderful photograph for the cover, taken in New Mexico, August 1997.

Thanks also to my many pre-publication readers, Alexandra Hart, Vic Walter, Leeya Nora Thompson, Linda Loos, Kate Ludeman, John Nelson, Angela Werneke, and Frank Mansfield. Your suggestions and encouragement along the way were invaluable.

Thanks, too, to two very special people, Gayle Seminara and Howard Mandel, of TRANSITIONS BOOKPLACE, in Chicago, who have given us and so many other authors, healers, and practitioners, a platform to present our ideas and our books.

~ Hal Zina Bennett, 1998

Dedicated to the Spirit of
Trickster Rabbit, whose teachings
of the invisible were the
first to penetrate the shadow
of my arrogance.

I still listen.

CONTENTS

Awakening brings its own assignments,
unique to each of us, chosen by each of us.
Whatever you may think about yourself
and however long you may have thought
it, you are not just you. You are a
seed, a silent promise.

~ Marilyn Ferguson

Ancient Prophecies

Professor Tara Fairfield found the envelope on her desk when she returned to her office with lunch from the Chinese deli. Eying the red, white and blue mailer, she sat down, opened her take-out carton and inhaled the earthy aromas of her shrimp fried rice. With chopsticks she tweezered a single pink shrimp from the box and popped it into her mouth. In an instant the sweet juices of the fleshy crustacean oozed over her tongue. She was famished.

The address on the envelope was face down against the desk blotter. Tara turned it over and stared at the careless scrawl. A tangle of old feelings knotted in her belly. The writing was her father's, Drake Fairfield. The postmark was Gallup, New Mexico. But this could not be. Drake had disappeared over two years before. The last she'd heard from him had been a postcard from Charla Mather's gallery in Albuquerque. No one had heard from him since then, not even the tabloids for whom he'd been writing for more than twenty-five years. For all intents and purposes, he had disappeared from the face of the earth.

The envelope bulged at one end. Tara jammed her chopsticks into the rice, leaving them protruding from the carton like two pale leafless stalks. Taking the envelope in two hands, she shook it gently. Stones or broken bits of clay rattled inside.

Once more she studied the address label. There could be no doubt about it. She would recognize that careless scrawl anywhere. It was Drake's all right. But this was impossible! Surely if he was alive he would have contacted her during the past twenty six months. It was not unusual for him to disappear for two to three months at a time when he was on assignment...but never this long. There could be other explanations, of course. This envelope might have been lost, perhaps in some cheap motel in the back country of New Mexico or Arizona. Then, finally, after all these months some Good

Samaritan had found it and mailed it. What else could explain it? Surely if he'd been hospitalized, in an accident, maybe suffering from amnesia, he would have contacted her by phone when he came out of it, not with something as anonymous and impersonal as this envelope.

From the top drawer of her desk she removed a pair of scissors with orange plastic handles, to which was attached an oversized artifact tag that read: "*Orangum Scissorum. Circa, late 20th c. Return to Fairfield collection.*" She had discovered that a little imagination and humor helped to keep her office partners from permanently borrowing her things. In her six years at the university she learned that anthropologists had better things to think about than who loaned you the scissors or the stapler or that bottle of aspirin.

Tara neatly severed the top of the envelope, reached inside and slipped out a second envelope labeled, "Photos. Don't Bend or Fold." *Too late for that,* she noted, seeing that whatever made the lump in the package had also creased the photos. She upended the mailer and spilled its contents onto the top of her desk. Two clay potsherds tumbled out, along with a single bone.

She picked up the potsherds first. Judging from the condition of the clay, they had to be at least 1,500 years old. The curvature of the fragments told her they had come from a large pot, with a capacity of at least three liters. The decorations were too elaborate for a utilitarian vessel. She felt her hands tingle as she held them, the way they always did with certain ancient artifacts. It was all imaginative, she told herself, these tantalizing sensations that she felt when she found important pieces from the past. Her entire body vibrated with excitement with the prospect that these small bits of clay connected her in some mysterious way with people who lived long ago. There were few things in the world that fascinated her more than touching life in the distant past. It was almost enough to make her put her questions about her father out of her mind.

Tara pressed the two potsherds together, noting a place where their edges interlocked perfectly, establishing them as segments of a contiguous design. She studied the potsherd in her right hand. The image preserved in the clay was a portion of a bird's wing and the edge of what had probably been a sharp beak, characteristic of birds of prey. Because the pieces were incomplete, it was difficult to determine what kind of bird the artisan had intended--owl, hawk or eagle.

Even though the profile was only partial, she decided the portion of the beak that she could see suggested an owl. She was well aware that the ancient cultures of the area around Gallup associated the owl with sorcery and magical powers. Legends taught that these birds were envoys between the world of the living and the spirits of the dead.

The design on the second potsherd had a slightly raised portion, like a *bas-relief,* forming the edge of a female breast. Downward-pointing chevrons painted across it, represented feathers. Tara knew the designs of the ancient Southwestern cultures very well. An expert on these societies, she had spent hundreds of hours studying the decorative techniques of different tribes. She mentally reviewed thousands of designs she'd studied over the years and could not find a single one that matched this sample. Not even close!

She tried to imagine the intact pot and how this mysterious effigy, part woman and part bird, might have originally looked. It was a clear reference to hermetic themes, a shape shifter symbol, with the figure being halfway between two species. Though she knew it was impossible, the only comparable image that immediately came to mind was the Egyptian Thoth. But the Thoth was always portrayed as having the body of a man and the head of an ibis. Creatures of this kind--part human and part animal--were associated with the ability to see beyond everyday reality. Found throughout the world, they were symbols of special powers, largely the ability to transcend limits of the physical world for purposes ranging from divination and healing to cheating death itself.

Not that Tara believed in the mythology such pieces represented! But as she held the two artifacts, neither of them larger than a playing card, her hands trembled, however slightly, conveying her excitement about their anthropological significance. There was no doubt in her mind that these two fragments could be the most important find of her career. If there were more pieces where these had come from, she might be able to prove a theory she'd proposed for over ten years--that there was a secret society of shamans in the Southwest who served a function comparable to the Oracle at Delphi, in ancient Greece. Like Pythia at the temple of Apollo, these medicine people foretold the future and interpreted the past. They could reveal secrets of a culture long buried.

She didn't remember when she'd first gotten the idea for seeking this secret society. But it had been long ago, perhaps in childhood. History was filled with tales of lost civilizations, but they were pure mythology. Ever since she was a young student losing herself in the libraries on the university campus near her home, she'd spent endless hours searching for evidence of these extraordinary shamans. It was odd, she sometimes mused, how something you'd read or heard someone say could become your passion, your life's mission, though you might not even recall the original source. As ludicrous as it might seem, the dream of one day finding this esoteric society had gotten Tara through three grueling years of graduate school. How ironic, she mused, that her father, whose very existence she'd often denied, would supply her with the breakthrough clues she had sought in the archives of the world's greatest universities.

Drake had known of her interest in this secret society of shamans. Perhaps he had found these artifacts just before his disappearance and had wanted her to have them. He could have left them somewhere, with a friend perhaps, maybe with Charla Mather in Albuquerque, maybe with his friend Chocko, in Zuni. She doubted very much that Drake himself had mailed the envelope. He had addressed it. There was no doubt of that but anyone could have mailed it. You heard about that sort of thing all the time, of letters delivered even a hundred years later because they'd been lost in an old piece of furniture, or in a desk drawer.

Her attention turned back to the potsherds, entranced by the image on their worn surfaces. These could easily constitute a breakthrough in her work. What strange twist of fate had delayed their delivery all this time? As she held the ancient pieces, her hand literally trembled with excitement. It was as if a ghostly hand had reached across the ages, inviting her into this secret society of shaman-priests.

Legends that many scholars said were only empty rumors suggested there had been a group of such people, both men and women, who communicated with the forces of nature and performed miracles rivaling those of any saint. But the more Tara discovered, the more the mystery deepened. Why was there such scant evidence of an oracle on the North American continent, one that was comparable to the Oracle at Delphi? And why would no one in her profession even discuss this fact? Everywhere else in the world, oracles had determined the fate of whole nations. It was impossible to think that there wasn't a similar tradition on this continent. The only feasible explanation was that the oracle took the form of a society of shamans, that is, medicine people sequestered in a small, secret mountain retreat. There were hundreds of small, unexplored sites throughout the Southwest, sites considered too small and *archaeologically insignificant* to deserve a study grant from any of the large universities. Any one of these could hold the secrets Tara was seeking, and all of them could remain unexplored forever, given the way funding worked these days.

To be the one to bring this society of shaman-priests to light could truly make Tara's name. Fame, however, was not all that drove her quest. As a child she heard that shamans possessed magical powers. They knew how to control invisible forces, to cause lightning, bring rains, cause volcanoes to erupt. They could disappear before your eyes or induce a trance in which you could dream about your own future. During her investigations she had seen shamanic feats no one could explain, such as stones the size of softballs rising in the air and flying around the room, and ceremonial rattles that shook themselves as they hovered overhead. She'd even met a healer, a woman in her eighties, who physicians from a nearby hospital called when there were birth complications. She could turn breech babies in the womb simply by placing her hands gently on the mother's belly and massaging lightly.

Every legend Tara heard about ancient shamans and lost villages triggered her passion. Whenever she heard stories about the City of the Mists, the Seven Cities of Cibola, or secret *kivas*, Tara's ears always perked up. Any mention of mythological people or places could be the clue she'd been seeking all her life. And now these potsherds arrive!

At last Tara picked up the bone. It was about an inch and a half long and as big around as a pen. Quite definitely human, its configurations established it as the middle joint of the index finger from a fairly large hand. She examined the sun bleached white surface of the bone with a magnifying glass. Still smooth, with minimal decalcification, it couldn't be very old. Numerous scratches indicated that small rodents had stripped the flesh from it.

She held it in her hand as she often held other artifacts. But what she felt wasn't the tingling she experienced with an archaeological revelation. Far from it! What filled her imagination, she was certain, would hold more interest for a criminologist than an anthropologist. Her mind filled with the ghastly imagery of a huge bird whose shrieks were more like that of a modern machine than a thing of nature. The caustic impressions of violence and human depravity it exhibited sent a shudder through her entire body. Were these images clues telling her of her father's fate? She set the bone back on her desk and returned both scissors and magnifying glass to the top drawer. Staring at the bone, she wondered if it could even be from her father's hand. Her mind recoiled at the possibility.

Was it possible that this package from Drake was nothing more than a dark joke? He had certainly been capable of that, of sending her artifacts from other countries, teasing her with the possibility that they were from New Mexico. He was an expert at weaving hoaxes. That, after all, had been his business, writing stories about space creatures and babies born with animal heads, for the supermarket tabloids. He was shameless, yet a skilled writer with one of the wildest imaginations in the world. Moreover, he seemed to enjoy teasing Tara about her own work. "Life is too short to take yourself

so seriously," he'd often said.

For a moment, she was overcome by a mixture of feelings, resentment, relief, elation and bitterness. It was possible, she speculated, that this envelope of arcane objects, along with Drake's two-year absence, were part of a cheap tabloid hoax her father was creating. She would never have imagined that he would go this far, causing his family to worry themselves half-sick for all this time, even allow them to mourn his death, just to fabricate such a sham. *But damnit, he would!* This could be his crowning glory, his swan song in a much checkered career.

She turned the potsherds over in her hands again and again. She was certain they weren't fake, and she was certain they were from the Southwest. She had spent enough time looking at artifacts from New Mexico and Arizona to recognize the clay found in that region.

The decorations on these potsherds were not typical of these areas however. Fifteen hundred years ago, the peoples living there rarely decorated their pottery with representational figures. Their embellishments were usually abstract, symbolizing waves of energy or movement, such as the jagged surge of lightning across the sky or the gentle waves of a river through a canyon, or the undulations of a snake across the dry desert floor. These movements were considered by the Indians to be spirits of Nature, symbols that were integral to their religion. The zigzag and wavy designs in their pottery paid homage to these spirits and, like prayers, sought their spirits' support and goodwill.

The bitter irony was that Drake had somehow stumbled upon these fragments, and probably the bone, during his search for a cheap tabloid story. Just a little over two years ago, he had dropped by her office as she was laying out some old photographs of petroglyphs that she had just received from the Smithsonian. They were of cave art recorded by the U.S. Bureau of Ethnology from an expedition organized by General John Wesley Powell in the mid-1800s to document the indigenous cultures which were fast being wiped out by the Western movement of European settlers.

Drake had leaned over her shoulder, examining the photos, and had suddenly thrust out a finger, pointing to what Tara knew was a classic drawing of a shaman wearing a moon mask.

"That looks like a spaceman," Drake had said, making a circle with his finger around the head of the figure.

"Dad," Tara chided, "Please don't start with that stuff."

"I'm serious," he said. "It looks like he's wearing a space suit, you can see that!"

"It's a mask and ceremonial costume," Tara tried to explain. "It dates back about 1,500 years, way before space travel."

"Sure, sure," he exclaimed. "But what a great story it could make. Think about it. You put this beside a photo of a modern spacesuit, with a big caption, 'New Evidence of Early Space Travel.'"

"Oh, lord! Just leave it alone, would you?"

"Honey, hey! These things are just in fun. No harm done. Who takes any of this stuff seriously anyhow?"

"I do, Dad. Your little hoaxes make it very difficult for legitimate researchers like me to establish credibility."

"We're all just storytellers," he argued. "We're all just telling each other a bunch of lies to pass the time."

She'd turned away from him, stifling an urge that came from deep in her gut, to punch him in the face. Not just to slap his face for the insult to her profession but to punch him in the mouth, to shut him up so that he would never utter such outrages again. She could never quite decide if he was an outwardly abusive man or if he was just cloddish and insensitive.

She knew her father didn't believe the stories he concocted for the tabloids. He cared about only one thing: Did it make a good story? He loved going to New Mexico, especially to Roswell, where he found an endless supply of the most preposterous claims about space aliens. Each story he came up with was even more improbable than the one before. Once, when she attacked him for his absurd involvement with space aliens, he told her he was doing it for her. She was furious. But he stood his ground, saying that someday she would understand his motives.

"Don't ever say you did those things for me," she'd chastised. "Don't you dare."

Tara reached for the carton of Chinese food and took a tentative bite. The food was cold now and her appetite was gone. She set what was left of her lunch, along with chopsticks, into the waste basket beside her desk. She folded her father's envelope in half and dropped it in the basket, too. Then she placed the potsherds and the bone off to the right of her desk and opened the second envelope, marked "Photos."

A sheet of paper slipped from the envelope. It was an undated note in Drake's hand, scrawled on motel stationery--The Gallup Inn. The note urged Tara to come to Charla's retreat out at Coyote Mesa, just south of Gallup, New Mexico. She was to call Charla's gallery in Albuquerque. Drake would leave a message at the desk. Obviously, Tara reflected, Drake fully expected her to respond to his invitation! But when had he written this? It could have been days ago or two years, for all she knew.

Tara quickly reached for the phone and dialed the number for the gallery. The phone rang several times, then an answering machine clicked on, telling her that it was Monday morning, and the gallery would be closed until Tuesday at noon. Patrons were asked to call back. Tara broke the connection and called information to get Charla Mather's home phone, which she immediately dialed. After four rings there was a pause and then the call was forwarded to the gallery answering machine. Frustrated, Tara set the phone on its cradle and turned her attention back to the objects on her desk.

From the envelope that had come inside the red, white and blue mailer, Tara slipped out an 8" x 10" black and white print and two color snapshots from a processing lab in Albuquerque. Again she searched the backs of the photos as well as the photo lab envelope for a date, finding nothing. She studied the first color photo; it showed three tall rock spires rising from a deep canyon floor. The three spires looked for all the world like ancient sentries carved in red rock, guarding she knew not what. Someone had used a ballpoint pen to draw a stick figure of a man beside them, apparently to note the scale of the spires. On that basis, Tara estimated each rock sentry was over a hundred feet tall!

On the back of this photo was an odd sketch of a figure that resembled a crippled old man leaning on a cane, his back bent in an awkward arch. Tara guessed it was intended to represent Kokopeli, the legendary flute player of Hopi, Zuni and Navajo mythology. Drawn off to the side of this figure was a crudely-rendered map. The map-maker had apparently used a cheap ballpoint pen that skipped in several places, etching the paper instead of leaving a clear blue mark. An arrow pointed toward Gallup, orienting the reader to the Northern quadrant and the town 120 miles West of Albuquerque on Interstate 40. Tara knew the area well.

The second color snapshot alarmed her. A scattering of bones lay in a rocky niche, protected from the sky above. Most puzzling of all, there appeared to be some sort of junk scattered around them, something that looked like mangled aluminum deck chairs or maybe a hang-glider. Tara immediately wondered if this was the site of her father's demise. Were these his bones? But that didn't make sense. If they were his bones, who had mailed the envelope?

The third photo, the large black and white print, appeared to have been shot from a great elevation. It was as if the photographer was attempting to show something at the bottom of the canyon. If there was something important to be seen, Tara could not make it out. She saw the tops of the three rock sentries depicted in the snapshot, along with a few rocks or boulders that might indicate the lines of an ancient trail. But their significance, if any, was not clear.

Tara hurriedly glanced over the photos, establishing that they had all been taken in and around the same site. She reached for her

Rolodex and flipped through the cards until she located her father's cell phone number, a number she hadn't even thought about for months. Finding it quickly she dialed for an outside line and then punched in the number. The line rang a dozen times. No answer. At least it was still in service, though she was well aware that after all this time it probably would have been reassigned. Only if Drake was still alive, hiding away somewhere as he perpetuated this gigantic hoax, could he possibly answer her call and tell her what was going on. She set the phone back on the hook.

*   *   *

Downstairs, in what students referred to as the "catacombs" of the anthropology department, Tara roamed through the labyrinthian aisles of steel racks holding tons of cataloged and uncatalogued artifacts. Fragments of pots, cardboard boxes filled to overflowing with bones, and piles of squared off rocks from ancient buildings threatened to spill from the curious disarray.

In a far corner of the sprawling basement room, Tara found Dr. Poynter at a workbench, sitting on a metal stool and peering through a six-inch magnifying glass at a fragile-looking chunk of painted wood, about the size of a common brick. On the floor beside his chair an electric heater glowed, and within it a small, noisy fan struggled to drive away the dampness of the moldy room.

"Dr. Poynter," Tara called out, not wanting to startle the professor.

Poynter looked up, squinting at her over the top of his tortoise shell reading glasses. "Yes, Dr. Fairfield," he answered coldly, turning back almost immediately to his examination of the painted wood. "What brings you down here?"

"I'm wondering if you'd take a look at something," she said, coming up to his side and holding up the potsherds, one in each hand. "What do you make of these?"

Tara didn't particularly like Poynter and guessed that the feeling was probably mutual. But he was one of the few people in the department who didn't think her theories about the society of shamans were a complete waste of time. He, too, believed it odd that there had never been any research done on pre-Columbian oracles on the North American continent. He at least shared her belief that shamanistic religions had existed on the American continent as far back as 7,000 years, predating even the Aboriginal cultures of Australia.

Poynter turned his head away from his work long enough to glance at the two clay fragments in her hand. "Where'd you get those?" he asked, his voice raspy and carefully controlled.

"Someone sent them from New Mexico. Do they look familiar?"

She did not want to tell him how they had come into her possession.

Poynter glanced at the potsherds, then plucked them from her hands. "Unusual pieces," he drawled, subjecting them to his magnifying glass. "They're very old."

Tara sensed Poynter's excitement. "How old?"

"I can't be sure. We need to carbon date them. But I'd say at least 500 B.C. Can you verify their source?"

"I'm going to try. I think they're from down around Gallup."

"Could be, maybe further south, maybe brought up from Mexico. I'd have to do some assays on the type of clay to tell you for sure. Unusual designs, though."

"Part human, part bird."

"Shalako."

"What?"

"You know, one of the Shalako. Zuni mythology. Bird monsters. Warrior chiefs of the Pautiwa."

Tara remembered the legends about the monster human birds who visited the village of Zuni, represented by costumes and masks more than twelve feet high.

"But look at the beak," Tara said, pointing to the edge of the first fragment. "It's long and straight...downward pointing."

Poynter looked more closely at the potsherd, showing genuine interest. "Uhunh! Interesting. You can't be certain. Part of it is missing. But if it was an eagle or hawk, you know, it would be wider where it joins the skull. Otherwise, you'd have an owl here, and that wouldn't be consistent unless you have stumbled upon a *nest of sorcerers...*" Poynter looked up, eyebrows raised, a silly half-grin on his thin lips, signaling Tara that he'd just made a deliberate pun.

She smiled back. "Good one," she said, acknowledging his dry humor. "What do we actually know about the witchcraft of that region?"

"That far back? Not much. Not much."

"Any guesses? Were they into black magic, casting spells, that sort of thing?"

Poynter got a look of disgust on his face. "You *are* joking, I hope?"

Tara shrugged.

"Dr. Fairfield," Poynter said. "You know as well as I that reports of witchcraft among these cultures are mostly the fabrications of European missionaries whose chauvinism has been responsible for the decimation of important artifacts that we will never recover. What they called black magic and witchcraft was perhaps nothing more than the indigenous people's worship of the natural forces. They are animists, after all."

"Yes, I'm aware of that. But the owl..."

"A messenger, that's all," Poynter concluded. "Nothing so dark about it except that it was believed to speak to the dead." He paused, becoming thoughtful. "You've seen the *New York Times* this morning?"

"No."

Poynter reached under his work table and produced a dogeared copy of the paper, which he handed to Tara. There on the front page was a panel illustrating petroglyphs from the Mojave desert. A headline under the panel read, '*Desert Reveals Old-Time Religion. Mojave Caves Provided Canvas for Shamanistic Art.*'

Tara quickly scanned the report. Several familiar names popped out at her. "Those bastards!" she said.

Poynter took the paper from her hand, adjusted his glasses and started reading aloud: "'Leading archaeologists have found evidence for what appears to be the oldest, continuously practiced religion. From the last ice age to early in the 20th century, indigenous peoples of the desert have practiced a religion in which shamans entered trance states to commune with the spirit realm and seek counsel for the people. Estimates are that this practice is 12,000 years old.'" He stopped. "Want to hear more?"

Tara nodded, though she churned inside. These revelations echoed what she had been saying for years--that one day there would be evidence to show that the shamanic traditions on this continent predated both Christianity and Judaism by at least 2,000 years.

Poynter resumed his reading: "'David Black, an expert on petroglyphs, says these peoples had a rich and complex mental and spiritual system.'"

"I can't stand it," Tara exclaimed. "David Black let them crucify me at the Southwest Society of Archaeology three years ago. He didn't even open his mouth to defend me. He knew I was onto something. He knew I was!" She took a deep breath. "Those sonovabitches..."

"All's fair in love and war," Poynter crooned. He shook the paper noisily, then resumed: "'John Lawrence, anthropologist and scholar of rock art at New Mexico State University, verifies Black's findings and states that shamanistic religions can be found as far back in human history as 25,000 years. These belief systems have influenced the development of virtually every major religion that we know today. Many indigenous peoples still practice these beliefs today...'"

"Enough," Tara said. "I'll read the rest later. But they are wrong about one thing. I'm still convinced the center of these practices was New Mexico, not the Mohave desert."

Poynter shrugged. "You'll have to prove it. Time to gather

evidence for your lost tribe theories." He tossed the paper under the table and went back to his work. "Anything else?"

"I'm taking off for a few days," Tara said. "Could you step in for me?"

Poynter didn't even look up from his work. "Same schedule as last semester?"

Tara handed him a sheet of paper on which she'd already printed out the times of her classes for the coming week.

"Through Wednesday," Poynter said. "I can cover you through a week from next Wednesday."

"Great. I'll clear it with the powers that be."

Poynter turned away and bent over the painted wooden artifact he'd been examining when Tara came in.

"What is that?" she asked.

"The left leg of Jesus," Poynter said. "From a Spanish mission not too far from where you're going, down South of Albuquerque. Looks like the rest of him got used as firewood."

* * *

When Tara got home that afternoon, Viveka, the housekeeper, had not yet returned with Maya from school. Tara bounded upstairs to her home office and glanced at her answering machine. The blinking red light indicated there was a call. Tara sat down and pressed the playback button. She heard only static at first, and for a moment thought there was something wrong with her machine. But then a voice came through the static, a voice she knew only too well. It was her father! But something was seriously wrong. The connection faded in and out. The voice sounded as if it were coming from a different world. Sentences came through the static in bits and pieces, like the scattered artifacts at an archaeological dig. She replayed the message several times, writing down Drake's words on a note pad beside the phone.

"Tara...to get down here...more up your alley than mine. You were right..."

There was a series of clicks and then only continuous hissing. For a moment Tara sat on the edge of her chair, unable to believe what she had just heard. He was alive. Drake was alive! This message was proof. Or was it? Someone could be toying with her, playing back a recording of Drake's voice. She began to feel suspicious. If it was a recording being played back into the mouthpiece of a telephone, it would not be unusual to hear so much distortion and static. But why, she asked, would anyone play such a cruel trick on her? Tom? Unlikely. He did not have the wit required for such a prank. If it was truly Drake, why had he returned now, at this moment?

The words she'd heard on the answering machine triggered pictures in Tara's mind, of Drake digging around some ancient site on the desert, oblivious to the fact that he was violating sacred ground and in a damn good position to get his head blown off. The looting and desecration of ancestral graves was no joking matter. Not that the fear of death ever deterred him from pursuing a hook for his stories! But he sounded so solemn. And was it possible that she detected an edge of fear in his voice?

Tara pressed the playback button on the answering machine again. Drake's words were so fragmented it was as if he was speaking in code: "It must have been a...breezy...from hell...but bones not old enough... This can't explain...nobody's belief..a risky, risky...crucial timing...something for your career...with a flute...map and photos to the house, we'll meet you...never find the place alone...East...dare the glyphs...gotta go...lu..."

Tara jotted down the entire message, ran the tape forward and back, but there were no more messages. For a moment she stared at the words on her note pad, attempting to make sense of them.

The front door slammed. Maya came running up the stairs and raced into Tara's office with a picture she'd made at school. The picture was of their family, she explained excitedly, four figures in all: Tara, the Mama, Viveka the Nanny, and Tom, the papa who lives so far away. And, what else," Maya exclaimed, with a twinkle in her eye "Here's Maya herself, who is just a wonderful child!"

"Do you know why she is so wonderful?" Maya asked, teasingly.

"I think I do," Tara said, hugging Maya and lifting her into her lap. "But you tell me."

"Because I have magical powers," Maya said. "Do you want to see, Mama?"

"Yes, I do!"

Maya jumped down and produced a shiny new penny from the pocket of her jeans. She turned her back briefly, reached into her pocket again, and then turned back to her mother, placing the penny on her desk. Judging from her exaggerated movements and manner of speech, Maya had been well-rehearsed by Viveka, who certainly had a flair for the dramatic.

"You see here an ordinary shiny new penny," Maya said, pointing to the coin and sounding for all the world like a stage magician. "Now, do you see this? You may look at it, if you wish." Maya handed her mother a thin red block of plastic with green felt on one side. Tara looked it over and handed it back, amused by her daughter's histrionics.

"I shall now place the block over my penny," Maya said, in a theatrical tone that made her mother smile. "And then I say these

magic words. Hocus pokus, dominy, yokus! Change my penny to a dime."

Maya quickly lifted the red block and there on the desk, instead of the penny, lay a bright shiny dime!

"That's wonderful!" Tara said.

"Because it's magic," Maya explained. "It came for me in the mail today. Viveka read the instructions and showed me how to do it. Do you want to see how it's done, Mommy?"

"You say it came in the mail?" Tara asked. "Was there a note or a return address?"

"No," Maya said. "It's just a present from somebody, I don't know who."

Maya was not interested in discussing who'd sent the trick. She insisted on revealing the trick, how the penny was actually hollow and how it covered the dime. A magnet in the red block lifted the fake penny off, revealing the dime under it.

A moment later, Viveka appeared in the doorway of the study. "You didn't give the secret away, did you?" she exclaimed. "A good magician never tells her secrets, Honey."

"But you can tell your mom," Maya said, apparently quite clear about that.

"Okay," Viveka said. "Moms are okay to tell."

That evening Tara took Maya and Viveka out to dinner at the Cat 'N Fiddle in Sausalito, where she told them that she would be leaving for Albuquerque early the next morning. Maya was not at all happy with the news and Tara was reminded, all over again, that co-parenting with a man like Tom, Maya's father, wasn't easy.

In a pleading tone Maya said, "I want to go with you."

"I'm sorry, Sweetheart, this is for Mommy's work," Tara said.

"You're *always* going away, and you never take me," Maya whined. "It's not fair!"

Even coming from her own daughter's mouth, said in perfect innocence, the words stung. What would it take for the world to appreciate the significance of this work? Finding the City of the Mists or any other proof of the society of shamans would rewrite history. Proof that she was right about this North American oracle, that she had been right from the start, would turn the tides. One day it would happen, she was certain of it. To prove that an oracle did in fact exist was worth any sacrifice, even the insults she suffered daily at the university.

"Maya, listen to me! You are not going with me, and that's that," Tara said. She had only intended to sound stern but her tone betrayed the anger and upset she was feeling.

"I can stay with my dad," Maya implored. "I haven't seen him for *so long!*"

For a moment Tara was speechless. Maya's sadness was real. Tom hadn't visited her for over a year, and he'd spoken to her on the phone no more than a half-dozen times. His contacts with Maya had consisted mainly of presents he'd had sent directly from the stores where he purchased them, for the obvious holidays, Christmas and Maya's birthday.

"Honey, I'll tell you what," Tara said. "I'll have a meeting with your Dad tomorrow night. Then, let's you and me go down to New Mexico for Christmas. We'll drive up to Taos and maybe go skiing, if the snow is good. If they possibly can, maybe Margarette and Tom will join us. In any case, we'll have a good visit with your dad. Okay? He loves skiing. I'm pretty sure he'll go."

Maya sank back in her chair and looked as if she'd just been told that the world was coming to an end. Pouting, she turned her head and looked up at Viveka. "I'll only go if Viveka comes, too."

"Of course she can come. Do you want to come, Viveka?"

"If you're not going to be running around after savages," Viveka said, derisively. "I'm not much for poking around that sort of thing."

"It will be strictly a fun trip," Tara promised, amused by Viveka's response. It wasn't the first time the older woman had made disparaging remarks about Tara's research subjects.

Viveka reached across the table and touched Maya's hand. She smiled at Maya and nodded.

"Okay, I'll do it," Maya said.

Later, Tara phoned Tom, just as she'd promised. But there was no answer. She left a message on his machine, saying she'd be in Albuquerque the following afternoon and would like to have dinner with him and Margarette, his wife, at El Tecolote, a restaurant Tara had enjoyed in the past.

That night, unable to sleep, Tara remembered her old phone book in the bottom of her bedside table. She quickly dug it out from beneath a stack of articles torn from magazines during her late night reading, mostly ideas for remodeling the kitchen, clipped from housing magazines. And there it was, her personal phone directory from two years ago. She thumbed through the dogeared pages. Drake's name popped out at her, and there, as she'd hoped, was his old cell phone number! It was a long-shot but why not give it a try? On the third ring, to her utter surprise, she heard a muffled hello and shouted into the phone: "Dad, is that you?"

His voice came through, breathless and garbled with static: "Tara. I can't believe this! Listen, you've..."

A buzz told her she'd lost the transmission. She screamed into the phone but to no avail. The connection was gone. She dialed

back immediately, and Drake's voice came through once more, but this time like a record played back in reverse, accompanied by an electronic squeal that rose higher and higher, then ended in a gentle pop. For a long time she just stared at the phone. It was bizarre, like a message from another world, a surreal distortion that belonged in a science fiction movie. More than ever, she was convinced that what she was hearing wasn't Drake's live voice. Rather, it was a recording, and someone was playing a vicious game with her.

She lay back in her bed, Drake's distorted voice echoing in her brain. She thought about a message he'd left two years before, saying he was poking around some ancient ruins. If that were true, it wouldn't be unusual for him to come across human bones. Corpses entombed for centuries could pop up after a storm, the rains washing away the last protective layers of dirt and rock. But these bones were not old, Tara was certain of that. *Not old* suggested foul play or a tragic accident.

She swept back the covers and reached for the phone again. After a moment's hesitation she dialed. A young woman's voice answered, surprisingly cheerful for 2 a.m. When the voice asked, How may I help you, Tara answered, "I'd like to make reservations for Albuquerque. Preferably a morning flight." ~

Flight

Ten minutes out of Phoenix, flying toward Albuquerque, Tara peered out the tiny square window on her right and watched a huge rain cloud hovering over the desert. From her seat on Southwest flight 617, originating in San Francisco, the cloud looked for all the world like a huge, mythological bird. She gazed at it for as long as it stayed in sight, spellbound as the rain cascaded from its wings, pouring heavy showers down over the arid landscape.

It was easy to understand how ancient peoples, unaware of the illusions of nature, mistook images such as this for sacred deities and made up myths about them. Skies like this could have birthed legends of Quetzalcoatl, the Aztec's feathered serpent god. Tara remembered a line from the *Codex Vidobonensis*, a rare pre-Columbian document that escaped the fires of the Inquisition: "...his mask resplendent in precious stones, on his back he carries a woman, just as a bridegroom would carry a bride." Images like this inflamed the early missionaries, steeped in their legends of virgin birth. And if Tara's own experiences were any indication, they still outraged some people.

Tara smiled as she remembered the first conversation she had with Viveka, when she tried to describe the passion she felt for her own work at the university. Viveka sat at the kitchen table staring over the breakfast dishes, a look of quiet consternation on her face, not yet comfortable with the rhythms of the house.

"And what do you hope to be learning from these savages?" she had asked.

Disarmed by her housekeeper's naivete, Tara's answer had been wry. "Oh, nothing much. The secrets of the universe."

Tara had watched Viveka's brow furrow, as she asked, "Why would you trouble with all that sort of thing?"

"I don't know when it began," Tara had said, deciding to take the question seriously. "But when I was a very small child somebody told me about these special people, this society of shamans. I don't even remember who it was. Mother knew so many famous people, who stayed at our house when they came to town. I learned that on every continent there have been fortune-tellers, people like priests, highly spiritual people, who saw into the future. They studied the stars, the earth, the courses of history, and this was their purpose in life. We don't know all the ways they came up with their knowledge. But their advice was sought by every leader of every great civilization. And whenever it was not followed that great civilization fell. The oracles knew. They were infallible.

"What was the source of their wisdom? How did they know so much? And why was there never such a group found on this continent? You know what? I think that we've been afraid to look! But we need to look. And the secret is going to be found in our earliest cultures, in the societies that were here for thousands of years before the Europeans came. *They were our oracles.* They knew. And if I'm right, they left behind a record about the past but also about the future. They will speak out of the past with a message for our future."

By the end of her speech, Tara was standing, pacing the kitchen floor in a high state of excitement.

Viveka had appeared stunned, and Tara had been afraid that maybe she'd scared her off.

"That's Black Magic," Viveka had said, fearfully.

Tara had felt the older woman drawing away from her. "No," she had tried to assure her. "I'm certain this society of shamans had absolutely the highest motives. They had access to wisdom unparalleled in history, surpassing even the most famous seers of all, the Oracle at Delphi, in ancient Greece."

"I don't know, Ms. Fairfield," Viveka had said. "I think you'd better watch out for yourself."

Tara smiled as she remembered the conversation. She wondered how far she'd get with that same topic if she tried to present it to anyone on this plane.

Lightning shot across the sky, way too close for comfort, flashing through the interior of the plane in a blinding glare, setting off a collective gasp that rippled through the passengers' compartment. The gasp turned into guarded laughter as people expressed their sense of relief, realizing the danger had passed. For a brief moment the plane groaned, sent out a metallic shudder of respite, and finally moved smoothly through the sky.

Tara loved the rain, the way it cooled the desert, leaving behind the fresh, earthy scent of dampened adobe and rising ozone. There was something frankly primal and sensual about the wetness and warmth transforming the usually arid and sinewy landscape. With the heavy fall rains she understood why the Indians called the earth Mother. Ordinarily she thought of the desert as a man. This sometimes crude and harsh male could be unrelentingly demanding and even abusive. But when the rains came, he melted into the atmosphere, like a mirage, and allowed this great, steaming female power to take over.

The thought of driving out to Gallup all alone in the rain filled Tara with an odd mixture of melancholy and adventure, something she'd felt since she was a small child. She never could understand the feeling. Sometimes it was almost as if she was leaving behind someone or something she had once deeply loved. But she could not name it except when it was attached to a real incident in her life. During her final separation from Tom, she was certain his absence caused the feeling, even though she had been in favor of ending the relationship. When her mother died, it was the same. But the fact remained that this strange mixture of melancholy and sense of adventure came to her even after her mourning for these losses was complete.

Somtimes the feeling turned into foreboding, like a premonition that she was moving toward her own death. But she had encountered that premonition thousands of time before and never took it seriously. On the contrary, it was a private joke with her. The simple fact that she was still alive after thousands of these so-called premonitions proved her apprehension irrational. Perhaps the feeling was nothing more than her own struggle with the fact of her own mortality. People had struggled with this verity since the beginning of human awareness and to her knowledge there were very few who'd ever made their peace with it.

In the meantime, she found comfort in the myriad signs that life was forever renewing itself. When she thought about this her attention turned back to her daughter Maya and suddenly her heart felt full. The little girl was the delight of her life. Gentle, blond and blue-eyed, Maya was the antithesis of the dark skinned peoples after which Tom and Tara had named her. Looking back, it had probably been sentimental and impulsive to name their daughter after such a powerful people. But Tara still loved the name, and each time she looked at her beautiful daughter she relived that wildly romantic summer with Tom that brought this lovely being into her life.

As the months passed and the baby swelled in her belly, Tara had realized her relationship with Tom was over. They both knew it, but only spoke of it once. They pretended nothing was wrong until two weeks after Maya's birth, when Tom left for his job in Albuquerque. Tara didn't try to stop him. But for several weeks after Tom left, she brooded over his departure. Sometimes she still missed

him, ached for him, though she told herself it was only her memories
of their early romance that she mourned.

Startled out of her reverie, Tara suddenly remembered that she
hadn't confirmed her dinner arrangements with Tom. She reached
into her handbag for her credit card and removed the air-phone from
its seat bracket. She slid the card through the scanning slot and
dialed Tom's office. A sudden crackling in the receiver told her the
storm was going to interfere with reception. Tom picked up on the
first ring.

"Hi," she said. "It's me."

"Tara, honey, it's great to hear your voice! What's going on?"

"Did you get my message?"

"I sure did. Where are you, anyhow? Sounds like a wind tunnel."

"Sorry. I'm on the plane. We're on for five-thirty then?"

"I didn't get the last part."

"I said we're on for five-thirty."

"Yes, yes," Tom said. "It'll be good to see you, it really will!"

"I've been putting together Christmas plans," Tara said,
wondering how much she could trust Tom's apparent enthusiasm
about her visit. "I'm making reservations up at Taos. And, Tom,
Maya wants to see you. I told her maybe we could get together. You
might want to meet us for a little skiing."

"Could you repeat that?"

Tara did, slowly and a little louder in an effort to be heard above
the wind and static.

"Oh, Lord!" Tom replied. "I haven't been on skis in three years
or more."

"Then you're interested?"

"Oh, sure, sure! You know me. I'll check with my better half
here. We'll work it out."

Tom's voice faded. At first Tara thought it was the phone
reception, then realized Tom's mood had suddenly shifted.

"You understand Margarette's working on her dissertation," he
said. "Got a bug up her boodie to finish this Spring. Don't tell Maya
the ski trip is definite. I'd hate to disappoint her if it doesn't come
off."

"Try to make some space for her," Tara said. "She doesn't make
many demands on you, Tom."

"Darling, don't guilt-trip me!"

"I don't want her going through what I did at that age..."

"Don't burden Maya with your issues, for god sake! We always
get into this." Tom paused. Then, in an upbeat voice that was too
loud, too agreeable, he added: "I miss you all! You know that, don't
you? You are my loves. If Christmas doesn't work out, we'll make it

next summer. I promise to put it on our calendar. How about that?"

Tara felt her stomach knot up. Tom was politely and gently telling her no about the Christmas plans. It was his way, this quiet manipulation that really drove her crazy. In less than a minute he'd not only rejected her and Maya's plans but had shifted the responsibility for the failure into her lap. It was an all too familiar tactic. But she didn't want to deal with this side of him. As always, she would do everything in her power to keep their conversation civil. She'd pretend that she was going to take his comment at face value and not confront him. If she did confront him, he would be certain to say no, and then she would really be angry with him. Besides, he might have information she wanted. She considered asking him if he'd seen the *New York Times* article, then thought better of it. She was not sure why she didn't want to discuss it with him but a strong sense of self-preservation prevented her from revealing her interest in David Black's work.

"I'm driving up to Coyote Mesa," she said, changing the subject. "Could you tell me something? In the past couple years, has there been any kind of new activity out there, new digs, anything at all?" She felt an old familiar tug and reflexively pulled back from sharing with him her excitement about the potsherds and her bewilderment over the photos and the phone calls from her father. Her discoveries, going all the way back to her higher academic position when they were still students, had always been the source of conflict between them. There were fears she would have liked to share with him--with anyone--about the mysterious calls from Drake. The idea that he might still be alive was almost too much to hold in. But the fact that he might be leading her to the society of shamans wasn't something she wanted Tom to know. Unlike most anthropologists, he had believed in her theories, and she would have loved to have his support now. However, how he'd take the news that Drake might be alive was another matter. They had never gotten along.

"New digs?" Tom replied. "No. None at all. Strange territory out there, not anthropologically significant. Wasn't your Dad out there, just before he disappeared...chasing UFOs or babies with two heads, whatever it was." He paused. "I'm sorry. I didn't mean to bring that up." Tom's voice trailed off until Tara wondered if she was losing the connection. Then he said: "Sweetheart, let's talk at dinner. We're looking forward."

After she hung up Tara realized something really was wrong. There was a tension in Tom's voice she hadn't heard in years. It wasn't just his evasiveness and his obvious manipulations. There was something else going on. Tom was lying to her. A few months before, she'd read an article in an obscure professional journal about

Tom helping the people of the Zuni, Hopi, and Acoma pueblos put together a collection of artifacts for the Indian museum in Albuquerque.

Surely, through his familiarity with the general area he would know about Coyote Mesa. So why had he been so evasive when she asked him about that place? He wouldn't have overlooked that region. If nothing else he was thorough in charting out the territories he worked.

Tom was hiding something. His vagaries when she asked him about the mesa reminded her of what happened at the dig they'd visited in Peru. He'd uncovered a gold figure, dating back before the Spanish Conquest. It was Incan, for sure. It stood about five inches tall, the figure of a bird of prey, missing its head but otherwise intact. Nobody saw him uncover it from the hole he'd been working. He pocketed it and brought it back to their tent. That night, in the light of their small lantern, he'd handed it to her to examine.

"It's worth a small fortune," he'd said.

"It belongs with the other artifacts," she'd replied sternly, admiring the intricate features of the obviously female statuette.

"Don't you get it? I know where to sell stuff like this. We could pay off our student loans, for god sake! It could give us both a good grub stake in the future. What harm could it do?"

"We're anthropologists, not grave robbers!"

Tom had exploded with anger. He had suddenly grabbed the golden icon from her hand; a sharp edge snagged Tara's palm. Stunned by his sudden violence she had just held up her hand, out in front of her, as blood coursed down over her wrist, staining her tee shirt and shorts. The next day Tom logged in the statuette. That night she went back to their tent early, saying she was turning in. When he came in two hours later, he discovered that she had separated their sleeping bags and was already sound asleep. Whether he knew it or not at the time, this moment was the beginning of the end for them. Tom had tried to awaken her. Tara had pushed him away.

The plane dipped suddenly, banked for a turn and Tara looked out the window. Through the rain clouds she could once again see the rugged desert range. Her mind drifted and she found herself basking in the memories of the summer she and Tom spent in Peru. They'd been kids, young, just finishing graduate studies, out on their own in a strange land, filled with dreams about the future. Idealism and sex...what a lovely combination that had been! Everything was possible that summer. The future was theirs to mold as they wished.

Before the incident with the statue, Tara had enjoyed a closeness with Tom that she'd always dreamed of having with a man.

Tom and she had long talks that stretched into the wee hours of the morning, comparing the experiences of their young lives, certain they were the first people on earth to ever share such intimacy.

Tara longed to share that kind of closeness again. She wanted someone who would help her put back all the pieces of her life. Increasingly, those pieces were becoming too scattered, too complex, tearing her apart. All the delicious dreams of her youth were being buried by career pressures, house loans, appointments with the pediatrician, meaningless paperwork and university politics.

Her thoughts turned to Drake. Her own father had never offered her much relief or comfort in the pressures she felt growing up, learning to become an adult, a mother. In fact, he had only added to the pressures she felt. When he first mentioned his trip to New Mexico, two years before, he'd said it was about a UFO story. "You know," he said, "There's evidence they were communicating with the early Pueblo peoples." The *they* he was talking about were extraterrestrial, beings from some faraway planet that he imagined, outside our solar system.

"Dad, you're going to use the photographs you saw in my office, aren't you? You got your own copies. I know you."

He had shrugged. Shrugged! She'd shaken her head in disbelief. "Please don't use me this way."

But what good was it to argue with him? He lived in a world all his own, a world where fantasy overruled the realities of everyday life. In her childhood, she'd suffered from terrible dreams about alien abductions, which her mother said were brought on by her father's wild stories. When Tara tried to talk with Drake about it, years later, he had tried to win her to his cause. He brought her a book written by John E. Mack, a Pulitzer Prize winner and Harvard professor.

"Explain the hundreds of interviews with abductees," Drake had implored her. "Do yourself a favor and read this book. Normal, healthy men and women, like you, Tara, are convinced they were abducted, and nobody has uncovered any evidence that they are lying, mentally imbalanced or the victims of a hoax. They've taken polygraphs and their stories check out.

"Mack thinks the UFOs actually come not from outer space but from a different reality. Maybe they've always been with us, even guiding us. He says there's evidence that other worlds exist within our own, whole universes that go undetected most of the time. We are unable to see, hear or touch these worlds because they exist in a state of being beyond the limits of our five senses."

More to poke holes in his theory than out of any real interest, Tara read the book. She couldn't find the holes she'd hoped for but she nevertheless remained skeptical.

"Delusional," she concluded. "The man's gone over the edge."

Drake laughed. "Prove to me there isn't a reality out there that we can't see, hear, taste or touch--not because it isn't there but because we don't have the capacity to see it."

"Dad, you know I can't," Tara had replied, too proud to give in to him.

Since her parents divorced when she was young, Tara never got to know Drake well until her mother's untimely death. A small plane in which Helen was flying with a friend, lost power and crashed into the mountainside.

Drake came to the funeral, even stood up and spoke eloquently of Helen's accomplishments as a university scholar and mother, straddling career and motherhood and excelling in both. For the first time ever Tara saw a different side of Drake. Hidden behind his mask of bombast and derring-do was someone who cared. Why, she wondered, did he hide this part? Why did any man?

"I've been angry with you for as long as I can remember," Tara told her father when they got together after the funeral. "But I've read every article you ever wrote." She stopped. Grinning, she waited for his response and was surprised to see tears in his eyes.

"That stuff..." He paused, wiping the corner of his eye with his index finger before he added, "Never mind."

But that, too, seemed so long ago.

Tara remembered the note Drake had sent her with the photos, instructing her to call Charla Mather's gallery. That woman was a definite point of contention for Tara. A wealthy importer, Tara suspected Mather of trading in objects obtained by pilfering sacred Indian sites. Indeed, Mather had been accused of selling some pre-Colombian figures smuggled into the country by Jose Haera, whose shadowy reputation extended even to the University of California Anthropology department, where Tara had done her graduate work. Eventually, Charla was acquitted of all wrongdoing, though Haera, a resident of Guadalajara, was banished from ever returning to the States.

Tara reached for the air-phone on the back of the seat, scanned in her credit card and punched in the number for the gallery, which she'd written down in her address book before leaving home. After several rings, a male voice answered.

"Bruce MacFrey. Mather Gallery."

"Charla Mather, please."

"I'm sorry, she's out of town. May I help you?"

"I need to get hold of her. I'm a...a friend."

"You need what, dear? You'll have to speak up. You've got a terrible connection."

"I need to get hold of Charla Mather or Drake Fairfield, either one."

"There's no phone service at her place," MacFrey said. "There's cell phone service only as far as Gallup. There's an instrument in her car also, but it's of no use at Coyote Mesa, as I've said."

"When is the last you heard from them?"

"Them?" he asked. "And your business is..?"

"I'm Dr. Tara Fairfield, Drake's daughter."

"Fine, but that doesn't cut much ice with me. I don't know any Drake."

"Look. My father and Charla Mather are friends. I was invited out to their place at Coyote Mesa. I'm trying to tell them when to expect me. It's important." If Drake indeed had been with Charla recently, this statement, Tara conjectured, should have drawn MacFrey out.

"Oh, for goodness sake!" the young man said, his tone sardonic and catty. "I didn't realize how urgent this really was! You should have told me."

"My father said to call you when I got to Albuquerque. He said he would leave information about meeting him in Gallup tomorrow."

"Well, guess what? I don't know the man."

"He hasn't called you? That's impossible!"

"Shall I send out the Pony Express for you?"

"Look, Bruce. This is all very cute. But would you just try to get through to them? Or else give me her number and I'll do it myself."

"Not even Jesus gets that number."

"Please."

"Did you actually say *please?* Oh, you've found the magic password!"

The line was silent, and for a moment Tara thought he'd hung up. But a beeping sound in the background gave her hope that he was actually dialing Charla's number on another phone. Then, "No connection. Hmm! Now didn't I just hear someone say this would be the case? If they should happen to call in, I should say Miss Whozit is coming down?"

"Dr. Tara Fairfield."

"And remind me, please, your business?"

"Drake Fairfield's daughter. Do you know what they're doing out there?"

"Honey, what Ms. Mather does out there is no business of yours or mine. And I'm sure she's not looking for company."

"You think she's alone, then?"

"I try not to meddle in other people's private affairs."

"Fine, Bruce. You've been so very helpful! I'll be sure to tell your

employer what a charmer you are."

"You do that."

She hung up, steaming. If she could get even a single message through--to determine if Drake was out there mucking around at the ruins he'd apparently found--she would have felt a hundred percent more at ease.

The flight attendant leaned in from the aisle and asked Tara to check her seat belt. Tara gazed out the window. The Albuquerque airport was already in sight. The aircraft shuddered slightly as the pilot let down the landing gears. The machinery locked into place with a hollow clunk. Moments later, the plane touched down, bounced slightly, and then braked, with engines roaring.

The plane's engines wound down and in an instant, it seemed, the air in the passengers' cabin began to heat up. Tara unbuckled her seat belt but then decided to wait while the plane emptied out. She hated fighting the crowds. She sat back and watched as the aisle filled with passengers, opening the overheads, dragging baggage out, clumsily jostling each other. Tara turned to stare out the window. It was raining lightly. Baggage handlers in yellow slickers were off-loading the plane, tossing bags onto a waiting trailer.

A figure of an animal, a wet, bedraggled dog, moved across the tarmac behind them. What could it be doing out in the middle of the airport in the rain? As she peered through the rain she saw it was not a dog at all but a coyote, trotting at a pretty good clip along the edge of the tarmac, heading toward the open land beyond.

Tara glanced up at the front of the plane. The profile of a man at the center of the compartment caught her eye. It was Drake! She was certain it was him! But there was a whole plane full of people crowded into the aisle, pushing toward the door. How could it be Drake? She stared after the crowd. He was gone. But surely her eyes had played tricks on her. She hung back, not wanting to believe what she thought she'd just seen. She had to pull herself together, not be thrown off by false hopes. The flight attendant called to her. "Do you need assistance, Ma'am?"

"No, I'm fine."

By the time Tara reached the baggage claim area, the man she'd thought was Drake was nowhere in sight. Retrieving her suitcase she strode quickly to the street, bumping into a figure standing at the curb, briefcase in hand. It was him, the man from the plane! He turned suddenly and Tara backed away, embarrassed. It was not Drake at all! In fact, the face under the hat belonged to a woman, not a man. She wore huge glasses that filled her face, making her look rather owlish.

"May I help you?" the owlish stranger asked.

"I'm sorry," Tara said. "Please excuse me."

She felt like a fool! Twenty feet away she turned back to take another look at the owlish woman, just in time to see her climbing into a white limousine.

Still fuming about the phone call to the gallery and Bruce MacFrey's rude treatment of her she raced to catch the van for the car rental office. She'd drive out to Coyote Mesa alone. If Drake were to be found at all, she would find him tomorrow and put a stop to his nonsense. He had to be told how his disappearance had affected her, how upset she had been for at least a year and a half, believing him, most assuredly, dead. But that wasn't all. He had to stop calling and sending her packages with inadequate explanations. And he had to be stopped from poking around that obviously significant anthropological site before he completely ruined her chances of exploring what he'd found. ~

 Spirit Circle

Initiation

A Nat King Cole sound-alike was crooning *Moon River* over the scratchy P.A. system at the car rental office. Feeling increasingly irritable and tired, Tara took her place behind a dozen fidgeting people waiting for their moment at the counter. When she finally got to the service representative she was sizzling with complaints about her long wait; after all, she told them, she had reserved ahead. Apologizing profusely, the agent upgraded her reservation to a white Chevy Camaro with a car phone. Throwing her bags into the back of the car she raced off to the Desert Springs Motel, in the center of Albuquerque. It was ten after three when she checked into her room. Having slept only four hours the night before, she looked forward to a nap and a good night's sleep. She also wanted to see Tom for dinner that night, and if possible repair any damage their last conversation had caused.

She felt giddy, anticipating the meeting with Tom. In spite of all the grief they'd caused each other, she was always amazed to discover that there was still some of the old chemistry between them. Every time they met she felt it. And she was pretty certain Tom did, too, though he'd never acknowledged it directly. Just as well! Margarette had the instincts of a junk yard dog when it came to Tara and Tom's feelings for each other. Between that, common sense, and Tara's simmering anger about Tom's neglect of Maya, she was sure she'd be able to maintain her rigid boundaries. She could only imagine what it might be like if it were not for these obstacles.

When she opened the door of her room at the Desert Springs Motel her attention became glued on the obviously new drapes and bedspread. They were matching prints, decorated with hot air balloons in red, white and blue. Balloons! Tara stood in the center of the room and shook her head in disgust. Here was an entire state, rich with dramatic desert landscapes, ancient Indian ruins and art,

heavenly skies and picturesque mountain villages. And what did this motel choose to feature in their newly redecorated rooms? Balloons, hot air balloons!

She appreciated that the annual balloon festival brought in an extra 50,000 tourists every summer, but it was not exactly a Southwestern image. She was appalled by the idea that they would pass over million-year-old natural marvels, and the beauty of cultural artifacts dating back several hundred years, in favor of phenomena that had become popular in this state less than a decade before.

Tara dropped her bags on the floor and reached for the telephone. To her this gross commercialization was an affront to her sensibilities. In her mind, such disdain for the past was reprehensible. She'd have her room changed! She pressed the number for the front desk and listened as it buzzed once, twice, a third and then a fourth time. A recorded female voice answered, apologized for the necessary wait and announced that she hoped her guests would enjoy a musical interlude. Muzak. Tara dropped the receiver to her side, sighed, then tossed it back onto the hook with a clatter. "Never mind," she counseled herself. "You can live with it for one night." There was no point in arguing with the Chamber of Commerce or the motel's interior decorator. She'd dim the lights and ignore the decor.

She placed her overnight bag on the long, mirrored dresser and carried her suitcase to the room's single closet alcove. She meticulously checked the bathroom, removing the paper sanitary ribbon from the toilet seat, folded it and dropped it in the plastic-lined wastebasket. She returned to the main room and sat down at the tiny desk. She set her purse to her right, removed her address book and reached for the phone. She called El Tecolote Restaurant to confirm her 5:30 dinner reservations.

In a little over an hour she'd be seeing Tom again and maybe would pump him for information about Coyote Mesa. She'd also nail him down about his visit with Maya over the Christmas holidays. The restaurant confirmed her reservations quickly and Tara dialed her home number. In an instant Maya's voice came on the line.

"I knew it was you, Mommy. Did you see my dad?"

"Not yet, sweetheart. We're meeting for dinner."

"I drew a picture at school today for my art teacher. It's about skiing with you and Daddy. But you know what?"

"What, baby?"

"I had this terrible dream. That's why I made the picture, Mommy. Viveka says it's just my imagination. I don't know if I should tell you."

"Tell me what?"

"Well, it wasn't a nice dream. Because I dreamed I went to see my Dad and Margarette but he wasn't there any more."

"Sometimes we dream things like that. It's okay."

"But something else..."

"Yes?"

"You had changed, Mommy. I didn't know you any more. You were all different. I cried a lot. The dream woke me up and I was crying, too."

"I think it just means that you miss us."

"But if you didn't come back...if you weren't my Mommy any more..."

"I'll always be your Mommy, sweetheart. Just keep nice feelings in your heart for me and your dad and all of us. You'll see, everything will be fine and during the holidays we'll go to Taos, and maybe your dad will come, too. We'll have fun."

"Viveka put my picture on the refrigerator door. I'm going to look at it every day so I can know it's just pretend."

"That's good, Honey."

"Viveka says it's good to look at it. That reminds me it's not real. I just made it up in my head. It's just pretend."

"Sometimes when we're feeling afraid or lonely we make up scary stories in our minds."

"I know it. But what if they come true? Sometimes I have dreams that come true! Viveka says that's not so. She says it's just super...super...*stitchun*, but I know it's real. I've had it happen lots of times."

"Honey, please don't worry. When we're children, dreams can seem very real. But when you grow up you begin to understand that they are mostly about being afraid. Our dreams are like little stories about what scares us. That's all they are, Honey. They don't tell about what's going to happen in the future, not really. If you are worried about it, you tell Viveka and talk to her."

"That's what I do." There was a pause, then: "I get lonesome for you, Mommy."

"I know, Sweetheart. I get lonesome for you, too. But I'll be back before you know it."

"I think you're mean not to let me come."

For a moment, Tara felt a twinge of guilt. But she knew better than to let Maya manipulate her that way. "I love you very much," she said, then added, "Would you ask Viveka if there were any phone messages for me?" She asked it as much to change the subject as anything else.

She heard Maya call to Viveka, an exchange of voices, then Maya came back on the line.

"Viveka says no. Nobody called."

"Okay. I'll call you tomorrow and tell you all about my meeting with your dad."

"Bye, Mommy."

"Bye, Honey. Don't you worry anymore. Remember what Mommy told you. Dreams aren't real. Okay?"

"Okay. But, Mommy..."

"Honey, they really aren't real. You sleep good, now. I love you very much."

"Mommy..."

"Sweety, I know what you are going to say, that your dreams really do come true sometimes..."

"They do so! You don't know everything."

Maya's plaintive, argumentative tone nearly broke Tara's heart. "No, you're right. I don't know everything," Tara said, humoring her daughter. "But I do know one thing, I love you *berry, berry* much."

"Berry, berry, berry much!" Maya giggled, playing a word game that Tara usually reserved for bedtime. "All the berries in the world!"

"Good night, Sweetheart."

Tara hung up the phone, troubled by the conversation, wishing she could be home to comfort her child. She stood up and opened her overnight case, removing the photos, the bone and the potsherds from Drake's envelope. She picked up the two clay fragments. They were like calling cards beckoning her back to the place of their origin. She sat down on the edge of the bed, holding one in each hand, admiring them. It was an amazing feeling to hold something so old in your hands, to realize that hands not unlike yours had molded these pieces, hundreds of years ago. And hundreds of years ago these pieces had been part of a large pot that played a central role in an important ceremony.

Images of the society of shamans filled her mind. She imagined their place high on a mesa, their ceremonial kivas and adobe pueblos climbing up along the cliffs, blending in with the red rock. From this place they could gaze out in all directions, to where the horizon blended with the sky, and imagine that they were truly sitting on the roof of the world. At times she could almost taste the air of this place, hear the drum beats of evening rituals, and smell the *pinon* fires and aromas of the evening meals being prepared, which would be eaten just before the sun had set.

But mostly she wondered, who were these people? What magic did they invoke, allowing them to see beyond what scholar-philosopher William James had once described as the "filmy veil" that separates everyday life from this other reality that theologians and spiritual leaders have been exploring for centuries? And what records did these ancient shaman-priests leave behind?

What artifacts? Somewhere out there, hidden even from probing aircraft, this ancient village, perhaps already buried under centuries of decaying adobe and desert dust, waited for her to pull back the veil and reveal its secrets.

Tara slipped the potsherds back into the envelope with the photographs. She got up, crossed the room and switched on the television set. Then she fell back on the bed, wanting to get the local weather report. It would be good to know tomorrow's prediction. The desert storms could be treacherous this time of the year.

But there was something wrong with the set. Whatever channel she chose the screen was snowy. She was about to turn it off when an image appeared. The pouty face of a young man stared back at her! It was crystal clear, as if he was actually gazing right into her eyes. There was no doubt about it. The young man she saw was the movie actor James Dean. Tara smiled as she contemplated his image. In her youth she'd loved James Dean's movies, no doubt because he reminded her of her dad. Drake's early photos looked a lot like Dean. With her young father little more than an elusive specter in her life, the actor had become Tara's father substitute. Admittedly, Dean was better looking than Drake ever was, but there was a clear resemblance, or so she had always believed. As a teenager Tara bought all of Dean's films on video. She and her friends played them over and over.

On the snowy television screen now the actor's lips moved, his mouth turned up at the corners in that characteristic smirk of his. But there was no sound. A second later, the screen was all snow again, then something else, entirely unrelated to that image appeared. It was an old black and white movie from the 1940's. Tara was annoyed at first, then intrigued, since some of the images from the movie seemed familiar. She recalled being about eight years old and watching this same film, yet she had no memory of where she'd seen it. It had probably been at a friend's house, she decided, on their VCR. The reception on the TV was bad again, filled with snow. She felt drowsy, her eyes heavy, her body sinking deeper and deeper into the soft mattress. She struggled to pull her attention back to the TV screen. But it was no use. It was as if some invisible power was pulling her down, forcing her to close her eyes.

Feeling herself drifting, spiraling downward, dizzily, she suddenly became frightened. Was it the movie that frightened her, or the memory it evoked, or... She tried to force her eyelids to lift. But it was as if they were frozen shut. Indeed, her entire face felt cold. *Cold! What is this? I must move,* she told herself, *must get up!* Yet she could not move so much as a finger. The pictures in her mind flittered about like the imagery in a kaleidoscope. Sometimes she was in the motel room with its hot air balloon motif. Then she seemed to be in the movie itself. Next, she was reliving the events of her past few days. Everything was a hopeless jumble. At last she surrendered to sleep. From time to time she'd hear bits and pieces of the TV sound track. Try as she might, she couldn't make sense of what people were saying. Even the music defied the rhythms and tones to which her ear was accustomed.

She soon lapsed into a dream. An airplane or helicopter--some sort of aircraft--had landed outside a small town in the Sierras where she was visiting. She was with her grandparents. She couldn't remember why her mother wasn't there. It was all very real, frighteningly so, though she was young and impressionable. Creatures like something out of a cartoon had gathered around her, strange, naked-looking beings with grayish skin. Had they gathered around her, or around the character in the movie? Was that her, or an actress? It was their eyes she remembered. They were more like pools of tranquil water or mirrors than human or animal eyes.

Some men from the Army came and kept everyone out. But for some reason she was right in the center of it. She didn't understand why. People were yelling all around her, just as if she was *in* the movie rather than watching it. Only now, it no longer seemed like a movie. Then she felt someone pick her up, a soldier or policeman. She remembered the prickly feeling of her face pressed into the scratchy shoulder of a uniform as she was placed in the back seat of a car. It smelled of stale sweat. Soon afterwards the car raced off.

She was being brought into somebody's home. People there were weeping and wailing. Were these her grandparents? They seemed terrified. She could not understand all this fuss over going to a movie. It was just a movie. It was all pretend, nothing to worry about.

Slowly, what had seemed to be a reality faded into a dream. The dream became the old movie again and she could smile about her fears. She thought how odd it was that childhood fantasies could seem so real, even after all these years.

Lying half-awake in the motel room in Albuquerque, surrounded by its gaudy decor, she realized it had been a long time since she'd seen that movie, or experienced the strange drift between dream, movie, and reality that was so often associated with it. And she had no idea why it all came back to her now.

There was a strange knocking. Someone was knocking at her door! Her startled response brought her back to the motel room.

She heard mumblings in the hallway, and recognized Tom's voice. She looked at the clock. It was 7:40 p.m! Tara felt panic. More than two hours past her date with Tom and Margarette at the restaurant! Drowsy, rubbing her eyes, she stumbled to the door and pulled it open.

"Oh, god, I fell asleep. I had no idea it was so late."

Tom hugged her. "We thought you'd been kidnapped. You look terrible. You been drinkin' again, Sweetheart?"

"Tom, don't be rude," Margarette said.

"It's okay," Tara told her. "He knows I don't drink. I'm just so drowsy...lost in dreamland." Her body felt leaden. She turned on the lights and invited them into the room. The television set was no longer on. *Did I turn it off?* she wondered, distractedly. Tom stepped in while Margarette hung back, hesitant to enter.

"Have you guys eaten?"

"We ordered, figuring you'd show up. We rang your room but there was no answer. They said you were out. So we ate, then decided we'd better check up on you. I guess you forgot about us. What do you think, Margarette? I suspect we're not on Tara's A-list anymore."

"You'll have to excuse Tom," Margarette said. "He's had a few Margaritas."

"This is embarrassing as hell. I overslept! I never do that."

"We're just sorry you weren't able to meet us for dinner," Margarette said, doing a decent job of disguising her annoyance. "Maybe we'd better leave you alone."

"I'm just groggy." Tara rubbed the back of her neck. It felt stiff and sore to the touch. Her skin felt sensitive as from a slight sunburn. Probably cramped from lying on it wrong.

"Maybe you're coming down with something," Tom said. "Anybody coughing on the plane? You know, flu viruses and God knows what all travels in the air-conditioning."

"I don't know," Tara said. "Would you mind if I called you in the morning? I'm just feeling off."

For a moment she felt a twinge of guilt and wanted somehow to assure them she hadn't been drinking. That was the truth. She hadn't touched any alcohol and hadn't eaten anything since eight o'clock that morning. Surely, if she'd ingested some sort of drugs they would have acted upon her long before this! On the plane she'd eaten only the usual snack. Oh yes, she'd had water from a bottle she bought in a convenience store right around the corner from the motel. But that couldn't have done it. Who would want to drug her?

"Maybe you should see a doctor." Tom touched her shoulder and studied her eyes for a moment. He seemed genuinely concerned, and in spite of her punchy state, his compassion triggered the old chemistry. It was nice, slightly arousing, to feel that somebody cared, that somebody was actually looking out for her welfare. But was he, really? Or was this just his way of getting on her good side before he dropped the bomb, before he told her he couldn't make it up to Taos for Christmas? She turned away. She didn't want to get too deeply into that, into the cross-current of old affections and present grievances that she knew were hovering very close to the surface.

"I think we should let her get some rest," Margarette said flatly.

Did Margarette sense the spark of intimacy her husband had just put out, Tara wondered.

"She's right," Tom said. "We'll call in the morning. I'll check my schedule at school tomorrow. Call me, will you?"

Margarette had already turned away from the door and was several steps down the hall.

Tara nodded vaguely, said goodbye and closed the door. She sat down on the edge of the bed. Slowly, as she gathered her wits about her she began to focus on her body. She felt a stinging behind her right ear. She fingered it gingerly and found a small bump, about the size of pea.

Her profound drowsiness had been caused by--by what? Perhaps some exotic spider? She thought about this a moment. Shivers undulated down her spine. Was it possible she'd been bitten by an arachnid that had been flown in from some exotic locale weeks before, a stowaway in the folds of the seat where she'd had the misfortune to sit? That explained it! Just a stupid spider. She tried to remember what people did about spider bites. Some could be quite toxic, even fatal. She wondered if she should see a doctor, as Tom had suggested. Probably not, she decided. They'd only make a big deal of it and keep her quarantined for twenty-four hours. She'd never had a friend who'd complained of anything but a little swelling from spider bites.

She made her way to the bathroom. Her head was clearing nicely. Really, she felt fine--perfectly rested and fully alert, actually as if she'd been given a miracle cure. In fact, she felt more rested than she'd felt in years! She decided she shouldn't worry about the spider bite. If it was serious she wouldn't feel as good as she felt now, having slept so well and so deeply for a few hours. Still, a hot shower would be great. That would surely clear her head.

In the bathroom, she leaned against the sink and stared at her face in the mirror. Except for the mussed tangle of her short blond hair she looked fine. She stripped down, surveying her naked body in the mirror. Had she lost weight? When they first met, what now seemed like ages ago, Tom had called her anorexic. God knows, she was skinny as a rail at the time, almost boyish except that she'd always had shapely breasts. She guessed she'd put on ten pounds since then. Most of it muscle, she told herself, thanks to daily runs and a good workout at the gym twice a week. Tom would be surprised to see her naked now. The thought of him seeing her now aroused her, in spite of the ambivalence she felt toward him.

She had always liked her own figure and so far it had improved with the years. There weren't a whole lot of women, or men for that matter, who could say that. At five-four, her 115 pounds had a supple, athletic look. Tom and she had dated before she'd developed much muscle on her arms and legs. She even knew some martial arts maneuvers now, which gave her a certain grace and confidence in her movements. The truth was, she'd never been happier with her body. Why, then, was she still single, still without a man in her life? She slipped into the shower.

She felt strangely anxious as she bathed but could not figure out what was bothering her. Something in the movie...but what movie? The television set had been turned off when she woke up. She had dreamed it. That was the only explanation there could be. Maybe there'd been no movie at all!

She turned her back to the showerhead, directing the stream of soothing warm water to the swelling behind her right ear. The warm water was comforting. Then an odd thing happened. A black stream of something poured down over her shoulder, pooling on the floor of the shower. It was like black ink. Like the ink from squid when you are cleaning them. But where was the ink coming from? Somewhere in her travels she'd walked under a dripping pipe or maybe just the edge of a roof. Something had landed in her hair. That must be it. Maybe something dripped on her head from the overhead compartment of the airplane. Somehow it had gotten in her hair. There were a million reasonable explanations. No mysteries here.

As she stepped from the shower and toweled off, she felt hungry. She glanced once more at the clock. It was now nearly nine. She decided to get dressed and go downstairs to the coffee shop. At least she could get a sandwich.

She opened her overnight bag and searched carefully through the contents, trying to decide what to wear. She chose something that wouldn't make her look too much like a tourist--jeans, with a sweatshirt her father had sent her from Albuquerque a few years before. She was glad she'd brought it. It was black with a small, stylized eagle in full flight over her heart. She laid the jeans and sweatshirt on the bed, then absently snapped on the TV. Nothing but static and snow on the first channel. She flipped to others. None of them worked, either. Snow and static on every channel. Frustrated, she switched it off and for the second time since she arrived picked up the phone to complain to the management.

She lifted the receiver, pressed it to her ear, started to dial, then stopped as before. She could talk to somebody at the desk when she went downstairs. Better to do it in person. She paused, her thoughts turning to Tom and Margarette, then to her dad's mysterious package, then back to Tom and Margarette. She reached to dial the phone again, thinking, *my mind is going a mile a minute, flitting from one thing to another. This is not like me at all!* She was always so focused. Punctual. Drake always teased her that her mind ran on steel tracks, never wavering off course. Steady, dependable, practical minded, responsible...oh, that was her, all right! She finished dialing the phone from memory. She listened as it rang, once, twice, a third time. A voice answered and at first Tara couldn't remember who she'd dialed.

"I...this is Tara," she said, falteringly. "I'm so embarrassed..."

"Oh, I was about to call you. We just stepped into the house. How are you feeling?"

"I'm fine, really. I took a shower and feel fine now. I guess it's just fatigue."

"I'm glad to hear it," Margarette said. "Tom checked his calendar. He's got a school meeting in the morning, and I've got to get to a doctor's appointment. So breakfast is out. Tom was wondering about lunch, maybe over near campus. I have to meet with one of my dissertation advisors, so I'll be able to be there, too."

Tara was surprised by the depth of her own disappointment. She hadn't realized how much she'd wanted to spend time with Tom. And she had hoped that Tom would be the one to answer, not Margarette. "That's not going to work," Tara said. "I'm so sorry. I need to get on the road as early in the morning as possible." She hoped she didn't communicate exactly the emotions she was feeling.

"I'm sure Tom will understand. Call us tomorrow night, would you? We'll be around. Maybe we can get together on your way back."

Did she detect a little cattiness in Margarette's voice? Someday soon it would be good to sit down and have a long talk with her, woman to woman. It didn't do any good to disguise the feelings she still had for Tom. If the three of them were ever going to be friends, Tara knew she had to admit what she felt and assure Margarette of her loyalty, that she would honor their marriage always. Unless, of course... Unless what? Tara asked herself. What kind of fool was she to cling to old romantic feelings with a person she not only had rejected long ago, but whose charm and sweet manner were mere camouflage?

"I'll call you from Gallup," Tara promised. "Margarette, I hope you don't think I'm a complete flake."

Margarette laughed. "Oh, no, not at all, not at all. Tom explained everything."

For a moment Tara felt a sense of horror. What was it Tom had explained? she asked herself. What could it possibly be? He certainly didn't know her mind, never had. But now Margarette was saying goodbye, saying something about really having to run.

"Goodbye."

"Yes, sure. Goodbye."

*   *   *

Half an hour later, Tara stood at the door of the motel coffee shop, staring at the closed sign in disbelief. She'd had her heart set on getting a sandwich and a glass of milk, and her stomach protested loudly at this unexpected change of events. She crossed the hallway to the front desk. The young woman on duty seemed surprised to learn the coffee shop was closed so early, though from where she sat she could clearly see the door of the cafe and the closed sign on it. She told Tara about a fast food restaurant two blocks away.

"I almost forgot," Tara said. "The TV is broken in my room."

"Oh, really?" the desk person said. "I'll leave a note for maintenance."

No apology. No offer to take something off the rent. No offer to change rooms. Not that Tara cared that much about the TV. But the desk person's apathy outraged her. How could people in her position be so indifferent to those she was paid to serve? Without patrons like Tara the young woman wouldn't have a job at all. It reminded Tara of that worn out joke at the university--that teaching would be a great profession if it weren't for the students.

Outside the motel office, the air was heavy and still but beginning to get chilly. The sky was perfectly clear, filled with stars. The weather in New Mexico was always so unpredictable this time of the year, storming one moment, clear and crisp the next. Tara decided to walk the few blocks to the fast food place instead of taking her car.

She turned a corner and found herself suddenly on a dark, abandoned street, less than a block from the motel. A shriek overhead sent a shot of adrenalin through her veins, stiffening her body with fear. The sound was like something from another world, a banshee cry, ghostly and terrible. A dark shape plummeted out of the sky, silent and eerie, only a shadow at first, then taking the shape of a large bird. She ducked, dropping to her knees as it plummeted toward her, veering off at the last moment.

Ghostly wings swept within inches of her face as the huge bird dove past her. She jerked her head up in time to see a large sewer rat race across the lid of a steel trash container in the alley behind one of the stores. The rat leapt toward a row of garbage cans in an effort to escape, landing with a heavy thud on the loose metal lid, which in

turn clattered to the ground, spinning across the alleyway in a cacophony of raucous metallic explosions that bore into Tara's brain.

The bird, an owl, snagged the neck of the hapless animal in its talons just as the rat rebounded from the metal lid. The rat squirmed furiously, in one last labor of survival, but the powerful bird rose into the sky undaunted by the efforts of its quarry. With soundless strokes of its powerful wings, it rose like a ghost toward rooftops four stories above the street.

Trembling, Tara watched as darkness swallowed up both the hunter and its prey. Slowly, the sounds of the city returned. Down on all fours in the middle of the sidewalk, where she'd crouched to escape what she had thought was an attack on her, she knew how the rat must feel. Ordinarily, she abhorred rodents. So she smiled at her sudden willingness to identify with its plight. Finally, she rose to her feet and brushed herself off. *You're ridiculous,* she muttered, relieved there hadn't been anyone on the street to witness her overreaction. Still, anybody who'd been in her position would have done the same, she decided. It was, after all, not something that happened every day. In fact, it was very unusual to see such a bird in the middle of the city.

Though shaken she continued on her way, keeping an eye in the direction of the rooftops. The chances of the bird returning were virtually non-existent, weren't they? And because owls were fiercely territorial, the possibility of an attack by a second bird was unlikely. Still, she found herself scouring the star lit heavens as she walked. Her mind tumbled from one thought to another. Many Indians associated the owl with witchcraft, she knew. They said it was a bad omen, and used rituals to ward off its dark influences. But there were others who spoke of the owl as an ally, an honored animal who acted as a messenger between the seen and unseen worlds.

Tara remembered an Indian woman she'd bumped into at Machu Pichu, when she and Tom were in Peru. It started when Tara had an argument with Tom--over what, she could no longer recall. Tara had wandered off, wanting to be by herself. She'd found a small, square stone structure, less than half the size of an average garage, tucked away in one of the minor ruins. The walls of the building were made of rock. The roof had partially collapsed and the place had only a single doorway. Noting that it had no windows, Tara thought the building might once have been a store room. Wanting to investigate, she had poked her head inside. As she did, there was a frantic flapping of wings; a huge owl rose from the center of the room and escaped through a hole in the roof.

Shaken and trembling from the sudden appearance of the bird, Tara had nevertheless stepped inside. As she waited for her eyes to adjust to the darkness, she had the eerie feeling that she was not alone. Someone or something was there in the tiny building with her! In a moment, she saw a figure. At first Tara had thought it was nothing more than a pile of rags. Then the pile stirred and a voice emerged from the gloom.

"*Que de passo?*" Tara had asked, in the most colloquial Spanish she knew, her voice shrill and trembling. *What's going on?*

In a voice that crackled with age, Tara heard, in Spanish: "Why have you come?"

"*No importante*," Tara had answered, in her broken Spanish. "I'm a visitor. I was just looking around."

"Go away. Owl is angry with you being here. You come too soon." The crone mumbled several more words, something Tara could not translate. It had something to do with Tara having too much culture, something about not being wild, or of not being *natural*. The old woman's Spanish was mixed with idioms Tara had never heard before, and some of her words were in an unfamiliar dialect.

Tara had asked the old woman about the bird she'd seen. The crone had laughed, a sardonic, condescending laugh: "You are a very ignorant young woman!" Then the crone said something about the bird being her helper from the other side. It was taking her to the place of the dead. Tara had interrupted her journey.

Tara had asked the old woman if she needed medical assistance, and the crone only cackled, ordering her once again to go away. Tara didn't know what to say. A full minute passed in silence. Then the crone said something very peculiar, the memory of which now sent shivers up Tara's spine: "I have seen the owl and the rat together. It is a sign. The Dark pursues me. She brings me Death like a treasure. In the future Owl will speak to you. She will speak."

That was all. Tara had retreated, back to the parking lot. She found Tom waiting for her in the car. She opened the door and climbed in, eager to tell him what she'd seen and heard. After listening to Tara's story about the owl and the crone, Tom had simply smiled.

"It's an old legend, a myth," he said, then added in a singsong voice that belittled her experience: "The Crone, the Owl and the Rat. Surely you've read about it. You just forgot."

"But I really saw it," Tara had protested. "I'm not dreaming!"

"Strange things happen around here. I'd be willing to bet if you went back there now she'd be gone. Did she ask you for money?"

"No, she didn't ask for money! What's the matter with you?"

"That's what I love about you, Tara. You're so damned gullible! It's charming. I mean it. It really is."

"And you're an ass, Tom."

"It's a test."

"What are you talking about?"

Tom had shrugged. "You know, a test. The spirits want to know which world you're living in."

"Did you set me up? Did you pay that old woman?"

"Me? My darling, how could you accuse me of such a thing?" He had started the engine of the car and was twisting around looking out the rear window as he backed out of the parking place. His big toothy grin told her he was going to stonewall her.

Had he hired some old beggar woman to put her on? It wouldn't be out of character for him. But then, what about the owl? He wouldn't have been able to fake that!

"Stop the car," she'd said. "Let's go back there right now. I want to talk to that old woman. I want to know the truth."

"Come on, we've got to get back to the hotel." He reminded her of their scheduled dinner meeting with a group of anthropologists from the university. Driven by her own sense of duty and youthful enthusiasm for meeting with other professionals from her field, she'd dropped the subject and soon enough let go of her anger at Tom.

Tara had never followed through with her questions about the old woman. In a way, she'd been reluctant to probe further, fearing ridicule from Tom. He was quite capable of setting her up, more to prove his superiority than to prove a point. At the time he fancied himself a modern day shaman--more witch than priest, she thought--and took every opportunity to play with people's fears and fantasies. He loved to create the impression that he possessed magical powers. In the beginning of their relationship, she believed he was just joking around with his shamanic posturing. And there was certainly the possibility that it had started in fun. But over time he'd begun to take it seriously, and she had come to despise his little games.

Now, however, having been scared nearly out of her wits by the appearance of an owl and a rat on the streets of Albuquerque, she wished she had pursued those questions. Could the owl and the rat together be a real curse or omen, as the crone had said it was? Not that she believed in such things! She'd run across many allusions to such beliefs in her studies. She tried to remember what, if anything, she'd seen in her books about rituals to protect oneself from maledictions of that kind. Even as she was thinking these things, she was amazed by her own reaction to them. It surprised her that she'd even remembered the encounter with the crone. It was curious how one responded to ancient superstitions when events like this occurred. Perhaps the owl and the rat were merely evoking some deep unconscious fears, like the primeval fear of snakes.

By the time she'd reached the restaurant Tara had calmed down. Her stomach growled, craving food, but all she could think of was the owl on a rooftop somewhere, tearing bits of flesh from the still warm carcass of the rat. Pressing her disgust to the back of her mind, she ordered a chicken sandwich with fries and hot tea. She sat all alone in an orange plastic booth, picking at the food.

I have seen the owl and the rat together, she mused, remembering the old woman's words. Her food hardly seemed appetizing now. She ate a half-dozen fries and less than half the sandwich. Suddenly she stood up and tossed her dinner into the chrome-topped garbage can near the door.

As she walked back to her room in the dark, she felt strangely restless. She'd felt like this before, just prior to her lecture presentations. Maybe it had something to do with Tom. Or maybe it was her worry about the adventure into which she felt herself being drawn by the artifacts she'd received in the mail. She wondered, was Drake really alive? She'd given him up for dead months ago. If he wasn't alive, it meant that someone was playing a very cruel trick on her, or worse, that they were deliberately drawing her into...into what? She could not even imagine why someone would want to harass her this way. It just made much more sense that Drake was alive. When she caught up with him, the first thing she'd insist on would be answers. She hated the idea of a showdown with him but certainly that was better than the alternative--to discover that there was a deeper, more sinister source of intrigue behind these elusive contacts with him. Over the years she'd grown used to his little dramas--vague plans, plans changing at the last moment, long waits, big hurry-ups, melodramatic insights that turned out to be nothing more than the product of his imagination.

Nothing ever happened with Drake the way it did with ordinary people. It was difficult to imagine she shared his genes. He raged through life, stumbling, pushing, leaping into adventures she would never choose for herself. And here she was, once again, drawn into his chaotic little world. Adventures, he liked to call them!

*   *   *

She checked out of her room the next morning at nine-fifteen. She tossed her bag in the back of the car, got a complimentary cup of coffee in the motel lobby, along with a soggy Danish, then climbed in behind the wheel of the rented Chevy and laced her way through morning traffic. The car ran smoothly, with plenty of power. She pushed it up to ten miles an hour over the speed limit, keeping one eye in the rearview mirror. The cops in New Mexico could be tough on speeders. But she'd always been lucky, able to spot them before it

was too late.

She nibbled the Danish, holding it gingerly between her fingers, pushing back the cellophane wrapper as she ate. The paper coffee cup teetered unsteadily in a small recess on the dashboard. Steam rising from the hot contents fogged up a narrow triangle at the center of the windshield.

On interstate 40, heading west, she watched the traffic creeping into town and was grateful not to be there. Heavy, gray clouds hovered over the desert. A half-hour later a hard-driving rain enveloped her, the white car fading into the ground fog that rose from the warm desert floor. ~

Standing Alone

The glowing green numbers on the Chevy's dashboard clock said four-twenty. Tara rubbed her eyes. They burned from peering through the rain and the silver-gray fog. She glanced once more at the digital numbers. They couldn't be correct! She lifted her wrist from the steering wheel and glanced at her watch. Four-ten, the dial said. The clock was right, at least within a few minutes. And Tara definitely remembered resetting her watch on the plane when they crossed the time zone. She quickly calculated the hours she'd been traveling. She'd left at nine-fifteen. Something was definitely wrong. Seven hours to drive the 140 miles from Albuquerque to Gallup made no sense at all, not even in the rain.

What was it she'd forgotten? She wracked her brain, trying to recall where she could have spent so much time. This was insane! At most the trip should have taken three and a half hours. The only explanation for the lost time was that she'd stopped somewhere along the way. But she had no recollection at all of a stop. Her stomach growled, proof that she had not even had any lunch, which could have accounted for an hour, at the most.

She glanced at the gas gauge. The indicator was riding between the one-half and one quarter full. So she couldn't have even stopped for gas. Perhaps she'd stopped to rest along the way. It was conceivable. She might have pulled off the road to rest her eyes, then overslept as she'd done at the motel the night before. If she'd done that, however, she surely would have remembered waking up and getting started again. She usually looked for a good strong cup of coffee after napping, and there were plenty of small towns where she would have gone for that. But she had no memory of it.

Then she remembered the strange bump behind her right ear, and her hand went up reflexively. It was still slightly painful but the swelling had gone down. As she touched it, she remembered the strange dream she'd had back in Albuquerque at the motel, then the black inky substance that had appeared when she showered. Were the two connected, the bump behind her ear and the ink? Maybe the ink had come from the bump and the same had caused her to hallucinate, and to lose all sense of time. She took her fingers away from her ear and rubbed them together. They felt a little oily. But that could be normal. She touched the sore spot. For a second she had a vivid image of James Dean's face, just as it had appeared on the television screen at the motel. When she pressed the sore it stimulated that image.

For a moment she panicked. Then she reminded herself that she'd seen her doctor less than a month ago, and had gone through a complete workup, so she was quite certain she didn't have some dread disease. A spider bite was the most plausible explanation. She'd heard of arachnids that caused quite serious swelling without posing any serious threats to a person's health. But could such a bite really be responsible for lost time, hours passing when she had no recollection of what she had done or where she had gone?

Surely something very strange was going on in her mind! Narcolepsy. Could that be it? She'd heard about people with narcolepsy just dropping off to sleep in the middle of a conversation. When they woke up they had no memory of sleeping or what they had been doing moments before they drifted off. But that was un-likely, too. If she had been driving the car when that happened she would have driven off the road or veered into oncoming traffic and crashed.

Besides, she had no history of narcolepsy or any other illness. Nor was there any kind of illness with an hereditary link in her family that could have explained what she'd been experiencing. Not that this proved she couldn't have it. But what was it? Other than feeling a little tired, she felt great, physically and mentally. Better than usual, if the truth were known. She must have pulled off the road and slept for a period of time. Eventually she'd remember it, she was certain. It was only a brief memory lapse.

The only thing in her memory now was a vague recollection of the movie she'd seen at the motel the night before. But what a strange thing to remember--a grade "B" movie! And what a coincidence to see a film from her childhood, or at least a fragment of it. It didn't make sense. What made even less sense to her was why the film stuck in her mind. She had vague, fragmented memories now of other scenes from the movie, scenes she hadn't previously remembered. There was a small room. She was alone in it. Someone was talking, a disembodied voice. Maybe a voice over the loudspeaker, like on the plane when the pilots speak. But more than one person was speaking. Their thoughts raced around in her head, as if they were her own.

"That's ridiculous," she said aloud. Then, hearing her own voice in the confines of the car, she added: "Great, now I'm talking to myself!" In spite of herself, she found this amusing.

As her mind cleared, she felt her own excitement rising. If she could find Drake, or trace down where he had been, new possibilities would open up to her. After the long drive, this prospect was like a breath of fresh air, revitalizing her. Never had she felt closer to her dream of finding the society of shamans and collecting artifacts to reconstruct enough of their culture to prove their existence and their importance. With a little luck, she'd take back enough proof of their existence to apply for funding and begin the search for a crew of archaeologists to work with. She would have to choose her team carefully, avoiding people whose ambitions would create power struggles. Yet, she would need people with enough credibility in the business to guarantee that the work was respected by her peers.

As she passed the sign announcing that Gallup was ahead, there was a momentary break in the weather. She reacted as if on automatic pilot now, turning south toward the frontage road and the row of businesses along the highway. Halfway down the strip, past curio shops, cheap motels and gas stations, she spotted a small Mexican restaurant. The windows were decorated with colorful paper cutouts of donkeys, cacti, and people wearing huge sombreros. There was a subtle irony in the way these figures were designed and arranged. Somebody inside had a good sense of humor.

Tara parked at the curb a block away, made certain her doors were locked, then walked briskly, stretching her legs. She passed the window of an electronics store. Staring out at her was a huge TV screen, at least four feet across. A man's face filled the screen. He was holding a microphone and talking. But no sound was piped out onto the street so she could not hear what he was saying. Now she saw a crowd behind him, with emergency crews milling about. Suddenly the images on the screen began shifting, as if somebody was surfing the channels. The imagery went from color to black and white. For a second it showed a bright object in the sky, flittering about between the clouds. She stopped directly in front of the store window, staring at the screen as it flipped through more channels. Then the screen filled with snow. For a moment, the same movie she'd seen the night before appeared. Strange that it was being repeated here, 150 miles from Albuquerque!

She looked beyond the screen to the inside of the store. As near as she could tell, the place was empty. She spotted a sign on the door. Closed at four o'clock. Odd hours. But perhaps this time of year there wasn't much business. She turned and walked on. She

shivered. A few steps away she caught herself thinking that, out of the corner of her eye, she'd seen the man with the microphone reappear on the screen. But she could not be certain. And anyway, why did that seem so important to her?

As she entered the Mexican restaurant a bell jingled over the door, a cheerful greeting. She could use some good cheer. Besides, it was warm here. She smelled corn tortillas, beans, rice and chicken stewing. What a wonderful mingling of odors! It was as though these delicious scents had been absorbed by every surface in the place, from floor to ceiling, over many years. Somehow the entire ambiance was charming and comforting, if not exactly a health inspector's dream.

The walls were painted light green, with turquoise and coral trim. A narrow shelf ran around the perimeter of the main room, high up on the walls, beyond most people's reach. On the shelf were hand-decorated bowls and plates facing outward. She recognized them as the traditional low-fire earthenware from Mexico, the kind readily available in native markets all across that country. Along with the plates there were hand-painted metal cutouts of howling coyotes and ravens so dignified they seemed to be in formal wear.

Tara took a seat in a red leatherette booth at the front of the room, facing the highway. The table in front of her was covered with a red and white checkered oilcloth, worn smooth at the edges. As she sat down, she glanced out the window. Suddenly the sky lit up, thunder clattered, and in seconds rain was pouring down again, pelting the plate glass window.

Outside, two men dressed only in tee-shirts and jeans ran past, racing toward a pickup truck parked at the curb. The rain soaked their hair and their drenched tee-shirts clung to their muscular backs as they leapt into the truck. Tara shivered, sympathetic with how they must feel, caught in the downpour and chilled to the bone.

A young man, no more than fifteen years old, came over to her table and flashed a toothy smile. He was dark skinned, with big brown eyes. Not Indian, she speculated. He was most certainly from Mexico.

"Have you driven far?" he asked.

Even with those four words she heard the accent in his voice. She was good at accents. This one was from central Mexico, probably Mexico City.

"Pretty far," she said. "From Albuquerque."

"It's a bad storm. My grandfather went down there last night to see the doctor. He's old. He worries about his health. Sometimes I go with him. It's very bad for him to go so far alone."

Tara looked up, surprised by the boy's candor. "You're very fond of your grandfather."

"He's a very stubborn old man, you know? He tells me I have to stay and help my mother."

Tara smiled. "You're very sweet."

The boy looked down, fidgeted with his order pad, a tight grin on his face.

"I'm sorry," she said. "I didn't mean to embarrass you."

He shrugged. "*Esta bien.*"

Tara ordered the Super Chicken Burrito, the dinner special, then asked, "Have you ever been down to Coyote Mesa?"

"Yeah, a coupla' times." The boy looked nervous. After a moment he dropped his gaze again, studying the order pad and doodling with the stub of a yellow pencil he clutched in his fingers.

"You have any friends down there?"

"No, Ma'am." He smiled but something in his demeanor had definitely changed. He seemed more reserved, not as outgoing.

"Is something wrong? What is it about Coyote Mesa?"

"I don't know. I'm supposed to help in the kitchen."

The young man turned away and disappeared into the back of the restaurant. Tara recognized his voice, speaking in Spanish to someone in the kitchen. He sounded excited, distressed. A moment later a thin woman with salt and pepper hair trapped under a black hair net came over to the booth. The young man held back. He leaned against the open kitchen doorway watching.

"Excuse me, *senora.* You asked my son about Coyote Mesa."

"Yes."

"Do you have friends down there?"

"My father. Why?"

"Excuse me. It's not so good for women to go down there alone. Pretty rough place."

"Why? What's at Coyote Mesa?"

"If your father is there, it's okay maybe."

"And if he wasn't?"

The woman shrugged her shoulders. "There are places not for a woman alone. *Cuidado!* Be careful, *senora.*"

"Thank you," Tara said. She returned the smile and the woman turned away, joining the young man at the kitchen doorway, then disappearing inside again. Tara wondered if there was something about her own demeanor that caused older women to want to protect her. Though she never paid too much attention to such warnings, she seemed to get them wherever she went. Perhaps it was just that people in undeveloped areas were not accustomed to seeing younger women traveling alone. Several times she had received such cautions during her trip to Peru. In Lima, during a short stopover on

her way to Cuzco, a well-dressed Peruvian woman in the airport warned her against traveling by herself. The woman opened her carry-on case and displayed a *pistola* which she explained that she always carried when business required her to travel alone.

"How do you get it past security?" Tara had asked.

"*Mordita*," the woman had answered. "You pay the guards not to see it. They understand."

The story of the encounter in Lima did nothing to help Tara feel more secure. Up till then she'd never feared traveling alone. She'd always been able to take care of herself. The idea that it was so easy to get a gun on the plane gave her nightmares every time she flew after that. She had visions of being hijacked in the Andes and getting diverted to some godforsaken place in the Amazon.

She hated guns. Tom had one that he had carried in his backpack when they first met. It was for protection from animals, not people, he said. He had purchased it at the marketplace in Cuzco. She made him get rid of it. He'd given it away, actually, to one of the laborers they'd hired to carry their gear into the back country. That didn't do a lot to put her mind at ease either. After that she had visions of getting robbed by the hired help. Guns were no good. Whether you carried them for personal protection, war or mischief they always spelled trouble.

In less than twenty minutes the young man, her waiter, returned with her plate, holding a folded towel under it. His smile was back but he was clearly not as comfortable and outgoing as he had been. He warned her that her plate was hot and disappeared. Was he not supposed to talk with the customers? Or did it have more to do with Coyote Mesa? She thought about probing mama a bit but dismissed the idea, deciding the whole thing was blown way out of proportion. It was probably associated with a superstition about the area, something they did not want to talk about with a stranger. If anybody could find out about any special problems in Coyote Mesa, it would be Tom. She'd call him after checking into a motel. The weather being what it was, she decided not to drive on to Coyote Mesa that night.

Meanwhile, the food the young man had placed on her table was delicious. She ate slowly, savoring the fresh tomatoes, cilantro, garlic, tomatillos and jalapenos that flavored the sauce. It was surely not out of the can but very possibly from an old family recipe. When she was done eating she had the boy bring her a *flan*. It came in a saucer, still warm, exactly as she liked it. Thin, dark caramel sauce had been artfully drizzled over the top and down into the saucer. Perfect.

Twenty minutes later, it was still raining and the idea of leaving the warm restaurant, with all its delicious smells, was the last thing Tara wanted to do. She ordered a cup of coffee and found a tabloid which a previous customer had left in her booth. It contained a listing of Indian markets, with profiles of various crafts people from the area. A calendar showed that most of these events were over for the season. She read a profile, however, about a woman from Zuni who had won a prize for her fetish carvings at a fair in Taos. There was a photo of her with one small animal carving she had made. The animal was a mountain lion, a long, sleek figure with its tail curled over its back. As Tara studied the carving she could imagine the real animal in the wild. It seemed female to her. She decided it was hunting, crouched low, close to the earth, lithe and agile and powerful. She jotted down the name of the carver in her notebook and promised herself that if she went to Zuni she would find that woman. She felt an attraction to the mountain lion and to the woman who'd carved it, and thought perhaps she could buy one as a talisman.

As she was putting away her notebook she remembered her father's friend, Chocko, who lived in Zuni, or at least had lived there during her last visit with her father. Why hadn't she thought of him sooner? Drake would surely have contacted him if he'd been in the area, and Coyote Mesa was located just a dozen or so miles beyond the southernmost border of that reservation. She promised herself she'd call Chocko the first chance she got.

She was definitely interested in the Zuni fetishes. Each one played many useful roles in the Zuni culture, roles that had been maintained for perhaps thousands of years, passed down through the generations by rituals, stories and even in the decorations on pottery and weavings. She knew about the mountain lion, knew that it was said to be the master hunter and the Guardian of the North. It stood for wisdom, the knowledge that only came from the ancients, and from the trials and victories of one peoples' entire history. Wisdom, she'd once read, was that *knowledge which applies to all equally*. It was universal knowledge and therefore sacred truth which must be held as holy and unimpeachable.

Tara had first learned about animal fetishes while she was still in graduate school. It was the first hint she had that there was a tradition of divination among the Pueblo peoples. She'd found reference to them in some obscure reports to the Bureau of Ethnology, dated from the mid-1800s. A man by the name of Frank Hamilton Cushing had been sent to the Southwest to study the cultures of the indigenous peoples and collect artifacts for what became the Smithsonian Institution. Cushing, a self-taught, intuitive anthropologist had done an excellent job of collecting and documenting the Zuni culture. In fact, he had become so enamored of this society, and they of him, that he became an honorary chief and lived among them for many years, until his death at the turn of the century.

In Cushing's writings, which were extensive, Tara had found evidence for her theories about the secret society of shamans. For various reasons, she doubted that the actual oracle priests were Zunis. But the tradition of animal fetishes among the Zunis, their reputation as great fetish carvers, and reports of ceremonies, recorded by Cushing, for blessing and empowering the fetishes, suggested that the Zunis might have provided these objects for use in secret oracle ceremonies performed by Tara's hypothetical society of shamans.

Tara felt strongly attracted to the picture of the mountain lion fetish. But why this powerful attraction? First and foremost, she told herself, this was a magnificent, powerful animal. She had seen them in the wild only twice, but each time she was awed by the animal's strength, its sleek beauty, and its graceful, confident movements. While she thoroughly disliked superstition, she respected sacred truths. And surely the fetish carving captured the sacred truths of this animal's beauty and power. What's more, she understood why the fetish carvers of old had chosen the mountain lion as Guardian of the North. It was not only the guardian but also a seeker of truth, a hunter and tracker. Tara loved the idea of having a fetish of this animal; she felt a close identification with it. There were times in her work that she felt herself to be a seeker, as tenacious and resolute as this great animal.

She glanced out the window to see if the rain was letting up. No. It pelted the glass noisily. She left a ten dollar bill on the counter with her check, allowing a two dollar tip for the boy.

Nobody came out to collect. Judging from the sounds in the kitchen they were busily preparing for the dinner crowd. She decided not to bother them, and just left.

Outside, she shivered, then held the tabloid she'd been reading over her head and made a run for it. The sky lit up again, the thunder roared, and the rain came down harder. She fumbled for the keys, dropped them on the ground beside the car, and as she knelt to pick them up the cold rain ran down her neck. The chilling riverlet raced down her spine, sending shivers throughout her body. Soaking wet, she unlocked the door and slipped in behind the wheel. She squirmed as her wet clothes clung to the prickly seat covers.

She started the engine immediately and turned on the heater. But the engine was cold and only cold air blew out of the vents. A few blocks away she saw a neon sign declaring *Desert Sky Motel.*

How comforting it would be to jump into a hot shower and then a warm bed. What a luxury it would be to slip between crisp white sheets in a warm room out of the weather. Besides, she was feeling groggy and disoriented again. Sleep would be a blessing. Maybe the weather would even clear tomorrow and she'd have a better chance of finding Charla Mather's place. Granted, it was a long-shot, but Tara knew that Drake had stayed there many times. For all she knew, Charla herself had been the one to find Drake's envelope and drop it in the mail to her. But then there were the fragmented phone calls. How did one explain those? All the evidence she had so far pointed to the fact that Drake was still alive and that he was probably staying with Charla at Coyote Mesa.

Given the weather, it was foolish to even attempt the drive out to Charla's tonight. At another time she might have driven the distance without a moment's hesitation. She enjoyed the desert at night, the broad skies and the silence. Even with the rain, it was a good chance there would be stars. But from what could be determined on the map there were no accommodations along the way. She could imagine driving all the way out there in this storm and be unable to find Charla's house, thus having no place to stay. Even if she did find the house and Drake was around, it would not be unusual for him to disappear, leaving no word where he was going or when he'd return. Tara didn't know much about Charla Mather's but she suspected that anyone who spent time with Drake had to be a lot like him, or they would never be able to put up with each other.

Tara sat shivering, waiting for the heater to warm up, wondering what Charla's house would be like.

Two years before, Drake had described it to her. Based on his description she had drawn a crude map, whose details she still remembered. The house was off the main highway, out a road that was nothing more than two dusty wheel ruts worn into the desert floor. When it rained, the road turned into two muddy riverlets, barely passable in the car she was driving, owing to its low clearance. She would have been much better off renting a utility vehicle with four-wheel drive.

Besides muddy roads, there was always the danger of flash floods during the rainy season. The desert, seemingly flat and desolate from the distance, was actually covered with endless arroyos, shallow canyons carved into the earth. A road such as the one to the Mather house might cross several such cuts, stretching for miles through the desert. During the rainy season, they filled with water in an instant and washed away everything in their path. A road through an arroyo could be completely safe one moment, and the next turn into a raging torrent.

Seven years before, while exploring the back country with her father, they set up camp on a ridge above just such an arroyo. It was another of Drake's wild escapades. He'd gotten a lead from his editor at the *World Enquirer* that some rock hounds in a four-wheeler had come upon what looked like the wreckage of a UFO. He'd been so anxious to get into the back country where it had been spotted that he decided to chance the storm that had been building for several days. He seemed nearly oblivious to danger when he was onto a good story, particularly if he knew he was the only one pursuing it. Tara had been visiting him in Albuquerque at the time and had no intention of going out on such an escapade with him. In a way, he'd tricked her into it, telling her the storm was clearing, that there were wonderful old ruins where they could camp. It was partly true; they did find the ruins. They did not find the UFO wreckage, however, and they did not escape the storm. That he could have put his own life at risk that way enraged her, as it always did. But what made matters worse was that he'd risked her life, as well.

She had to admit, however, that he had taken her safety into account. Perhaps it was that, or maybe it was just that he respected natural disasters more than ones made by humans. She had to give him credit for taking precautions when they came to a flooded arroyo. Because of the rains, he had explained to Tara, he was hesitant to cross it, though the gulch itself was less than a hundred yards across. So they lay, dry and warm, in sleeping bags inside their tent, watching the arroyo fill with water, waiting for the storm to pass.

From their vantage point, they saw a small camper shell mounted on the back of a Toyota pickup truck drive out of the hills, lumbering along slowly and cautiously in the rain. It stopped at the edge of the arroyo, and a couple in their late 50's got out. They walked down to the water and the man waded out a ways, measuring its depth. It was only ten or twelve inches deep. In spite of the rain, Drake left his tent and walked over to warn them. Because of their out of state license plates, he thought they might not know the dangers of the desert. Tara stayed behind, warm and dry in her sleeping bag.

"I wouldn't chance it," Drake yelled to the couple. "Flash floods this time of year."

"We've seen worse," the man yelled back. "We've got four-wheel drive."

"It's your life," Drake said. "I'd wait till morning. Watch the water."

The man returned stubbornly to the truck and climbed in. He

revved the engine and lurched forward. He moved tentatively at first. Drake stood watching gravely and shaking his head. Halfway across the gully the left front wheel of the truck dropped into a hole. The whole rig shifted to the left, heaved over at an angle and skidded around, rear end facing downstream. The driver raced the engine, and all four wheels churned. Mud and water flew from the spinning wheels. But the vehicle didn't budge.

Facing upstream, water crashed against the grill, spewing up over the hood and against the front of the camper shell. The engine raced again. This time the truck leapt forward a foot or two, then veered back and around, broadside to the flow of the river and heaving over at a precarious angle.

Again the engine raced, all four wheels spinning, searching for traction and not finding it. Then the engine choked out and died. Drake ran past the tent, leapt into his Jeep, and drove to within a few feet of the water's edge. Tara watched in horror as he leapt from the cab, then hurled a huge coil of rope toward the campers. She couldn't imagine what he was trying to do. Perhaps he'd throw them a line so that they could cling to it as he pulled them out. It was clear to her that it was already too late to save the truck itself.

Then, off in the distance, she heard a terrible roar, a pounding like the plunging waters of a distant waterfall. She heard the dull, unmistakable rumble of boulders tumbling and crashing together as they were carried downstream. She screamed a warning to Drake. He scrambled madly up the bank of the arroyo just moments before the wall of water hit the side of the precariously teetering truck.

The woman was crawling out of the open window of the truck. It appeared she was trying to climb onto the roof, aided by the man from behind. The water hit her full force, flipping her onto the hood instead. For seconds, the man's arms protruded from the window, clawing at the slippery metal, trying to pull himself out. Then the truck rolled over onto its top, trapping the man inside. Thrown clear, the woman flailed above the muddy barrage of water and rock, then disappeared beneath the surface, consumed by the frenzied churning of water and rock. Fifty feet downstream the camper shell split away from the truck and came apart, spilling its contents. Canned goods, blankets, clothing, and household belongings boiled downstream into the raging torrents. Like a drowned cow the truck rolled over one more time and lodged between two boulders.

From her tent, Tara watched in horror as rocks and mud piled up against the stranded truck. For a long time, Drake stood in the rain, staring out at the upturned truck with its driver pinned inside, under the water and the mud. Tara saw the tension in her father's back as he stared at the tragedy which he had come so close to averting. She began to shake all over, stunned by the power and speed with which it had all happened.

The flood was over in minutes, leaving the arroyo with only a few inches of water in the aftermath. Drake took his rope, lashed one end around the bumper of his Jeep and waded through the shallow water to the door of the flooded out truck. She could not understand why he would risk it now, since there wasn't a chance that the driver had survived. Even from her vantage point she could see that the cab of the truck was filled with rock, washed into it by the sheer force of the flood. If there was a body in there it was now packed in amidst a ton of mud and rock.

Giving up, Drake shuffled back to the tent, thoroughly shaken.

The rain had let up but as he stood outside the dry tent, water ran down his face. Tara wondered if some of it was tears. She'd never seen her father cry and couldn't be certain he was crying now. But his face looked anguished. He was truly shaken by this event, just as she had been.

After a while, he climbed into the Jeep and changed into dry clothes. Then he came back to the tent and slipped into his sleeping bag.

"If they'd only waited another twenty minutes..." he'd said.

In spite of the horror of it all, there had been something clean and inevitable about what had happened. Nature swept in to claim these lives, with no rancor, with no desire to cause pain or grief. Never before had Tara seen people die--not right in front of her eyes. Though friends and loved ones had died in her life, she had never witnessed death's sudden, sure entrance like this, sweeping two lives away as swiftly and impersonally as she might kill a spider or an ant. Numb and trembling, she had never felt smaller or more helpless. All she could think of was a line from Albert Camus' writing: "The benign indifference of the universe." She said it aloud.

Drake put his arm around her and hugged her. She could feel his body shaking but could not tell if it was from cold or fear or grief. Maybe it was all of those together. She did not want to look at his face. *Just be my anchor now,* she had thought. *Just be larger than me!*

"Don't follow in my footsteps," he had said. "Don't follow in anybody's footsteps."

What did he mean? She had thought about his words for a long time, puzzling over them, not knowing what he'd meant or why he had said it when he did. She had thought he would say more, that he would go on, but he never did. Still, she thought about these words often and wondered what it was in the flood and the loss of two lives that had prompted him to say what he did at that moment.

By the next morning the rain had stopped and the desert looked dry and stable again. They walked for half a mile or so down the arroyo, their feet barely making a sound on the damp, hard packed earth. Once or twice large, gangly jack rabbits leapt out of nowhere, materializing magically from the desert floor, to lope across the open ground. A lone hawk circled in the distance, nothing more than a dark silhouette against an opal sky.

They found the woman's swollen body face down in a small pool of muddy water. Tara watched as Drake waded into the pool, grabbed the corpse's ankles and dragged it to high ground. Then Tara and he walked silently back to the Jeep. They returned a few minutes later. Tara helped Drake wrap the body in a blue plastic tarp. They loaded her onto the front fender and lashed her down like a trophy deer, having no other place for her in the already cramped cab.

During the night the waters had shoved the hapless truck downstream another ten or fifteen feet. But the cab was still under water and they could see no sign of the driver.

By ten o'clock the sun was out, warm and bright over the eastern horizon, bringing comfort to Tara's thoroughly chilled body. They had no trouble crossing the arroyo in their own Jeep now.

"There'll be other victims," Drake said. "Young deer get caught in watery bogs. Even rabbits and coyotes. They crawl under rocks or into caves, looking for shelter. But too late they find they're in the path of the floods. Look!"

He pointed up into the sky. A half-mile away vultures circled, having caught the scent of fresh carrion. Tara counted them. There were six.

That was long ago, Tara reminded herself. But lessons like that didn't die. From that grim experience, she'd gained infinite respect for Mother Nature. Some said the Universe was a loving, nurturing place, she reflected, as she drove in the rain down the frontage road in Gallup, toward the motel. She could not wholly disagree with that way of thinking. But lessons like the one she learned at the arroyo also sent a message that the world was a place in which every creature had to look out for itself. The universe didn't extend itself in the form of a mother's love, protecting all creatures from physical harm, any more than it extended itself in the form of a father's wrath, always punishing the guilty. Perhaps, she reasoned, this was the single lesson everyone had to learn: respect for nature's powers and for one's limitations and sheer fragility.

The horn of a semi behind her blasted her rudely out of her daydream; she pulled over to let it pass. The huge truck, pulling an empty flatbed trailer, rumbled past, spraying the side of her car with muddy water from the street. For a moment, she was blinded. The windshield wipers took nearly a full minute to clear the glass.

By the time she'd checked into the motel, it was after six o'clock. But even as early as it was she decided to settle in for the night. She bought a local paper in the motel lobby then went to her room. She switched on the TV to watch the news. When the set warmed up she saw a man out on the tarmac at the airport, an umbrella over his head. It was nearly the same image as she'd seen on the TV screen on the frontage road more than an hour before.

"The loudest sound out here tonight is the rain on my umbrella," he said. "All planes have been grounded since three o'clock this afternoon. No change in sight with the weather..." Static interrupted the sound portion of the report, then: "...tomorrow morning." Static.

The screen went blank for a moment, then the channels started shifting, flickering from one image to another, some in black and white, some in color. She glanced at the bedside table, looking for the controller. Obviously, something was wrong with the cable setup. But there was no controller that she could find, other than the buttons on the set itself. Suddenly, just as had happened in the electronics store before dinner, the screen went to pure snow and the sound went haywire. Maybe it was the storm. It appeared to be causing transmission problems all over New Mexico. The same thing had happened in her motel room back in Albuquerque.

She stared at the flickering spots on the screen like a fortune teller staring into a crystal ball, and saw her hero, the young James Dean. Some Albuquerque station must be having a revival of his movies, she noted. Dean looked directly into the camera, grinning the way only he could do, which always convinced her he was looking directly at her. He puckered his lips and she puckered hers. His mugging like this made her grin. "Hi, James Dean," she said, smiling self-consciously at her own foolishness. He grinned back at her.

She got up from the bed, crossed the room and switched off the TV. If she'd been a TV fan she would have complained to the management, though she had doubts it would have done any good. She guessed that because of the storms reception was thrown off throughout the state. Nothing the management could do about that.

She stripped off her damp clothes and jumped into the shower. The steamy water on her naked flesh flushed away all the tensions of the past few days. It was sheer bliss to stand under the warm stream and luxuriate in this way. As she bent her head, allowing the water to wash over the back of her neck, she gingerly touched the sore spot behind her ear. It was still swollen, and still slightly painful, even though the swelling was definitely diminished. She took her hand away, somewhat relieved but promising herself that she'd see a doctor about it as soon as she got back home. It would be okay. There was no sign of that terrible black dye that had oozed from it the night before.

She stayed in the shower, turning this way and that, letting the warm water flow over her back, then down over her breasts and belly, until she began to feel guilty that there would be no hot water left for the other guests. As she stepped from the shower she went over to the mirror and peered at the sore area as best she could. It looked normal. No redness. Thus, the chances were good that it wasn't a serious infection. She wished she'd brought along a hand mirror so that she could get a better look, but for now she'd have to assume that whatever it was, it was slowly healing.

She dried herself off, using the two fluffy oversized towels the motel had provided. She dropped the wet towels on the bathroom floor and crawled into bed naked, snuggling down under the covers so that the blankets nearly covered her head. The cool sheets against her warm flesh, still moist from the shower, awakened sweetly erotic feelings. She thought about Tom and how beautifully their bodies had once fit, and how well their sexual appetites had matched. That had been the one thing that kept them together, and it had been the most difficult to leave. Soon after Tom went off to New Mexico, she had felt relieved that he was gone. The baby more than filled her days, and she found the powerful energy of her sensuality satisfied in the pleasures of mothering. For months she hadn't given Tom a second thought, except to phone him now and then to give him reports on their baby's progress. It was only when she heard about him and Margarette getting married that she got in touch with her hurt.

It took Tara two years and twice that many hastily chosen, disappointing love affairs to make her see that she was not celebrating her freedom so much as punishing herself for breaking up with Tom. It had been stupid to give him up so easily. But what was done was done. Tom and Margarette had moved on with their lives. They seemed happy enough, and Tara knew she had to let go. It was the most difficult thing she'd ever had to do. Intellectually, she was a perfect saint about it, respecting their marriage. However, her stubborn heart made her a fool and told her she could still get Tom back if she had the guts. Her own feelings tore at her. Why do I want him? she asked herself. He had hurt her in so many ways. It was even possible that he was abusive with women, though she'd seen no indication of it with Margarette. But it was hardly the sort of thing a wife shared with her husband's ex-partner. Still, Tara wondered. It was almost as if there were two Toms, the one she continued to hold in her heart and the one in real life who, again

and again, had proved he was not worthy of her love, her commitment.

She'd been through all this a million times before. And each
time she got new insights about herself. She didn't beat herself up
about it as much as she once had. Still, the old ache for him came
back to haunt her at moments like this, when she least expected it.
Two years ago she'd screwed up her courage enough to share her
heartache with her Dad. He listened attentively, then told her: "No
guarantees, baby. Life comes *as is*. Just like a used car. No
guarantees. You've gotta do your own repairs." Somehow, those
words had helped, though she couldn't say exactly why. What he
said seemed callous at the time, an empty statement whose underly-
ing message was probably, "Leave me alone. Don't drag me into your
problems."

Like the subtly erotic feelings of crisp clean sheets against her
naked flesh, small comforts had taken on a larger importance in
Tara's life since Tom married. Tara learned to take her pleasure
where she could find it, just as she'd done in the Mexican restaurant
tonight. She could thoroughly enjoy a good meal--even a meal alone.
As Julia, her therapist, pointed out, flying solo at times had its own
merits. The best antidote to life's ills was to live in the moment, to
take in whatever each new moment offered. Let the past go. Soak up
all the pleasure you can. Be present. Chances were good that there
would be very little pleasure once she got to Charla Mather's place.
From what she was hearing, there was no great surplus of luxury
down there.

But her efforts to relax were frustrated. She lay in bed staring at
the ceiling, wondering about the potsherds and Drake's mysterious
phone calls. Were the fragments real, and was he in trouble, as his
voice seemed to indicate? As she thought about his message on the
answering machine she remembered hearing the roar of an engine in
the background. Maybe it was highway noise, but the more she
thought about it, the more she doubted it. The engine she heard on
the tape was running at a constant speed, the way a generator or
industrial pump might do. She remembered the sound from one of
the digs she'd visited in Mexico as a student. They had a huge
generator set up so that they could work around the clock. All night
long the generator had rumbled on, and those who slept during the
night shift had to plug their ears.

Lying awake in the quiet motel room, Tara began to remember
fragments of a conversation she'd had with Tom a year before. He
had made an offhand remark about a story he was investigating on
some public land that lay between two reservations. There was a
lawsuit pending by one of the tribal governments which claimed it

was sacred land that rightfully belonged to them. Time had blurred the details, however, and Tara couldn't remember if he'd ever said exactly where it was. Surely Tom should know something about this. She reached for the phone on the bedside table and dialed for the line out. In an instant, Tom's voice came on, a familiar, shrill, excited voice with a slightly devious quality.

"Tara, what's up?" Tom virtually shouted into the phone: "You okay out there? Feeling any better? When we saw you at the motel, you looked like something the cat wouldn't bother to drag in. You sure you should be out there at all?"

"I'm fine, Tom," she replied, noting his excitement and reminding herself that when he was under pressure he usually became excited and devious. It was one of the things that most annoyed her about him. He shifted in and out of different personalities, depending on the pressure he was feeling and his mood.

She resumed: "It's just that I don't know quite what to make of this message I got from my Dad." She hesitated, wondering if she was doing the right thing, then went on to relate all that she knew of Drake's latest escapade and of the message he'd left on her voice mail. She asked Tom about an area somewhere around Acoma, which she believed could have been Drake's destination...though her memory of this was over two years old.

"Listen, I'm concerned about you wandering around out there in your condition," Tom replied, evasively. "You're the mother of my child, sweetheart! I'd rather you went home and took care of yourself..."

"And her," Tara finished his sentence for him. "That's what you really mean, isn't it? Look, I don't want to get into a big thing with you about my responsibility as a mother. In fact, when I get back you and I have to sit down and talk about the role you're playing in your daughter's life."

"Oh, geez, Tara! Will you give it up? I'm under a lot of pressure these days. It's not easy, this extended family business."

"Well, I manage, and I'm under as much pressure as you."

"You're not married."

"What's that supposed to mean?"

"Can we talk about this another time?"

"Sure. Sure we can, Tom. Why not? Along with everything else we have been saying we need to talk about later..."

"Look here, my love, you and I aren't an item anymore. I am not going to pretend we are, and I'm not going to waste my energy working out our past."

Tara was dumbstruck. Her first reaction was to tell him to go to hell. If he was going to pull back into non-communication--that always had been his best weapon--then maybe she would... Would what? Prevent him from seeing Maya? That was hardly what she wanted. Having a child with this man had certainly taught her the vexatious benefits of humility.

"Forgive me, Tom," she said, hoping the sharp edge to her voice got softened a bit on its way to his ear. "But think about Taos for Christmas. Margarette would love it, wouldn't she? It would be okay. Do it for our daughter, even if it's just for a day or two."

"You've got to respect the fact that my wife..."

"I'm just asking you to think about it."

"I'll think about it."

"Meanwhile, my crazy father has resurfaced and he's going to start a new Indian uprising if I don't get him out of there. Are you sure there's nothing going on out there, any new digs, anything he might have gotten himself into?"

"Sorry," Tom said. "Never did much around Coyote Mesa. It's not even on the maps."

"It's on my map! I'm sitting right here with a map from the auto club, and it shows it plain as day!"

"Well, it's not on mine. Just a big zero, zed, *nada*."

"But, Tom, I read something about a project you were doing out around there. Don't you..."

"Oh, that. You're talking about the arts council out there. It's no big deal, Tara. I'm just on a committee."

"A few months ago, you told me about a lawsuit over some property on the southern border of the reservation. That must be the general area, I would guess."

"Might be. Did I really talk about that with you? I guess I could have mentioned it a while back. Not much to it, though. Guess it slipped my mind. Not much of a thing."

"I can't believe this! You even told me how much the Indians got from the government, that it was several million dollars. It had something to do with reclaiming sacred ground stolen from them a few hundred years ago. You were so excited about it. You said you were going to do some investigating because you thought you'd maybe be able to turn up evidence proving your theory about the Seven Cities being underground, in caves or something. You don't recall that?"

"Sure. It was pure speculation, you know? One of those things you do to meet your publishing quota at the university."

There was that deviousness again. It was more than deviousness, Tara thought. Her instincts told her he was covering something up, that for some reason he didn't want her going out there. She was silent for a moment, then decided to prod him one more time. "You told me flat out that the suit had something to do with secret ceremonial caves."

"Oh, well, I think that's more myth than reality. It made a good story for their defense, you know how these things go. And like I say, it was pure speculation. Pipe dreams. I saw an opportunity to publish an article. You'd be surprised how much pressure we get from the department to publish."

"Did you ever talk with my Dad about these things? Did he contact you recently?"

"You know how he feels about me."

"Tom, he made his peace with you years ago!"

There was a moment of silence, then Tom said, "Depends on what you call peace, my darling. In any case, I've not heard from the old boy. Besides, if he was out there poking around, wouldn't he be under contract with some magazine or whatever? Why don't you contact one of them? They can tell you what he's up to...maybe even tell you what leads he's following."

Tara had, in fact, given this some thought. But she knew how her father worked. He'd probably finagled money out of three different tabloids and a TV producer or two. He'd probably convinced each of them that they had an exclusive on his story, that they were the only ones in the world with whom he'd shared his secret. If she started poking around she'd probably get him in a lot of trouble. And the idea that they would let out this kind of information to somebody calling in by phone didn't strike her as likely, either.

"The people he does business with put a high priority on protecting their stories," Tara told Tom. "If Drake has a story for them, they aren't going to risk losing it. How do they know I'm really his daughter?"

"I've got to go, Tara. Margarette's working on her thesis. Got her a new computer today. You know how that is, getting it all up and running."

"Good night, Tom." She could not disguise the disappointment and suspicion in her voice.

"Tara, darling, are you sure you want to get into all this? I mean, a single woman wandering around out there all alone..."

Tara hung up the phone. Tom's conversation left her fuming. He was clearly holding out on her, in more ways than one. But was it out of his desire to protect her? She had her doubts. More likely, he was protecting his own interests. She felt terribly let down, knowing that either way he was not being honest with her. She kept dreaming, fooling herself into believing he would change, that his deceptive self would one day magically go away and the part that she loved would fill the space it left. She was a fool, she decided, to keep hoping, to hold out for such a remote and distant dream.

But that was not all that troubled her. She believed that there really were ceremonial caves and that they had been the subject of a big lawsuit. And she knew a story like that would have intrigued Drake. It was the perfect opportunity for a great story, hoax or not. Tara knew what little regard he held for the Indians' feelings about sacred sites, that he would start poking around no matter who he offended. Besides, he definitely knew the area, and even had friends among the Hopi, Zuni, Acoma and Navajo communities. God knows why any of them wanted to be friends with him, given that he had so little reverence for their ways. He had never taken anybody's religion seriously, except maybe what it offered by way of a sensational story.

She thought again about Drake's friend Chocko over in Zuni. Chocko Tedlock. His real name was actually Charles Tedlock. If Tom wouldn't help her, maybe Chocko could. Surely he'd have some ideas. There was a good chance Drake would have contacted Chocko and surely Chocko would know about Coyote Mesa. She picked up the phone again, dialed information and in seconds had Chocko's number. She dialed again and Chocko's voice came on the line.

"Chocko, this is Tara Fairfield. Do you remember me?"

"Tara, of course I do! I saw your Dad a while ago. He talked about you. He and his lady friend were heading down to Coyote Mesa."

"You're saying *a while ago*, what does that mean?"

"Oh, I guess it's been several months, maybe even a year."

"I haven't heard from him in two years," Tara said. "I need to find him."

"Two years! I'm sure it's not that long since I saw him. Just last year he came through, I'm sure of it. Maybe not even a year."

"So, you saw him maybe a month or two after we last talked." Tara tried to jog Chocko's memory, that fifteen months before she'd called all Drake's friends trying to locate him.

"Yes. I think that's right. I told him you'd called. You tried calling him? He had one of those new cell phones with him."

"I tried, yeah. I just get a lot of static."

"Well, that will be true if he's out there on the mesa, that's right. It has something to do with a freak magnetic field. No phones, no nothing. You go out there you might as well be on another planet. You want to leave the face of the earth for a while, that's where you go. Good place to vanish, escape from the law. Even the law doesn't go in there. They don't go anywhere they can't have radio contact with the front office."

This was not the sort of thing Tara wanted to hear. She thought about the mass murderer Drake had befriended a few years back and realized he could very well be pursuing that kind of person in a place like Chocko described.

"Listen, do you know what Dad was doing out there?"

"He didn't say a lot. We talked about that big legal settlement the Zunis had over some land down around there. But I didn't get the sense he was all that interested. Just curious, you know? Passing the time."

"Or he was just playing possum, pretending not to be interested when he really was."

"I dunno. He asked about the caves that are supposed to be out there. I told him what I knew but he'd never find the place."

"I'm going out to Coyote Mesa in the morning and see if I can locate Charla's place. I'll call you from there, if it's okay with you."

"No you won't."

"What?"

"No phones, no radios. Unless you got pony express you aren't getting any message to me."

"Sorry, you're right. I'll drop by on my way back, if that's okay. I'm sure I can clear this thing up. You'll be around?"

"Yeah, I'm here."

"See you soon."

"Yeah. See you."

*　　*　　*

Tara awoke at 6:30 a.m. totally rested. For the second day in a row, she noted, she'd gotten up this way, in spite of the fact that her sleep had been troubled. As she stepped outside, it was still dark, with heavy rain clouds hovering over the desert, blocking the sun. She ate a quick breakfast at the counter of an all-night truck stop next door to the motel, then got into her car and headed south toward Coyote Mesa. It had begun to rain again.

On the trip she'd made with her father, six years before, he'd introduced her to Chocko and a couple other people in Zuni, whose names she could not recall. Drake had worked with people in that community over several months, getting permission to write an article on Alex Setowa, a local resident who had dedicated the past twenty eight years of his life to painting a mural depicting the Zuni Katchinas at Our Lady of Guadalupe mission. Drake had at first been turned down by the tribal council. But he had persisted in his request, telling them that he would honor any limits they might want to place on him. In time they agreed, and the article, with photos, had come out in the *National Geographic*, documenting Setowa's amazing accomplishment.

It felt good to know Chocko was there, a loyal friend of her father's. He was a strange man, Chocko was. Drake had known him in college. That's where Chocko had gotten his name. It was a nickname, actually, given him after he, Drake and a group of friends made a weekend trip to Chaco Canyon. Chocko spelled it differently. "Like chock-full-of-nuts," Drake had said, in his own cynical way, poking fun both at his friend's name and the legends surrounding the ancient site. Chocko, as she recalled, wasn't of Zuni descent, nor of Hopi. But he was definitely from one of the Pueblos.

As she thought about the conversation she'd had with Chocko the night before she was tempted to drive over to Zuni and hunt him down. Maybe in person he could shed more light on Drake's whereabouts. Maybe he'd be willing to share with her something he might know about the society of shamans. If it became clear to her that her father was doing little more than chasing the shadows of half-truths and hoaxes, she'd go back home. The more she thought about it, the more agitated she became. Her father had spent his entire life circling around the *lunatic fringe*. All her life she'd tried to pretend he was someone he was not, denying that this man, whose love and respect she had once wanted so desperately, lived in a world she herself could neither love or respect.

Still, as she raced through the rain, windshield wipers working overtime, she could not deny that the thought of poking around and questioning people about her father's whereabouts excited her. She began to see correlations between the investigative work she enjoyed as an anthropologist and the investigative work her father engaged in to get a good story. Perhaps, after all, they shared more than she wanted to admit. Maybe his old warnings, following the flood, were intended to warn her about just such attributes: "Don't follow in my footsteps. Don't follow in anyone's footsteps."

She remembered there being something urgent and tender in his voice at that moment. Perhaps even then he'd recognized a part of her she'd only now begun to know. ~

Raven's Wheel

Past Vanderwagen, south of Gallup, the early morning rains settled into modest but steady showers. Ground fog clung to the road even as the sun squeezed between the jagged eastern horizon and a heavy, slate-gray sky. Long, even fingers of sunlight, like piercing beacons, cast bars of light across the road in the distance while fog softened the rugged landscape, as in a photograph taken slightly out of focus.

Out of the corner of her eye, Tara saw a dying pinon tree less than a hundred yards off the road. It seemed out of place there, alone on the mesa. Yet it rose at least forty feet in the air, confirming that it had survived in this barren land for at least a hundred years. Once it must have been a proud and magnificent sentinel. Now its scrawny branches were reduced to thin black lines etched against the gray sky. Even in its present configuration, however, it supported life. A dozen ravens perched in its branches, each of them a black silhouette. One bird rose, lifted into the wind and others followed, filling the sky with the abstract, flittering movements of their dark wings. Seconds later they settled down into the tree again. Tara wondered what this odd ritual of shifting and changing could mean. She had never seen ravens flock like this in nature. As far as she knew, this behavior existed only in mythology.

She recalled a story an old shaman told her while she was in Peru. He said in the natural world realities constantly shifted. Birds adjusted to change by fluttering from branch to branch while humans clung to their single perches, never looking beyond what they already knew. The raven, however, was always on the move. He was always changing his perch. The shaman's lesson had to do with what he called *shape shifting,* that is, experiences that force us to look at the world in new ways. He emphasized that these experiences were always accompanied by mystery and fear.

"Change your branch one-thousand-and-twenty times," the shaman said. "Each change brings you closer to the truth. It is like sitting at the medicine wheel. To find what is real for you, you must see from every direction. Every flight brings Raven new eyes, new ears, new scents, new winds." Remembering this lesson, Tara felt somehow closer to her destination, that she was moving ever-nearer to the secrets of the oracle, which for centuries had remained hidden from the world.

As she drove toward Coyote Mesa, a gentle rain produced a black and white atmosphere, seductively cool and enticing. She was grateful for the protection of the car and the warmth of its heater. But more than that, her quiet solo journey lifted her spirits, lulling her into a sense of security that all but quelled the fears hovering so near the surface. She felt a quiet excitement that rose out of her fears, taking wing, just as the great, dark birds on the ancient tree lifted from their lofty perches and spiraled momentarily over the land. Like those birds her fears seemed to be searching for a place to settle, a niche where they could perch, perhaps to see the world with new eyes.

The narrow blacktop road through the reservation was badly pocked, rough and sorely in need of repair. Jolting potholes forced her to drive slowly, allowing her to feel her own presence in the desert. There was little traffic, none on her side of the road. Only an occasional vehicle passed, usually a rusty, battered pickup truck going in the opposite direction. The miles elapsed easily, time dissolving, primordial and dreamlike. The land around her became more and more sparsely populated. She counted eleven homes--a few adobes, a few mobile homes--in the twenty-plus miles that she drove through the reservation.

Occasionally the sunlight illuminated the mountains west of the road, revealing coarse striations of red rock, with sharp cliffs chiseled into the stone by the winds. Figures appeared in the landscape, bold sentries memorialized for eternity, as ancient as the earth herself, rising toward the sky. Broad plains of wild grasses caught the light. Like nature's prisms they projected waves of color--green and purple and yellow and pink--celebrating the damp earth.

Tara was not certain where the Zuni's boundaries ended, but gripping the steering wheel tightly in her tense hands she noted the odometer reading. A quick calculation indicated she had come thirty-two miles since the turnoff that would have taken her toward the Pueblo. Her father had described this point to her once, though two years had passed since then and she was not at all certain her memory served her correctly. Still, what he had described at the time had seemed so bizarre that she had been convinced she would never forget it. She gazed ahead, through the rain. Another mile passed, then another. At the point when she was certain she had missed her landmark she spotted it off to her right. It was just as her father had described it, a spire of rock rising ten or twelve feet, less than a dozen yards from the roadway.

Balancing atop the spire, as if placed there by a gentle hand, was a rock formed roughly in the shape of an animal. Drake had called it "Coyote Rock." He'd said it looked like a coyote had tried to leap over the rock but had become impaled on it instead.

Though it took considerable imagination to say the rock resembled a coyote, Tara was certain that what she was seeing now was the mark for her turn. A formation of rock swept around the side of the coyote's reclining body like a long, stringy tail. Facing westward, a narrow head with a pointed nose sniffed the air. Around its neck somebody had wound a garland of rusty barbed wire, and from the rusty wire there dangled a huge bunch of matted feathers. It twisted and turned in the breeze. Even from the road Tara could see that it was the half-decayed corpse of a raven.

She stopped the car at the intersection and studied the eerie adornment for a moment. Somebody had placed it there purposefully. The dead raven dangled from the wire circling the coyote's neck. A piece of twine was lashed around the left wing, then looped through the rusty collar, allowing it to twist in the wind. Bringing to mind the sacred knowledge she recalled of the Southwest cultures, she could interpret the ritualistic adornment in at least three ways. First, it could be someone's sick idea of a joke, in which case it meant nothing. Or, if taken seriously, it could mean that Coyote, the trickster, dominated here and had Raven under his control. In that case, it could be a dark warning that one should be cautious of vanity and human folly. Or it could mean that in this place Coyote wore Raven like a collar, the latter being the animal who in legend often worked as a guide to the dark side of the human soul. In the legends, Raven was also depicted as wiser than Coyote, whose vanity constantly got him, and others around him, in trouble. Raven's ability to outwit Coyote was a warning to humans about following the four-legged canine's vainglorious path.

As she toyed with these possibilities, Tara had an eerie feeling. Tethered by a strand of rusty barbed wire, Raven's fate could not in any way be interpreted as a good omen. She could not help but wonder if Drake had placed the raven there, not as a ritualistic sign but as a way of poking fun at what he would consider to be people's superstitions. It would be just like him. He had a way of mocking the very things she and others took most seriously. He was nothing if not an iconoclast. Helen, Tara's mother, who had been a pretty good judge of people, said Drake was a man who couldn't make up his mind to believe in God or the vast indifferent universe, and so he didn't believe in anything, not even himself. Helen had added, "He'd just love to believe in the extraterrestrials and other spooks he writes about. But you know, at heart he's too much of a pragmatist to cross over that line." Remembering this conversation, Tara touched her foot to the accelerator and the car leapt forward, putting the coyote and raven behind her.

She smiled as she drove, shaking her head as she imagined Drake rigging up the barbed wire collar and attaching the raven's dried corpse, which he had probably found in the road. It wouldn't have been an easy job. He would have had to climb, clinging to the rock spire for ten or twelve feet until he could straddle the stone coyote's neck. She could easily imagine him, astride the coyote, like a bronco rider in a rodeo.

Tara glanced ahead through the mud-smeared windshield, dirty wipers flicking back and forth, leaving feathered streaks across the glass. The narrow gravel road wound up into the hills and disappeared behind a promontory of smooth red rock, several miles ahead. She estimated that she would gain another two hundred feet before she reached that point.

The road, called Coyote Rock Trail, was well-traveled for the first mile or so, branching out into pathways leading up to small houses spotted over the countryside like nomadic dwellings. A few scraggly head of cattle grazed on the hillside, clustered together as if for protection from predators, or perhaps from the weather. In various fields she passed, she counted a total of seven horses. Judging by their prominent ribs and bony withers they weren't getting the best of care, and the stingy desert land was not enough to support them. One of them, a spirited buckskin mare with a white flame pattern on her forehead, galloped along, parallel to the route of Tara's car. She tossed her head and seemed to delight in the race, until a border fence stopped her. Tara looked up into the rear view mirror and watched the animal, who stood with her chest pressed against the fence, watching the passing car.

It seemed odd but the houses appeared to have been placed as far from one another as possible, with at least a quarter mile of desert between each one. Some houses were adobe with metal roofs. A few were mobile homes made of corrugated aluminum, standing up higher off the ground than the others. An accumulation of makeshift buildings and sheds surrounded most of them, with an occasional wrecked car or pickup truck rotting slowly into the desert.

If there was a sense of community here, Tara speculated, it had to be based on an agreement that each person would maintain a respectful distance. The houses, she further noted, had no electrical or telephone service going into them. In fact, she realized that she had not seen service poles for over an hour. Residents in this region apparently had scarce contact with the outside world. One had to assume this was the reason they lived out here.

As she passed slowly through the area, she saw not a single person. An occasional light, produced by gas or kerosene lamps, she guessed, glowed within the homes, proving there were people living and working here. But perhaps because of the weather they were not outside where she would have seen them. Still, it seemed odd that she hadn't spotted a single car on the road, or a face peering out a window as she passed through.

The weather was cooperating with her. For the moment, at least, the rain was little more than a drizzle. The road, hard packed gravel, was pocked with deep ruts but stable enough, even for the rented Chevrolet, with its low clearance, which certainly wasn't designed for back country travel. Even so, the going was slow, the wheels spinning from time to time as she braked for a deep pothole and then accelerated again.

The road climbed, with several switch backs, through a barren, rocky terrain. Scrubby clumps of sagebrush and chaparral garnished the otherwise naked aridness as she moved into the high desert. As the road climbed, it also narrowed, at times leaving barely enough room to squeeze between desolate cliffs on one side and narrow shoulders on the other. Tara drove cautiously, wondering what would happen were she to meet another car. Who would back up? There was surely not enough room for two vehicles to pass. She had gone past places where there was nothing even resembling a turnoff for a half mile or more.

She maneuvered carefully through a series of sharp switch backs, then dropped the transmission into low gear to grind her way up a long, steep grade, the engine groaning against the effort. Without warning the road leveled out onto the top of a high mesa. She drew a breath, at first from relief, and then in response to the sheer beauty of this place. From this airy plateau, she gazed out onto a vast panorama, which seemed to go on for hundreds of miles. She guessed she was four to five hundred feet above the main road through the reservation, which was now only a narrow black line drawn on the landscape. Though the skies were dark and brooding, with spots of rain to the east, the land itself was simply magnificent. Great red cliffs and rocky spires as symmetrical as church steeples gave the impression of being carved by master artisans. Nowhere in the world were there more spectacular skylines, with sharp cliffs, gray and somber in the haze, forming an endless array of contours stretching out toward infinity.

Tara had always wondered what drew the ancient ones to this seemingly desolate land so long ago. Why here, where food was scarce and cultivation all but impossible? Why did they not migrate to those places they surely knew about, where life might be so much easier? But here was the answer, spread out before her eyes. For the first time in her life she realized that these lands, testaments to Mother Earth's deepest mysteries, nurtured much more than the body. The ancient ones had made a choice between nurturing the body or energizing the spirit, and perhaps wisely they had chosen the latter. In this land that seemed so miserly when it came to providing for the flesh, they had found a veritable feast for the soul. As an anthropologist she was intrigued. As a woman her heart was moved. For a moment she felt herself at one with the women of a thousand years ago who'd made this place their home.

After a few minutes she became aware of the house across the road. Less than a hundred yards away, it was an ancient dwelling made of adobe bricks, typically plastered over with uncolored mortar made from the same materials. The dwelling was almost invisible against the cliffs behind it, given that their colors nearly matched. There was a wide deck across the front of the place, upon which sat large, terra cotta flower pots, perhaps twenty of them, each spilling over with weeds.

For a long time she sat in the car, leaning on the steering wheel and staring at the building through the rain and the foggy windshield. In many ways it resembled the adobe houses down below. But this one was different. Someone had obviously spent a lot of money restoring it. It had a relatively new terra cotta roof while the houses down below had cheap metal roofs. The porch across the front was made of concrete, not earth or rotting planks. And this house had a stone chimney that looked like a piece of art, each separate rock placed carefully, the mortar trimmed and molded neatly.

She closed the door of her car and crossed the open field toward the front porch in the rain, stepping in deep ruts worn into the hard earth. As she drew closer to the house, she saw that the clay pots actually held herbs. She recognized cilantro, thyme, rosemary and oregano, all of which she cultivated at her own home back in Berkeley. In addition, there were several pots with tiny red peppers drooping like dragons' tears from frail green branches. This herb garden had been lovingly tended until quite recently. Now the house had the hollow, haunted feeling of a place that had been abandoned.

Halfway up the driveway Tara stopped in her tracks. The house was boarded up! What she'd first taken to be shutters proved to be boards nailed across the front door. Huge spikes had been carelessly driven through the planks, splintering the doorjamb in several places. This work must have been recently done, Tara surmised, and by somebody who had little concern for the property. The nails were still shiny and new, and the wood doorjamb which the nails defaced had obviously been painted not too long before.

Stepping up onto the porch, she saw that the doorjamb had once been decorated with hand-painted flowers. Tiny daisies, they were, with white petals, bright yellow centers, and with leaves and stems of vibrant green. Against the turquoise paint of the doorjamb, they looked strangely out of place, flowers of a different climate, a different region of the country.

There were large windows on the front of the house, which faced south, characteristic of desert homes. In the winter, the windows caught the heat of the low sun while in the summer, with the sun high overhead, the windows stayed relatively cool with the narrow roof over the porch protecting them. Tara moved around to the east side. Here there were two small windows. Once again they were both boarded over. She walked around to the back, the northern side, and here again found windows, two larger ones and a smaller. All three were boarded up, this time with huge plywood sheets which nobody had bothered to square up or cut to size. Whoever had done the work had been in a hurry, displaying almost no skills as a carpenter. Several nails were bent over and hammered against the wood as a child might do, without the skill to pull them out and start over again. Finally, on the western end of the house, Tara found two more windows and a narrow doorway. Again, all three were covered with plywood sheets.

Out of the corner of her eye, she noticed a small plot where somebody had apparently started a garden. The dirt appeared to have been turned over quite recently, probably just days before the rains came. The dirt looked rich and fertile. Somebody had turned in humus and commercially prepared soil, clearly with ambitions for planting in the near future. A few rocks the size of fists had been placed randomly atop the overturned soil, and in the rain the dirt had settled, leaving a slight indentation in the earth, roughly in a five foot circle.

Odd, Tara thought, for a person to board up their home and abandon it in the middle of starting a new project like this. She walked around to the front of the house again and sat down on the porch, looking back one more time to study the front door. Why, she asked, would the place be boarded up like this? And then her hands began to tremble. This had to be the place her father had described to her. There was no other. The road ended here, did not go on into the mountains above her. The fact was, there was only a single road on or off this small plateau. And the closest dwelling was at least two miles back. She tried to reconstruct the conversation she'd had with her father so many months before. The map she made in her mind at that time matched what she saw now. There was no mistake. This had to be Charla Mather's place.

Tara recalled stories about the Navajo's superstitions concerning death. They vacated the houses in which relatives had died. They looked upon death as an evil power, a sort of demon with a life of its own. Those who followed the old ways still held to the belief that it was bad luck to utter even the name of a person who had died. In the old days--and perhaps even now in some remote locations, she speculated--they not only vacated the hogan where a person died, they destroyed one wall so that the spirit of the deceased would not be trapped inside. To enter such a place was certain to bring terrible misfortune to the trespasser, and the idea of anybody ever taking up residence in such a dwelling again was unthinkable. The living dared not mingle with the ghosts of the dead.

Tara faced the boarded up entrance. At the top of the door, peeking out between the planks, she saw some writing. The door was relatively low, scaled to people whose average height was under five foot three. With considerable effort, she reached up, curled her fingers around one board and pulled it back. The nails in the splintered plank gave little resistance. She pulled it away enough to reveal the painted letters of a familiar name, adorned with the same daisies she saw around the lower portions of the doorjamb: Charla Mather. There could be no doubt about it now. But what had happened here? Where had the occupants gone?

The newly installed boards and the still vibrant plants in the clay pots on the front deck offered clear proof that the residents had left not long before. But why not just lock the doors and walk away? Surely, there could not be any great danger of trespassers up here, at the end of a road too precipitous for all but the most ambitious driver! What other explanation could there be but that someone had felt the need to follow old traditions? Sealing up the house could mean only one of two things: either someone had died here or someone thought it awfully important to keep people out.

In spite of the sealed doors and windows, Tara knew she had to get inside and search for any clues that could tell her what might have happened. Her resolve became even more firm now. She knew her father had owned a laptop computer. He always sent his stories to the tabloids on diskette. If he had lived here, there was a chance that he would have left a diskette or two behind, which could provide her with clues about what he'd been doing.

A thousand questions raced through her mind. When Drake sent her the envelope with the artifacts and photos--and *if* it was he who sent them--would he not have known about this place being boarded up? Not necessarily, she reasoned. It was very possible that he was not staying here at the time. But that didn't make sense either. Nothing was coming together for her. His fleeting messages seemed to indicate that he was assuming she would know where to go--to the place he'd told her about two years before. Charla's place at Coyote Mesa was, after all, his last known residence. But she was willing to bet the house had been boarded up a week or two before. If he'd been living there when he sent her the package, he surely would have mentioned this fact in his note. Still, Drake was un-predictable and so self-involved that he might not have even thought about telling Tara these details, somehow making the assumption that she already knew. As crazy as that sounded, Tara had no illusions about her father's character. Drake had always been careless of others' feelings and needs. Why would he change now?

Tara pulled at other boards blocking the front door. The end of one or two came loose easily while others resisted her efforts. She glanced over the front yard for something that might work as a lever, a pry-bar to help her release the boards. Her eyes fell upon a rusty steel fence post supporting a scraggly tree. Its leaves had dropped and its branches were withered and dry. With a few sharp tugs on the post, the soft damp dirt gave up its trophy. Tara carried the steel fencepost back to the front door. With the help of her rusty lever, the boards gave way. Then she turned the knob hard and leaned into the door. To her surprise the latch popped open easily and as the door swung open she stumbled inside, nearly losing her balance.

She found herself standing in the foyer of a fully furnished living room. The house was decorated with surprisingly good taste, in the Southwestern style one would expect in an expensive condo in the city, rarely in an ancient adobe out on the edge of Indian country. There was a leather couch, two handsome pine chairs with pillows covered with fragments of handwoven Indian rugs. Tara had seen pillows like these in the Santa Fe decorators' shops, selling for upwards of three hundred dollars each. It seemed preposterous to find such artifacts out here. She moved past the living room into a small but well furnished kitchen. Expensive copper pots and kitchen gadgets hung from a wrought iron rack over the cooking range. Dirty dishes, crawling with bugs, were piled in the kitchen sink. The place smelled of rotting food, telling her the residents had vacated only several days before, and apparently in a hurry. The good news was that they, or *someone*, was here recently. Tara could not be too far

behind them.

There were two doors down a long, narrow hallway. The first stood ajar and as she cautiously approached, her heart pounded, anticipating what she might find. She stopped, leaned forward and peered inside the first doorway. It was a bedroom. A single twin bed stood in one corner, neatly made up, sporting a Pendleton blanket with a traditional Navajo pattern. Tara recognized the blanket as one she'd given her father as a Christmas present several years before. She was touched that he still had it--or had until very recently. She stepped into the room. Like the bed, the space was neat and well kept.

"I should have paid better attention," she said aloud, startled by her own voice in the empty house. There could not be even a shadow of a doubt now. Drake had been staying here. But then what? Why was he no longer here? And if he had been living here, until very recently, where had he been the last two years? What had prevented him from contacting her until three days before? And why had he vacated, apparently during the same period of time he had begged Tara to come? She wondered if he had been actually hiding out here--but from whom, and why? As negligent as he was of his fatherly responsibilities, the only reason she could imagine for his not contacting her over those many months was that he needed to protect her from any knowledge of his whereabouts, should someone decide to question her. But that seemed far-fetched to Tara, too much like something from a bad movie.

She made a circle around the room, pulling open drawers, swinging open the doors of the large pine armoire that stood across one corner. If anything was missing, it was impossible to say what it might be. The drawers of the single dresser were empty and clean. In the armoire she found a light canvas jacket, her father's, and a heavy full length sheepskin coat she did not recognize though it was his size.

"The laptop!"

She glanced furtively around the room. But there was no sign of the computer she knew Drake prized. She opened drawers, looked under the bed, pawed through a stack of magazines at the bottom of the armoire. Nothing. No sign of it. Maybe she'd find it in one of the other rooms. As she turned to go into the hallway, she felt something crunch under her foot. She gave a start and looked down.

She had just stepped on a computer disk, destroying its protective plastic case. She reached down and picked it up, examining the damage. There was no label, so perhaps there was no data on it anyway. She pocketed it on the outside chance that it could be repaired and the data retrieved. It was a long-shot, but she'd take any shot she could at this point.

The second room was also a bedroom. Judging by the clothes she found there, this was the master bedroom where Drake and the Mather woman slept. The blankets on the king-sized bed had been thrown aside, as if it had been vacated only moments before. Nobody had bothered to make it, and the covers being in such disarray left the impression that the residents of this place had in all likelihood intended to return.

The clothing styles in the closet, and bottles of makeup atop one of the two dressers in this room, indicated the tastes of a woman accustomed to expensive things. The closet also contained her father's sparse wardrobe, consisting of a well-worn, brown suede sport coat, a single pair of Western-cut slacks, and several pairs of jeans creased and laid across coat hangers. He had never been one to wear ironed jeans but Tara chalked it up to his new life with Charla Mather, whose tastes were obviously far more refined than Drake's. Tara could even imagine Charla Mather being the kind of person who'd send her father's jeans off to the cleaners.

Tara began pulling drawers open again, peeking into the back of the closet, under the bed, even throwing back the bed covers, on the outside chance that the computer might be there, buried amidst rumpled bedding. It was then that she spotted a photograph on the bedside table. It was propped up against a lamp made of an ancient Indian pot filled with black feathers. She reached out, picked up the photo and held it to the light. In spite of herself, she let out a gasp.

It was a picture of herself and her father leaning against a Jeep. It had been taken the year they saw the two people die in the flood. She had shot that picture with her own camera, setting it on the fender of a car in the parking lot of a guest lodge where they'd stayed a few days before the fatal incident on the desert. The camera's automatic timer triggered the shutter as she ran back to stand beside Drake. She had the photo framed when she returned from that trip. The following Christmas she sent it to her father as a gift. Surely he would not have knowingly left this photo behind! Drake had been in Florida at the time she gave him the photo. He was looking for a private boat owner who'd ferry him to Cuba. He'd managed to get in touch with Fidel Castro's people who granted him an exclusive interview with the Cuban prime minister. The trouble was the State Department wouldn't give him permission to go over there. So he had found his own way of getting across.

The remaining rooms of the house consisted of a bathroom and a small utility room. In the latter she found several small wire baskets of herbs suspended from the ceiling and set out to dry. There was laundry still in the clothes dryer. In the bathroom, she discovered toothbrushes, hairbrushes, cosmetics and even a hair drier. Finding all these personal items troubled her. These were not the things people knowingly left behind, particularly not in a house they intended to board up upon leaving.

Tara sat down on the rim of the bathtub. Her heart was pounding and she became aware that she was breathing shallowly, terrified by prospects she could not even allow herself to entertain. There was only one reason she could immediately give for a person leaving behind personal grooming items in this way. She flashed back to a story her father had written, published in one of the few reputable papers that took his material. It was a story about the day his father--Tara's grandfather--died, a dozen years before. The hospital had called him to come in and pick up the old man's belongings. He was handed a shopping bag containing a blue plastic throwaway bedpan, a spit tray and a tumbler. At the bottom of the bag was another package containing his father's dental bridge, a toothbrush, a comb and a half-used bottle of mouthwash. Suddenly, the terrible meaning of these mundane objects had struck him. He told Tara his impressions, how these objects, taken so much for granted in daily grooming and care, were no longer of use to anyone. The soul who once used them had moved on to some other form, a form nobody in this life had ever seen.

Glancing around the bathroom, Tara saw all the toiletry items in this same light. But she was not ready to accept death as the reason that her father's objects had been left behind. Neither could she imagine that Drake or Charla Mather would have boarded the place up. Surely they would not have left things in such a jumble before nailing boards to the windows and doors! But why? None of this made sense to her. None of it.

Suddenly she became aware of a sound outside the house. An engine idling! She stood bolt upright, alert, adrenalin pumping. The engine stopped. A car door gently opened, then closed, not far away. How had it gotten so close without her hearing it?

Footsteps plodded across the soft dirt. They came closer and Tara recognized the sound of riding boots crossing the hard cement floor of the front porch. A flash of hope turned to anxiety as she realized these footsteps could not be Drake's. She knew her father's gait; he always walked with a slight limp, favoring his left leg, injured in a motorcycle accident years ago. The footsteps approaching the open front door were regular, firm and aggressive.

Her first thought was to get away but she instantly realized that with the house boarded up, the front door was her only escape. She heard the footsteps stop with a slight clatter as the visitor stumbled on one of the boards she'd pulled off the door.

"Hello!" she called. She thought her voice sounded shaky and fearful, though she'd tried her best to hide what she felt. She stepped out of the bedroom and into the hallway. There, framed in the front entrance, silhouetted against the dim light of a threatening sky, stood a dark-skinned man dressed in jeans, a denim jacket and a green baseball cap with a beer logo emblazoned across the crown. Her gaze was drawn to a huge Bowie knife with a handle of white staghorn strapped to his right side.

The man did not speak. Tara stared at his face, trying to divine his intentions. Her legs wobbled under her. She could barely breathe. The man's face betrayed nothing of what might be in his mind, his eyes expressionless and cold. He nodded, staring back, then said something she did not understand. It took her a moment to realize he was telling her his name. John Whitecrow. He moved a few steps closer and extended his hand. Tara took it hesitantly. His skin was dry, like leather left out in the weather. She pulled her hand away and managed to slip by him, out onto the front porch. She was aware of Whitecrow following her.

"This place," Tara said. "Why is it boarded up?" She turned slowly, forcing herself to face Whitecrow, but barely able to focus on his eyes, dreading what she might find there.

Several seconds passed in silence, then Whitecrow asked, "She kin of yours, the Mather woman?"

"My father lived with her."

Whitecrow nodded and a slight smile played at the corners of his mouth. "Fairfield. That guy? He asked a lot of questions."

"*That guy*, yes," Tara said. "What kind of questions?"

Whitecrow showed no desire to continue this conversation. "We don't take much to anthropologists poking around," he said.

Tara gave a start. She knew the Indians' sentiments about anthropologists only too well but was surprised by Whitecrow's statement. She had not mentioned being an anthropologist.

"What gives you the idea I'm an anthropologist?"

"Not you. Your father. They come around looking for stories, then write up lies about us."

"My dad's a journalist, not an anthropologist," Tara corrected. "He's more likely to write about UFO's than your people."

"What happens down here is none of his business. None of yours, either."

"How long since you've seen him?"

"A couple weeks maybe."

Tara glanced toward her car, parked on the opposite side of the narrow trail to the house, calculating how quickly she might cover the distance. Judging by Whitecrow's size, she was certain he could outrun her. Directly in front of her car was a late model Jeep with a canvas top and side doors.

"My father contacted me by phone in the last couple days," Tara ventured. "He wanted me to come here right away."

"He didn't call from here."

"Why do you say that?"

"No phone service."

"He has a cell phone."

"No radio reception. No TV. No nothing."

"I don't understand."

"They say there's a magnetic disturbance, something like that."

"I heard an engine running in the background, like maybe a large generator or a pump. Any place like that around here, where there might be a large engine running?"

Whitecrow shrugged. "Down the highway, south of here, maybe ten miles." He stepped down from the front porch and looked up toward the sky. "Storm coming. You staying up here?"

Tara glanced up at the sky. Billowy, slate-colored clouds were gathering overhead. She'd seen enough desert storms to know what was coming--not just more rain but a downpour, a veritable downpour. The road could wash out, and leave the car stranded up on the mesa for days until the road dried out. The prospect of spending the night in this empty house hardly appealed to her.

"Do you know why the place was boarded up?" she asked Whitecrow. "It seems strange, them leaving everything behind and taking off like this."

Whitecrow shrugged. "She does what she does."

"Do you have any opinions?"

Whitecrow dropped his gaze to the ground. "She isn't Navajo."

"Meaning she probably didn't board the place up because of a death."

"Meaning, she has her own reasons for doing things. Not something I'd know about. I work for her sometimes, that's all."

"You do what...like repair work?" Before Whitecrow answered, a bolt of lightning shot across the sky, not a half mile away, and as if responding to a prearranged signal, they both ran for their respective vehicles. Whitecrow's Jeep was already moving past her as Tara got to the door of her car and yanked it open. The thunder rumbled menacingly as she followed Whitecrow's Jeep down the narrow road toward the highway, maintaining a safe distance. Through the back window of Whitecrow's Jeep she could see what looked like a large toolbox and what might have been gardening tools.

The full force of the storm didn't hit until they were down off the mesa. Then it came with a vengeance, thunder and lightning accompanying the torrent. It was as if the sky had exploded, dropping tubs full of water. Tara heaved a sigh of relief, grateful to see the pavement ahead. Wanting to rest, she pulled off at a row of mailboxes a few yards back from the highway. She watched Whitecrow's Jeep turn and go north, its taillights quickly vanishing in the gray curtain of rain. The downpour stopped as suddenly as it had begun and what had been a violent storm became a drizzle.

*   *   *

The map showed the actual town of Coyote Mesa ten miles south. She drove in a trance, barely aware of the rain or the passing landscape. If there were other cars on the road, she didn't notice. A break in the rain revealed a turnoff ahead, indicated by a hand painted sign and an arrow pointing to the left. The sign said "Party Store 1/2 mile." She turned, moving east now along a narrow gravel road, across what appeared to be the floor of the desert. Just as suddenly as it came, the storm ceased. Ahead she saw a gravel turnoff and a wide parking apron in front of an old mobile home. The rain was light now, just a gentle shower. A faded sign in a front window of the building, depicting a rugged-looking cowboy on a horse, advertised Marlboro cigarettes, and announced that the place was open.

Tara parked the car beside a battered old pickup truck with a young calf tethered in the back. As she got out, the calf bawled, as if crying for her attention. She reached out to pat its nose but it withdrew, its hooves clattering noisily in the slippery metal bed of the truck as it pulled against its tether trying to get away from her. The rain came only in a drizzle now, but the calf's coat was soaking wet, as if it had been standing alone in the storm for many hours.

There was only one other vehicle in the parking lot, a black, mud-spattered car with U.S. Government license plates and a decal in the lower corner of the windshield on the driver's side. The decal was bright yellow with a single number in the middle: 55. The decal attracted her attention because it stood out in sharp contrast to the anonymous-looking car and the gray light.

Tara crossed in front of the truck with the calf in the back and reached out to open the front door of the store. She stepped into what she guessed had once been somebody's living room. Now it was a makeshift grocery and dry goods mart. There were shelves made of planks with concrete block separators. These were sparsely furnished with a few bakery and canned goods. One shelf contained a small variety of pastas, crackers and chips. Along one wall were four refrigerators, the kind found in most homes. None of them were alike, each one salvaged from a different source, probably the secondhand stores back in Gallup. Somebody had labeled the white doors with a black marking pen. One said "DRINKS," another "FOOD", and the third "DAIRY." The fourth had no label.

A young woman sat in a chair behind a counter near the door. A gas lantern, hung from a metal hook in the ceiling above the counter, provided the only light in the room, except for the little that filtered in through the dirty windows from the slate gray skies outside. The woman had been reading a book which she closed as Tara walked in. The title of her book was, *You Can Make A Million in Real Estate*. Like Whitecrow, the woman wore jeans and a denim jacket. Tara guessed her to be in her mid-thirties, an attractive, dark skinned woman with raven hair falling loosely over her shoulders, brown eyes and a pleasant smile.

"Ma'am?" she said, her voice raising at the end, making a question. "Can I help you?"

Tara glanced around the room, looking for something to buy. She decided on a sack of corn chips and a can of Seven Up. "I was looking for my Dad, who is supposed to be staying around here. I can't find the place where we were supposed to meet." She set the items she'd selected on the counter. "His name is Drake Fairfield. He's been living up the road, north of here about five miles."

The young woman shrugged, the pleasant smile quickly fading from her face, replaced by a stoic stare. "I don't know anybody up there."

"Do you know a woman named Charla Mather?"

"White woman?"

"Yeah, I think so. Older woman."

"Maybe. I could have seen her."

Tara laid a five dollar bill on the counter and the young woman looked at the items she was purchasing and quickly made change from a metal cash box. Tara left the change on the counter as she popped open her soda can. "My father was staying with her. He's been working on a research project up on this side of the Ramah Reservation."

"Don't know them. I've heard about the white people living up the road. Never talked to them, though."

Tara remembered the black car in the parking lot and thought it strange there was no sign of its driver in the store. He or she could have been in another room, however, perhaps a small office whose door was hidden from view. "Is there anyone else around who might know them?" Tara asked.

"Only me."

"I thought maybe the driver of that car might be around." Tara swung her head in the direction of the parking lot. "Is he around?"

"I haven't seen them."

Them, Tara thought, *the woman said them. So there must be at least two people.* "They didn't come in here?"

The woman shrugged. "I haven't seen them."

Tara thought she noticed the woman glance down the dark, narrow hallway to the right of the counter.

"The calf out there in the pickup," Tara said. "It looks half drowned. Is it okay?"

"Well, that's the way it is. She's going up to my uncle's place tonight for a ceremony."

"What ceremony?" Tara tried to remember if there were any holidays coming up. Perhaps it was a wedding. The calf was to be butchered for a wedding.

The woman behind the counter shrugged. It was not a gesture that said *I don't know.* Rather, the message was that it was none of Tara's business.

"Look," Tara said. "I'm really worried about my dad. If there's any way you could help me..."

The young woman shrugged again. This time it was for a different reason. "I think I saw him and her once. The woman you talk about and maybe this man."

"How long ago?"

"Not long. Maybe a few days. They were in her car up the road. I passed her, that's all. She was stopped at the highway."

"She was going north?"

"Maybe north, maybe south. She was waiting to come onto the highway. I didn't notice which way she went. She's got one of those English jeep things. A Range Rover, that's what it is. I've seen them on television. All leather inside. Really nice. A dark green one. I remember. It was green."

"You're certain of that? A Range Rover is an expensive car."

"Sure. I think she's a pretty rich lady. She likes fancy things, you know. She comes around the rez sometimes. Some friends of mine, they sell her pottery and paintings and things. They say she has a house in Albuquerque, real big place out there along the Rio Grande. She has horses but she never rides them. That's what they say."

"Do you know John Whitecrow?" Tara asked.

The young woman studied Tara's face for a moment, her brow wrinkling. Then she laughed nervously. "White crow?"

"Yes. I'm sure that's his name."

"There isn't any such thing as a white crow."

"What do you mean?"

"Somebody's playing with you."

"Charla Mather knows him."

"Maybe she knows *some* Indian guy. Not white crow. That's a joke. Crows are black. They're never white."

"Why would somebody call himself that?"

"Maybe he's a white guy. I don't know any Indians named that."

"The house," Tara said. "Do you know any reason a person would want to board up their house around here?"

"Somebody dies, they board it up sometimes. Some of the old people, they still think that way. What they do is none of my business except I'd just be sure to stay away if I saw that."

Tara tipped back the can of pop and swallowed a mouthful of the fizzy liquid. It was warm, as if it had not been refrigerated at all. "The soda isn't cold," she said.

"The power goes off sometimes. It just does that."

Tara held the can in her hand, considered asking for her money back. She glanced at the four refrigerators and wondered why the woman even bothered to put anything in them if she couldn't depend on the power.

"I'll be staying up at Gallup," Tara said. "If you hear anything about Ms. Mather or my father, would you mind giving me a call? I'm staying at the Desert Sky Motel. I'll be up there tonight and tomorrow night. If you give me your number here I'll be glad to call back and keep in touch."

"No phone."

Tara remembered what John Whitecrow, or whatever his name was, had told her about phone service in the area.

"I might drop by again," Tara said, moving toward the door. "Thanks for your help."

"Change."

"What?"

"Your change," the young woman said. "You forgot your change." She scooped up four dollars and some coins from the counter, then touched Tara's hand and held it gently for a moment before dropping the change into it. "Good luck finding your father." For a moment the woman's eyes locked on Tara's, communicating a deep sadness. Then she whispered, "I lost my father when I was just a little kid. He went overseas to Vietnam. He should never have gone there. He was a beautiful man and they killed him for nothing."

"I'm very sorry," Tara said.

The woman withdrew her hand and held it to her chest. "The men, they like war. I think they like it."

"I hope not. But yes. You may be right. Maybe they do."

*   *   *

Tara was ten miles north, on her way back to Gallup, when the thought struck her: What about the soda at the store? Cold or warm, there sometimes was electricity at the store. She tried to remember if she'd seen power poles around the place. She didn't think so. What ran the refrigerators--four of them--when they did run? A generator. There had to be a generator nearby. Maybe it didn't work all the time, but it had to run some of the time! And it would have to be a fairly sizable generator, run by a large engine, if it was expected to keep four refrigerators working. A large engine like that could make the kind of sound she'd heard in the background of her father's message. Somewhere nearby there had to be a generator. She pulled off to the side of the road and stopped. She reached for the cell phone on her console, switching it on. There was only a slight hiss, the sound she knew came from the instrument itself when it wasn't connecting with a transmitter. She lay the phone in her lap and made a U-turn.

It took only minutes to get back to the party store. But even as she approached it she saw that the pickup truck with the calf in the back was nowhere in sight. How could it have disappeared so quickly? The sign in the window with the Marlboro man had been turned around and on the back someone had scrawled "Closed" with a thick black marking pen. She stopped and parked where the truck had been sitting only a few minutes before. Once again she pressed the phone to her ear. For a brief moment, there was the familiar hum that she had learned to associate with a connection being made with a transmitter cell, but then it switched off and she heard only a hiss. She backed the car up, moved slowly to the south a dozen yards, holding the instrument to her ear. As she did, she heard the hum of a connection but then static broke up the signal and the hiss returned.

She put the car in Park and shut off the engine. It was possible that Drake had a better phone than hers, one that was capable of picking up and maintaining the signal from somewhere nearby. She swung the door of her car open and stepped out into the rain again. For a moment she just stood there, slowly turning in a circle as she surveyed the area. She spotted no power poles. So she was right. The power for the refrigerators had to come from a local generator.

She walked around to the back of the building. There was no second building which might house a generator as she'd hope to find. But then she saw something she'd missed on her first visit. An orange wire came out of the side of the building, just below the windows. It stretched along the ground, going east over the desert. It was a thick utility cord, the kind used at construction sites to carry electricity over long distances to heavy duty power tools. She quickly returned to the car, backed out of her parking place and abruptly stopped.

Something felt wrong. For a moment she sat with the engine idling, trying to figure out what it was that bothered her. She glanced in her rearview mirror at the empty parking lot behind her. That was it! The parking lot was empty. The pickup truck with the calf in the back was gone. But she'd noticed that before. The woman had said she was going to drive the calf up to her uncle's house. And then it struck her. The black government car was gone, too!

She distinctly remembered asking the woman at the counter about the driver of the car. The woman had answered that she hadn't seen *them*. But if she hadn't seen them, who drove that car away? Tara was certain there hadn't been anyone hanging around outside the store. She would have seen them if they'd been there. There could be only two explanations: either the woman was lying, and the drivers of the car had been somewhere in the building, or somebody in still another vehicle had dropped the driver off after Tara left. But it all seemed so strange! It had been only a few minutes between the time Tara left the parking lot and now, and she had seen no other vehicles on the road. How could the woman in the store and the driver of the black car have gotten away so quickly? Tara could see for miles in every direction and there was no sign of another vehicle coming or going. Bewildered, she dropped the car in gear and turned up the narrow side road, away from the main highway.

A hundred feet up the road she stopped again and got out, walking out onto the desert a few feet back from the road. Following the wire with her eyes, she spotted a power pole, then a second and third. The power cord from the store was plugged into a utility box on the closest pole. The road beside the pole continued up into a narrow canyon a quarter mile away. She returned to the car and drove again, until she came to a driveway heading south. She turned in. A thousand feet off the road she saw a rooftop. Somewhere back in there was a house and it was a very good bet that she'd find a large generator there as well. ~

Off Limits!

Sunlight broke through the clouds and suddenly the entire desert was bathed in golden light, bringing out the rich, myriad colors of the land. The deep earthen reds of the nearest cliffs. The rich blues of distant skylines seen through the stormy haze. Tara was accustomed to dramatic weather changes over this spectacular land but she was always surprised when shifts such as this came so suddenly, so unexpectedly. In perfect concert with the light she came up over a sharp rise in the narrow roadway and there before her was one of the most beautiful canyons she had ever seen.

Canyon walls to the east and south climbed several hundred feet straight up. They towered above a cultivated valley floor, green and lush against the striated red rock. The roof she had seen belonged to a large adobe building, painted to match the salmon-tinted cliffs behind it. It glowed in the center of the valley, facing the north. It rested a hundred feet back from a narrow riverbed, through which a swift current raced, fed by the rains.

The house itself was new, and extravagant by local standards. Tara guessed it to be at least 5,000 square feet. Great expanses of glass looked north and west over a well-manicured lawn. The land around the house was fully landscaped. There were fruit trees, hedges and flower beds. Several trees were filled with apples, their late fall yield waiting to be harvested. Others were already barren, having given their bounty earlier in the season.

To the south of the house was a complex of metal buildings. They were painted a dull beige that blended in with the land around them. Most were seriously in need of a fresh coat of paint since large areas had peeled or flaked away, leaving an olive drab undercoating that Tara associated with military installations. Curiously, the ground around the foundations of the buildings was sprinkled with a fine white powder. Tara guessed it was some kind of insecticide and wondered what sort of infestation it was warding off, and what might be stored in the buildings that needed this kind of protection.

These buildings were of the kind that were quickly fabricated, often used by the military because they could be easily taken down and trucked out. The largest of them was two stories high. Rows of narrow windows looked to the west, each window painted over with flaking white paint. The painted windows reflected the afternoon sun and the distant landscape. This was eerie, Tara thought, out of sync with everything around it. These were city buildings, the kind she'd often seen in warehouse districts and behind suburban shopping centers.

The main compound was surrounded by a chain link fence at least twelve feet high. Coils of rusting razor wire topped it all around. Nevertheless, an open gate invited her in. She drove through and stopped at a small building that looked as if it might house a guard. If it served that purpose, there was no guard there now. Papers on a clipboard rested against the doorjamb as if someone had recently set them down. They rustled in the breeze and Tara wondered, momentarily, if they were going to get wet when the rain returned, which it was sure to do. A number stenciled on the wall in black paint, next to the door, identified the structure as *Building 7-A.*

She paused within twenty feet of Building 7-A and reached for the cell phone. She switched it on. The hum she heard in her ear clearly indicated she was getting through to a transmitter here. She punched in the number for her own electronic mail back home. In an instant a recorded voice came on, asking for her code. She punched it in, and immediately heard a recording telling her she had three messages. She pressed the number to listen to them, excited by the prospect that one might be from Drake. The first message was from Viveka, saying that she couldn't find the checkbook. The second was also from Viveka saying to disregard the previous message; she had found the checkbook in the laundry room. The third message was from a professional association in Chicago, asking if Tara would be attending their next conference on preserving cultural artifacts.

Nothing warranted her immediate attention. She considered calling Maya, glanced at her watch, and realized her daughter would be at her swimming class. She punched in Drake's cell phone number. It rang several times, then a message came on, saying that the owner of this number could not be reached. Disappointed, Tara set her own phone back on its cradle. For what it was worth, one thing was now clear. Drake could have called her from this area. Probably there was a large generator, or some other power source here, that could account for the sound of the engine running in the background she'd recorded on her answering machine. For a moment she sat thinking as she surveyed the compound ahead of her.

All the ground within the fenced area was blacktopped and clean, almost spotless, in fact, as if it had been scrubbed that same day. She slipped her car into gear and moved forward, noting there wasn't another vehicle to be seen. It was eerie. No sign of life anywhere, yet she somehow felt that she was being watched. She drove slowly toward the center of the compound and was about to honk her horn when she noticed the back of the black car she'd seen in the parking lot at the party store. There was no doubt in her mind that it was the same car. She saw the same yellow decal on the driver's side of the windshield with its stark number "55." Even the mud spatters looked familiar.

She thought about honking her horn to get someone's attention. Then she noticed that the huge sliding door on one of the buildings to her left was ajar. She set the parking brake of her car, got out, and stepped toward the door, noticing it was extraordinarily bright inside. The entire interior was snow white, shiny and clean, and at the center of the warehouse loomed what appeared to be a kind of huge boiler. Large enough to hold a small airplane, Tara's impression was that it was a special kind of sealed room. A small round observation window in the side reminded her of a ship's porthole.

As she stepped inside the warehouse, a loud bell began to ring, sounding an alarm somewhere outside. Apparently she'd set it off when she walked into the building. Surely somebody would come now! As she peered toward the observation window in the great tank, a white figure appeared on the other side of the murky glass. For a moment it stared back at her, but then quickly disappeared, as if frightened by her appearance. It was an odd-looking figure dressed in some sort of costume, complete with goggled eyes. *Perhaps a workman dressed in protective garb. But what were they doing in there?*

Frantic footsteps of boots on pavement were fast approaching. She spun around, heart pounding and found herself staring into the barrels of two rifles. The men holding them wore green uniforms with gold embroidered patches on their shoulders that revealed nothing except the number 55.

"Identify yourself!" one of them barked at her, the voice of a young man, no more than twenty, and much impressed with himself.

"I'm sorry," Tara said. "I just drove in. I was looking..."

"Show your identification," the young man barked again, stepping closer, the barrel of his gun waving within inches from her face.

"Look," she said. "There's no need for the gun..."

"Identification!"

"It's back in my car. Just get the damn gun out of my face." Tara slapped at the barrel of the rifle, wanting to swat it away, but the kid held it surprisingly firm. Her palm stung as it smacked against the cold steel barrel.

"Go check out her car," one of the men said.

Tara lifted her hands as the second man moved toward her car, feeling that somehow her show of submission would keep her youthful guard from doing something foolish.

The man at her car reached inside and pulled out her purse. In a moment he withdrew her wallet and started thumbing clumsily through its contents, tossing papers and credit cards onto the driver's seat. At last he found what he was seeking and held up the wallet as if to show the world.

"Her name's Tara Fairfield, down from California. She's got an ID here from some university."

"I'm a college professor," Tara offered weakly.

The young man tossed her wallet and purse carelessly back into the car.

"What do you want here?" the young man in charge demanded.

"I just wandered in. I'm sorry. The gate was open."

"Shit," the second man said. "Who the fuck left the goddamned gate open?"

"Shut up!" the first man said. "This place is off limits to civilians," he announced, turning back to Tara.

"I never would have guessed," Tara said. "And I suppose you shoot us civilians for asking questions?"

"Excuse me, Miss. We're just doing our job here."

"You and Adolph Hitler!" Tara said.

"Shit!" the second man said.

"What's going on here?"

Tara turned abruptly, in spite of the gun still being leveled on her. This third voice belonged to a slender man, graying at the temples, dressed in civilian clothing. He wore tan pants and a dark brown dress shirt with a monogram on the breast pocket. Except for the fact that he seemed over-dressed for his surroundings, he appeared normal enough. At least he wasn't pointing a gun at her.

"How'd she get in here?"

"Gate was left open, sir."

"Yeah? Where were you guys, out playing *tiddly-winks*?"

The sound of the words *tiddly-winks* was truly anachronistic coming from this man's lips. Tara had an idea that he'd had something far less elegant in mind but changed what he said in deference to the presence of a woman.

"Sorry, sir. It won't happen again."

"My name's Guy Perry," the gentleman in the brown shirt told

Tara. The men with the guns stepped back as Guy Perry extended his hand to Tara.

The man's friendliness seemed forced, to say the least. She'd encountered this kind of feigned affability once or twice before on Army bases. It was the result of a certain training that men of higher rank apparently received. In spite of his pretension of friendliness, Guy Perry projected a clear sense of authority that put her on notice that there was a very thin line she must not cross.

"I was looking for the woman who runs the party store," Tara lied, trying to sound as light as possible. "I'm dying for a cool soft drink or a bottle of beer. Thought she might live up here. I saw her power line leading back this way and followed it back. I thought maybe..."

"That's a lot of bullshit," Perry said. "You just came from there."

"I was on my way back..." she began, trying to cover herself but the effort seemed lame even to her. "The truth is, I'm looking for my father who I was supposed to meet in Coyote Mesa. He's staying with a friend, a woman named Charla Mather. Do you know her?"

"I don't know her or anyone else. You never should have gotten in here. Somebody's head will roll for this."

"What do you do here?" Tara ventured, already pretty sure what the answer would be.

"We ask people like you to butt out," Perry said. "These men will escort you to the gate."

Perry stared blankly at Tara for a moment. His face was frightening. There was not a hint of emotion in it. It was easy to imagine that he was comfortable with killing, a soldier blindly dedicated to his cause. The two young men with their guns moved ominously toward her. There was nothing to do but walk slowly toward her car. The moment she touched her hand to the door handle, she heard a rumbling sound behind her and she turned her head to see Guy Perry sliding the big door of the building shut. This done, he turned back to his young soldiers.

"Get her the hell out of here," he said. "And make sure the gate is secured." He strode across the compound, heading in the direction of the house.

Tara opened the door of her car and started the engine, as her two guards looked on, their guns still aimed in her direction.

"Drive slowly," the first guard said.

She set the car in gear, a soldier on each side of her, inches from the front fenders, walking with her toward the gate. She drove slowly out of the compound, fearful that if she drove too fast she'd get her tires shot, or worse. Once she had moved beyond the gate, the two guards shouldered their weapons and pulled it shut, bolting it with a

 Spirit Circle

heavy brass padlock.

*   *   *

By the time she got back to the highway, Tara's heart was pounding with anger, fear, and a growing sense of defiance. A knot had formed in her stomach, tightening against her ribcage. It was outrageous that Drake would lure her all the way down here and then neither leave a message with the gallery, nor make any arrangements to meet her at Coyote Mesa. Discovering the boarded up house was outrageous enough but then to stumble on this covert military operation, and to have her life threatened in the process...it was hardly what she'd bargained for.

It wasn't these events alone that troubled her, though any one of them was distressing enough for a lifetime. What she realized was that this exquisite combination of danger and intrigue was exactly what Drake loved. It was what he lived for. If he'd gotten wind of the activities at the compound behind the party store, he would have jumped into the middle of it. He would have picked locks, scaled walls and bribed guards to find out what was going on there.

What were they hiding up there? Tara wondered. *Who or what was the strange white figure inside the tank?* And why the armed guards and the secrecy? This was peace time, after all. Security was greatly relaxed in all military installations.

The white figure in the tank looked familiar to Tara, though she could not place where she'd seen anything like it before. It might be nothing more than a person in protective clothing, cleaning out this tank that held...what? It was ridiculous to speculate. It could be anything, some deadly chemical perhaps.

She thought about the Indian woman in the party store, trucking the calf off to her uncle's place for a ceremony. How was she involved with the operation at the compound? Certainly she was involved somehow, if only as an employee. She knew something more than she told Tara. And there was a good chance that the woman in the store knew perfectly well the whereabouts of the drivers of the black car. But here were two worlds that, at least on the surface, could not be further apart--a woman on her way to a ceremony who was also involved with some high tech government operation.

Nothing added up. All this had nothing to do with her own objective, discovering where her father had found the potsherds. These completely unrelated intrigues had all the earmarks of a story that Drake Fairfield would see as the chance of a lifetime. *The Mystery at Area 55!* She could almost see the headlines. The story would make her father the prince of the tabloid journalists again, restoring him to a position he'd held probably a dozen times in his life. You never stayed a prince for long in that business. There were always new princes vying for the position.

She was pretty certain Drake had already found the compound. Her little test with the cell phone seemed to indicate that. It was very possible that the compound could provide her with the clues she needed to trace him down. But getting in there--that was another matter. She was not going to risk her own life by going that route to find him.

As Tara drove toward Coyote Mesa, she couldn't help but wonder what Charla's involvement was in all this--whatever all this was. Did she know about the compound and Guy Perry? And if Drake was maybe a captive there, had Charla met a similar fate? What was going on behind the painted over windows in those buildings on the compound? Tara quickly censored herself again, chastising herself mildly for going off on a wild tangent. It was, after all, quite possible that there was legitimate research going on behind those walls. Military scientists had a penchant for insisting that their work was top secret. They had to protect their creations at all costs. Industrial spying and espionage had become major threats to every research and development group in the world, not just those associated with the military. Ideas themselves had become the most valued commodity in the industrialized world because good, marketable ideas, developed privately or with public resources, would ultimately become the fountainheads of fortune and power for individuals as well as governments.

Tara knew about this kind of spying and espionage because Drake had written a feature article on the subject--one of his more serious efforts, she thought--published in "Today's Issues" three years ago. As she sped along the highway, her eyes dropped down to the cell phone. She picked it up again, switched it on and pressed it to her ear. She heard only the hiss made by the phone itself. It was again beyond the range of a transmitter. She'd driven less than five miles from Guy Perry's place, where she'd been able to receive an active connection, but now she got nothing. What was going on at the compound that allowed her to get through? She switched the phone off and set it back in its bracket.

She saw Coyote Rock ahead, marking the road up onto the mesa where she had found Charla Mather's boarded up home. Without thinking, without being aware of having made the decision to do so, she slowed and turned into it. Where the blacktop ended, the road became soft and unstable. Her car fishtailed as she moved further up the hill, the tires spinning in the soft slimy mud. By the time she reached the first switch back, climbing toward the mesa, the car was making little headway, though Tara had dropped it down into first gear. Unable to go on she stopped, shifting the transmission into Park.

Staring straight ahead, she estimated it was a quarter-mile, perhaps a little more, to the top. On foot she could make it in ten minutes. Could she make it up and back before the rains started again? There was no way to tell. The sky was etherically blue, not a cloud for as far as she could see. But that didn't mean much, not this time of year when storms appeared to manifest out of nowhere, without warning.

In her mind's eye she kept seeing the little plot of ground on the west side of the house where somebody had been digging. Something was pulling her to that spot, perhaps her own fears. She didn't like what was in her mind now, but there was no way to get it out except to examine that place close up. Why hadn't it occurred to her earlier, when she first saw it? She didn't know. Maybe she had not wanted to even entertain the possibility at that point. It had been too horrible to contemplate. But she had to face facts. If there had been foul play, what better way to keep away probing strangers than to board up the house, Indian style, indicating at least to those who still held to the old ways that Death had been here. Tara wasn't that familiar with how modern Indians were affected by traditional ways but from what she had pieced together the sealing up of a house would have been a dire warning for them to stay away as well.

And what about John Whitecrow? If the woman at the party store was right, that wasn't his real name. Could she trust that? Tara tried to recall if she'd ever heard the name Whitecrow before in her travels around Arizona and New Mexico over the past decade. If she had heard it, she couldn't remember. She did remember, however, that stories of the crow were often confused with raven stories. Like the owl, crow and raven were associated with ancient legends that had to do with the secret mysticism of many Pueblo peoples. Suddenly she felt very much out of her element, in the midst of several complex societies whose ways she only vaguely knew. She wished she'd paid more attention to the many bits and pieces of cultural information she'd heard over the years. As she attempted to put the puzzle together now she recognized that there were huge gaps in her information.

She recalled an odd story about crows, an ancient legend a friend had told her. The story said that in ancient times crow became intrigued by his own shadow. He pecked at it and pecked at it. Then one day his shadow woke up. In an instant crow was eaten by his shadow, and ever since then, the crow we know is Dead Crow, the crow of the dark side. It knows the mysteries beyond the physical world, the mysteries of change, of life and death, the mysteries of the eternal and the illusions of the finite world in which we humans live.

If the legend of the crow was important to a person, Tara mused, and if he or she believed this story, why would they take the name of White Crow, suggesting the opposite side of Dead Crow--crow before he was eaten by his shadow? Dead Crow was also identified as a Guardian, protecting one's left side, the intuitive and mystical. Would that then mean that White Crow was the Guardian of the right side, the down-to-earth, empirical side that wished to stay near what could be known?

During her trip to Peru with Tom they had interviewed a shaman in the Andes. He had said, "All life has a feminine and a masculine side, a side that is light and a side that is dark. There is the sky, the earth, and the underground, and we must know them all. Those who know only the light are prey to the darkness. In the darkness are many powers. If we reject them, or deny they are there, we fall victim to much evil and much pain."

She did not know exactly what the shaman meant. Maybe some of the problem was in the translation. But the words bubbled to the surface from her memory as she thought about Whitecrow. Why the dead raven tied to Coyote Rock? Why this name that was no name at all but a trick somebody was playing on her?

"Mind games!" Tara whispered hoarsely. All of it was pure speculation, struggling to interpret the symbols of a way of life so foreign to her own that they might as well have been on different planets or the expressions of a different species. She could speculate forever, frighten herself, or make herself feel good, all by manipulating icons and imagery--with her ignorance and half-truths. That was the challenge of the anthropologist, she mused, trying to piece together the fragments of an alien life. While she lived on the same planet as the Zunis, Navahos, Hopis, and the people of Acoma at Sky City, they lived in very different realities. How presumptuous to claim the power to cross from one to another, to pretend to have what it took to translate the symbolism of worlds outside your own!

She rolled down the window, slipped the Chevy's transmission into reverse, leaned out and carefully backed down to a wider part of the road. Content that she was leaving enough room for a second vehicle to pass, she locked the car doors and walked to the rear where she opened the trunk. Unzipping her suitcase, she rummaged through its contents until she found the parka she'd packed away. She folded it into a neat bundle and stuffed it into the side pocket of the small backpack in which she carried her notebook, a few personal items and reading material for the plane. She emptied out these less essential articles and stuffed a warm sweater inside.

Swinging the pack over her left shoulder, she shut the trunk of the car and stepped out into the center of the road.

As she turned to go back up toward the mesa, she glanced out toward the highway. A black car pulled off onto the shoulder. As Tara watched, it turned onto the mesa road, drove a ways, then stopped a hundred feet or so from the turnoff. The passenger's door opened and a man stepped out, standing beside the car to urinate. Then he got back in, leaving the door slightly ajar. Judging by the color of the vehicle, and the white license plate on the front, the car could be from the federal motor pool. Maybe they were following her. But if so, what did they want?

She shivered. A sharp wind caught under her canvas jacket and lifted it up, chilling her to the core. Tara stopped, turned her back to the wind, zipped her coat tightly around her, then turned again in the direction of the mesa. Glancing at her watch, she calculated that she had just a little over an hour before the sun set. Enough time to find out what she needed to know, though it might require making her way back down the road in the twilight. If for some reason her task took longer, it would be dark by the time she got back to the car.

She felt tired and hungry. There was nothing she would rather do than be at home with Viveka and Maya. She could imagine having a light dinner with them, maybe just a sandwich, then lounging around in the living room, perhaps watching one of Maya's favorite programs on TV.

For a moment, gloom swept over her. The sense of despair and foreboding that came with it were not unfamiliar to her. It seemed as if she was repeating a very old theme with her father, searching for him or waiting for him to show up. If she was wise, she brooded, she'd drop the whole thing right now, return to Albuquerque, get on a plane and fly home. But she knew she wasn't going to do that. Like a hundred times in the past, her mind clung to fragile hopes that somehow things would get better between her and Drake.

If it gets too late, she thought, *the drive back to Gallup is going to be a long one.* She hardly cherished the idea of driving the long, dark road back to the motel, particularly if it rained again. There were several rather treacherous stretches in and out of the deep canyons, narrow roads that snaked along the sheer mountain walls. The worst that could happen, she decided, is that she would be forced to sleep at Charla's house. But the thought of doing that sent shivers up her spine. She remembered the words of the woman in the party store: "If the place was boarded up I'd be sure to stay away." Superstition or not, Tara decided it was good advice.

Somehow it seemed a lot less threatening to consider camping out for the night, perhaps curled up in the back seat of the car. It had been years since she'd roughed it that way but if it came to that it wouldn't be the first time she'd improvised. The year she and Tom went to the Andes they'd spent many nights sleeping on airplanes, buses, and once even curled up on the hard floor of a train terminal. She'd manage. Regardless of what happened, she'd manage to find a place to sleep. Tears began to pool in her eyes, clouding her vision. But anger burned there as well. ~

 Spirit Circle

Coyote Mesa

It was darker than Tara had anticipated when she reached the top of Coyote Mesa. Heavy gray clouds moved swiftly across the sky from the northwest, and the sun, already low on the horizon, was barely more than a sanguine stain along the edge of the earth. Tara stopped for a moment and looked back down the road she'd just climbed. Below her, the long trail from the highway, across the canyon floor and then up to where she stood, reminded her of a line scratched into the earth by a boy dragging a stick across the sand. It snaked back and forth, slithering into the high country, seeking the sun or trying to escape it, depending on one's perspective. It was a beautiful sight, filled with the kind of lonely mystery that drew her back to the Southwest desert again and again. What Tara saw down on the road, however, troubled her.

The black car was still parked on the mesa road, out near the highway. From her vantage point it appeared that its occupants had left the vehicle. But there was no sign of anyone on foot. Her mind galloped into fantasies about who had been in the car--perhaps the two young soldiers with their guns, or maybe Guy Perry, or...her mind was running wild. Tara chastised herself. There was no evidence, after all, that this car had anything to do with her. Her mind was simply playing tricks on her. If the car's occupants were government men investigating what she was doing in the area, so what? She would simply explain the whole thing. It was a private matter, nothing to do with them!

As she started to turn away from the road, she saw a second vehicle approaching the Coyote Mesa turnoff from the north. About a half mile from the cutoff, it stopped and pulled onto the shoulder. At first she thought it could be John Whitecrow returning. Instinctively, Tara moved behind a large rock that lay a dozen yards from the road. The rock towered over her, its wind-sculpted top a good ten feet above her head. She felt certain that she could not be seen from this vantage point. The driver's door of the Jeep swung open and a man stepped out, his body partially hidden by the door. He appeared to be looking toward the mesa road with binoculars pressed to his face. In a moment, he climbed back into the Jeep and made a hasty U-turn, heading north again. Instantly, the black car backed onto the highway, tires smoking as they hit pavement, then raced north after the Jeep.

Tara sighed, satisfied that she was going to be left alone but curious about the relationship between the two vehicles. It seemed fairly obvious that whoever was driving the Jeep wanted to elude the men in the black car. Whatever was going on, she could not imagine what it might have to do with her.

She turned toward the house, crossed the road and walked slowly up the driveway. As she walked she looked for any movement around the house or in the mountain that rose behind it. But she saw nothing. Then her gaze settled on the circle of freshly-turned earth on the western end of the building. As she approached it, she noticed something she'd missed the first time.

Someone had carefully placed a circle of smooth rocks around the edge of the little plot of earth, and there was a smaller circle of rocks in the center of that circle. The smaller circle, she estimated, was no more than three feet in diameter. As she studied it, she realized the pattern was familiar to her. She'd seen it many times in her anthropology texts. It resembled the medicine wheel of many Native American peoples, constructed to mark a place for ritual work, for healing a rift with the natural forces or to seek solutions from the Four Directions. Usually a medicine wheel was large enough to accommodate a dozen people or more inside its design. This one was much smaller, and Tara wondered if the ritualized pattern was simply a coincidence.

Then she noticed that in the center of the smaller circle, someone had inserted a stick about a foot-and-a half-long. The stick was as big around as Tara's index finger. It had been stripped of its bark and stained dark blue, probably in the traditional way, with berries or a root. Three brown and white feathers--which because of their size, color and pattern she guessed could be from the wing of a hawk or an owl--pointed toward the sky, attached to the stained shaft by a thin leather thong. There were dozens of turquoise and coral beads, the kind known as *ishi,* strung along the leather thong, producing a striking, irregular pattern against the smooth surface of the dark blue stick.

Tara thought it odd that she could have overlooked all this before. She wracked her brain, trying to reconstruct the memory of her first visit to this place. Had the rocks and the stick been there then? It didn't seem possible. And yet, she had to allow that she could have missed them. She had been nervous, disturbed by the implications of the boarded up house. As Tara studied these objects and the ground around them, she had no doubt that someone had painstakingly arranged the two rock circles and placed the feathered shaft at their center. The task had obviously been performed as a ritual. For what reason, she couldn't say, but here was this stick with feathers and beads which somebody had gone to a great deal of trouble to make, stripping the bark, staining the wood, stringing the beads on the leather thong, then wrapping the three feathers to the shaft.

If the rocks and the feathered shaft hadn't been there on her first visit, somebody had set them in place quickly. In the time between her first visit to the house and now, she had driven toward Fence Lake, stopped at the store, then had gone over to the ranch where she met Guy Perry. It was difficult to believe that somebody had constructed the medicine wheel and performed all the appropriate rituals during the interim. She'd seen tribal preparations for medicine wheels. Some took days to install, with prayers and rituals for each rock they placed on the ground. It was a painstaking process, one that she only came to understand when she began studying the literature on the subject of medicine wheels. The rich spiritual symbolism of each rock, and the teachings associated with each of the four directions, were renewed each time the sacred medicine wheel circle was created. When, at last, participants sat down at the wheel, there were more prayers and rituals, and each person now brought her or his own unique *medicine* into the circle, offering it in the service of a *greater power*. This greater power could be anything from Mother Earth herself to the one spirit over all.

It was her study of the medicine wheel literature that had convinced Tara that Pre-Colombian shamans possessed systems of divination at least as sophisticated as any found in Europe. She did not fully understand their workings, but there was a rich magic involved in the use of the medicine wheel that definitely allowed one to transcend the limits of everyday awareness.

She looked up, scanning the rugged country above her. Ridges carved into the cliffs by Mother Nature suggested a presence, people or animals who blended into the landscape, born to this country and knowing how to make themselves invisible if need be. If she was being watched, however, she did not feel it, or at least did not feel threatened. It was hard for her to imagine that the locals would wish her any harm. If there was a danger to be reckoned with, it would more likely be found in the person of John Whitecrow or the people in the black car, whoever they might be.

Tara had spent enough years in Indian country to have assimilated many legends about the early cultures of the region. She remembered stories of prayer sticks which the Pueblos planted in the ground--for various reasons. For example, she recalled how ancient hunters planted these sticks wherever their prey had fallen, marking the spot where a deer or elk's heart had ceased to beat. With the ritual sticks properly placed in the earth, the hunter knelt down, uttering his prayers for the spirit of the animal, thanking it for its sacrifice and asking that its soul might enjoy a safe journey to the other side, and that it would be reborn again soon so that it could rejoin its deer family on Mother Earth.

But prayer sticks were used for many purposes. They were used in ceremonies to pray for rain, ceremonies for the crops, for fertility, for harmony in the community and for the darker side of the shaman's art: witchcraft. Now Tara stood up and took a few steps back from the little plot of ground. While she did not believe in the dark magic of witchcraft, what she saw before her began to make a kind of sense she would have preferred not to see. The feathers! She looked at them more closely. Though she could not be certain, she did not believe they were from a hawk. Judging from their pattern, she was willing to bet they were from the tail or wing of an owl. They were soft and fluffy on the ends, unique to the latter bird, whose silent wing had won it the reputation as a ghost, allowing it to sweep in upon its prey with hardly a sound. Depending on which culture the person who performed the ritual belonged to, the owl could be considered an ally in the practice of witchcraft, or simply an intermediary between the invisible world, or the spirit world of the dead, and our own. On a more mundane level, the owl was perceived as a protector of the home. Was this prayer stick nothing more than that, a home protection device in the old tradition?

She remembered a story she'd heard at the Native American museum in Albuquerque three or four years before. The story told of a young man who fell in love with a beautiful young woman from his tribe but by some tragic accident she was killed. While he was grieving his great loss, an owl came to his rescue, promising to escort the young man to Spirit Lake, where spirits traveled after death. There he could retrieve the soul of his beloved and bring her back to his village where she could be with her grieving lover. The owl warned that the young woman would seem to be truly alive. But while he could feast his eyes on her great beauty, and could speak with her as he had previously done, he could never touch her. If he did, she would disappear and he would never see her again.

Eager to reclaim his love, to have her in his life no matter what the cost, the young man agreed to go with the owl to the sacred lake. After many trials and tribulations, the young man plunged down through the deep waters of Spirit Lake to the hidden city where the souls of the dead lived, waiting to be reborn. The owl helped him find and communicate with the soul of his beloved, who the young man then escorted back up through the deep waters to the land.

For two days they traveled together, the young man blissfully walking at the beautiful young woman's side, always careful not to touch her. Secretly, he yearned with all his heart to take her in his arms, just as he'd done before her death. However, he remembered the owl's warning and did his very best to obey.

On the second night, as the beautiful young woman slept, her lover gazed upon her gorgeous face in the moonlight. Moved by his great love for her and for the longing he felt in his heart, he leaned over and kissed her lips gently. His heart raced and joy flooded every inch of his body. In celebration of his love he cried out to the universe, his voice rising in song. Then came a sound that struck terror in his heart, the beating of heavy wings in the darkness above him, and as he drew back in horror the owl swooped down and swept away the soul of the beautiful young woman. In that instant, the young man knew she was gone forever. He would never see her again. Grief stricken, the young man returned to his village. In penance for his error, he never allowed himself to cast his eyes upon such beauty again. Though he became a great hunter and warrior, he remained forever faithful to his lost love.

At first Tara could not grasp why she had thought of that story. What was the original theme, the moral it was intended to teach? It had to do with acknowledging and respecting the boundaries between the living and the dead. Or was it something more? The ancient peoples held the idea that there was an invisible world, a different reality than everyday existence. This unseen world, though non-material and incorporeal, nevertheless could have an impact on one's life, particularly if one violated its boundaries.

Tara knelt down at the southeastern quadrant of the circle and gazed into the center. As she studied it more carefully, she noticed a cluster of ivory-colored beads wrapped around the prayer stick and held together with the single dark hair. These were quite possibly made of bone. And the presence of the bone, combined with the three owl feathers, strongly suggested that witchcraft indeed was involved here. Witchcraft violated the boundaries between the living and the dead. In certain Navajo traditions, beads of bone or bone dust were used to cast spells, to place a curse on one's enemies. In spite of the fact that she did not believe in such things, Tara became more cautious, inwardly drawing back from this site.

Briefly, she thought about finding a shovel to dig at the center of the medicine wheel and see what had been buried there. But now she wanted only to distance herself from this place. The idea of disturbing this ground was unthinkable. Superstitions aside, she felt reverence, awed by what she saw. In spite of the scientific detachment of her profession, it was impossible not to feel moved by the old legends and to respect the metaphors, signs and symbols that told of truths buried under the hard realities of modern life. If nothing else, Tara was unnerved by the two circles of rocks and the prayer stick. This ground had been sanctified--for good or for evil--as surely as the grave of a loved one would be sanctified by the most reverent Jewish or Christian funeral. Though she might maintain a healthy, scientific skepticism about such rituals, she could not bring herself to violate this site in any way. It had to be respected.

She heard the engine of a car drawing near. Though it was still some distance away, there could be little doubt that it was heading in her direction. She glanced quickly around, suddenly afraid. Her heart pounded. *Why fear?* she asked herself. It could be her father or Charla. But something told her it wasn't either of them. It didn't make any sense but a small voice within told her to flee. Run! Hide! The car would be breaking up over the top of the hill in minutes. She glanced furtively around. For a moment she considered hiding in the house, but dismissed the thought immediately. If the person coming was Whitecrow, that would be the first place he'd look. Besides, the idea of entering that place again filled her with dread. Was it superstition, linked to the tradition of sealing up houses where people died? She tried to dismiss that possibility but could not. Then, behind the house, she spied a series of steps carved into the rock, random risers and plateaus that formed an easy path into a high rocky landscape above, where she could hide and watch.

As she turned away from the house, moving toward the trail, the sound of the approaching car's engine grew stronger. She moved more quickly, finding a well worn footpath, or perhaps game trail, threading between gigantic boulders. Within moments she was high above the house, looking down at the rooftop. Breathless, she paused and studied the lay of the land across the almost perfect plane formed by the mesa. There was the roof of the house, a terra cotta rectangle raised above the land. Off to the right was the circle gouged into the dirt. From here it clearly gave off the impression of being an important ritual site.

As she watched, careful to keep hidden behind the rock, the Jeep came over the last rise, raced across the mesa, turned up the driveway at the house and stopped. She heard the racheting sound of a parking brake pulled on and the engine switching off, then for a moment a profound silence blanketed the desert. Tara waited nervously in this silence, waiting to see what the driver of the Jeep would do. At last the car door swung open and a man stepped out. He wore a wide-brimmed cowboy hat that shielded his face from Tara's sight, a dark blue sweat shirt that boasted a large printed shield that she could not make out from that distance, blue jeans and western-style boots. He glanced quickly around, strode toward the house and disappeared from Tara's sight. Presumably, he had gone inside. She heard him calling but could not make out his words. In a moment he emerged from the side of the house and strode toward the garden.

From her vantage point, Tara could not clearly see the man's face or be certain of his stature. A line of sage brush partly obscured her view. If it was Whitecrow he had changed his hat and his shirt. She was not even certain it wasn't Tom or her own father.

The man knelt down at the edge of the rock circle. Though it was difficult to tell exactly what he was doing, it appeared that he had reached out and plucked the prayer stick from the ground. Standing again, he tossed it away, dismissing it as if it were no more important than a common weed. He stepped into the center of the circle and kicked away the smaller rocks. Having done this he returned to the Jeep, reached into the back and withdrew a shovel, which he carried back to the rock circle. First removing his hat and setting it aside, the man proceeded to place the blade of the shovel against the earth and set his right foot on it.

Tara was amazed and troubled by the way the man worked. She thought, surely he'd seen her car parked beside the road as he drove up. It seemed to her that a normal person, particularly one who was up to no good, would have been concerned about possibly encountering its driver at the top. Such brazen behavior chilled her. Was his mission so important that he didn't care if he was dis-covered, that someone might come along and confront him about trespassing, digging on Charla Mather's property? She was somehow certain he was intruding, that he was not here in the service of the owner. He was more like an armed thief, determined to get what he'd come for, even if it meant killing anyone who tried to stand in his way.

Tara watched as the man threw his weight against his right foot. The thin steel blade of the shovel broke through the soil, penetrating deep into the earth. Bending over, the man lifted out a shovelful of dirt and heaved it carelessly aside. At the same instant, Tara saw a small movement out of the corner of her eye. She turned to look but whatever it was leapt behind the house, eluding her. The man with the shovel placed the blade against the earth and again lifted out a clod of soil, rapping the blade against a rock this time to remove the dirt which clung to the shiny metal. Again, Tara saw a movement out of the corner of her eye and turned to look at it.

It had to be an hallucination, Tara thought. What she saw was a figure too fantastic to be real. It appeared to be a man dressed in a costume, but a costume so bizarre that Tara did not trust her eyes. The person or creature--whatever it was--appeared to be seven or eight feet tall! Its feet were wrapped in knee-length boots made of straw or some kind of thick reeds. It wore a skirt of the same material, with a breastplate of elaborate colored feathers and a belt adorned with a huge metal crest that caught the thin rays of the light filtering through the clouds. But most extraordinary of all were the creature's mask and headdress. Round like a full moon, and stark white, the mask itself had two huge eyes that seemed to stare out into infinity. Below them black lips with outlines of gigantic teeth appeared to be frozen in a passive grin. All around this ghostly face were huge eagle feathers, so that the mask itself gave the appearance of a sunburst, or perhaps it was meant to represent the moon.

As quickly as it appeared, the creature disappeared. Yet, it did this in a very peculiar way. It was as if the figure was like the flame of a candle, dying out for a moment, swallowed by the darkness, then suddenly reigniting and becoming bright again. Tara rubbed her eyes and looked away thinking that in her fatigue her own senses were perhaps playing tricks on her. But that was not it. Once more the figure flickered in and out, the image dying and reappearing in the same mysterious way. Then it was gone.

Since it was so elusive, Tara could not decide if she'd actually seen a figure or not. She turned her attention back to the man with the shovel, who had now removed several more clumps of the heavy soil. The hole he'd produced looked to be two or three feet in diameter, and about a foot deep. The man stopped, stood up straight as if alerted by a sound. He glanced to his left and right, called out something which Tara could not understand, waited for a second, then returned to his digging.

For several minutes, Tara watched the man digging and then the flickering figure with the round white mask was suddenly standing only a few feet from him. It stood with its hands on its hips, watching the man work. Yet, the man with the shovel was totally unaware of its presence.

The sky was growing darker by the moment and Tara could barely see what happened next. The man stopped digging and seemed to look straight through the costumed figure. He did not react at all. How could this be? Surely he couldn't ignore such a strange presence! Maybe the two of them were working together.

But that was the most preposterous explanation of all.

The figure in the mask now began moving from side to side, weaving back and forth, at times actually dancing a few steps, lifting his feet a foot or so, as if tamping down the earth, weaving first to one side of the hole and then the other. It no longer flickered in and out but maintained a constant form. At times it seemed to move right through the man with the shovel, as if one or the other of them had no physical form. Tara noticed that the figure moved in a circle around the medicine wheel, from the West side, to the North, back to the West, then to the South, and around the entire circle again. he digging man continued his work undisturbed. Then he stopped, tossed the shovel aside and leaned over, peering into the hole. He reached down and with his bare hands lifted something out. It appeared to be an object wrapped in plastic about the size of a small mixing bowl. He sat down on the ground with it, pulled the wrappings apart and reached inside them. In a moment he was holding the object in his hands, pressing it once or twice to his lips, as if to kiss it, and then holding it out at arms length to admire it again.

Whatever the object, it was dark and quite plain looking. Though it was impossible to say for certain, owing to the dimming light of the setting sun, the object appeared to be coated with a slightly shiny surface. It might have been the deep patina of an ancient metal that had been buried for centuries in the earth, or a hard glazed finish. The latter did not seem likely to Tara since she knew of no ancient tribes who used such glazes. Whatever it was, the hard surface caught the light of the fading sun as the man turned it around and around in his hands, admiring his discovery.

Unseen by the man on the ground, the creature in the bizarre costume began dancing in a circle again. Now the creature's arms waved in the air, the way a child does when it is pretending to fly. Indeed, as Tara watched, this phantom was transformed into a gigantic bird--a bird in body and wings but with the face of a man! Like a huge owl it hovered over the man with the dark artifact, still unseen by him. As Tara watched the great birdlike creature, she was reminded of the other owls that had appeared in her life: the owl that had swooped down from the rooftops to pluck the squirming rat from the garbage can in Albuquerque, the owl that had risen on powerful wings in her strange encounter with the old woman at the ruins in Peru. Why owls? Why were these creatures coming into her life now? Being night hunters, they were rarely seen by people. But this latest apparition was the most disturbing. Nothing in her experience could have prepared her for this.

Her heart pounded. Dozens of times she'd read accounts of people who claimed to have witnessed such events. Native peoples she'd interviewed had sworn they'd seen shamans transform themselves into animals and even become giant birds, like this one, that could take flight. Often they claimed that the shamans were actually owls who'd transformed themselves into men or women who brought wisdom from the *unseen world* to their people. It was sheer superstition, of course. As an anthropologist she knew that many of the tales the native peoples told were like parables with morals to teach. They were passed along from generation to generation the way parents once scared their children with stories about the bogey man to make them behave.

But this was no legend. She saw this figure transformed before her very eyes. It *had* to be a trick! Though she had never believed that she was susceptible to hypnotic suggestion, it was possible that fear, the cold, and her memories of all too many ancient legends, had mixed together in her mind to fabricate this weird imagery. But how could that be? she asked herself. Everything else around her seemed so clear, so reasonable.

The man who'd been digging held his treasure in his hands and straightened up, letting the plastic wrappings fall carelessly to the ground. And then, as the bird creature hovered above him, he walked back to the Jeep, clutching his bounty to his chest as a mother might hold her child. He opened the passenger's side of the car, placed the object carefully on the seat, as if it were extremely fragile and valuable, closed the door again and returned to the hole. He picked up the shovel, carelessly kicked dirt back into the hole and returned to the Jeep.

A huge bolt of lightning ripped across the sky to the south, and like a gigantic preying mantis it appeared to squat momentarily over the earth. Instantly, the skies opened up and the rain poured down, splattering in gigantic drops off the hood of the Jeep as it headed back down the hill. Momentarily, Tara saw the huge bird flying above the Jeep, like a night hunter silently stalking its prey, un- disturbed by the storm.

Bewildered and shivering, Tara turned away and climbed further up the mountain toward a cave she had spotted an hour before, during her scamper up the hill. Better to get out of the storm for a while. She dreaded the thought of threading her way back down the rocky trail in the rain. The footing would be slippery, and it was now growing quite dark. She could easily injure herself. If she sprained an ankle or broke something, it could be days before anyone found her up here. She considered waiting for the storm to subside, then going back down the trail to spend the night in the house. It would be warm there, even comfortable. The plan seemed more and more inviting. Why not chance it? She might make a fire in the wood stove she'd seen in the living room. But not now, not now. The thought of being in Charla's house again made her stomach queasy. There was something dark and forbidding about that place, even more off-putting than the idea of crawling into a cave.

Finally at the mouth of the cave, she picked up a rock and threw it inside, as she'd seen their guide in Peru do, to chase out any animals that might have taken up residence there. She waited in silence, then hearing nothing, she stepped tentatively inside.

The cave was mercifully dry, providing welcome protection from the storm. Though she could barely stand up in it, it cut back deep into the cliffs behind her, farther back than she could see in the dim light. She did not dare venture into its depths for fear of falling into an unseen shaft or hole, from which she might never escape. Instead, she sat closer to the opening where she could see the sky. Though she could not feel the wind, it groaned past the opening of her sanctuary, each gust reverberating deep in the bowels of the earth like an angry god. Was she sitting in his mouth?

She thought about the specter she'd just seen on the mesa below. Surely it was a figment of her own imagination. There was nothing else it could be. Searching for assurance she recalled the vision quest she'd been on in the High Sierras when she was a teen. Friends had persuaded her to go with them, guided by a man who claimed he was a shaman. Tara had been skeptical of all this excitement about Native American spirituality, but she had gone along. In the morning they'd done a "sweat," seven of them crammed into a crudely made lodge fashioned of willow branches and covered with blankets and plastic tarps. In the steamy darkness, stinking of sweating bodies, burning sage, and sweet grass, she suddenly broke out in song. She had never sung before, and couldn't believe she was doing it then. It was more of a chant than a song, but the leader of the group called it a song. She sang of lost love and lost opportunities and a certain hollow grief she felt for humanity. She sang of a loneliness and longing which could not be described with words. Later, outside and away from the heat, her friends embraced her, congratulating her for what, she knew not.

She felt embarrassed, vulnerable, humiliated. But her venture was not yet complete. The second leg of her initiation would be a vision quest. In the evening she would go out from the campsite, alone in the darkness, and sit for the rest of the night. The shaman told her she would sit in silence for a long time, with no activity to distract her, and soon she would find her own inner voice. It would come in the form of fears, regrets, grievances with others--all the issues we avoid in daily life. Out of this experience, he explained, would come a vision, a dream, which would guide her in ways she could not herself even imagine. The shaman warned her that this dream would be like no other she'd ever had.

That night on the cliff where she'd staked out a camp for her vision quest, she'd sung her song again. It touched something deep, a secret place within her, something she'd never known was there, thoughts she would never share with any other person. Later in the night she'd nodded off, awakened in a few hours by the sound of a creature near her camp. A large beast had ambled through the brush, and she had not moved, hoping it would go away. Instead, it came closer, until she saw what it was, a black bear, not much bigger than a very large dog, except for its great bulk--which reminded her of an obese woman. The bear walked to within ten or twelve feet of her and stopped, staring directly into her eyes. It moaned, bellowed really, making a sound that she thought was more like a cow than a bear. And then it sat down opposite her at her camp, resting back on its haunches, supporting its ponderous upper body with its front legs. For what seemed like an hour or more woman and beast contemplated each other, each silent, each a bit restless, frightened, each patiently waiting for the other to break the spell.

The next day, when she'd returned to the base camp where the various members of their group were to share their stories, Tara told of her confrontation with the bear in a flat, matter-of-fact voice. Her friends had interpreted her experience for its symbolic meaning. She did not object but felt certain she had not had a dream. None of it mattered. She could not understand why they would want to make so much of it.

That had been long ago. Twenty or more years had passed. As she thought over this extraordinary experience, Tara began to have her doubts. Bears did not mingle with humans in this way. Her *vision,* as they called it, must have been an illusion, an apparition, a trick of the mind, nothing more. She decided there must be times in a person's life when some neurological aberration, a storm in the visual cortex perhaps, caused a change in her chemistry that made it impossible to distinguish between reality and fantasy. In fact, there were theories that the schizophrenic mind was caused by just such storms, resulting in the victim's inability to distinguish between reality and fantasy.

Was her experience tonight sheer craziness? It was certainly possible that in the frenzy of her quest to find Drake, and pursue the secret society of shamans, compounded by her discoveries at the house, she had somehow set off a series of neurological events in her own brain. She could no longer trust what she saw or heard. Reason told her there was no such thing as costumed men who turned into giant birds of prey. Surely her imagination, fueled by fear, had been set into motion by the circles of rock she'd found so carefully placed around the little plot of dirt down by the house. In addition, there had been that elaborate prayer stick placed at the center, suggesting a mystical link with everything else that was going on--the disappearance of her father and Charla Mather, the boarding up of the house, and the curious object the man had dug from the ground and taken away in his Jeep. But what did it all mean?

Tara crossed her legs and leaned back against the wall of the cave. Outside, the weather gave no hint of subsiding. If anything, the fury of the rain was escalating, the lightning and thunder booming every two or three minutes now. The sky had grown dark and shadows formed over the landscape below. Oddly, she had no fear at the prospect of spending the night holed up in this cliff. She felt, in fact, that she was protected, as if she was somehow completely invulnerable to the night and the storm and the occult forces that were showing themselves.

She could not explain the feelings she was having now. All reason told her she should feel afraid, that any sense of wellbeing under the circumstances was completely irrational. False euphoria or not, she welcomed the hope that came with it, desperate to be freed of the knotted clump of fear that had formed in her belly over the past forty-eight hours.

As the night wore on she felt pressured, a sense of urgency rising within her. Wrapping herself in her extra sweater and parka, she warmed, assured by this small comfort. She was hungry, but it didn't matter. In the morning she could satisfy that. But the urgency she felt was more. In her mind's eye she pictured Drake at the bottom of a long shaft, deep in the center of the earth. Then she dismissed this image, or rather drove it from her mind. Obviously, she reasoned, she had gotten this premonition from news stories she'd heard over the years about men getting trapped in mine shafts, or children getting stuck in old drainage pipes. The papers always said the person would perish if not rescued in the first twenty four hours. And sometimes they did perish, of course. Sometimes help did not arrive in time.

She started to tremble. It wasn't the cold. Her body in fact felt warm. But the shaking continued and in a moment she bowed her head, pressing her chin against her chest, choking back the tears. But tears came anyway, flooding her eyes, streaming down her face. Why is it always like this with you, father? How many times when I was a child did I awaken in the middle of the night, terrified, wanting to be able to feel your presence in the house, in my life? She reminded herself that she was an adult, a professional woman. There was no reason for this terror and anger to persist. What craziness kept her pursuing him, knowing that his first love was danger, not his family. Everything else ran second for him. *Edgewalker.* He was an edgewalker. She could not remember where she'd first heard that term, nor was she certain what it meant. But Drake had turned his back on a normal world where people loved and cared for each other, where they went off to work in the morning and came home at night to play with their children and talk over the day's events with their loved ones. Drake lived for the excitement of the shadows, feeding on crisis, doom, high risk and even human degradation. He made no excuses for how he lived. Drake had once said, "If you're not living on the edge, you're taking up too much space." He laughed, apparently thinking it was very funny. But the same statement sent chills up Tara's spine.

Yet, she could not deny it; there was a part of her that followed in his footsteps, that liked living at the edge, too. Not exactly his edge but an edge, a place of mystery and risk nevertheless. As much as she loved her daughter, she knew that the prospect of exploring an ancient dig in some remote mountain or desert area would pull her away every time. It was Drake's legacy to her. Maybe she didn't seek out mass murderers, or race off into some back country town to interview a family that claimed to have been abducted by space aliens. No, she didn't do that. But she did disappear from her daughter's life every time she heard of a new project where she might uncover evidence for the society of shamans.

Tara knew the price Maya paid for her long absences. But at least, Tara reminded herself, she was not putting her own life at risk as Drake had done during her childhood. At least her daughter did not lie awake at night, terrified that her mother might never come back. At least Maya wouldn't have to spend her adolescence reading about her father's exploits in a cheap supermarket tabloid, which made him seem to her like a man drawn to the most precarious edge, beyond common sense, even beyond all credibility, playing the edge like a tipsy tightrope walker.

She did not have to follow his example! She was an adult woman, after all, a respected professional with a family... Her family! When she thought of Maya, a dark cloud of regret and melancholy filled her. Never before had she seen so clearly that as Maya's parent she was passing along the very legacy that she herself was trying to escape. Maybe it was not quite as toxic. But how did one break the chain of moving from danger to danger and crisis to crisis? There was, after all, only one way. She had to sever the invisible threads that joined her life with Drake's. She had to give up all hope that he would ever be anything more than he already was, an edgewalker, one who sought a precarious existence.

Tara tried to put her father out of her mind. She did not want to think about what might have happened to him, why he had not returned to the house, and why he had sent her the package from Gallup. But the pull she felt to find evidence that he was okay wouldn't go away. It was not just that she wanted to find the society of shamans. She wanted that even more than she wanted to find Drake.

There was something in her makeup that delighted in the adventure, in risking whatever she must to find proof for the existence of the society of shamans. She could not escape this mission. It drove her even as the heroin addict was driven by his dark appetite.

A sense of foreboding came over her, enveloping her in a feeling she had not experienced since her childhood. She was certain Drake was in trouble. He had gone beyond even his own edge of safety and could not get back. She had to move swiftly, but darkness and the storm prevented her, at least for now, from pursuing him. The cave, which had been like a nurturing womb, now became a dungeon, locking her into a gloom of inaction and self-doubt. ~

 Spirit Circle

The Cave

Tara catnapped, slipping in and out of sleep. From time to time thunder or a particularly noisy downpour jolted her awake. She slept fitfully, dreaming sporadically. Her dreams wove back and forth between her father, boarded up houses, lost Indian civilizations, the society of shamans, and James Dean. Each time she was awakened by the storm, James Dean's image filled her mind. Once she imagined him at the mouth of the cave, grinning in the moonlight, almost mischievous in his demeanor, mouthing the words, "I'll protect you."

As quickly as the figure appeared, it vanished. But the phrase "I'll protect you," echoed in Tara's mind. Anger welled up in her heart as these words triggered memories of her father's erratic, sometimes completely crazy behavior, his seemingly miraculous ability to escape disaster and...at the top of his list, broken promises. *Did he ever really protect me? God knows, there were a million times I sought a safe haven as a child. I wanted a sanctuary and he certainly wasn't there!*

But who, after all, had protected whom? She knew in ways that were almost too subtle for her to hold onto that she had protected him, had protected him from her own anger, and from her mother's anger. They had both loved him. Both had clung to their own separate illusions of what he *could* or *should* be in their lives--Tara seeking a hero and a shield from a world she found threatening, Helen a lover and companion, a foundation. *But why did an adult woman, proud of her own accomplishments, still dwell on such things? Old wounds lingered far too long.*

In Drake's absence from her young life, Tara was left with her own fantasies about who her father really was. In her childhood mind, he was always the bright knight. He was exactly who she wanted him to be. And so, when he came to visit, or took her away for a vacation, she was always disappointed in what she found. Or, rather, what she didn't find. Now, shivering in this cave, she felt herself flooded with the truth, of all the promises he never kept, of how lightly he had always taken her love and her need for him. Yet, in spite of it all, she also felt an imponderable connection with this man. Something constantly drew her to him, just as the tug of the Earth's magnetic flow pulls the needle of a compass North.

Drifting in and out of sleep, her mind played tricks on her. She dreamed she was with Tom at the dig in Peru. She remembered the love she once felt for him, fueled by the wonder and innocence of youthful idealism. That had been a very special time in her life, and if it had ended sadly, the poignancy of that time was still a powerful memory. Outside the cave a stone tumbled down a slope, rattling and clicking, gathering momentum and dislodging other rocks as it went. She strained to hear if footsteps might follow...animal or human. Her body tensed in anticipation. For a moment she imagined a crouching mountain lion returning to reclaim her lair, or an Indian his sacred cave, and she felt like the intruder she was.

As an anthropologist, she knew that in ancient times, when the land was still held as sacred and alive, a vital and spirited entity rather than as property to be owned and bartered, the elders viewed the caves as sacrosanct. They were seen as places of human trans-formation and healing, where old conflicts between tribes or in-dividuals could be repaired. Caves were the earth's sanctuaries, above the reign of human law, human differences and troubles. In the most poetic myths about the caves they were described as wombs within Mother Earth where one literally went in times of trouble, praying to the gods that they might be reborn.

In the cosmologies of the first people of this region, it was from Mother Earth that the original humans had come. So going into the earth, actually slipping beneath her skin once again, was never taken lightly, was indeed undertaken with a sense of reverence and awe. If a woman allowed herself to receive the cave's gifts--Mother Earth's loving succor--she might be able, at least for a moment, to feel a higher truth than she was able to experience on her own. *Yet, where is that comfort now?* Tara asked. Perhaps, not being from the bloodline of those who shared this reverence for the cave, she was unable to receive its gifts. Though she tried to dismiss these thoughts as pure superstition, the fact remained that she became immersed in the feeling that somehow she was left out, alone, abandoned. The gods or goddesses who had been so generous and loving in ancient times were no longer willing to receive her. Here, in this life, she was alone.

In the solitude of the cave, fear came and went with each sound, each movement of the shadows. In her mind's eye old memories came to the fore; she was a child of five or six, alone and fearful, feeling an emotion that she had learned to call abandonment. Her heart was filled with feeling from the past, feelings she had convinced herself were in the past, all but forgotten, dismissed as no longer useful. But nothing was lost, nothing. Why did these hardest of all memories bubble forth at times like this, when one needed strength, not the cold, relentless nagging of regret and fear, fear that choices, many of them made during moments of anger or frustration, had been wrong, terribly, terribly wrong? For her this cave, once the source of comfort for others, had become for her a callous, even ruthless theater where her regrets were being paraded before her without mercy.

Abandoned! That word lodged in her mind. The feelings surrounding it spun backward into her consciousness, haunting her. It was a portent--*foreboding* her therapist had once called it. She was not proud to be harboring such feelings, nor was she proud of the fact that this same foreboding seemed to draw her to men who were exciting but ultimately untrustworthy, if not dangerous. The men in her life, she reasoned, drew her into adventures that tore at her fragile illusions of security, of loving and being loved, that she had tried so desperately, yet so unsuccessfully, to weave into her life.

When she dwelt too long on these issues, she began to feel guilty, guilty for the way her own hangups had deprived Maya, the person she most loved in the world, of having a trustworthy and empathic father in her life. Certainly Tom was no more trustworthy as a father than Drake had been. In truth, he had never related to Maya as his daughter. As for her grandfather, Drake, poor Maya barely knew him.

A certain pain, a longing and a sadness that Tara had come to almost accept in her childhood, closed in around her. Ordinarily, her work insulated her from these feelings. But the safe buffer of her professional role had now faded away. Without even that stern comfort, she was left to face the barren truth of her yearning.

The light from the night sky, spilling through the mouth of the cave, was suddenly blocked, perhaps by a rain cloud drifting in front of the moon. But for Tara it was a warning, a portent. She turned her head, staring out, feeling the fear but unable to identify its cause. Surely there was a reasonable explanation for the dimming light. Part of her knew it was a cloud passing over the moon. But then she saw the outline of a human figure standing in the entrance of the cave, less than twenty feet away.

Every muscle in her body tensed. Was it human or merely her own ghostly fantasies? The image of the form flickered in and out of her consciousness like a flame dying and mysteriously reigniting in the darkness. Its shape nearly filled the opening of the cave, its head reaching the top of the arc. *Of course, it could not be real. It simply could not!* It had to be the product of her own dread. There had been no footsteps. She heard no rustling of clothing, no sound of breathing as it moved.

She forced herself to her feet, trembling as she did. Dare she move forward? She had no choice. There was no other direction to go. She stepped forward cautiously, not knowing what she would do but knowing that her only escape was through the very space now blocked by the figure. The shadowy form moved slightly to the side and she saw beyond it. In the distance the sky glowed dimly, lit by a billion points of light. Far away the desert floor merged with the sky, dissolving into infinite space.

A rock rolled under her foot, and she looked down reflexively. When she looked up again the figure was gone. It had disappeared silently, without so much as a whisper. She listened but heard no sound outside the cave. *So, it cannot be real. It is only in my mind. There is nothing to fear...nothing real,* she told herself.

Standing at the mouth of the cave, she leaned out, staring into the star lit night. Nothing moved. Nothing! She shivered. She had to get control of herself! Her legs wobbled as she clung to the rock wall of her uncertain refuge. *It was the exertion,* she told herself. She would not give in to her fear! She would not yield to the foolish fabrications; they were nothing more than the products of her own most foolish dreams.

Tara grasped for that state of mind which had served her so well in her work--her objectivity, her intellectual detachment. Trance, she reflected, that's what I'm experiencing...an altered state produced by my own fear...not mystical...not mythical...only my own fear... I won't be seduced by this... After all, I am not a superstition-bound primitive who has fallen victim to her own fantasies, confusing premonitions for the real thing. Nothing these walls tell me can be trusted, nothing!

In the past, she'd been able to talk herself out of her own fears. But this time it wasn't working. She reached deep into her rational mind for assurance that she was okay, reminding herself that when people spent too much time around ancient digs, they had a tendency to let their minds wander and invent, to identify with the mythology of the place. She'd always been able to resist that. So many others she'd known had not. Instead, they'd fallen victim to such fantasies, the myths touching a frail and vulnerable place in their minds. She was a strong woman. She would not let this happen!

She moved unsteadily toward the rear of the cave. She sat down, back against the wall, hugging her knees. One just had to be calm. Wasn't that always the solution? No reason to panic. She stared out beyond the opening of the cave at the night sky. Trembling, she clenched her jaw to prevent her teeth from chattering, though it was not cold that caused this reaction. Sobbing gently, her thoughts turned to Maya and home. But even here she did not find the comfort she so desperately sought.

Tara remembered the dream Maya had the day after she left on this trip. Maya had dreamed that Tom was gone and Tara had changed. She had tried to sooth Maya, assuring her that dreams weren't real. *But perhaps they were! What if the boarded up house meant that something had happened to Drake?* No, she would not let herself dwell on such irrational forebodings. Certainly a child's dreams could not be prophetic! And yet...and yet, what? What if dreams... *No! No, she would not give in to these fantasies, these products of fear and superstition!*

Determined not to be victimized by her fears, it occurred to her that the wisest thing to do was to go back down the hill, get into her car and race back to Gallup for the night. The looters were gone now. There was nothing to fear. She could spend the rest of the night at a safe and warm motel, then drive back to Albuquerque whenever she woke up. Then she'd catch the first plane home. She would end this foolishness once and for all.

Was it really so important to find Drake or the site of the society of shamans? No. And yes. They were two different issues, joined at the center by the very real possibility that Drake would blunder into trouble at this site he had found and would, at the very least, ban anyone else from ever investigating the place. In spite of her discomfort, she still felt bound by her original purpose for coming here. Why couldn't she let it go? She searched her mind for an explanation but there was none. It was pure folly to believe Drake really needed her. But she couldn't let go of the fact that he had called her, not just requesting her help but pleading for it.

Her mind jumped from one thing to another. She could not hold her focus. She worried about the figure she'd seen standing silently at the mouth of the cave only minutes before. Surely she had fabricated this image. Hallucinations of this kind were wish-fulfillments, nothing more, a trick of the mind, an illusion it had created to quell her fears and satisfy a secret wish.

At this moment, however, she wished nothing more than to have a real protector, one of flesh and bone, not dream stuff. Suddenly she was dozing again but heard a voice as clearly as if another person was standing before her.

"*No tengo cuidado*," James Dean told her in Spanish. "They will not touch you. You are one of them, more than you know." The words echoed in her mind--*No tengo cuidado!*

She burst from the depths of her half-sleep, startled by the clarity of his voice. It was as if a real person were standing there. Perhaps, she reasoned, it sounded so real because she had been the one to speak the words. It would not have been the first time she'd talked in her sleep. But was it this, truly?

"No *tango...*" she said aloud, testing the sound of her voice. It was nothing like the voice she'd heard moments before, nor could she say exactly what the words meant. "*No tango que...*" That wasn't it! She knew the words were Spanish, knew they were telling her not to be afraid. But she could not repeat them. She did not know these words.

Maybe she was remembering a scene from one of James Dean's movies, which she had loved so much as a child, able to recall how he looked, what he'd said, and how his words had affected those around him, even though she did not know the exact translation of his words. That must be the explanation, she told herself. But which movie was this scene from? When would he have spoken Spanish? And what did he mean by *them?*

She had to get back to her car. It was raining outside but only lightly. The man in the Jeep was gone, she was certain of that. The worst danger would be the walk in the darkness down the long, slippery path to the abandoned house. She dreaded the idea that she might fall and injure herself. Besides, she was tired, exhausted really. She did not have to go. This fear and foreboding, these fantasies of movie star visitors, were all in her head. Of course they were! Silly superstitions, nothing more. Why have any anxiety at all about staying? She was a grown woman, a woman with scientific training, never given to hysteria like this. She did not need to fall victim to her own ridiculous fears. She would sleep until the earliest light of dawn, that was decided. It would be fine. Illusion or not, she trusted what James Dean had told her, that there was nothing to fear.

She probed her own knowledge for a token of comfort and support, an explanation for her fantasies, a rationale that would help her make sense of her present experiences.

Two hours slipped by as she drifted in and out of sleep. Twice she heard a voice in the distance, asking her to listen, to move beyond her fear of the invisible world. There was a tone of urgency in the plea. At some point she opened her eyes and stared out through the entrance to the cave. A light moved across the sky. It was probably an airplane or a distant satellite, perhaps a helicopter, a reflection. It moved back into view and then away again several times.

If the voice is mine, she reflected, why would I be telling myself to move beyond my fear of the invisible world? She wasn't afraid of that world. How could an intelligent woman be fearful of something that didn't even exist, something fabricated by primitive minds because they had no way of knowing the truth? The message made no sense to her, any more than her father's fragmented messages on the answering machine made any sense. *Yet...yet, what?* What did these invisible realities offer? What did they mean? She slipped toward sleep and was startled awake almost immediately by the voice again urging her to listen, to move beyond her fears.

"Let me sleep!" she wailed, her own voice echoing back to her from the walls of the cave. She felt embarrassed, then reminded herself she was alone. She could talk to herself as much as she wished and nobody would ever know. Her only fear was that she was losing touch with reality, slipping into an hallucinatory state from which she might never escape. No, of course, it could not be. She had confidence in her own rationality.

"To *not listen* is insanity. Listen and open your mind!"

These words were as clear as words from her own mouth. Indeed, she felt the vibration of James Dean's voice in her head: "The world you believe you have mastered is an illusion. Move beyond it."

Words from a movie I saw when I was a child... she tried to tell herself. But try as she might she could not remember any films where such words fit the story. She remembered long ago being called by an other-worldly creature into a reality she did not understand. It had happened again at the motel back in Albuquerque.

That was it, she reflected. That was the explanation--the movie that she could not erase from her memory, the movie from her childhood, with beings from another world! "Buck Rogers and his space travelers," she said aloud, satirizing her own quirky mind. But immediately, the answer came: "No!"

Moments passed and she again drifted off to sleep, a deep and very pleasant sleep, of a kind she had not enjoyed for days, not since receiving the package with the artifacts from Drake. Along with her sleep, she dreamed. In her dream Tara rose to her feet and walked to the mouth of the cave. She stood just inside looking out. The rain had stopped. A bright moon hung over the mesa, piercing rays like a midnight sun that bathed the broad New Mexico landscape in turquoise light.

In the dream Tara was a young woman. But she was not herself. She moved in a different way, her skin darker, her manner of dress unfamiliar. She wore a dark, heavy skirt, striped with bright colors. Over her shoulders she had draped a woven shawl, a *serape.* Her long hair was pulled back and bound behind her head, flowing down her back in a pony tail.

She strode silently out onto the rocky ledge outside the cave and looked out over the mesa below her. She saw the terra cotta rooftop of the little house, its earthen colors vibrant and bright. The house was new, the adobe bricks still fresh, red and whiskered with the chopped straw that had been mixed with adobe mud when they were made. In time the wind and rain and sun would shave away the straw whiskers, leaving smooth stones bleached by the sun.

She surveyed the scene below, feeling great love and reverence, gratitude beyond measure for the house and the natural beauty surrounding it. People she loved had built this beautiful house and had cleared this land and planted it. She picked up a handful of small pebbles, then, sitting cross-legged on the hard rocky ledge, she absently arranged them in a circle, creating a pattern of near-perfect symmetry, chanting prayers. At last she stopped and looked down, studying her handiwork. She had made two circles, one inside the other.

"Medicine wheel," Tara thought.

She pressed her palms together and raised them toward the bright moon overhead. She stared into the light and chanted, the sounds resonating in her ears.

"*Hom ton teh k'o, hanah, ahneek tchi ahnap tooh.*" Tara felt the meaning of her chant, bubbling up from a place deep inside. The sounds formed a prayer of gratitude for the light.

She stopped chanting, held her hands over the small medicine wheel she'd made, closed her eyes again and thanked the circle for its help. Satisfied, she leaned forward and brushed away the tiny rocks, erasing the medicine wheel she'd constructed. The pebbles rolled and tumbled down the slope toward the house, gathering speed as they went.

Fearfully, for the path was precarious, she picked her way down the narrow, rocky trail, finally reaching the firm footing of the mesa. She made one full circle around the house and momentarily stopped at the front door. A large white feather with a rounded black tip lay on the threshold, caught in a crevice between the tiles. She bent down and picked it up. An eagle feather! She once more turned her face to the sky, searching for the powerful bird who had deposited it there. She felt immense gratitude and awe.

As she held the feather she imagined new energy and strength moving up her arm, empowering her. She glanced nervously at the front door of the house and was suddenly filled with grief. Tears flooded her eyes, blurring her vision. The door was still boarded up, barring human entry. She knew she could never enter this house again. It was the way. Death was in this house, this beautiful place that had once been her home. Shaking off her emotions, she crossed to the west end of the building and stopped at the circle of disturbed earth. The rocks which had once formed the central circle of the medicine wheel were scattered all about, and the prayer stick lay trampled in the dirt. She stared at this disrupted scene, feeling strangely, brutally violated, as if her own body had been ravished. This was sacred ground! How dare any defile it?

She glanced over her shoulder at the house. Death hovered there in those rooms even though the physical body from which the spirit had fled had been removed and the proper ceremonies completed. All had gone well until now. Now something belonging to the spirit had been unearthed, had been wrenched violently from the ground.

Even as these thoughts and feelings swirled through her mind, there was a part of her that questioned it all. Where were all these ideas coming from? Old studies, old books, nothing more.

The hole the looter had made in the dirt lay open, filled with rain water that had not yet perked into the soil. Tara stood back from the hole, careful not to put her feet where she imagined the shadowy dancer had stood earlier in the night, and careful that she did not further damage this spot. This sacred place had been plundered, desecrated. Her heart ached as she stared at the broken circle and the prayer stick senselessly ground into the dirt. How could she ever forgive this transgression!

The discomfort she felt with the defilement of this site welled up in her gut. She wanted only to strike out, to punish the wrongdoer who'd committed this offense, to take back what had been pillaged. She wanted the thief to experience the loathing she now felt for him. He needed to stand before her and feel her anger, and he needed to make retribution. He had embraced the darkness in this act. He danced with the spirits of evil and sickness and death.

Now she moved automatically, reflexively, guided from within by ancient and mysterious impulses. She fondled the feather she'd found on the front porch, held it to her heart, then lifted it up to the bright moonlight for a moment. She felt the feather absorb the healing rays of the new moon, just as she'd been taught in the stories of the ancient ones. Then she leaned over and carefully set the feather in the ground at the center of the circle, quill end stuck in the dirt, the dark outer tip pointing toward the heavens. For a moment she just stared at the feather, feeling a rightness about placing it there. Perhaps the gods would recognize the purity of her motives and reward her efforts, mending the damage that had been inflicted here. For a moment the heaviness in her heart was lifted.

Immortals! Ghosts...gods... Suddenly Tara felt an intense need to escape from this dream, to return to the reality she knew and understood. This was crazy!

The dream ended. Wide awake, she basked in the darkness of the cave for a moment. But she couldn't get the dream out of her mind. It was all too real, a dream that was not a dream at all, a dream that connected her with a life she had never before witnessed first hand. Thinking about this Tara realized that the little plot of dirt where she'd planted the eagle feather was probably the ceremonial plot of a departed shaman. She'd heard myths about spiritual leaders who buried their most powerful *medicine* in shallow graves, preventing it from falling into the wrong hands. In this way, the power of those artifacts was slowly taken back by the spirits who'd originally given them.

Time passed and she dozed. Then sunlight announcing a new dawn was flowing into the cave. She rose to her feet and walked stiffly out onto the ledge. She looked out across the mesa at the rising sun and remembered a conversation she'd had with Chocko several years before. She had asked him questions about shamanism, about tricks and illusions they used in their ceremonies, illusions that seemed to provide evidence for the existence of an invisible reality but which in fact were mere slights of hand. Chocko had laughed, telling her that the shaman's reality could not be explained in those terms, though he recognized that this was what she was wanting to hear. The illusions of the shaman's rituals were not illusions in the sense that she defined that word. Tricks or not they provided small windows into a reality which she did not yet understand. Indeed, he was right about that; such magic, in her mind, was nothing more than deception.

Chocko said there were many stories of shamans who changed into animals--deer, elk, coyotes or mountain lions--and that some of these events actually occurred. To this day, Tara could not take Chocko seriously. He loved to tease her, make fun of her rational approach to the study of the ancient ways he had embraced.

Though Chocko had lived and worked in the modern world, he now adopted the same prejudices the reservation-raised Indians had about anthropologists, that they were intruders who misinterpreted everything they saw, everything they touched, bent on a singular purpose, to make a name for themselves in the academic community. Time and again Tara had heard such complaints, that the secrets of the ancient traditions could never be understood by the anthropologists' clumsy pokings and proddings. Tara was certain she was above such criticism. She was not one of *them*; she had a sincere interest in learning about primitive cultures.

In the dream, she had momentarily seen the world through the eyes of these primitive peoples. Dream or reality, hallucination and solid physical existence were now all mixed together in her mind. She searched for an explanation. The work of Gareth Matthews came to mind, a brilliant anthropologist whose studies of the Algonquins of the Northeastern coast included his lifelong study of their unshakeable belief in the *manitu*. He had been able to maintain a rational stance even as he left room for the possibility of what others labeled primitive superstition and trickery.

Gareth said the *manitu* were spirits, good and evil, which the shamans called forth both for healing and for casting spells on their enemies. These powerful spirits were evoked when the shaman donned a mask and other sacred garb that represented the spirit. Then, amidst much rattling and drumming, the *manitu* spoke through the mask, giving instructions for healing or for power over enemies. A potion of herbs was sometimes prepared from the *manitu's* prescription, which was duly administered to the patient.

As she considered these ideas, Tara looked down from the ledge outside the cave and studied the rugged trail to the mesa below. She was glad she hadn't tried to leave the ledge the night before. The rain had washed out the footholds and crevices that had helped her climb to this place the night before. Negotiating the path in the darkness would have been treacherous. Even now, as she moved toward it, she felt anxious. The first thirty yards were steep, slippery from the rains. Tara kept her attention focused only on where she placed her feet. But as the trail leveled out, and she began to feel more secure, her thoughts turned once more to Gareth Matthews' comments about the *manitu*.

He had documented over a dozen cases where shamans had healed diseases medical doctors of that period were unable to cure. But most of the evidence was anecdotal, passed down through several generations. It was impossible to determine the truth.

Matthews believed that shamans were magicians, masters of the slight of hand, who practiced their craft not so much to deceive as to induce a change of mind. Tricked, then shocked into new possibilities, Matthews speculated, the shaman's client was transported into an invisible world of dream and fantasy. In this altered state they shifted their own perceptions, like the ravens Tara had watched in the tree, circling above their roosts, then settling down to a very different view of the world. The bottom line, Matthews speculated, was that these tricks worked much as a placebo does, triggering the body's own self-healing mechanisms. In the final analysis, Tara noted, this was pretty much what Chocko had told her, that the tricks had a purpose, that they challenged our way of thinking and seeing...that they changed us.

As Tara made her way carefully down the last few yards of the path to the mesa, she recognized that the events of last night had given her new eyes. She had changed. Even so, she clung to the side of reason, the bastion of scientific objectivity upon which she had built her professional status.

She reminded herself of a trip she'd made up north, to the Dakotas, where she'd sat in the darkness of a huge sweat lodge. She'd gone there to authenticate a ceremony that few non-Indians had ever witnessed. The lodge had been fashioned from willow branches bowed in great arches, then covered over with blankets, all prepared in a sacred way. She inhaled the burning sage and sweet grass from the smudge sticks and the twelve bodies sweating in the hot, moist room. She recalled the intense heat on her skin, heard the sounds of the drums, and remembered the glowing light of the moon filtering through the outer skins of the lodge.

Twelve people sat in a circle as the shaman beat his drum. The drumming stopped and two assistants wrapped the shaman in several layers of blankets until he looked like a mummy. They carried him to a spot at the north quadrant of the circle where everyone could see him. Then the door of the lodge was shut, sealing in the heat.

Drumming started outside the lodge, moving in a circle and rising at times over the roof of the domed structure. Then a glowing figure rose from the living mummy sack that held the shaman. It danced inside the circle, chanting in a hoarse, rhythmic voice, shaking a pair of rawhide rattles, one held in each hand. Nobody moved a muscle, entranced by the mysterious performance. Finally, the dancer slowed and as the others watched his image faded away, like the glow of a campfire dying out. On the floor the rumpled blankets fluffed and filled up, and they were once again looking at the mummy-like form in which the shaman had been wrapped.

Now two assistants came to the blanketed form, lifted it upright and unwrapped it. Seconds later the shaman stood before them, grinning from ear to ear. It had to be a trick, of course. Was the shaman an escape artist, the Lakota version of Harry Houdini?

Many things could happen when you were surrounded by people who believed in the ritual. A certain magic rose from the collective hearts and minds of those who witnessed the performance. More than likely that was the explanation.

Walking past the boarded up house Tara felt curiously grateful for the dream she'd had during the night. It provided her with a useful model for her studies of these peoples. There had to be a scientific explanation for everything that happened, whether it involved magic or not. She had to believe that. ~

Defiled

As Tara approached her car, parked halfway down the hill, she sensed that something was wrong. It appeared to have been moved slightly from the place she'd left it the night before. Then she saw the problem. The left rear fender was damaged! The metal was creased, with part of the rear bumper peeled away from the metal. A smear of bronze-colored paint, about six inches high and three feet long, stood out against the white paint. She knelt down to examine the scraped fender. Even in the dim morning light she could see the injury had been inflicted by the Jeep she'd seen on the mesa the night before. There was no doubt about it. In the storm, the driver had apparently sideswiped Tara's car.

Her first reaction was anger. She'd have to pay the car rental agency $200, the deductible amount on her own car insurance. This was the second time something like this had happened to her in a year. Just a few months before, during a conference in Chicago, somebody had smashed the grill of her rented Nissan while it was parked on the street. Twenty years of driving without a collision claim and now this--two claims in a year! Her insurance carrier wasn't going to be happy about this. She was probably facing an increase in her premium.

What made matters worse was that she found no note on the windshield of the car. The driver who did the damage hadn't even had the courtesy to apologize, much less acknowledge his error and leave the name of his insurance carrier. It was a damned shame how people these days had no sense of responsibility. She wished she'd had the foresight to get the license number of the Jeep. It could have served her even if there'd been no damage to her car. She might have been able to trace the number to the organization that owned the two similar Jeeps she'd seen yesterday--John Whitecrow's and this one, whose paint now marred her fender. It also would have given her a clue to track down whoever it was that was so interested in the house on the mesa and who had taken the mysterious object buried in the garden.

Cursing her own lack of foresight, Tara unlocked the trunk and tossed her backpack inside. She opened the driver's door and climbed in, angrily inserting the key in the ignition. Having started the engine, she allowed it to warm up, then dropped the transmission into gear and edged forward. Rather than trying to turn around, she decided to drive to the top of the hill. There was a chance she'd missed something that could lead her to the driver who'd injured her car. If there was a clue of some kind, she'd trace him down. She'd demand payment for the damage and also probe the driver about what he'd taken from the garden.

The rain had let up during the night, and already the road to the highway was dry except for small areas of dense clay that would not absorb the water. Her wheels spun a little in places where the rain had pooled but she drove the distance to Charla's house without difficulty.

She pulled into the driveway and stopped. For a moment she was flooded with thoughts about Drake. Being so close, close enough to touch the personal items he'd left in the house, convinced her that though the departure had been hasty, it had also been deliberate. The clues she'd found thus far--personal items left behind, the house boarded up, the fact that he had actually made an effort to contact her by phone--made it clear that this time his disappearance was different than ever before. Prior to this he had simply not shown up for her, slipping away in the night, leaving the impression in her mind that he simply didn't value his connection with her. But this time he'd sought her help.

For several minutes she replayed in her mind the scene of the night before. She felt unsettled about the significance of her dream, with its persistent message about an invisible reality that she knew she could never quite accept. She swung open the car door and got out to take one last stroll around the yard. She had the nagging feeling that she had missed something, that regardless of how bizarre it seemed, it was true that her dreams sometimes alerted her to things she'd forgotten or overlooked.

In the morning air, she was struck by the profound silence of this place. The only sound she heard was the electronic squeal from the car itself, reminding her that the door was open and the keys were still in the ignition. She reached in, pulled them out, dropped them onto the driver's seat and slammed the door. Standing in the silence that closed in around her, she became conscious of her own breathing. There were no other sounds. It was unnaturally quiet. She looked around her, studying the immediate landscape. No birds. Not so much as a single insect in the air. Was it simply too early in the day for them? Were they waiting for the heat of the sun? No. Something was wrong here, something she couldn't explain.

Tara shivered as she walked toward the house. Usually when she walked in the high country like this, even early in the morning, she scared up at least a small lizard or two. But no living thing stirred here, nothing. Was this tranquility an omen? She chastised herself for falling into that superstitious way of thinking again. There had to be other explanations. Maybe it was the season. Maybe the birds flew to a special place this time of year, fleeing the cold winds and the rain. That seemed likely. But what about the lizards? They were cold blooded animals. They lived within the earth and under rocks. They hibernated in the country when there was snow, but it was too early in the year for that. Maybe owls or other birds of prey had wiped them out. As she speculated, she recalled the image of the figure from the night before, the dream woman who Tara had followed to the garden.

Hallucinations. Yes, that was it! She had been frightened by the storm and the prospect of having to spend the night in the cave. All this discomfort had contributed to a state of mind that could quite well have bordered on the delusional. The strain and anxiety about her father's safety, combined with all the events that occurred yesterday, could easily have produced a toxic state of mind...temporarily, she was sure. She was simply seeing things that weren't there. As soon as she got something to eat, and some proper rest, she'd be okay.

Now she had an odd feeling that she was being watched. Stopping from time to time, she looked up into the hills behind the house. Nothing. She could detect no movement. She knew there were several caves carved into the rock. A person could stand just back from the mouth of any one of them and not be seen in the dim light of dawn. Yet, she somehow doubted that was the case. More likely, it was just her state of mind causing her to feel fearful, even paranoid.

She walked over to the little plot of land that had been the focus of her dream the night before. As she drew closer she was stopped cold by what she saw. A white feather with a black tip stood in the center of the plot! She stared at it, remembering the dream and perfectly recalling the way she herself had planted it there. But that was a dream, and this was a real feather! It was a coincidence, that's all. Someone else had planted the feather there and she simply hadn't consciously noted it before. The only other explanation was that she'd been sleepwalking, that when she dreamed about planting the feather she had been acting it out. But as far as she knew she had never walked in her sleep, and she doubted that she could have made it down the trail from the cave in the storm. Of course, she couldn't have, she reassured herself. Besides, had she done that she would have been bruised, muddy and wet when she awoke.

She sat down at the edge of the circle, staring at its center for a long time, noting that the outer circle of rocks had not been disturbed, even though the looter had dug into the center. It was as if the larger circle had been reverently or even fearfully avoided. She turned and studied the rocky trail up to the cave where she'd spent the night. She wondered if there might be passages stretching deep into the earth, perhaps a tunnel where one might escape an enemy, or prepare for ceremonies. That might help explain what she'd seen last night, that what she had thought was a dream was an actual ceremony, witnessed in a deeply somnolent state.

She wished she had a strong flashlight. With a good one she might risk exploring the caves to satisfy her curiosity. But she did not have a proper light. Nor would she dare explore the cave without a companion or at least a guide rope to lead her back out. She wasn't exactly a spelunker but in her work she'd been deep into more than one cave, exploring archaeological finds. She loved exploring caves, the least well-known, and the hotter the finds, the better. Caves were thought to be sacred places among many of the ancient peoples she had studied. Caves provided natural protection from one's enemies and they were ideal places for hiding their most treasured sacred objects when they were being raided by adventurers or other marauding tribes. Caves were places of meditation and celebration. The shamans journeyed through the caves, deep into the heart of Mother Earth, certain that in the darkness they would be transformed. They would slip through the filmy veil to enter the invisible world which was a source of their power, and their mystique. When they emerged once again into the sunlight, they would be reborn in the eyes of their fellows.

As an anthropologist, Tara had often found wonderful artifacts in caves, precious not just because of their monetary value but because they revealed important secrets about past civilizations. She had no great interest in the monetary value of these objects, though she was more than aware that others did. Many of the world's greatest anthropological treasures were plundered by grave-robbers and treasure hunters who literally fought to their deaths over their spoils. To Tara certain artifacts opened up new possibilities, clues to lost civilizations, such as the secret society of shamans, and to rituals or ways of life that could tell us about our forebears.

As she sat at the edge of the circle, she tried to make sense of

what she'd witnessed these past three days. Nothing in all her years
of scholarship had prepared her for this. Or had it? Only a month
before she'd heard a lecture by Gareth Matthews, whose work she'd
always believed was impeccable. He'd spoken of how shamans ventured into the underworld through a hole in the earth. Surely he'd
meant this metaphorically! Or had he? He invited his audience to
entertain the possibility that the hole might have actually led to a
secret valley and a group of people untouched by the reality the rest
of us share. Isolated from the world these wise ones taught about the
use of herbs, rituals and other magic which shamans then took back
to their people. After all, such societies were constantly being discovered in the Amazon, in deepest Africa, and high in the Andes.
Why could they not exist right under our eyes, hidden in the rugged
terrain of the high desert country?

Tara was convinced Matthews was a closet mystic and felt a
degree of professional embarrassment about defending his work. Yet
she also took comfort from knowing that such a rational man, who'd
won the respect of researchers throughout the world, clung to a
belief in shamanistic truths and lost civilizations. You could not
ignore his work. He wove in just enough scientific validation to keep
alive one's conviction that evidence for the society of shamans and
the ancient wisdom of the oracle could still be found.

Sitting at the edge of the circle in the little garden near Charla's
house, Tara closed her eyes, feeling the heat of the rising sun on her
face. It was a wonderful feeling, warming and comforting. How sub-
lime it would be to lay out in the sun and sleep. As she sat in this
way, a smile lifted her face. She recalled James Dean who had
appeared in her dreams last night. Once again she saw his face but
this time she imagined him sitting across from her at the circle.
James Dean! Her university associates would ridicule her if they
knew that in her darkest moments she turned for comfort to
memories of her teenage idol. But she indulged herself anyway,
secure in the knowledge that her secret was safe.

For a long time, she did not open her eyes for fear of destroying
the comforting illusion. She imagined James Dean attempting to
communicate with her. What was he saying? *Please listen! Please
take the next step. Listen and believe.* But what could that mean,
she asked herself, except that there was a part of her that wanted,
like her father, to believe something that clearly wasn't real. Where
was the comfort in that! Perhaps it was a test of her own scientific
resolve, she decided, something that tempted everyone who studied
ancient societies. She would never allow herself to fall into that trap.

As she rose from the place where she sat, she involuntarily
looked up toward the mouth of the cave in which she'd spent the

night. The shadowy figure of a man stood just inside, watching her. She quickly looked down at the ground in front of her, knowing that what she saw was an hallucination, a product of her overwrought imagination. She would not allow her delusions to seduce her into actions she would later regret.

She turned back to the car. ~

Running for Help

As she sat in her car, turning events over in her mind, Tara realized that the only possible clue to Drake's whereabouts was hidden on the computer disk she'd found in the house yesterday. And she thought once more of Chocko, up in Zuni. With his background in computers, he'd surely know how to retrieve whatever information the disk might contain. If it contained anything at all!

Turning north at the highway, she was soon driving in the rugged terrain of the reservation. It was just after six a.m. A dark, brooding sky loomed overhead as she wound back and forth through a series of sharp switchbacks. The road narrowed, skirting a deep canyon on the right side of the car. She switched on her headlights. A few miles further, red and blue lights flashed through the trees on the shadowy side of a canyon wall. She slowed as she rounded the next curve. The dim silhouette of a tow truck, parked crossways in the road, blocked both lanes. A patrol car was parked beyond it, a bank of flashing red and blue lights on its roof. The officer and the tow truck driver stood talking beside the back of the truck. A thick steel cable extended from a large iron winch, anchored in the tow truck's bed, down into the canyon below.

Tara pulled onto the gravel shoulder, set the emergency brake, and climbed out. She started walking toward the two men operating the winch of the truck. They were staring down the cable at what appeared to be nothing more than a twisted mass of steel. And then she realized what she was looking at. It had been a Jeep, the same color as the one she'd encountered on the mesa the night before! As the winch groaned, drawing its burden closer to the road, Tara walked toward the two men.

The police officer, apparently noticing Tara for the first time, broke away from the back of the truck and waved his arms, indicating that she should stop.

"Keep back. If the cable breaks it'll snap like a bullwhip." Taking

Tara's elbow, he escorted her roughly toward her car.

"What happened?"

"Guy drove off the highway last night."

"Anybody injured?"

"Guess you could say that. Must have rolled a dozen times. Practically tore his head off. Neck broken in several places, severed the spinal cord."

"Drunk driver?"

The officer shrugged. "We don't know yet."

The winch on the tow truck groaned and stalled. As the demolished Jeep broke over the top of the hill, the left front wheel, its axle torn loose from the frame, flopped over lazily. The entire frame listed to the left and seemed almost to groan as it rested against the earth. They had dragged the vehicle up by the rear wheels, which now dangled from the cable at the end of the boom, the tires ripped to shreds and partially torn from the rims. Dirt, branches, sagebrush and rocks, pinched between creases of torn and mangled steel, attested to the violence of the crash.

Tara scanned the side of the Jeep. The right rear quarter panel was crumpled and torn, revealing a smear of white paint where it had scraped another car. She stared in disbelief. The paint clinging to the scraped metal was the same as on her car! There was no doubt about it. This was the same vehicle that had grazed the side of her rented Chevrolet. She looked from the Jeep to the man standing beside her and suddenly wanted to tell him the whole story.

"I saw this Jeep last night," she said. "In fact, he scraped the side of my car. Look. You can see for yourself." She pointed to the white Chevrolet, parked behind her.

The officer walked around the side of her car and leaned over to inspect the body damage.

"Whereabouts did this happen?" he asked. He took a small spiral note pad from his breast pocket. There was a pencil stub, like the kind used for bridge parties, held in the coils binding the pad. He tapped it out into his palm, then touched the lead to the tip of his tongue.

"Do you know Coyote Mesa, down south of here?"

The officer nodded. "Sure. Yeah. You have people down there?" He seemed particularly interested in her reply to this question.

"Not exactly. My dad was staying at a house out there. I was supposed to meet him."

"Lady, there are no tourist accommodations out there."

"I know. The house belongs to a friend, Charla Mather. But when I got out there the place was abandoned. Boarded up!"

"Your father's friend is Charla Mather?" The officer looked exceedingly interested now.

Tara shrugged, the officer's suspicion alerting her to be cautious about how she replied. "He said he was staying there, at her house. They've known each other a long time. But there was no sign of them when I arrived. No message. Nothing."

"You're sure of your date, the time?"

"Of course. I'm certain of it."

"So, you stayed where?"

"I camped out, in the caves above the mesa."

"I wouldn't advise going out there. That Mather woman's had people out there lots of times, doing ceremonies and such for her. Doesn't help. Best advice she ever got was to seal the place up, stay out of there. You live around here you gotta respect that sort of thing. Most of it's rumors, old superstitions. Maybe it's true, maybe not. Still, if it were me, I'd stay away from there."

"I did see something," Tara said. "Part of it was real, but the rest was a trick, I'm sure of it. Someone playing with my head..."

The officer eyed Tara with the same look of skepticism and cool indifference he might have reserved for a traffic violator. He held his pencil stub tightly in his fingers, poised at the edge of the pad.

Suddenly, Tara felt her hands trembling, and wondered if the officer was able to see. "The light was funny," she said. "But this man, the driver of this car...he was there, digging in the garden behind the house...and he found something, dug it up and put it in his car..."

The officer stared down at his writing pad, scribbling vigorously. "Did you see what it was?"

Tara shook her head. "I couldn't make it out. I saw a Katchina there when he was digging. It had a round mask, like a moonface."

"You mean a dancer?" The officer looked up from his writing pad. "Are we talking about the same thing?"

"Maybe it was the light...an apparition. Never mind. I thought maybe you'd know something about it."

"Are you telling me there was a second person, a person dressed up in a costume?"

"No...I'm not sure."

"Did you get a good look at this guy's face?" the officer asked, growing impatient. "Back at the mesa there. Could you identify the man who was digging in the garden?"

"I didn't see his face. Would I recognize him? He was tall. Tall and skinny, if that helps."

"Anything else?"

"When I first arrived, there was another man, a man named White Crow. He drove a Jeep like this one." She pointed at the heap

of tangled metal that the tow truck driver was now attaching to a dolly.

"White Crow." The officer jotted the name down in his notebook. "He from around here?"

"He said he did work for Charla Mather."

"Work?"

"Handyman sorts of things, I think."

"You said the place was boarded up when you got there."

"Yes."

"But you went inside?"

"Yes."

The officer made some notes in his pad. "You were given a key or what?"

Tara shook her head. "The door wasn't actually locked. Somebody had nailed boards across it."

"Technically, that's breaking and entering."

"Look, I was invited to meet my father there, to stay there as his and Charla Mather's guest..." Tara stopped suddenly, realizing she was being defensive and that this was very likely to arouse more suspicion.

"So you went inside and saw what?"

"It looked as if they'd left suddenly. Most of their stuff is there."

The officer studied her face for a moment. The flashing yellow lights from the tow truck made him look sickly and jaundiced. "I'll need your name," he said, "And your father's. You'll have to show me some identification."

Tara reached into her car and pulled out her backpack, then dug out her wallet and showed the officer her driver's license. He took the plastic card with her picture on it, peered closely at it, then squinted as he studied her face. Finally he wrote in his notebook and handed the license back to Tara.

"Do you have any idea where to contact your father or Ms. Mather? Could they maybe be off somewhere together?"

"I don't know. Charla Mather has a place in Albuquerque, but when I called there nobody had heard from her."

"And you don't know where your father is hiding?"

"Why would he be hiding?"

"Ma'am, a woman is missing."

"Are you talking about Charla Mather?"

"When was the last time you heard from your father?"

"Wait. What's going on here?"

"Answer my question, please."

"No. I don't think I will."

"Ms. Fairfield, you'll be saving yourself a lot of trouble in the long run."

"Meaning?"

"I'll have to take you in."

"Take me in! On what grounds?"

"We just want your cooperation."

Suddenly Tara had a mental picture of being locked in the back room of a makeshift police station at Coyote Mesa, questioned by a surly cop who stunk of cigarettes, stale beer and sweat. It wasn't an image she relished.

"I heard from my father five days ago. He left a message."

"And where was he then?"

"Down at Ms. Mather's place. He was following a story."

"What do you mean a story?"

She explained that her father was a newspaper reporter. "He was doing something on Indian ruins in the area." Reluctant to give details, Tara watched the officer's face cautiously. "He only said he was on assignment. I'm an anthropologist. He wanted my advice about something he'd found, but he didn't tell me what."

"I'll need a phone number where we can contact you."

Tara reluctantly gave him Chocko's phone number in Zuni. Behind them, the driver of the tow truck had mounted dolly wheels under the Jeep and was ready to leave.

"Could you call me if you have any news about my father?"

The officer shoved the stub of his pencil back into the spiral bound pad, then reached into his breast pocket and handed Tara a card with a "Sheriff's Department" seal printed under it. His name was Sam Loba. The address was Coyote Mesa.

"Give me a call tomorrow evening, after seven," Loba said.

"But there isn't..." Tara stopped herself.

"Isn't what?"

Tara shrugged. She knew there was no phone service at Coyote Mesa except near Guy Perry's place. If that were the case, what was the link between these two men, Sam Loba, Perry and his millitary playmates with their guns? Instinct warned her to keep her mouth shut. She got back into her car and tucked the officer's card into her purse. Then she pulled around the side of the tow truck and started up the hill on the road going north. A quarter mile past the wreck the road widened and she found a vista point where she could safely pull off. She parked and shut off the engine.

For a moment she just sat, barely breathing as she stared vacantly into space. With each mile of her journey, it seemed, she had felt herself descending further and further into a darkness she did not understand. Certainly this was not what she had intended. She abhorred intrigue. She never should have listened to her father's call for help, never should have responded. She thought about the wreck and the cop back in the road. To be questioned like a common criminal was humiliating! The entire event churned in her guts like some grotesque worm that had invaded her body.

She crossed her arms over the steering wheel and pressed her face against them. From within her chest came a deep, mournful groan that instantly turned into wrenching sobs. Tears flooded her eyes, soaking her sleeves. She felt alone and lost, drawn into a world she despised and resented--the dark underside of life that was Drake's passion. Whatever he found in the seedy discord between cops and bad guys was beyond her wildest imaginings.

She dried her tears and flung open the door. Swinging out of the car she rose to her feet in one graceful motion, then stared down the road she'd just left. If she was going to be drawn into this mess, she decided, she was going to do it with a vengeance, not sit around passively while others played their ridiculous games. Through the trees along the edge of the canyon she watched the tow truck pulling away, followed by the sheriff's car with its flashing lights. They were moving south. She stood and watched until they were out of sight, then walked back down to the place in the road where the Jeep had gone over.

The exact spot was easy to identify because the tow truck's cable had gouged deep scars in the earth. There was also a series of black skid marks all over the pavement. Trying to decipher what had happened in the tragic moment before the Jeep plunged over the precipice was like trying to decipher ancient petroglyphs discovered on the wall of a cave. It appeared that the driver had been conscious of what was happening and had desperately struggled to save himself. Skid marks crisscrossed both sides of the road.

It looked to her as if two or more vehicles had been involved, since two sets of skid marks marred the road. Nothing in the conversation with the sheriff had indicated that he knew of another vehicle's presence but that was certainly no proof that he hadn't already noted this for himself.

For a moment she just stood, looking down into the canyon. It was treacherously steep, mostly loose rock, with a few trees scattered here and there along the precipitous walls. It was difficult to see how the sheriff or the tow truck crew, or for that matter the ambulance crew the night before, had gotten down to the bottom where the wrecked Jeep and its driver had come to a final stop.

The sun was rising now, and there was just enough light to see the trail of debris left by the Jeep on its way down. Small bits of shiny metal marked the deadly journey. There was no way, Tara decided, to follow that trail except with the help of a rope and some sort of climbing equipment to assist her over the slippery rock.

The chances were pretty good that the emergency crew had the right equipment for such an adventure. They could have rappelled down with ropes, pulling along the cable that was attached to the Jeep. If that were the case, the climbers had left before Tara got there.

Surveying the landscape, she noticed what was apparently a game trail another quarter mile down the road. Starting at a lower elevation, it went down to a ridge about halfway up the canyon wall. From her present vantage point it didn't appear too precipitous for her to follow. She walked down the road to where the trail began and in less than a half-hour had made her way to the middle ridge. From there she looked down into the bottom of the canyon. It was a steep, dizzying view. She spotted a huge boulder which seemed to have been sprinkled with sparkling bits of crystal. Studying the boulder for several minutes she realized that the early morning light was catching the jagged facets of broken glass and shiny chrome that were scattered over the rock. It was a good guess that this had been the final resting place for the Jeep and its unlucky driver.

She would have given anything to know more about what they'd found in the wreck, besides the ravaged body of its driver. Had they found whatever it was the looter dug up in Charla Mather's garden? And was she right that this Jeep belonged to the man she'd seen digging in the garden? There could be little doubt about that. The scrape along its side, that contained the same paint color as the paint on her own car, was pretty solid proof of that. But it was not irrefutable proof.

She was dying to go further down the mountain, following the trail of debris. With luck she might just find whatever it was the driver had dug out of the earth the night before. But she knew this would be impossible without the help of someone with climbing experience.

With binoculars she might have been able to find some evidence along the trail of debris the Jeep had left. But as the sun rose, she was able to see amazingly well with the naked eye. She tried in vain to recall the size and shape of the object the man took from Charla's yard. Surely it would have shown up if it had been thrown out of the wreck, which presumably it would have been. After all, the top of the Jeep had been torn loose. It was now little more than a ragged stack of rubble. The crew that went down after the body would have found it, if it had been there at all. But maybe not.

Maybe. Maybe. Maybe. Suddenly her life was filled with maybes, pure speculations, nothing more. She was unaccustomed to operating in a world of treachery like the one into which she'd been thrown. A part of her simply couldn't accept what was happening. A part of her was convinced that the next time she got to a phone, or she got into an area where the cell phone would operate, she'd call home and discover a simple, everyday, logical explanation for everything that had happened. She'd find a message from her father clearing the whole thing up. She'd find out that he and Charla were comfortably lodged at some $200 a night bed and breakfast, and that everything that had happened to her since her arrival in New Mexico had been a series of absurd misunderstandings. But then there was the issue of the envelope with the artifacts, the bone and the photos. Whether she'd been mistaken about Drake's other fragmented messages or not, those items could not be denied. The potsherds still pointed toward the existence of a society of shamans, and the bone and photos only deepened the mystery.

She turned and glanced back up the trail she'd just taken. It seemed steeper than she remembered it coming down. There were a couple of places that looked downright dangerous. It had been foolish of her to come down. But there was nothing to do about that now, nothing but to hike back up.

It took her over half an hour to get back to the road. Breathless, she sat cross legged at the edge of the canyon when she reached the top. She gazed down, once more studying the land. If you could ignore the fact that a man had lost his life there the night before, it was really quite beautiful. She closed her eyes, hugging her knees to her chest. A strange whistling filled her ears. The wind? Suddenly there was heat and light on her eyelids. She lifted her arm and held up her hand to shield her eyes.

A bright ball of light hovered over the center of the canyon, down low, level with the road. The light was so brilliant she dared not fully open her eyes, peering at it through narrowed slits. Startled by its sudden appearance, but unable to see anything beyond the blinding light she could only guess what it was. Maybe a helicopter with an intense light beam searching the canyon floor, or some new high tech invention of the police force. But from the local sheriff's department? She doubted that. Who would be sending out such a high tech piece of equipment, and why?

A buzzing sound at the back of her neck alerted her to a large insect and she swatted it absently. Something popped, and she thought it odd but nevertheless took some satisfaction in knowing that she'd annihilated the pest before it could bite her. Then her thoughts returned to the strange light in the sky.

No, she decided, it could not be a helicopter! It made hardly a sound, just that eerie, low whistling sound, like the wind. Now the light seemed to get brighter, more intense, like a blazing hot sun on her face. She was certain, for a moment, that it was a large comet or asteroid and that she would surely perish when it collided with the earth. And then, just as suddenly as it had appeared, the light was gone. Tara opened her eyes. There was no sign of anything that could have made such a light. Nothing!

Her hand rose reflexively to the back of her neck, then to the spot behind her ear where she'd first found the lump two days before. Her fingers searched gingerly for the area that had been so tender. Oddly, the skin was now smooth and there was only a vague hint of discomfort. She took her hand away and examined her fingers. They were sticky, coated with a small amount of blood. She fingered the spot behind here ear again. No doubt about it, the skin felt smooth and cool, completely healed. She sighed, relieved that at least one source of anxiety was resolved.

She rose to her feet and returned to her car. It was parked, just as she'd left it, at the vista point. But now there was another car beside it. A woman and three children were standing near the low wall at the edge of the canyon. The woman had a camera and was pointing it at the children, telling them to smile and wave. All three, like the obedient, scrubbed creatures they seemed to be, did as they were told, and the woman snapped her picture.

As Tara approached her car the woman turned and smiled at her. Tara noted the plates on their car were from out of state--Colorado.

"Did you see that light?" Tara asked. As she spoke, her voice trembled and she realized for the first time how deeply she'd been affected by the incident.

The woman stared blankly. "Light?"

"Over the canyon. Just a few minutes ago." It suddenly became very important to Tara to share what had happened with someone, even if that someone was a stranger. She felt terribly, horribly alone.

The woman eyed her suspiciously. "We just got here."

Tara studied the woman's face, wanting her to listen, wanting her to hear the whole story about the wrecked Jeep and the light. She needed a sympathetic ear, someone who could help her sort out everything that had happened in Coyote Mesa. Instead, the woman turned her back and called out, "Kids, get back in the car. Time to move on."

Tara unlocked her own car and settled in behind the wheel before pulling the door shut. As she reached for the ignition, she noticed the clock on the dashboard. It was 3:15 p.m. "But that's impossible!" she said aloud. She furtively glanced at her watch. It was the same--3:15. She took a deep breath and pressed her body back into the seat. What was happening to her? Calm, be calm, she told herself. She began to check out every part of her body, how she felt from the tip of her toes to the top of her head. She felt fine. In fact, she felt great, except for the haunting sense that she was missing something important, some elusive piece she could not identify.

The car with the mother and three children pulled away and disappeared down the road, going south. Tara sat for a long time, calming herself. There had to be a logical explanation. Maybe it was just stress, tension. Maybe she'd walked further down the canyon than she'd thought. But how could she have possibly walked so far that she'd killed nearly eight and a half hours? Not likely. Had she fallen asleep? Maybe that was it, she decided. Down on the trail she'd rested. She'd closed her eyes and maybe when she woke up again several hours had passed, while she had the impression it had only been a few minutes. Possible. Yes, that had to be it. It made sense when she stopped to consider she probably hadn't slept for more than a couple hours the night before. Her body and mind had played tricks on her, just as they did with the dream of the woman on the mesa last night.

What other explanation could there be? She glanced at her face in the rearview mirror. Her hair was a mess, and her cheeks were smudged with dirt. Her mouth tasted like cotton, and she was certain her breath could kill a horse. Becoming aware of how she looked reminded her that her stomach felt hollow and raw, her lips parched and dry. With that came the realization that she had totally ignored her bodily needs for nearly two full days. She knew better. She was only too aware of the affects of altitude and the dry desert environment on a person not yet acclimated to it. One could easily become dehydrated, even during the Fall and Winter storm season.

She leaned forward, turned the ignition and the engine leapt to life. She had to get to a place where she could clean up, rest and pamper herself for at least a few hours. She glanced at the clock on the dashboard again. It was just a little after 3:30 now. If she took it easy, getting herself reoriented along the way, she could be at Chocko's, in Zuni, by 5:00. She would drive slowly, think things over, try to piece together all the bits and fragments of what she'd seen and done over the past few days. She was certain she could come up with a more reasonable explanation than she had so far. There seemed to be something in her mind that insisted on exaggerating everything that happened around her. Maybe the bottom line was that she needed to retrace her steps and go back home. Maybe she should see a psychiatrist! Maybe.

It now became more pressing than ever to get to Zuni, to talk with Chocko. She needed the reassurance of another human being, one with whom she had at least some personal contact, somebody to talk with who could make sense of what was happening to her. Chocko seemed down to earth enough, not given to these crazy flights of fancy. Besides, he knew the territory. He could assure her that things were not as they appeared. Maybe he even knew how to contact Drake. Maybe. Maybe. There it was again, just a lot more maybes. And maybe he could do something with the broken computer disk she'd found when she searched Charla's house. Maybe.

She reached for the cell phone. She had to call Chocko right away, make certain he was home. Then she remembered his phone number was in the book in her backpack. She swerved over to the shoulder and yanked on the emergency brake, then dug through her backpack for the book with her phone numbers. As she tossed the backpack aside, two snack bars fell out. She grabbed them, tore the wrapping from one with her teeth and shoved the whole thing into her mouth.

As she chewed she thumbed madly through her address book. By the time she found Chocko's number she'd devoured the first snack bar and was starting on the other, tossing the wrappers carelessly into the back seat. She reached over to the passenger's seat for the bottle of water she'd brought from Albuquerque and washed down what was left of the second bar. Gulping down the water she nearly choked. When she was done drinking the plastic bottle was empty. She tossed it into the back seat with the crumpled wrappers.

She punched up Chocko's phone number on the cell phone, waited a second, holding her breath. Amazingly, the call went through. She sighed with relief. Apparently she was out of the dead area, which she deduced must be limited to Coyote Mesa. The phone rang once, twice... After the tenth ring she hung up.

"Damn!"

She flung the cell phone onto the seat beside her, then reached for the ignition. As soon as the engine had roared into action, she dropped the transmission into drive and pressed the accelerator nearly to the floor. The car leapt forward, wheels churning in the gravel, then shrieked as rubber found pavement. ~

 Spirit Circle

Reunion

The Zuni Pueblo insinuates itself on the desert landscape as if its founders, five hundred years before, had felt apologetic about imposing themselves here, recognizing there was something special, something sacred and inviolable about this place. Even so, even knowing this, they knew also that they had to stop, had to put down roots, establish this spot, this *center of the world*, this point of beginning and point of ending. This was the place where they could be present, alone, centered, bound as one in community, from that day on, forever.

And so, even today, there is a gentleness about the way the buildings, mostly ancient adobes, resting close to the earth, blend with their surroundings, indeed, fashioned from mud and stone and dried straw just as the planet herself is, and so in that way inseparable from her, flesh of her flesh, deserving and worthy, honoring the imposition, even celebrating it.

In spite of all efforts to respect tradition, the modern world had made its mark on this place. Yet even this was polite. The most dominant commerce consists of the Zuni Arts and Crafts Co-op, housed in a neat storefront on the narrow, dusty main street which is also the highway going west, where it eventually links up with Highway 666, in Arizona. There are also two other privately owned trading posts, and a convenience store with a deli in back, plus a bank of electronic games and a rack of videos dating back to Humphrey Bogart's *Casablanca,* which could be rented for $1.75 per day. There were only thirty or forty video titles on the rack, and the residents of Zuni who own VCRs have seen most of them several times over.

A quarter mile past the convenience store a dusty road turning off to the right lead to the pueblo's only laundromat, about three blocks off the highway. Adjacent to the laundromat, off to the left, is a permanent trailer park where twenty or so trailers and weathered mobile homes huddle together on two narrow dirt streets. On the first street, in the last lot before the desert, is the newest mobile home, a sixty-five footer, a good twenty feet longer than anything else in the park. It is here that Chocko lives.

Chocko is not a Zuni but Mestizo, or mixed blood. It is not clear what that mix is and if he knows for certain he has never shared this truth with his friends. He and Drake had been roommates in college, thrown together not because they had anything in common, or because they had mutual friends, but because they were both assigned to the same room by the housing office at the college.

Tara had heard the story a hundred times. Drake was told, during the college housing interview, that Chocko was Indian. So when they first met, Drake thought this meant his roommate was from India. The fact that he had dark skin, Anglo Saxon nose and cheeks, and blue eyes, seemed to confirm Drake's original belief. It was some time during that first month, while they were getting to know each other and while they were still establishing their boundaries in the cramped little room they shared, that Drake learned his roommate was from Albuquerque.

"Oh, *that* kind of Indian!" Drake had said, his tone one of disappointment. He immediately regretted the comment, since Chocko looked offended. Bewildered, not knowing how to repair what he'd done, Drake stared down at the floor, so did not notice Chocko doing the same. It was a befuddling moment for them both, neither of them knowing what to say, recognizing that they had uncovered a prejudice neither of them wished to own, though both felt.

But the truth was that Chocko's Native American heritage was not the source of Drake's bias or his disappointment. Rather, at that time Drake had been studying Hinduism. He was reading books by Kristnamurti and had illusions of long dialogues with his new roommate about Eastern mysticism, a subject they would never, as it turned out, discuss. If there was bias, it was in Drake's assumption that just anyone from India would have an interest in talking with him about his spiritual destiny. The closest Chocko had come to any kind of spiritual training, which he would have gladly discussed, though not without a bias of his own, was from the Pentecostal Church of his foster parents, where the men handled poisonous snakes as part of the service.

It had taken Chocko several minutes to recover enough to say, in a tone almost remorseful, "I'm afraid I don't even know what kind of Indian I am. *Mixblood,* that's all I know. My folks never told me much about where they grew up or any of that. And now they're dead and I don't know any of my relatives. Down where I grew up they called me the Lost One. But don't ask me what that means, either, because the truth is I'm only interested in one thing, and that is making a lot of money and living the American dream."

"There must be somebody, some link," Drake had said absently, ignoring the rest of the subject, feeling embarrassed to be prying.

"Maybe, maybe not," Chocko said. "The people who are my foster parents take pretty good care of me, seeing that I get a good education and all. But they are pretty vague about where I came from. Everybody is. I didn't even have a birth certificate until the county made one up for me, along with some papers that say I'm a ward of the court and that sort of thing. My file just says I'm most likely part Spanish, part Anglo, part Portuguese and part Pueblo. So that can be most anything, you know, Pueblo I mean, because there are a lot of different Pueblos, just as there are a lot of different Spaniards and Anglos."

Chocko's major was Engineering, Drake's journalism. So there were few classes they shared. Still they remained roommates and good friends for the whole four years of their stay at the university, for reasons neither of them could ever figure out. They had discovered a bond. "Maybe you are my brother," Chocko once said, jokingly, swearing that if he found out he was a real Indian he'd see to it that Drake was made an honorary member of the tribe. "No matter how you look at it, we're both *mixbloods*," he'd told Drake.

At first with some jealousy, Drake had watched Chocko's career take off, even while they were still in college. Motivated by the American Dream, upon which Drake had soured even before he had thought to pursue it, Chocko was driven by financial ambition, and Drake's self-confidence dwindled as he watched his best friend celebrating his success with fancy cars, good clothes and travel.

By the end of their senior year Chocko was already working part time for a big electronics firm, involved in a multi-million dollar research project for the government. Chocko would only say it was connected with the space program. He had specialized in computer technology, eventually becoming one of the most sought-after software designers in the country. And then one day, eighteen years after graduation, he simply stopped. He sold his million dollar home in Malibu, bought a Winnebago motor home and went on the road.

One day he sent Drake a joke postcard from Wyoming with a picture of a rainbow trout so big it filled up the back of a flatbed truck. On the message side of the card, to the left of the address, Chocko had scrawled, "It was all wrong to send a man to the moon. Now we're all in deep doo-doo! Your friend, Injun Joe."

For reasons Chocko didn't know, and didn't even appear curious about, he gravitated to this place in Zuni, traded in the motor home for a mobile home and settled down. He made a meager living now, teaching computer classes at the cultural center and occasionally troubleshooting software systems on a freelance basis for a few small businesses in Albuquerque. Chocko did very little else for money. He didn't need much where he lived now, and had no desire for more.

* * *

Tara pulled in front of Chocko's home and shut off the engine. Judging by the fact that there was no vehicle under the carport at the side of the house, she decided her father's friend was either not home or the aging Jaguar roadster he once drove--the last remnant of his more opulent Malibu lifestyle--had finally given out. Tara reached for her cell phone, punched in the number of her voice mail service and waited as the transmission went through. The connection was made and she dialed in her code. There were no messages, not even one.

She dialed again, her home number this time. After the second or third ring, the line clicked over to the voice mail service. "Hi, Maya, hi, Viveka. Hope you're having fun. Everything's fine here. Raining a lot. I'll call you later."

She switched off the phone, clipped it back on the console and reached over the seat for her small backpack. Then she got out, locked the doors and walked around to the desert side of the house. Chocko had built a pine deck across the front of his place, complete with a picnic table where he could sit and eat his dinner in the evenings, gazing out over the desert and, on the best and luckiest days, watch the setting sun.

Four years before, during Drake's last visit to the Southwest, a trip he'd made with Tara, the two of them had sat with Chocko in this very spot. The deck was brand new then. They watched a spectacular sunset, the sky aglow with the most amazing colors--golds, peaches, and pearls, with violet shadows cast over the salmon and terra cotta earth below. They'd eaten a pair of rabbits from Chocko's freezer, which he'd shot earlier that summer not a hundred yards from his house. He'd barbecued them on spits over mesquite, in an improvised cooking pit in his back yard. The rabbit had been good, the taste of the gamy flesh enhanced by wild sage, fresh garlic and Chocko's own homemade salsa mixed with a cup of thick, dark molasses.

"Life is good here," Chocko had said. "I'm home."

They'd talked about "El A," as Chocko called it--Los Angeles being El A just as New York is the "Big Apple."

"It's called that, the Big Apple I mean, because it is what happens to you after you are banished from the Garden of Eden. They are two places very much alike, *mi amigo*, the Big Apple and El

A. Trouble is, you don't know what it is when you're living in it. It's the serpent turning on you, you know what I mean? It's the serpent turning on you and laughing his fucking head off cause he's already sunk his fangs in you and injected his poison and you're none the wiser for it but you're dyin' fast."

"You should complain," Drake had said, grinning. "It made you a damned millionaire."

"A millionaire with an ulcer, high blood pressure and a two-hundred dollar a day coke habit. A millionaire with no soul."

"I didn't know about the coke," Drake had said.

"It's okay," Chocko said, brushing it off. "It went away with the rest of it, with the ulcer and the high blood pressure and fancy cars and fancy dope and beautiful white ladies and the house on the Pacific. I'm back to the Garden, now. Look at this, man. I mean look at this!" He'd stood up, waving his arms in gentle, sweeping gestures that were sensuous and loving, like a great mother bird spreading her wings over her brood, indicating the entire landscape, the infinite desert, the mountains rising beyond, and now a colossal display of stars over their heads. "I'll never leave it. Not for anything."

"What about the American Dream?" Drake had asked.

"Yeah, how about that!"

                    *   *   *

It was almost time for another sunset when Chocko arrived, pulling into the carport in a ten-year old Ford pickup with two mismatched front fenders, one black, the other dark green, the rest of the body an oxidized tan. As he climbed out, the door groaned in protest and made a snapping sound that suggested a broken hinge. A large yellow dog leapt down from the cab of the truck and ran across the yard to lift its leg and pee against a tiny sapling. Chocko slammed the door of the truck behind him and strode stiffly toward the deck where Tara sat awaiting his arrival.

He was of medium build, with the suggestion of a pot belly beginning to show. He'd put on a good thirty pounds in the thirty years since college--a pound a year. But he kept himself in shape and mostly carried the extra weight well, like a linebacker whose bulk was an asset. He wore a dark blue sweatshirt with the faded seal of the University of New Mexico on it, with cutoff sleeves revealing well-muscled arms and dark, dusty, leathery skin, dry from too many hours in the sun.

"You been here long?" he asked.

"Half-hour or so. You sell your Jaguar?"

The dog had turned back toward the house. It sniffed at Tara's ankles, then looked up expectantly, nudging her hand with the tip of his nose. Tara patted the animal's head automatically.

"The Jag is gone," Chocko said. He bent down and slapped the dog gently across its backsides. "Go lay down, Melvin!" The dog skulked away and lay down under the edge of the picnic table.

Chocko gave Tara a cursory hug. "There's this Navajo guy up in Gallup. He's a great mechanic, been going to him for years. Traded me for the truck. It's got some rough spots but a fresh engine, good brakes and brand new tires. With a cheap paint job one of these days it'll look okay, won't disgrace the neighborhood."

"Midlife crisis?" She meant it as a joke but felt embarrassed once the words were out of her mouth and she heard her own sarcasm.

Chocko shrugged. "Maybe so. Some friends and I, we started a cooperative garden up the road, a big community project. Back to the land, you know? The Jag wasn't much good at hauling horse shit and fence posts. Besides, if you're going to be a real Indian, you've got to have a truck." He stopped and grinned back at her. "You want a beer or something?"

"Thanks. No. I'd take some water, though."

Chocko took a key from a narrow ledge above the door and turned it in the deadbolt. Melvin the dog watched patiently as his master put the key back. The animal made no effort to follow them inside as Tara and Chocko entered the house. The room they came into served many purposes: kitchen, computer work room, living room and library. A half-assembled portable generator shared the kitchen table with a greasy Styrofoam tray full of well-cleaned chicken bones from the convenience store in town. The place smelled of gasoline, apparently from the carburetor of the little engine that powered the generator.

Chocko pulled open the refrigerator door, reached in and grabbed a short, stubby bottle of imported mineral water and a long-necked bottle of beer. He set the cool bottles on the counter, opened a drawer, rummaged through a scramble of kitchen gadgets and came up with a bottle opener. He topped the bottles and handed the mineral water to Tara. Then he placed the beer to his lips, tipped it up and swallowed about a third of its contents. They stepped back outside, onto the deck, then sat down opposite one another at the picnic table.

"You seen anything of your dad yet?"

Tara shook her head. Over the next few minutes, she filled Chocko in on what she'd found at the house on the mesa--the windows all boarded up and most of her father's stuff still there in-side, as if he'd left in a hurry.

"Navajos used to do that when somebody died," Chocko said. "I mean, I'm sorry to suggest that but it's odd, don't you think? It doesn't necessarily mean that."

"I've got to assume he's okay."

"Of course. Of course. And chances are he is. I'm just saying, it's peculiar."

"The house belongs to this woman from Albuquerque. Some of her stuff was there, too." Tara reached into her backpack, which she'd previously set down under the table. She handed Chocko the computer diskette she'd found back at the boarded up house. "Can you do anything with this? I found it there on the floor. It's Dad's, I'm sure. I stepped on it when I was going through Charla's house."

Rising from his seat, Chocko took the diskette, removed a red-handled knife from his pants pocket, and pried open the broken casing. Then he pulled out a thin plastic disk with several wrinkles and scuff marks on it where the protective envelope had been crushed. He beckoned her to follow him back inside where he flipped on the computer, resting on a battered pine table in one corner of the room, and proceeded to carefully pry open a second computer disk, using the blade of his knife again. Removing the new disk from its casing, he then put the disk Tara had found inside, taped the casing closed and inserted it in the drive slot of his computer.

"This'll take a couple minutes. You might as well relax."

Tara eyed the TV set across the room. "Do you mind if I turn on the television?" she asked. "I'd like to see the news."

Chocko turned around in his chair, looked at her briefly, glanced at the television and then back to her. "It's broken," he said. "I need to take it into the shop." He stood up suddenly, crossed the room and leaned behind the television set to pull the plug from the wall. When he looked up again he was smiling cordially. Tara thought maybe too cordially. "I should have taken it in a week ago. Something was smoking back there. I don't want to do any more damage."

Tara turned, went back outside and sat down, leaning both elbows on the table. It briefly crossed her mind that Chocko was overly jumpy about the TV set. She took a sip of water from her bottle. The cold, carbonated liquid fizzed in her mouth. It tasted good, ice cold, with a pleasing bite as it went down. She didn't ordinarily like carbonated drinks but she'd been thirsty and dry for several hours. Melvin the dog eyed her, she thought, longingly, then edged forward and set his head on her knee.

She remembered the dog from her previous visit. It had been a puppy then, half its present size. She recalled that Chocko had explained it was the first pet he'd ever had, and he didn't know if he liked the idea or not. He said it was unnatural for animals to like people and live with them. Judging from the dog's behavior, Chocko and Melvin had gotten over that impasse in their relationship. ~

 Spirit Circle

Journey Beyond

Behind her Tara heard the unmistakable buzz of a printer and in a moment Chocko came out, handing her a thin packet of fan-fold pages with the dotted tractor feed margins still in place. As she read what was printed on them she absent-mindedly tore off the dotted strips.

"That's all there was?" she asked.

"That's all I could get for now. Maybe with a little playing around I can get some more. But not much. It'll take time."

"Did you read it?"

Chocko nodded. "Some. Enough to see that it was recorded this year. But I figured you better read it first."

She flipped back to the first page and proceeded to read aloud what she found printed there:

Sept. 29 How do you admit it to yourself, much less commit it to paper? One has to assume I haven't gone completely mad. If I were mad, would I even consider recording this? But mad or not I cannot deny what I have seen with my own eyes. Hundreds have sought it for centuries and centuries, and have never been fruitful. But I believe I may have found it...it...what to call it, that's the problem! What else but a door, a passageway into a very different reality.

What a strange and wondrous place it is! Here, even the placement of the stars in the sky is different from our own!

It lies near the center of the ruins we stumbled upon three days ago as I was tracing down the reported landing of three UFO's. One expected, what? Burned ground where the craft had landed, if the report was accurate, as these things never are. Maybe little green men emerging from shiny silver disks? Ridiculous quests of a lifetime...well, it has made for some magnificent stories for the masses, nevertheless. No matter. This find is worth all the abortive pursuits of a lifetime.

Where to begin! There is a single wall, constructed of ancient adobe, which Charla speculates may have once been a roundhouse, a building where the ancient ones, the earliest inhabitants of this place, once held their occult ceremonies. The wall stands alone now. However, there remains a line of worn bricks, nearly level with the ground, completing the circle where outer walls stood. Standing at the center of this circle one finds it easy to imagine the dark ceremonies, the dancing and the drumming and chanting of costumed figures performing their arcane rituals, their spirits departed many long centuries past.

Charla told me about ancient spiritual communities, some whose beliefs survive even to this day. She speaks of those who still practice these teachings, maintaining them even as civilization presses in with all its impositions. Her stories echo ones Tara has told me about the tribes still living high in the Andes, whole communities bound to the old ways, convinced it's their destiny to pass along the ancient prophecies. How, one must ask, do they hide from the rest of the world, with thousands of airplanes in the sky and satellite photography mapping the globe. Yet they do! Are these mere phantoms, disembodied souls of a substance that remains undetected by all our modern surveillance systems? Perhaps so.

Charla has not been comfortable poking around this spot. I tried to convince her it was a wonderful opportunity to find objects or even potsherds that she might sell at the gallery. But she will have none of it. She assures me she has no intention of treasure hunting in this area. Something about this place frightens her. She informed me this evening she will not come back with me tomorrow.

Oct. 02. I must continue recording my find, though it is difficult to contain myself enough to write. All day yesterday, two days after my find, I sat alone on the cliffs behind Charla's house here on Coyote Mesa. Charla left early last night. She is very angry, accuses me of dabbling in matters I know nothing about. She may be right but one would be a fool to turn back now. Choose between her and this, my discovery, she said. I could not do that, I told her. That's when she said she was leaving. "I'll see you back in the city," I told her. "No, you won't," she said, and I knew that was the end of the conversation. She would not say more. All very mysterious, I counseled myself, having the good sense to not argue with her. I hate it when a woman uses silence and secrecy to get back at me! *God protect me from feminine guile!*

Just staring off into the distance, wondering if I should tell the world what I have seen. Even a week ago, this seemed the answer to a lifetime dream, the story that would free me from the cares of the world. Pulitzer Prize. But today all this has changed. Who would believe me, beyond that lunatic fringe that has paid my rent all these years? And if they did believe what I have seen here, what then? It would change the world...for the better? I'm not so sure. Reason tells me to keep silent, yet I would love nothing better than to stand on the highest mountain and shout it to the world.

I know there are dangers if I reveal all I now know. But can they pursue me beyond that wall that separates our worlds? I have to believe they can't. If they could I am convinced the story would have been made public by now. Someone from there would have leaked it. If nothing else is clear to me it is that human weaknesses exist in both realms. No matter, the bottom line is that I must record what I've experienced. If they find my record it could mean trouble. I keep thinking that if they think I don't believe what I have seen maybe they will leave me alone. Maybe I can go on with my life as if nothing happened...the only price my silence. The trouble is that I can't imagine ever keeping the story to myself. I'm dying to tell it. I go back and forth between deciding to keep it a secret forever and telling it regardless of its impact on us all.

Oct. 03. I am sitting alone at the ruins, just outside the perimeter, the wall. No word from Charla. Maybe it's just as well for now. Four days have now passed since my last visit to this place. That is when it began, when I saw the figure standing outside the window as I approached the ruins. His back was to me and he wore what I took to be a woven vest, of many colors. His arms were bare, his long black hair brushed neatly down over his shoulders. When I was within twenty or thirty feet of him, I called out. He turned his head and seemed to catch sight of me. For a moment he just stared at me quizzically, cupping his hand over his brow as if peering into the sun. Then he just disappeared. When I say disappeared, I mean that. He was there one moment, gone the next, dematerialized in an instant.

I ran to the window, thinking I could catch up with him. But as I approached, something very strange occurred. At one moment I was gazing up over the wall into a vast New Mexico sky. It was one of those brooding days, with heavy, flinty-grey skies threatening a storm. The next moment I was staring out through the window in the stone wall at a sky that was clear and blue, as in the middle of a bright summer day! But that's not all. Now I also saw a

 Spirit Circle

beautiful village.

*The vision was not like one that comes fleetingly in a dream.
On the contrary! I stopped and stared for a long time. At least five
minutes passed! I saw the blue sky, the warm sunlight on adobe
buildings that appeared fresh and pink in the stark desert bright-
ness. There were people going about their daily business. A woman
walked past the window carrying a large earthen pot on her head,
yet she seemed totally unaware of me staring back at her. Half
naked children played in the plaza at the center of this village.
Some distance beyond the pueblo a dozen people worked in a field,
harvesting their crop of corn or maize. It could not be, but it was!
This was an ancient pueblo, not a reproduction but an entire
community going about their business just as they had hundreds, or
even thousands of years ago!*

*Then I noticed that to the right and left of this wall, which was
only thirty feet wide at the most, I saw nothing but the same
brooding gray sky of my own, everyday reality. It was the same
overhead and behind me. The buildings, the people, the children
playing, the people in the field, the blue sky and sunlight, could
only be seen through the space framed by the window. I would
have said it was like looking at a movie screen that had been set up
just within the window. But it wasn't exactly like that, either, because this world extended past the limits of the wall, past the limits
of a two-dimensional screen. I could see for miles in any direction
through that space. But when I stepped back, even a few inches, it
all disappeared, and there was only the gray, brooding sky again.
Even through the window itself I could only see the pueblo if I
stood in a particular place. Otherwise I saw the brooding gray sky
that formed the roof above my own world.*

*I called to people on the other side but they were not able to
hear me. At one point a young Indian woman, perhaps in her
twenties, approached the window and looked directly at me. She
was very beautiful, with dark brown skin, innocent eyes and the
sweet expression of a person who knew nothing of the pressures of
modern life. Her face reminded me of Tara's, when my daughter
was still a child. She reached out as if to touch me but suddenly
withdrew her hand. Her face took on a troubled expression and she
turned and ran away. I called to her but if she heard my voice she
didn't respond. I moved closer to the window with the idea of
climbing through and pursuing her but as soon as I set my hand on
the window sill the entire scene simply vanished. Afterwards I
attempted to get back into the right position where I'd seen all this
but I couldn't. It appears that I found the window and then lost it.*

Oct. 05. *I can't exclude the possibility that all this is some kind of trick. Why does this vision appear and disappear as it does? For the third day in a row I've returned to the ruins but with no more extraordinary encounters.*

Before she left Charla lectured me about the dangers of poking around this place. When I questioned her she said only that she thought I was having hallucinations, maybe a psychotic breakdown. I told her that if that were the case I was certain I'd be much less coherent. She speculated that maybe I was being affected by something in the wind, maybe a gas of some sort, or even a pollen, that caused a neurological change. I wonder now, was Charla right? But if what I've experienced is an hallucination it is like no other hallucination I've ever had. What I have seen did not come from my own psyche but from a reality I am certain is not of my own making.

No! In my heart I know she is wrong. I know what I saw. I cannot deny it, even to myself, though it might be nice to do just that, to withdraw into denial and disbelief, to return to my un-enlightened space. That would be the safest course by far! If what I've seen is true, it could change the world as radically as the world was changed by Columbus' voyage to the New World.

Oct. 06. *Today at the ruins there was only the wall again, the single wall, the last remnant of the village that had stood there so proudly just a few days ago--or was it centuries? The window looked out onto the mountains beyond, mountains that I saw even when I stepped out from behind the wall. There was nothing more extraordinary about this vista than the magic of Nature herself. I saw no ancient pueblo, no people walking around, nobody at the window. I explored the area for several hours, picking up a few potsherds scattered around the ruins but nothing important. At last I went back to Coyote Mesa. Once again the empty house, where I begin again to wonder about my own sanity. Did I really see what I think I saw just a few days before? Maybe Charla is right. Maybe I am delusional, the first signs of Alzheimers or senile dementia. It is hard to believe that I have aged so fast, that only yesterday these musings were a joke. Today they are real possibilities. Yet, I also find myself wishing that what I've seen might be passed off as a medical problem. Such a mundane diagnosis would release me from the turmoil of wanting to tell the world what I have seen these past few days.*

Oct. 07. *It is over a week since I found the opening. I now know I must tell the story. I write this sitting on the ground near the wall, the window, my computer in my lap, my back supported by the cool, shaded adobe. It is a beautiful day, the skies clear, the air clean, the weather almost springlike. I love the New Mexico desert on days like this, after a light rain the night before.*

But I am procrastinating. I need to get this down...

On that day, as I approached the window, I was aware of something different, something in the air, the path I'd taken to the ruins...something. I had parked my Jeep about a half a mile away, then walked to the top of the hill, passing a terraglyph of a flute player. I followed what appeared to be an ancient footpath, indicated by a shallow indentation in the hard ground. Though it might have been mistaken for a game trail its width, depth and a handful of potsherds I found along it, proved to me it was the path the ancient ones had traversed to reach this place, this other dimension.

At the top of the hill, I came to the edge of the wall, or rather what is left of it, extending around the entire site. Now it is little more than a few weathered adobe bricks, the largest one about ten inches high. This time I walked through what once must have been an entrance to this place, an opening in the exterior wall. I imagine that one day, long ago, there were heavy gates here keeping out intruders.

As I passed beyond the boundary defined by the ruined wall, I had a sudden attack of vertigo. I stopped, pressed my eyes shut in an effort to clear the feeling. For a moment it crossed my mind that Charla had been right, that my "visions" were not that at all, but the symptoms of a disease. However, when I opened my eyes again, it was as if I had been transported into an entirely different place and time. I dropped down to my knees, panicked, wondering if I was at the threshold of my death. Down on all fours, crawling along the earth like an animal I began concentrating on my breathing, as I had learned to do in a stress management class I took many years ago. My breathing, surprisingly, was even and steady, and within seconds the vertigo passed.

Gradually, I eased myself to a sitting position and rested with my legs crossed, hands on my knees. I looked around me. I was sitting just inside the gates of an ancient village! This was the village I'd seen before, through the window. But now I was inside the walls, not outside looking in.

The sky was no longer bright, however. It was late in the day, and already stars were penetrating the gauzy film of the gathering dusk. I studied the heavens for a moment, trying to orient myself but the patterns of stars were like nothing I had ever seen. I thought for a moment I must be on some sort of stage set prepared by a designer who knew nothing about astronomy, but this was not the case. The heavens were different because this was a different universe than the one I knew.

I collected myself as calmly as I could, trying to recall how I'd arrived at this place. But I was slightly amnesiac. I could not remember. And with no memory I turned to logic. The first, most reasonable explanation was that I had suffered a lapse of memory, that I had come to this place in a normal, non-extraordinary way, and something had happened that simply wiped out all memory of what went on before.

Slowly my memory cleared. I recalled every foot of my passage to this place, as if it had become suddenly very critical for me to remember. I recalled walking up the hill from the Jeep, then passing through the opening in the ruined wall, or rather the wall I imagined once being here. I speculated that whatever vertigo I'd suffered hadn't been caused by a mental or physical breakdown but by my mind's inability to accept what had just happened to me!

My heart beat furiously. This was THE STORY I'd been pursuing my entire life, the one that would win me every journalistic accolade my profession offered! I had to get it all down. I rose to my feet unsteadily and began looking around. Almost immediately, I became aware of voices a little ways off in the distance, across a narrow roadway. Because of the layout of the buildings, the labyrinthian walls and paths leading to this place, I realized that only the memory of these surroundings--perhaps from a previous lifetime?--could have guided me here. I never would have imagined myself saying this, but I believe I once lived here. It was not sheer dumb luck that brought me to this place.

Ahead of me I saw the single wall with its single window. Only now the structure was complete and new, not the remnants of an ancient ruin at all. Moreover, I was not outside looking in but inside looking out. The window was at the western quadrant of a perfectly round building with an umbrella-like roof made of twigs and branches. I was standing within the village I'd seen through the window! Because I'd previously viewed it from a distance, but now stood inside its borders, it took me several minutes to get oriented. There could be no mistake about it; even in the gathering dusk it was quite clear to me that I had slipped through some portal separating our two worlds and was now on the other side!

Voices were coming from the round building but as far as I could see nobody was on the narrow dusty streets in the immediate vicinity. Shadows were forming in the spaces between buildings and I wondered if some of these darker corners might be hiding observers who could watch my every move. I saw nobody in the *fields or in the plaza at the center of the pueblo. The entire village appeared to be abandoned, except for those voices in the round-house. I searched for a way into this structure and found a single, narrow door made of stripped saplings lashed together with what I guessed to be willow branches. I did not dare open it for fear of being detected.*

I moved cautiously toward the window opening but soon discovered it was sealed with heavy shutters made in the same manner as the door. I raised myself up far enough to peer into the room between the saplings, careful not to expose myself to any person who might be inside.

A fire burned in the center of the round room. Smoke rose up through a small hole in the roof but the truth is that the room itself was murky with smoke. The only illumination was provided by the glowing coals of the smoldering fire. The unmistakable, sweet scent of burning sage and sweet grass crept out between the cracks around the window.

I crouched in the shadows, peering in at the strange figures seated in a circle and talking in turns. I counted a dozen figures, about equally divided between men and women. They were dressed in garments like ones I'd seen in paintings of native peoples at the Indian Museum in Albuquerque, with shirts and pants, or blouses and skirts woven of many colors, ranging from rich, earthen browns to bright greens and purples. Their feet were bare, and they sat crosslegged on the ground. Both men and women wore jewelry--necklaces and bracelets--decorated with beads made of colored seeds, tiny stone carvings of animals, and nuggets of turquoise.

As my eyes grew accustomed to the darkness, I became aware of a figure sitting in the shadows not six feet from the window behind which I hid. I heard its voice first, and it was not the voice of an ordinary human being. It was hollow and deep, resonating like the lowest registers of a cello. I could not understand its words, yet the others in the circle fell silent, as if in awe at its message. As it spoke, it rose and started moving around the outside of the circle, shaking a large gourd rattle that made a gentle husha, husha, husha sound.

This bizarre creature was bigger than life, perhaps eight feet tall, towering over the others. It wore a huge black mask that rose nearly three feet above its shoulders, with a long red tongue that hung down over its black beard. Its entire body was painted black, with yellow shoulders and arms. It wore a kilt made of long grasses that rustled when it moved, this kilt suspended from a waist band made of long, red fur. It had a necklace of fresh spruce around its throat, twigs of spruce stuck in the sash around its waist and tucked in woven bracelets on each wrist. All in all, a frightful appearance!

When it at last finished its speech--or perhaps prayer--this figure sat down just to my left, its back toward me. It was then that I noticed, for the first time, two more, similar figures sitting outside the circle. So there were three figures in all dressed, as I took it to be, in the traditional costumes and fantastic masks of the Katchinas.

A second life-sized Katchina sat opposite the first. As I became more aware of it, it was as if a special light had been turned on, illuminating its features. Was this my imagination or did my very attention create this light or cause the creature to be illuminated in this way! I could swear this was the case. It wore a mask painted turquoise on the left, yellow on the right, with a long blue snout that apparently served as both a mouth and a nose. Its body was painted turquoise, as well, with large circles of coral all over its upper body and limbs. From time to time this one made an odd sort of snorting sound, long breathy exhalations that the others took in with eyes clamped shut and intense expressions on their faces, as if they were listening to the most sacred utterings.

The third Katchina had a large, flat-faced mask painted pink, with black clouds for eyebrows, huge green ears, a white snout and large, fang-like teeth. This one had a head-dress of eagle feathers and wore grey feather ruffles around its wrists, ankles and neck. It held a large, round hand drum which it struck every second or so with a beater whose shaft was decorated with brightly colored feathers, blue and green and red, long tail feathers from a wild pheasant, that jiggled and caught the light of the flickering coals as it drummed.

I am not a great student of these cultures, but I know these figures represent spirits that the Indians believe rule their lives. Even the word Katchina tells of their importance--ka, meaning respect, china meaning spirit. I was once told they supposedly come from a different planet than our own and take up residence within the masks and costumes that people don at certain times of the year. When not in use, the people treat these costumes with great reverence, feeding them, praying to them and keeping them in good repair, as if they contained the spirit, waiting to animate their earthly shroud.

Even as I watched, spellbound and slipping into the same trance these people shared, I imagined the Katchina spirits return-ing to Earth earlier that day. I imagined an ordinary person, the caretaker of the mask and paraphernalia, putting on the costume,

*then the mask, and the spirit coming down from some faraway
galaxy. In that moment, as the spirit moves in, the person beneath
the trappings fades away, his spirit moving aside to make way for
this entity so much greater than he. Instantly, he seems changed,
his body transformed by the dominating spirit of the Katchina. At
least, that's how I imagined it to be.*

*Each of the Katchinas radiated a peculiar light whenever I
turned my attention to them. Their energy glowed in the darkness,
a powerful, purplish aura that expanded out from their bodies
several inches. Even their movements were super-human! From
time to time they faded, their forms rippling the way the mirage of
a tree in the distance will ripple in the desert heat in the summer.
At one point, the figure with the turquoise and yellow mask raised
it arms toward the heavens. A beam of beautiful golden light
streamed through the roof of the round house, as if its burning
power had pierced a hole in the branches. The great, golden light
seemed to flow into the hands of the Katchina. For several minutes
this continued. Then that Katchina rose slowly and moved around
the circle and as it moved, this incredible band of golden light
enveloped the participants. Surely these figures were not life forms
I knew, not beings who belonged in my mundane universe.*

*I looked for a spot of skin beneath the costumes that would
betray their disguise. But if there was human flesh beneath these
masks and heavy garb I could not find it. I was in the presence of
a magic that went far beyond my mere human understanding. If
not mere mortals, who or what were these beings?*

*Then it struck me. These were not people. They were
goddesses and gods! I was in the presence of beings who had no
counterpart in my own reality, entities whose existence lived on in
my lifetime only through stories and ceremonial dances wherein
their effigies were animated by human dancers. But these were no
dancers or actors! Even in the dim light within that dark space, the
eyes of the Katchinas burned with a power and intensity far beyond
anything I'd ever witnessed in man or beast. I dared not look into
these faces for more than an instant, knowing the force which
burned there was not of a world I understood. My vertigo returned
and I rested a moment, trying to grasp what all this meant.*

*Fearful of dwelling on the Katchinas any longer I turned my
attention to more mundane things. I noted the walls of this place
were lined with crystalline formations. The light from the glowing
fire at the center of the room danced across a billion facets, forming rainbows of color even in the near-darkness.*

*Above the heads of the people sitting there was an object that
seemed completely out of place in this arcane setting. It was a*

huge, shiny, metallic disk, about twenty feet in diameter. It
hovered there, over their heads, as if controlled by an invisible
force. I thought there must be thin wires holding it up. But during
the meeting it changed elevation several times, at one point
lowering to eye level and sending out a beautiful stream of sounds,
much like the musical notes of a celestial harp whose gentle
reverberations had somehow become fluid, airy and smooth.

For that brief instant I was able to see the body of this disk was
some sort of highly polished metal, the glow from the fire playing
across its shiny surfaces. My first impression was that it was a
model of a spaceship. But how could this be? If my eyes weren't
deceiving me I was looking at a convergence of the most ancient
and primitive and the most advanced of technologies. Yet, was this
so impossible? In another dimension of reality, our perceptions of
time and space, of dimension and meaning would most assuredly be
shattered! And yet...there was so much that was like the world I
knew.

On either side of the doorway, at the opposite wall from where
I crouched, I saw what at first appeared to be an elaborate
petroglyph depicting a dozen or more coyotes in a large pack, their
fangs bared, their faces turned toward the door...an ominous image,
to say the least. I got the impression that they were guardians
protecting the entrance. Indeed, as I stared at them in the soft
light of the glowing embers that groaned and popped from time to
time at the center of the room, the coyotes began to mill about,
restless, agitated, alive! And yet, they were not alive! They were
drawings, but also much more than drawings. They were holograms
of some mysterious sort, three dimensional images of coyotes, twice
life-sized, acting very much as living coyotes behaved. But these
creatures were projected from the crystalline walls of this room. I
do not know how to explain their existence. Maybe like the
Katchinas they were ghosts or spirits, each with a life of its own.
For a moment I feared that they had detected my presence and
that their agitation would signal the others of my whereabouts.

The occupants of the room spoke in very low voices. The odd
thing is that they spoke a language I have never before heard, yet I
understood exactly what they were saying. How could this possibly
be! I have heard of people who suddenly recalled and understood
bits and pieces of ancient languages they themselves had never
heard. But I could still not believe that I could experience this with
a race of people with whom I had no blood bonds. I am fairly
certain my gene pool did not include these people.

A part of me wished Charla was there to witness all this. Then
she would have to believe my claims! She could never again accuse

me of suffering from delusions. This was not a dream! These were not the symptoms of a disease of the brain. The buildings, the figures in the round house, the metallic space craft hovering over the circle, the coyote spirits, the smoke and the scents...all of it was so real!

However, I cannot forget the purpose of the meeting. It, even more than the rest, fills me with trepidation. The discussion of the people and spirits seated around the fire centered on what was to be done about interlopers who'd invaded their sanctity. I crouched in my hiding place as they debated this issue, a wave of nausea and dizziness spreading over me. They spoke of thieves who'd carried away treasures from a place they called the third vestibule. There was much disagreement about which course of action to take, whether to defend their world and the ancient prophecies or allow the outside world in. Some on the council argued the outsiders were not prepared to receive the sacred gifts; others argued that unless they risked letting the outsiders in, the evolving world beyond their walls would be destroyed completely by ignorance and greed.

There were several who argued that they must do everything within their power to defend their borders, while others said that these borders were dissolving of their own accord and nothing could be done to refortify their walls. Time itself, which had helped to maintain the walls for so many centuries, was itself decaying. The great illusions of the physical world were slipping away, and even if they did nothing to defend or relax their boundaries, the moment was near when separate universes would collide.

Hearing these words sent chills down my spine, for I did not know what they meant by all this. How did time itself decay? Time is real! We can measure it in terms of our movements through the heavens and by the discharge of atoms from matter. How could they speak of time forming barriers and of universes colliding? And how could these primitive souls, gathered around a firepit in an ancient village, possibly know of scientific concepts that were still only half-proven theories to quantum physicists, even in my epoch, which was so far advanced compared to theirs? Not that I myself understand the principles of quantum physics, but I understand enough to know they were speaking of this sort of phenomena.

Suddenly one of the men rose to his feet. For a moment I was certain he'd seen me since he stared directly at me as he spoke. His voice rose in anger and he punched at the air as he ranted on. He said that a way must be found to ferret out those among them who no longer honored the ancient prophecies. And they must destroy the intruders, the thieves who were carrying away sacred treasures.

As he spoke, his anger rose to a fever pitch and I realized that this wasn't a game I was engaged in but an adventure I might pay for with my life.

I crouched at the window listening for as long as I dared, then made my way along the wall of the round house toward the space where I'd entered. As I approached my exit, however, I was startled to find huge plank doors blocking my way! These were sealed shut by long poles lashed in place. I considered scaling the poles and going over the top, a height of about 15 feet. But I was pretty certain the meeting at the round house was about to break up. If they left the building as I was scaling the wall they would surely see me and the chances were great that I would be captured.

I began working my way along the wall, taking every advantage of the shadows, when I heard excited voices behind me, coming from between two buildings. I turned in time to see three figures, young men I believe, pointing toward me and shouting to someone behind them who I could not see. Fearing for my life I fled along the wall, and in a moment was surprised to discover I was not being pursued. At least, I could detect no footsteps.

I could see no opening in the wall. It curved around the pueblo for nearly a quarter of a mile, with some structures nearly touching it. It seemed to me that the wall, and the narrow pathways crisscrossing the pueblo itself, formed a carefully engineered labyrinth, from which I might never escape. I turned away from the wall and was slipping up a narrow passage between two buildings when I came face to face with a young woman. I believe it might have been the woman I saw at the window the day before, the one who looked like Tara. My heart raced as we looked into each others' eyes, hers as terrified as mine, I suspect.

For what seemed like an eternity, she just stared back at me. From a distance I heard men's angry voices and hurried footsteps speedily approaching me. I was certain the young woman was going to cry out and I was considering clasping my hand over her mouth to silence her when she beckoned me to follow.

Why she assisted me, I do not know. I was led in and out of narrow corridors, through many rooms within stark, adobe structures, and finally to a mountainside that formed one protective portion of the wall around the pueblo. All this time, I was aware of the angry voices pursuing us but I did not stop to question whether I could trust my escort or not. I had no choice!

She pulled aside a bush and pointed to a narrow space in the rock, a tunnel perhaps three feet in diameter. I grabbed her hand, thinking that she would go with me, that surely she was in as much danger as I, having aided this interloper. But she pulled away from

me and fled. I thought of pursuing her but gave it up when I heard
the angry voices again. Without a second thought I climbed into
the hole that had been pointed out to me. I crept along on my
knees, feeling ahead of me in the darkness. I could not have been
more than fifty yards into the mountain when the ground gave way
beneath me and I felt myself falling, tumbling endlessly through
space. Seconds later I was simply sitting alone in the center of the
ruins again, bruised and cut but otherwise intact!

Oct. 9: As I write this, back home on the mesa, I am lounging on the bed in the room that has become my office. I have
barely entered the other rooms of the house now for several days. I
know things are in chaos out there, that I should take the time to
straighten things up, just in case Charla returns. She would be
furious to see how I have neglected everything.

I am lounging around in my shorts, still swabbing the bruises
on my legs with witch hazel and tea tree oil Charla left behind. She
would not believe my story were she here. How could she believe
it? I myself would not believe it if she was the one telling me. She
is convinced that either I am somehow ingesting or inhaling a
powerful hallucinogen or I am cracking up. I wonder if there is
anything I can ever do to convince her it is otherwise.

The idea that we are always but a breath away from this other
reality fills me with dread but also with great awe. I cannot say for
certain whether this reality is one that belongs to our dream world
or to the physical realm. But I do know that it is real, in its own
right. It is always there, touching us in ways we do not even know.

There are gentle spirits in this place, including the young
creature who helped me escape. But there are also those whose
intentions are savage and unpredictable. In the round house they
debated the fate of interlopers, of grave robbers and treasure
hunters, of those among them who can no longer be trusted. There
is confusion among them, much anger and vengefulness as well as a
genuine desire to bring their ancient teachings into the modern
world. But in many ways it is all very dark, very troubling to me. As
much as I am repelled by what I have heard and seen, I cannot
leave it alone. I feel repulsed by the thought that our universe is
not at all as it appears. If what I've seen is true, then all of us on
this planet must completely rethink how we live.

Charla is furious with me. Her last words before leaving were
that she wanted me to go back with her to the city and check into
a hospital for tests. But I told her I knew there was nothing wrong
with me. Tomorrow, I will return to the ruins and look for the
passage to the other side again. I need proof of my vision. I think it

*may be possible to bring back an artifact, something that will
clearly show that this other reality exists. I'm not certain this is
possible...but I have to try. Dare I try? Maybe that's the real question. Do we share a physical reality where objects can pass back
and forth? It seems feasible since I am a physical being and I have
stood in both worlds, recognized by both. I have to go
back...There's no choice.*

*I remember seeing a small pot outside a doorway, not far from
the round house where the ceremonies took place. I think it is
probably small enough to tuck into my backpack. Am wondering
about pictures, too. I need something to verify what I've seen. But
does photography even work in this other reality? There are about
ten pictures left on the last of the three throwaway cameras I got in
Gallup...would give my left nut to get my Leicas back. Not much I
can do with those rinky-dink tourist cameras...not much choice in
the matter...*

*But the issue is...would they believe me even then, with the
best photo documentation and an artifact or two...after a lifetime
in this business of doctored photos and...if it's going to work at all
I'm going to need...*

*   *   *

Tara read to the bottom of the last page. The whole thing was
absolutely preposterous. Surely Drake hadn't been so desperate as
this, to create what was obviously a hoax of ludicrous dimensions!
Unless he had completely slipped a cog, even he must realize that no
one would believe a story this preposterous. Yet, certain things about
it troubled her, like the woman who looked like Tara but was an
Indian, who lead him out of the village. Tara thought about the
woman in her dream who, she had to admit, could have been a
mirror image of herself except for the way she dressed and wore her
hair. It had to be a coincidence! But what if it wasn't? What if there
really was a place like he described, and what if dreams like the one
Tara had experienced last night actually connected us with hidden
realities?

What Drake described was exactly the image she had in her
mind for the secret society of shamans, who she'd been pursuing her
entire professional life. She tried to recall if she had ever described it
to him, in which case he could be constructing this hoax from things
she had said. On the other hand, if what he described was true, he
had not only stumbled upon this society but it was still very much
alive. He had not literally stepped through a time barrier, though she
could imagine that to him it would appear that way if he had
stumbled upon a group of shamans who were still plying their trade,
undaunted by the fact that they were fast slipping into the 21st

century. She could not allow herself to even entertain the possibility that such things might be true! But what other explanation could there be?

"Most of this happened over a period of a week or so," she said, keeping her voice calm and making a point of sticking to the known and concrete, the world of substance and measurable time and space. She paused, thinking.

"The message he left on my answering machine," Tara said, "was five days ago. If he was at Charla's when he made his last entry, which we can assume is true because that's where I found the disk, it means he could still have been around Coyote Mesa maybe even hours before I landed in Albuquerque."

Chocko nodded. "That's right."

Tara suddenly felt as if a band of steel was tightening around her chest, constricting her breathing, her heart pounding. To be so close yet so far away! If too much time had passed, she might have to give up her search and go home. It would be painful, grievous, but being this close she might still be able to rescue him. Rescue! She hardly dared allow herself that thought. To rescue meant that he was in peril. But what peril? She was inclined to agree with Charla's appraisal of Drake's competence, that he needed medical care. She had visions of him wandering around in the wilderness, in the storms, unable to find help. Or, worse yet, trapped in a cave some-where. She tried to calm herself, took a deep breath and exhaled slowly, managing to successfully disguise her distress from Chocko.

"What do you make of it?" she asked, waving the pages he'd printed out.

"Maybe it's just like he says."

In spite of her effort to hide her shock, Tara gasped. "That's ridiculous!" she exclaimed, suddenly standing up to stride several steps out toward the darkening desert. She bit her lip, stepped off the deck and walked out away from the house. When she turned again, Chocko was standing, watching her. Melvin the dog had followed her and he now sat down, looking up at her. She reached out and patted his head.

"He's delusional!" Tara said. "You know that, don't you? He's delusional. Things like this don't happen. It's impossible."

"You could be right." Chocko was obviously not convinced.

"I *could* be right! What do you mean *I could be right?* You're joking, I hope!"

Chocko was silent. Melvin whimpered, reached out a foreleg and pawed gently at Tara's knee.

Tara ignored the animal's supplications and focused her atten-tion on Chocko, searching for a hint of irony that would betray what she hoped was nothing more than an ill-advised effort to soothe her. She desperately wanted to find irony in his expression. It wasn't there.

"You're serious," she said. "You think it's real."

Chocko nodded.

"You think this other reality really exists? He really saw this phantom pueblo? These people in the round house..."

"Sometimes *mescalito* allows you to see what you might otherwise overlook."

"*Mescalito*," Tara echoed. "Hallucinogens? I've never known my father to use drugs of any kind. He doesn't even like to take aspirin."

"I didn't mean to imply that."

"But you're suggesting that something is happening like that, something to cause him to hallucinate..."

Chocko shook his head. "Mescaline is an *entheogen*, not a hallucinogen. What that means is it doesn't make illusions, it strips them away. It pulls away the cobwebs from your mind and allows you to see the truth, to know God. Mescalito is the spirit of mescaline, like a spirit shaman."

For a moment, Tara was silent. "You actually believe this, don't you?" she said, thinking she was liking the direction of this conversation less and less. "Dad said you were always so level-headed, so down to earth. Are you sure these Indians haven't led you astray?"

Chocko laughed. "On the contrary! They brought me to my senses." He said this in all seriousness, then smiled, adding, "Your father always told me I was one of them, that one day I'd discover my true identity."

"I'm sure he didn't expect you to abandon all reason."

"*Abandon all reason, Oh Ye who enter here*," Chocko mimicked, waving his arms dramatically.

"It wasn't *reason*, it was *hope*," Tara corrected, realizing Chocko was quoting Dante, the great Italian poet who mapped out Hell. "*Abandon all hope, Oh Ye who enter here.*" She strode back to the deck and sat down on the edge of the picnic table.

"Reason, hope," Chocko said. "You'd be surprised what a fine line there is between the two."

It was a word game but not a game, one that she knew Drake and Chocko had played since they first met, thirty years before. It was what had drawn them together in the first place, Tara reflected, a sense of irony, a sense of the absurd, an appreciation for the contradictions in life, a way of standing back from their lives as if they had already lived them, completed them. "Irony and pity," one of Hemingway's characters had said. "Give them pity and irony, irony and pity." Drake had gotten that passage from *The Sun Also Rises,* remembered it from his college days, and had quoted it again on their last visit to Chocko's home in Zuni. "It became a slogan for us," Drake once told Tara. "We played with it at parties and in social settings, driving everyone a little batty, I'm sure."

Tara knew that dancing at the edge of Chocko's humor, his playing the word game again, just as he and Drake had done at college, there was masked a deeper concern for his friend. It was a concern that neither he nor Tara were willing to articulate because they were not ready to let themselves entertain the real possibility that Drake was dead.

"There was something buried in Charla's yard, down at Coyote Mesa," Tara said, thinking out loud. "Do you think Dad brought an artifact back from this place, to prove himself to her?"

"How do you know something was buried?"

"Somebody came and dug it up, then drove away with it. I saw them."

"Why didn't you stop them?"

She was silent for a moment. "Do I look like somebody who could go up against a 200 pound man who might have been armed, for all I know? Besides, it was storming. I was hiding in a cave above the mesa."

"In a cave?"

Tara shrugged. "I've done it a hundred times."

"How big was this thing?"

"Not so big that he couldn't carry it under his arm. It was a bowl, I think, something about the size of a large salad bowl. But he didn't make it very far."

"What are you talking about?"

Tara related the story of the Jeep that went over the cliff, killing the driver. She described all the details, about the scrape on the side of her rented car, clearly marked with the paint from the Jeep, and the scrape on the Jeep with the same color paint as her rented car. She told Chocko about the sheriff who said two men in a car with government plates reported the accident. She told him how the police crew found the driver with his head caved in and his neck broken. Somewhere, as the Jeep tumbled end over end down the long, steep slope, the cab got torn off and the roll bar, with which it was equipped, tore loose.

"It's odd. It's like John Baler. It may be nothing. One of the locals...he drove off the road, hit a tree. Not dead, not even physically hurt. But he was pretty shook up. He was drinking, though. I don't suspect there's anything so unusual about that."

Not knowing what to say, Tara was silent. Her fears played at the edges of her consciousness, raising images of her father wandering around on the desert half crazy. Or maybe worse.

"What is it about Coyote Mesa?" she asked. "What's the big mystery out there?"

"It's one of those things...stories get started and pretty soon they get twisted into legends. You know. Don't take it too seriously."

"What stories?"

"There's this group out there. Maybe witches. Around here, that's bad news. You don't even say the word. It's like invoking Satan at a Catholic wedding."

She did know all this. Within the Pueblo belief system, there were strict taboos about death. Death was dark and evil. One did not speak the name of a dead person, for example, for fear that their ghost would return. Even the ghosts of loved ones could be dangerous. By defying these taboos, and even going so far as to use the ghosts of ancestors to work their will, witches achieved great power. But it was a dark power and a power that eventually destroyed all who touched it. It was the equivalent in the Christian tradition of selling your soul to the devil.

"Are they Navajo, Hopi, what?"

Chocko shook his head. "Nobody wants to take credit for them. I tend to think they're mostly just outcasts from other tribes around here, you know? A lot of half-bloods like me. But the official story is they're the ragtag end of a lost tribe. They claim to have been around for thousands of years, maybe longer than anyone else."

"The Anasazi?"

Chocko nodded.

"Could be interesting. I mean as an anthropologist."

"Don't be so sure. Nobody out there wants anything to do with anthropologists. Around here you guys are almost as unpopular as witches or government guys. So watch your step, you know?"

"Tell me something. There are all these whisperings about the land out there being haunted."

"More likely some sort of magnetic disturbance. Geologists go down there and can't figure it out. Radios don't work. They've tried to get regular phone service in there a couple times, and that doesn't even work very well. They have trouble with all kinds of electronic stuff. Car radios don't even work."

"Nor my cell phone."

"Oh, yeah. Those things. Not bad enough we've got phones in our homes. Now we carry them around in our pockets. That's crazy, you know? People come out here to get away from it all but they walk around with those fucking phones on their hips, like cowboys' six-guns. I even know some Indians with them."

"What would cause that?"

"Fear of your own thoughts..."

"I mean the magnetic disturbance."

"Like I say, maybe it's true what they say. It's witch country."

"Like the witches my dad saw? Come on, Chocko!"

Chocko gazed out over the desert, obviously weighing this possibility and pondering ways to answer her.

Tara knew of the Indians' dislike for witches. They attributed all kinds of dark happenings to them, gave them credit for everything bad that ever happened. Disease, family problems, still births, drought, bad luck of every kind was accredited to witchcraft. Superstitions such as these made bringing modern medicine to the pueblos frustrating, to say the least. Particularly, many of the older people, who were most in need of medical care, had a fatalistic view of their illnesses, saying there was nothing to be done.

"They wouldn't be traditionalists," Chocko said, finally responding to Tara's question. "They wouldn't be protecting ancient prophecies. This Anglo friend of mine was studying storytelling with a man out there. Learned a lot of the coyote stories from him. They were the sacred stories that you are never supposed to tell except in the winter. In the winter you're preparing for the spring, for new life, and Coyote stories are teachings to help you in that. You are never to talk about these stories except that time of year, and certainly not with outsiders, with Anglos. It's very bad luck to do that. But my friend, he was learning them. I warned him about it but he flipped me off, said I was getting too caught up in Indian ways.

"So, about a year ago, this guy down in Coyote Mesa who told my friend all these stories started having real bad luck. His son got drunk one night and drove into a tree. Killed himself. About a year later, the storyteller's wife comes down with cancer and dies. Then my friend's wife loses her baby in childbirth. The cord wrapped around her neck and choked her. Around here they say that's caused by witches, by you violating the sacred laws."

"Do you believe all that stuff, Chocko?"

"It's too much of a coincidence. Since moving back, I can't ignore it. Maybe it just goes with the territory."

Tara fell silent. She came back to the deck and sat down across from Chocko. "I want to know about the caves. I have to know about them. What do the people around here believe about them?"

Chocko leaned on his elbows and stared into the distance, as if the story of the caves, this entrance to another world, was written out there, somewhere, on the gathering darkness of the vast desert landscape. ~

Invisible Connections

"There's a round house, a meeting place about fifteen hundred feet straight down inside Mother Earth's belly," Chocko said. "Legend has it that it takes days to get down there. People have gotten lost in that place. Grave robbers, you know. They hear about hidden treasures in these places, go down where they have no business being, and that's the end of them. Maybe somebody stumbles on their bodies later on, maybe not.

"There's only this handful of Indians who know the way, and they were trained in the journey from a very early age. The only maps of the place are in the heads of those folks, and they're dying out. The younger generation hasn't kept up the old traditions. You know how that is."

Chocko paused, studied Tara's face, then went on. "All of this is rumors, of course. Supposedly they converse with the spirits."

"Oh, yes, the spirits!" Tara said, seeking comfort in her scorn for superstition, yet not finding it.

"There are infinite stories about that land out there. We only know a small portion of the legends and myths surrounding it. This fellow I know from Albuquerque, Jack Milford, used to fly over that general area in one of those little breezies. I helped him set up a computer down at his place in Albuquerque. We became pretty good friends. He wanted to get on the internet, had this idea of exchanging information with people..."

"Wait," Tara interrupted. "What are *breezies?*" The word had come up in her father's message--breezy from hell.

"You know, ultra light aircraft," Chocko said. "Little thing run by an old Volkswagen engine. He built it himself from a kit. Anyhow, the crazy guy used to truck it out there, bolt it together and buzz around. They can fly at about thirty miles an hour and get close in around those canyons and such. There's millions of acres back in there that nobody's explored much. He was a photographer, you know? He used to sell his stuff to a place in New York. One of the tabloids, I think. And he himself was writing a book. He had these photographs of something he called *terraglyphs...*"

"Terraglyphs?" Tara said aloud. "Of course!" Two years earlier her father had written an article about crop circles, comparing them to the ancient terraglyphs found during archaeological expeditions on virtually every continent. Some of them were huge, stretching out for miles, usually depicting animals or humans, similar to the *petroglyphs* found on the walls of caves. The peculiar thing about the terraglyphs was their size. Art experts who'd see aerial photos of them had said they would have been impossible to create with such precision unless the artists had been able to look down at them from a great height. Further research showed that the artisans would have had to look down from an elevation of at least 2,000 feet, which in every case was impossible, since there were not even mountains nearby that would have afforded that perspective.

Nobody knew exactly what purpose these artifacts had served in the cultures where they'd been found since to a person on the ground terraglyphys would have been nothing more than occasional scratchings in the earth or rows of rock laid out on the land for no apparent reason. In Drake's article, he had claimed there could be only one explanation: terraglyphs and crop circles were messages to extraterrestrials. As proof of his hypothesis, Drake claimed that these "codes to the sky gods"--that was his phrase--were always found in areas of the world where UFOs had been sighted. He insisted that the terraglyphs identified landing strips for UFOs or that they sent messages about when and where it would be safe to land.

There was, of course, no real evidence for Drake's claim, a fact of which he was well aware. What's more, Tara knew that Drake had gleaned much of his information about terraglyphs from the anthropology library where she worked. He had ignored all the more responsible research about terraglyphs. For example, he'd totally dismissed Sir Arnold Berry's hypothesis that they were evidence for early land surveying and mathematical skills. Berry had shown how early peoples could have created grids and crude surveying techniques that would have allowed them not only to establish boundaries between tribes but to translate a small sketch on a flat rock into a terraglyph stretching over hundreds of yards. Why had they done this? It was still anyone's guess, except that most of the people who'd created such artifacts had believed that gods looked down at them from the skies. Perhaps these terraglyphs had been intended to appease the gods, to request their cooperation in the planting of crops or in the hunting of animals.

Chocko continued his story: "The photos this guy had from that area were not unlike pictographs of Kokopeli, the humpback flute player. One difference, the one he photographed out there covered about five acres. I'd guess it was maybe a thousand feet long, about a hundred feet wide, something like that. It was holding something out in one hand, like a square tablet of some sort, and it had glyphs on it, too, except they were partially scraped out or covered over."

"Chocko, listen. This is beginning to make some kind of sense. Dad sent me these pictures. I've got them in the car. Two years ago, the last time I saw him, he also talked about going in search of a flute player. I think he knew about these photos back then. Maybe he even knew this photographer you're talking about. That's why Dad came out here. That's what it was all about. He knew something. Maybe this photographer guy had found something that gave Drake an idea for a big story."

"Your Dad and I talked about this photographer guy, you know. Last time I saw him. But he seemed all skeptical at the time. He said the whole deal would have been too easy to fake, that they do it all the time at the papers where he works. He told me about investigating some terraglyphs down in Chile somewhere that turned out to be hoaxes. He even showed me one he and a friend mocked up. It's a simple matter of trick photography, sandwiching the negative of a common petroglyph over the photograph of a large strip of land. They can do it even better nowadays with computers, of course. But I can assure you the ones I saw from this guy in Albuquerque weren't faked."

"And this man you know still has the photographs?"

"Well, not exactly."

"What do you mean, *not exactly?*"

"He disappeared. Him and the breezie, too. They found his truck parked out on the highway but no sign of him, no sign of the breezie, either. He just vanished. The Civil Air Patrol went out there, looked around, couldn't find nothing. He is as gone as childhood, you know?"

"And the photos?"

"Gone, too. I've talked with Dorothy, his widow, several times on the phone. She needed money, so I lined her up a customer for all his computer equipment. We have to assume he's dead...looked through his home office for the photos. I thought they might help her out, raise a little money for her. Nothing. Not a sign of them. She hasn't turned up a thing."

"I don't know, Chocko, you get around a lot of people with wild imaginations and an ordinary tragedy suddenly becomes another urban myth...or in this case, a desert myth. It's that sort of thing that keeps my dad in business, and feeds the tabloids. You told him about all this, about the terraglyphs and the breezy?"

"Yeah, oh, yeah! We discussed it all. But he already knew about terraglyphs. He wanted me to poke around for him, ask the folks I know here in Zuni. I did. A lot of them say they've heard stories about the terraglyphs. Their grandfathers and great grandfathers passed the stories along. Supposedly there is a place out there where worlds overlap. That's how they talk about it, that it is what you or I would call a merging of different realities."

"What *you* would call it," Tara corrected. "Or what my dad would call it. You're bucking three hundred years of physical science, Chocko. I'm a skeptic when it comes to that stuff! No, more than that. I've got to tell you, I'm not a believer. If you look far enough into any of these stories you find reasonable explanations. These mystical worlds they talk about are in the mind, believe me. There's nothing to them. Science may not have all the answers, but it has freed humanity of a lot of superstitions that otherwise would have kept us in the Dark Ages forever."

Chocko ignored her. "The Indians say the cave out there is an opening, like they speak of with the Anasazi, the *ancient ones.* You've heard of the Hopi prophecies, of course, which tell about the evolving worlds?"

"I'm not sure, Chocko. Remind me." As much as she disliked the superstitions that ensnared the minds of the people of this area, the ancient stories and legends still intrigued her. It was just that she was not intrigued for the same reasons that most people were. Certainly there was symbolic meaning to be found in these myths. That much could not be denied, but to take them literally was pure folly, as childish as her daughter Maya's belief that her dreams foretold the future.

"Well, they say our culture is presently living in the fourth world, having emerged from the third only a few hundred years ago," Chocko said. "Some even claim that great seers from the third world still exist, though they live in a world most of us cannot see. It's a sort of underworld, invisible unless you pass through the secret opening, the *kiva* that takes you beyond your everyday reality. People much like ourselves still live there in this other reality, this other world, just as they did several hundred years ago. They say there's a big sky, a sun and moon, and all the rest, except it's there under the crust of the Earth."

"It's like the shamans talk about," Tara said. She kept her excitement hidden, hoping to draw Chocko out. "You have to take the magic with a grain of salt, you know, but as a cultural artifact it is definitely intriguing."

For a moment Chocko stared at her with an expression that was both impassive and contemplative as if he could look right into her mind. "You know, your dad is right about you. You're pretty stuck in your ways," he said.

"Drake told you that?"

"He loves you just the same." Chocko smiled. "Let's try it another way. Let's call it another reality, worlds invisible to us...where we are also invisible to those in the other world. But let me pose a possibility here. What if there really were interactions between the two, I mean, that we could actually travel back and forth between the two worlds? Let's say this other world, this world of...what should we call it, a dream world...was real though not tangible in the way the dirt out there is, you know, non-material."

"You're beginning to sound like Carlos Castenada! Have you ever read his books?"

Chocko laughed. "You mean, his talk about separate realities? Sure, why not? I thought a good anthropologist looked at all the possibilities, no matter how farfetched they might appear. Think of all the stories, the myths and legends, that tell of portals between these different realities. Around here people talk about occult ceremonies carried out by secret societies, even today, in which the high priests of the fourth world--our world--conjure up the high priests from the third world. You know, they just sort of manifest out of the vapor. Once a year they exchange information and insights. It is said there is a need to do this, to make amends for past injustices. Sacrifices are made, and these sacrifices are payment toward attaining peace in the fourth world and the next, the fifth, which is only now emerging."

"Sacrifices like what?"

"Some say animal sacrifices, some say human. There's not much evidence for the latter. I think I know enough about these people to say with some authority there isn't much blood sacrifice in this day and age. Not even animal blood. I mean, I'd be surprised if they were sacrificing anything more than a chicken, you know? Unless, of course, you count Shalako, when they slaughter a bunch of sheep to feed the people."

"Chocko, Dad told me once that you weren't raised in these old traditions. Just give me your honest take on it, would you? You don't really believe in this other realities thing, do you, I mean that it is an actual physical place?"

"I believe the legends may be telling us something the scientific world simply can't wrap their minds around. What if...I'm just saying, what if...there were a force that actually determined different patterns of behavior, that there were these templates of energy that, let's say, emerged from the consciousness of the Earth herself. Say the earth is like the old ones have been telling us for thousands of years, that it's not just a ball of mud but more like a being, a spirit, if you will. And perhaps our relationship with it is as interactive as they've been trying to tell us, that these templates of energy grow out of it, evolving from a complex relationship between us and it, or her, as the case may be."

"Chocko, I don't know you very well. But this is a fairy tale! It's not going to help me find my dad."

"Don't be so sure. Maybe you have to learn to entertain some other possibilities, let in the mystery of it. After all, even the astronauts, who are some pretty hard-edged techno types, came back from outer space with the belief that Mother Earth is literally a giant cell, a living being, you know, the Gaia myths, the notion of Earth as a living, metabolizing being, for which each of us is something akin to a piece of Her gray matter. Each of our lives is the stuff of Her dreams, stretching back through centuries to the beginning of time."

"But what are you telling me? And what does it matter what you or I or anybody else believes? I need a little reality check here, Chocko." She could no longer hide her frustration. "Ever since I got to New Mexico, my life has been topsy turvey. I don't get it! Just tell me what's going on at Coyote Mesa. Why all the mystery around it? What is it people don't want to tell me?"

"I don't know how to answer that. Something's going on out there, it's true. Electronic stuff goes all haywire out there. Phones and radios don't work. I think it's exaggerated but a lot of people from around here won't even go there anymore. They accuse the people who do live there of being witches, you know? The Navajos are particularly cautious about those people out there. Others I've talked with say they think a New World is going to emerge from there, you know, a sort of Second Coming."

"Fascinating!" Tara made no effort to disguise her sarcasm. But underneath this sardonic exterior, her imagination was sailing off into fantasies perhaps as preposterous as the ones Chocko described.

Chocko continued his monologue: "In modern times, there have been UFO sightings out there. The government had some research projects in the area and had strange things happen. Computers going down. Generators blowing up. Telephone and communication devices failing to function. People started disappearing..."

"Whoa. People disappearing?"

"Oh, they'd turn up again. But they were filled with all sorts of bizarre stories. The Army, which was conducting one project, finally pulled out and never came back. They said it was too isolated, that there was also some kind of magnetic disturbance there as well, and between the isolation and the technical problems that were coming up, people were going A.W.O.L. They couldn't get people to stay out there."

"What do you personally believe about all this?"

Chocko gazed off into the distance, as if seeking his answer there. "Since I came back here to live," he said, "I've seen and heard things that go against everything I ever learned in college. There is a kind of magic about this place. Where sacred sites are concerned, you've got to pay attention to the local beliefs and rituals. The mythology of this place must not only be taken seriously, in some cases it must be taken literally. You may not believe in occult forces. You can belittle them all you like. But they're a factor here, a strong factor. Maybe it's even a sort of mass hysteria, you know? Maybe all the stories and rituals that support them hypnotize us all into believing. I can't offer an explanation that's going to satisfy you, I'm sure of that. But the fact remains, the myths affect the lives of everyone who lives out here, and let me assure you, it's not just su-perstition, as you suggest. We have to respect and honor the myths. It's dangerous not to believe."

"Let's say I take a leap of faith," Tara said. "Let's say I go along with you. How does that help me find my father or determine what it was he found out there?"

"Drake was intrigued by these things. You and I both know that. He would love nothing better than to crack the mystery. But what if it won't crack?"

"Won't crack?"

There was a long pause. Then Chocko began talking again, in a hushed tone at first. Tara felt an urgency in his voice, an urgency mixed with patience, as if he knew he simply had to get it all out before she had the opportunity to protest.

"The story is this," Chocko said, "that a new reality was born about two hundred years ago. We are never more than a breath away from this new world. We are in it already, surrounded by it. We even share molecules with it. It's just that most of us can't see it yet. Why is it so hard for us to accept this? We know there are many phenomena in the universe that we can't perceive with our five senses. Why should it come as such a surprise to us that there's this whole world, maybe even a whole solar system we don't know about! Maybe that's the world we contact when we go to sleep at night and dream. Maybe dreams have an entirely different explanation than the one the social scientists like Freud and others have posed. When I think of it that way, I can't any longer say that such things aren't at least *possible.*

"Many people from our world, the fourth, are being prepared for the fifth. They're being initiated into this other reality. They are going back and forth between two worlds by altering their states of consciousness, some through meditation, some through dance, some through fasting, some through deliberately induced trance, and some through *entheogens* that grow near certain sacred sites."

"Entheogen. There's that word again!"

"Why are you so surprised? You're an anthropologist. These substances were used for spiritual insight even in biblical times. You must know about the early Christian mystics' use of *ergot*, the fungus harvested from wheat! For thousands of years religious leaders have known about entheogens and have used them to see beyond the limits of human reason. In modern times, psychologists have looked at them in a little different way. They say these plants produce hallucinations. But modern students of ethnopharmacology, like Terence McKenna, for instance, say that entheogens remove the *hallucinations of our everyday identities.* They help us see beyond the limits of our own perceptions and to come into direct contact with the reality beyond all hallucinations."

"Yes, I know. To literally see God. Right, Chocko, I've had this conversation before, with Drake."

"It doesn't matter how skeptical you might be of these things, Tara. I've experienced it first hand. It's not to be toyed with."

"You've *ingested* entheogens?"

"Some years ago, for the first time. You and Drake are the only ones who know about this, except for the woman who is my teacher."

"Your teacher?"

"An old woman, what you would call a Medicine Woman. She's the reason I dropped my business in Malibu and came down here to live. She is very important to me."

"She's a shaman."

"She's simply a very wise old woman."

"Who chews peyote and magic mushrooms and spins tall tales."

"Perhaps. But since working with her I had to take a personal stand. I had to come back to my people. And I have had to start looking at the ancient prophesies in a new light, from the vantage point that maybe they are all true."

"Chocko, tell me this, are you still using these entheogens, as you call them?"

"They are great teachers. Shamans throughout the world have been using them for centuries. And there's evidence that the world's great religions owe much to them. If we're going to probe beneath the surface of everyday reality, we've got to look at these things. We have to look at what they're telling us in quantum physics, too, because scientists seem to be proving that the ancients were onto something we've overlooked. For example, the evidence is mounting that our physical world is illusion and something even more elusive than energy is the real building block of the universe. It may very well be that the plants' gifts can reveal secrets that can carry us considerably beyond the limits of our present thinking."

Something Tom had said to her years before echoed in her mind. Flashing back to it, for only an instant, she felt the old charge around it, recalling old arguments that had to do with him attending a ceremony in Peru where plant substances that were said to produce hallucinations were ingested. She'd been furious with him. He argued that if anthropology was to move out of the Dark Ages, people like him and her had to experience the real magic of the past. Apparently, for Tom, real magic was filling your nervous system with narcotics that warped your view of reality.

It was an argument that never got resolved. He took any opportunity that offered itself to tell her she wasn't open enough to the magic. She accused him of being a metaphysician, not a social scientist, and that he was just one step away from alchemy in this harebrained approach to his profession.

"It's all superstition," Tara told Chocko now. "And I'll grant you this much, that people for thousands of years have been moved and manipulated by superstition. But for the sake of argument, let's say there's some truth in what you're saying. Let's say there are these different worlds, these other realities or whatever. Maybe they are just in the mind, you know, more metaphorical than actual. And let's say these entheogens do prepare us for transiting back and forth between these different worlds. What then?"

"I would like to believe we're on the cusp of change--change for the better. Because if we're not..."

"The Apocalypse! I'm sorry, but I'm a social scientist. We have thousands of documentations revealing how cults have manipulated people for centuries and centuries. The one thing common to all of them is the Apocalyptic prophecy."

"That isn't what I said, is it? I am of the belief that the world is on the cusp of positive change. If we don't make that change, our evolution will continue to go along as we're going now, led by a technology that's exploitive and that values technological progress above the life of the planet itself."

"Tell me. Have you met a single person who's actually made this trip to these other worlds, who has actually experienced these different realities? Produce just one person and maybe I'll take you more seriously."

She had a hidden motive for asking. Instinct told her if her father had heard any of this he would have seen a potential story. Whether it was true or not would be irrelevant for him. Drake would find a story in it if he could just put together a few interviews by people who claimed to have made these transitions back and forth.

"Yeah," Chocko said. "There's a street person who begs spare change down in Albuquerque. He says he's from Atlantis. And sometimes he claims he's the bastard son of Elvis."

"You're joking, I hope."

"Of course I'm joking. But maybe there's some truth in madness, you know, if we're willing to seek it out."

Tara's mind drifted. Was it possible that Chocko was right, that these ancient myths of other worlds, other realities, weren't just the stuff of dream and hallucination? She thought about her dreams of James Dean and shuddered. Was it possible there was a reality beyond these ancient symbols and metaphors that were found throughout the art of the ancients? Chocko wasn't the only one who seemed to believe in such things. Tom, too, was a believer, though he explained it in anthropological terms that Tara found more acceptable. The bottom line, however, was that if they believed these things, she could pretty much count on Drake believing them enough to look for a story. She could just imagine him roaming around the desert, probing around these sacred sites--these portals into the distant past or the next world, depending on your perspective. At the very least he put himself at risk with the Indians who guarded these places religiously. What was the price one paid for violating these protected spots? Her own studies offered plenty of evidence that trespassers often paid with their lives.

She remembered the prayer stick in the garden at Charla Mather's house. It had three beads made of bone attached to it. Bone and bone dust, particularly when derived from human bone, was known to be a witch's curse in the Navajo tradition. She also remembered the ghostly dancer, dressed like a Katchina, back at Charla's house. It looked like a Katchina but it was not one she recognized. It definitely wasn't traditional. This was all very puzzling but she was certain there would eventually prove to be reasonable explanations.

An image came to her mind of the calf in the back of the pickup truck, parked in front of the convenience store she'd found just south of Coyote Mesa. The woman inside had told Tara the calf was to be taken to her uncle's house for a ceremony. If there was any truth whatsoever in what Chocko was saying, there was a good chance that this calf wasn't headed for a barbecue at a wedding. It was going to be ritually sacrificed. With all these strange goings-on out there, it was no wonder people started rumors about the place.

"I saw this light out there," Tara said. "I figured it was a comet, or maybe some secret weapon they're experimenting with out at Los Alamos. Have you heard anything about that?"

"UFO, most likely."

"UFO, right!"

Chocko hesitated for a long time before he spoke again. "What I'm about to tell you is going to sound even crazier than your dad's adventure. You're going to say it's a conspiracy theory, but I have an idea that everything your father said on the disk is true. The Indians around here have been talking about stuff like this for centuries. Drake is nuts for stories like this. You know that. But what if he stumbled onto the real thing..."

"I'm sure he stumbled on *something*," Tara said. "And whatever it is could be an important anthropological find. But let's stay in the real world, Chocko. Life is weird enough without this overlay of superstition."

"Tara, you have to open your eyes. It's the only way you'll ever find Drake."

"Excuse me, but there's no way you'll convince me of this separate worlds thing. I wouldn't put it past my father to vanish into the mountains for a month or two, then show up all disheveled, claiming he's been abducted by people from this other dimension, or by little green men in a flying saucer. He's been working on his *story of a lifetime* for thirty years or more. You know what? I wouldn't put it past him to disappear for even two years to create such a hoax. He isn't a man bound by any other ethics except to produce a story more preposterous than anything you or I have even imagined."

For a long time, Chocko was silent. When he spoke again, he lowered his voice so that she had to lean closer to him to hear. "Listen to me," he said. "I have to tell you this, and I want you to pay attention. About two weeks ago, not far from here, there was a sighting over by the old town, out there at Black Mesa."

"A sighting?"

"UFOs. They came in pretty low and were spotted by at least a dozen people, probably a great many more than that."

"Oh, God, Chocko, I can't believe stuff like this. Wouldn't it be in all the papers if it was real?"

"It was in the papers--the *Global Enquirer, Sightings*..."

"I see. The tabloids," Tara said. "It's ding-dong time."

"Exactly. That's the point."

"What's the point?"

"If you were going to debunk somebody's story, what would you do? You'd go to the tabloids first. Who else is going to touch it after that?"

"I'm sorry. I don't get it."

"What's there to get? Release the story to those rags first and you'll be hard pressed to sell it to any first line publisher. It's the kiss of death."

"The perfect cover up, you mean. Sorry, I still don't buy it."

"Let's say I've not only thought of it, I know it for a fact."

"You mean the sightings, the UFO's?"

"If they were from our people, someone, somewhere, has mastered a technology I don't know anything about. And believe me, I've worked with engineers on the cutting edge. I may have been out of touch for the last ten years, but things don't move that fast. This stuff would have to be based on an entirely new model of physics. I'd know if it was ours. Believe me, I'd know. I'm sure of it."

"But you have no proof..." Tara's voice trailed off into silence.

"It didn't stop with these initial sightings. Ever since the incident two weeks ago, there are these peculiar looking helicopters, all black, no markings, cruising around the territory here, scouting like."

"Wouldn't that be natural enough, the Air Force, maybe NASA poking around, investigating?"

"Investigating what? The tribal councils of three communities around here arranged meetings with both NASA and the Air Force to talk it over. Black Mesa is sacred ground. There were agreements that the air space over that area would not be violated. The government promised it wasn't being violated, that they knew nothing about the helicopters. The council had photographs. The government claimed the aircraft weren't theirs, though they said there could be some stuff going on at NASA that they don't know about.

"They also said that anyone with the money--about two million dollars per--could buy some exotic looking aircraft, maybe from the French Air Force or something, minus some of the top-secret accessories. From what I hear, however, the Air Force was as concerned as the Council about the copters. You see, there were no identifying marks on them. None whatsoever. That's highly illegal, even for experimental military aircraft."

"It's crazy."

"Maybe. But what if there's another explanation?"

"Did Drake ever talk to you about things like this?"

"Yes, I'm afraid he did. Two years ago, he and I talked. He said that this was going to happen, said he had it on good authority there would be a landing. I have no idea where he got his information, and I never thought he'd go after a story so speculative, built around an event that was rumored to happen many months in the future. You know, it was just idle chatter. We were just passing the time, having a couple beers."

"I thought you knew my dad. Stories like that are his narcotic. He couldn't possibly leave it alone."

Chocko was silent. Then he said, "Listen, it's getting awfully late to drive back up to Gallup. Stay over. There's an extra bedroom, though you'll have to share it with some computer junk."

"I don't mind. I'd really appreciate it."

"No problem. No problem at all."

That evening, as she was getting ready for bed, he brought her a page from a newspaper. It was dated over three weeks before. There were photos of two men under a banner which read: "UFO Sighted Near Zuni."

"Do you know these men?" Tara asked.

Chocko nodded. "Fred Winfield lives just west of Gallup, off the highway. He runs sheep down here, has cattle on his own ranch."

"And the other..."

"John Baler. I told you about him already, the one who wrecked his truck." ~

 Spirit Circle

The Aliens

At 5:15 a.m. Tara left Chocko's, heading west toward the Arizona border and highway 666, on her way out to Winfield's ranch. Chocko had made the call for her, assuring her that Winfield would be awake at that ungodly hour. The weather and farm reports would be on the radio and Winfield, like most ranchers, would be listening. Without hearing Winfield's end of the conversation, Tara had thought the rancher wasn't overjoyed with the prospect of meeting with her. So when Chocko cradled the phone again, she was certain her visit was off. But she'd been wrong. Winfield told Chocko she could come but he didn't have a lot of time. He'd be working in the barn, and she could find him there.

It was a bright, beautiful morning. The rains were momentarily suspended and the skies already glowed with the sanguine flush of an early dawn. The desert atmosphere had a fresh, new feeling about it, instilling in Tara a kind of guarded optimism. Early morning life scurried and slithered over dry, reddish rocks, seeking warmth, excited by the prospect of a new sun and dry breezes that were the life source of the desert.

As she drove west, Tara's thoughts turned to her father again. As crazy and undependable as he seemed on the surface, there was a part of him who was a genuine seeker. She wouldn't argue that he warped his subject matter in the stories he wrote for the tabloids, but there was a part of him that wanted the truth. And if he had shirked his responsibilities as a father, at least for most of her childhood, he never denied his part in Tara's unhappiness. He had even admitted to her once that her birth, the fact that there was another person in the world who was bound to him by blood, had touched him more deeply than anything else in his life. After the divorce he had kept his distance, that was true. But there were reasons a man did that, mostly a matter of not wanting to reopen wounds that he knew would never heal.

It had taken Tara a long time to allow herself to understand her father's pain, to allow herself to see the connection between his absence from her life, his anguish and his love. Only with the death of her mother did she discover that all those years when he'd seemed so remote, he had not been indifferent to her; Drake had been seeking refuge. Upon news of Helen's death, he moved right into her life, at least for a short period of time. He arranged Helen's funeral expertly, caringly, and it was then that Tara realized he'd never quite gotten over the divorce.

When Tom came into Tara's life, Drake had opposed the relationship, for reasons she'd never quite understood. She accused her father of being jealous but he only scoffed, told her it was no such thing, that it was an issue of character, pure and simple. When she asked him to explain, Drake was evasive.

"You're a grown woman," he'd said. "I'm hardly the person to be handing out advice this late in your life."

No matter how she pressed him Drake would not discuss his dislike of Tom. In fact, she was aware of his position only because he made a point of not being around whenever Tom was with her. He made excuses, even canceled dinner dates with them at the last moment. Now, years after she and Tom had parted company she struggled with the idea that maybe she had rejected Tom in part because of her father's opinion of him. How could she ever be sure that she had been true to her own feelings in refusing to make her life with him? It was still a question in her mind, particularly when she let herself acknowledge the confusing passion she felt in Tom's presence.

Out of the corner of her eye a flash of brilliant light caught her attention. She reflexively turned in that direction but her view was blocked by a wall of rock. A few moments later she saw the flash again. Light glistened in the sky, far to the north, like a huge mirror. It was extremely bright, sending laser-sharp beams in her direction. She thought, this was the way rumors about UFO's started in the area. Obviously, it was an airplane or weather balloon or helicopter, which because of the angle of the light in the clear dry air, mirrored the rising sun in an unusual way. She leaned forward, turning her head to the right, to get a better look. Nothing. It had to have been a distant airplane or some quirk of nature. A small circle of light glowed in the sky where she guessed the airplane had been. Then it, too, faded. The New Mexico sky was like that, she reflected, remembering the light in the sky between Coyote Mesa and Zuni the day before.

Her thoughts returned to her father. Given what she knew of his lifestyle, it wasn't difficult to ignore his disappearance for three or four months. In the past he'd always turned up more or less unscathed, with a wonderful story to write. But he had never dropped completely out of sight for two years. And he had never sent her anything like the package she'd received six days ago, with fragmented clues to his whereabouts. And the notes on the computer diskette were nothing short of crazy, as near as she could tell. *Little green men,* she thought. Perhaps he'd had a breakdown and was delusional.

But that didn't explain the boarded up house, the personal belongings left behind, the stranger digging in the garden. The wrecked Jeep on the road back to Zuni might have been a coincidence, totally unrelated to her father's and Charla's disappearance. No, that was whistling in the dark. There had been skid marks on the road, suggesting a high speed duel between two vehicles, with one obvious loser. She couldn't allow herself to dismiss that evidence. A man had died in that wreck, and very possibly it was the same man she'd seen at Charla's house.

As she thought about her father, she felt a confusing mixture of fear and anger. It was not an unfamiliar feeling. She had felt it often as a child. After her parents' divorce she'd felt that her whole world had collapsed. There had been times when she brooded, inwardly raging at Drake for leaving. These feelings warred with others--a need to be with him, to have him near. She remembered a short period one summer when she first got to know his gentler side. The memory of it soothed her, lessening the panic.

She was seven years old. It was the first time in the two years following her parents' divorce that she'd been alone with her father for more than a few hours. He'd rented a cabin in a tiny village called Strawberry, high in the Sierras east of Sonora, California. At night she lay in bed and listened to him typing on his portable typewriter. Tara slept in an adjacent room. Often, she'd wake up and hear him working, sometimes pacing the floor, sometimes clicking away at the keyboard, and she'd wondered when he ever slept. He was always there early in the morning, cooking breakfast, teasing her about being a sleepyhead.

During the day, they hiked up to Pinecrest Lake where he taught her to fish. He'd bought her a fly rod of her own, wanting her to become a real angler, not a "worm drowner," as he called the other kind of anglers. Though the big rod was cumbersome for her she got so she could cast a dozen feet of dry line, straight and flat and quiet, out onto the water.

They fished side by side from a clear bank, where the water was deep only two or three feet out from shore, and there was no brush behind them to snag the leader. They caught three trout the first day, one of them on Tara's fly rod. She hadn't wanted to kill her fish. She'd wanted to take it home, put it in an aquarium and keep it as a pet. But Drake convinced her that some fish were meant as pets and some were meant to be eaten, and the fish they were catching were for eating. He showed her how to make a bed of tender ferns on the bottom of the woven reed creel. He helped her lay the firm bodies of the trout on ferns, then cover them over with damp ferns to keep them cool and fresh.

At night she helped him clean the fish, dust them with flour, and fry them in a big pan with butter until they were crisp and golden brown. She didn't like how the fish smelled when they were cleaning them but she liked how they smelled when they were cooking. Later, father and daughter sat at a plank table on the porch and ate fish. He deboned the trout for her neatly, and she pulled the tender white flesh apart in her fingers, putting little bite-sized chunks into her mouth, talking endlessly as she chewed. She told him about all her friends at school, about Jenny whose mother rode horses--English horses that jump over walls, she said--and Sierra whose father was a *hippy* who wrote poetry and lived in an old bus up in Portland. She talked about Mommy's friend, who taught biology at the college and had his students cut up frogs and make their legs jump with a battery, even though they were dead. She had seen it *really happen*, she'd said, because Mommy took her to his class to watch it.

Drake had listened intently, smiling, watching her eat and talk, saying nothing when she wiped her greasy fingers on her jeans. Her mother would have reprimanded her sternly for that. Looking back on it now, Tara wondered how Drake had felt that night when she told him about her mother's friend. She wondered if he'd been tempted to ask questions about his ex-wife's lover, to assuage his curiosity. But he never probed, never did anything that summer to spoil their time together.

As an adult Tara had learned about male jealousy. Even Tom had struggled with it after they broke up. He told Tara he had never wanted to marry her. Yet, he had probed. He had called often, wanting to know if she was dating. He called even after he married Margarette. Tara wondered what impulse for self-torture made divorced men obsess about their ex-wives' love life. Even more, she wondered why little children always managed to bring up such sensitive subjects. She was fairly sure it wasn't all that innocent.

Tara remembered sitting at the log table on the porch that summer long past, talking to Drake about her mother's friend. She knew that hadn't been innocent. She remembered watching Drake's

face out of the tops of her eyes, looking for something, some reaction, she knew not what. But as far as she could recall, he'd never
shown any jealousy and as she thought about it now she realized that
she'd been disappointed then. All he'd said to her, when she was
done, was: "You must like biology." Perhaps it was his way of getting
away from this talk about Mommy's friends. It had been a graceful
way to change the subject and escape the uncomfortable edge of his
own jealousy.

She remembered how she had answered her father, that yes, she
did like biology. She didn't like it when they cut frogs apart. But
since they were dead she guessed it wasn't hurting them. She'd
paused, poked at the tail fin of the ravaged trout on her plate, then
had asked, "Does it?" Drake had smiled and said no. Even now she
felt embarrassed by what she'd next asked her father.

"Do you like mommy's friend?"

He'd answered with a shrug, then: "I'm glad she has a friend that
you like, too." Today, Tara was sure it hadn't been easy for him to
say that.

She had smiled. "But I don't like what he does to frogs."

"I suppose the frogs don't either."

There was another long pause, and she had watched her father,
resting her head on her forearm, looking away from him, into the
distance, then back. "He's not my dad."

That had been the end of it.

It had been an idyllic summer, and whenever Tara got low, even
many years later, she recalled that time to her memory. Even now,
driving across the New Mexico desert alone, the memory raised her
spirits, though it also filled her with melancholy. It was, after all, the
one and only time in her early childhood that they'd been that close.
She had grown up too quickly, and as she moved into adolescence a
bewildering distance grew between them, when she would not even
return his phone calls. Even then, however, she often recalled that
wonderful summer with him, at the lake in the mountains. She
remembered it in a bittersweet way, wanting to be close but never
allowing herself to dream it could really happen.

Now thinking about Maya, Tara wondered if, as a mother, she
was duplicating Drake's pattern. Viveka was the mother this time,
Tara the distant parent, like the father who had slipped in and out of
her own life like a ghost. Was it really that way? Impulsively, Tara
reached for the cell phone clipped to the car's console, then glanced
at the clock and realized it was way too early to call. With an hour's
time difference between them, Maya and Viveka would be sound
asleep.

So much had changed. So much had stayed the same.

As Tara drove west out of Zuni that morning, her longing for her daughter was overshadowed by questions about Drake's remarks concerning the mysterious village and the meeting with the Katchinas. What he described on the diskette, about his encounters with these beings, sounded like something from a fantasy novel. Or, if real, it was possible that he had stumbled upon the legendary society of shamans which she was certain existed out there somewhere.

But what about Chocko's suggestions that Drake had somehow ingested an hallucinogen or--as he insisted on calling it, an entheogen. Chocko had spoken of *entheogenic* substances like peyote and *auyahuasca*, that the high priests of ancient civilizations once used to strip away the illusions of everyday life, presumably allowing them to see God. And she remembered *ergot*, a fungus that grows on rye, which reportedly aided the ancient Christian and Jewish visionaries.

Was it possible, then, that something in the cave Drake was exploring, a dust, a fungus growing on the rock walls, something, had triggered her father's visions of the ancient people and the Katchinas? Surely that was a more reasonable explanation than Chocko's theories about mysterious entities from another reality.

She could not afford to disregard any of this. Myths and superstitions all too often proved to be more than fantasies invented by a prescientific society. They were glimpses into other realities.

Other realities! Those two words had taken on new meaning in the last few days. The boarded up house on the mesa where Drake had obviously been living was another reality, not one where Tara felt comfortable. Similarly, seeing the looter digging in the ground at the abandoned house, then watching his mangled Jeep snaked up on a long cable from the rocky canyon were not events that she ordinarily found in her daily life.

Like the ravens lifting briefly from a dead pinon tree, then settling down on new branches to see life from a different angle, Tara tried to settle herself into this other reality. Perhaps, she reasoned, the shamans were correct, that only by shifting perspective, as the ravens did, could she begin to grasp what was happening. She instinctively knew that she was missing something important, and would continue to miss it, as long as she clung to the familiar and secure reasoning of her everyday life.

But where could she even begin to get a different perspective? What was the new *branch* that she should seek? Tara thought about Charla Mather, a woman whose reality could not have been more different than her own. Charla was a wealthy woman and a dealer in antique Indian artifacts. As an anthropologist, Tara could not fathom how a person could exploit the ancient past like that. What was Charla's view of reality? What would it be like to share the branch from which that woman viewed the world?

With wealth came power, visibility, and fame, at least fame within a certain limited circle. Charla's wealth might have made her a target. Maybe she had been robbed, her car stolen and stripped, prompting her and Drake to change their plans, to board up their house and sail off to god-knows-where. But wouldn't Drake have thought to notify Tara of these changes in their plans?

Like the raven, Tara imagined herself lifting on the wind, circling around each event she'd encountered over the past few days. She imagined herself at the motel in Albuquerque, watching the old TV movie, oversleeping and receiving a visit from Tom and Margarette, of driving to Gallup, then Coyote Mesa and finally up to Charla's, of finding Drake's disk, watching the destruction of the Medicine Wheel in the garden, and spending the night in the cave. She imagined herself flying over the canyon where the Jeep had mysteriously crashed. She imagined seeing it moments before the crash, coming up the mountain, through the switch backs, the silvery beams of its headlamps cutting through the darkness. From the raven's eye view of her daydream, the beams were long pillars of light jitter-bugging across the landscape. But the Jeep was not alone! A second car, traveling faster, approached at high speed from the rear. Rain pelted down upon the cars; it pelted on the wings of the raven, too. And what raven saw was a deadly duel between two metal creatures, racing along the winding ribbon of pavement far below.

Then they hit. There were sparks, and the raven circled closer, finding a new perch on a turret of rock, affording her a perfect view. The Jeep spun out of control, careened across the road, struck the shoulder and lifted into the air, as if to fly. Its long pillars of light shot toward the moon, then suddenly sank and were extinguished. A thunderous roar and a shriek of steel meeting rock startled the raven. She rose on panicked wings and fled.

Tara clutched the steering wheel, her fingers curled around the cold plastic. Her vision blurred, the dark ribbon of road becoming a mere abstraction. She slowed, pulled over to the side and stopped. Setting the transmission in Park, she leaned back in her seat and rolled down the window. She took a deep breath, closed her eyes and slumped forward.

What could be happening to her? The raven's flight above the crash sight had been pure imagination, an unguarded moment when she slipped into a pure dream state. Daydreams. Surely that was it! Nothing more. As an anthropologist, she'd always been careful about projecting too much into the known facts. She was disciplined, never reading too much into the artifacts dug up at an ancient site. Cultural anthropology required some imagination, but caution had to be taken to avoid wrenching the facts.

And now this. This was a perfect case of wrenching the facts, allowing her imagination to take over, to pull her into a prolonged daydream in which reality completely dissolved. A good scientist didn't allow that to happen. There was a fine line between the educated guesses of a disciplined academician and the fanciful flights of delusion that shamans employed to manipulate the primitive mind. She wondered if she'd crossed that line--and why. Sleep deprivation? No, the truth was she'd slept very well last night, long and deep, probably because she'd slept so fitfully the night before, in the cave behind Charla's house. In fact, her lack of sleep could not account for what she thought she'd seen at Charla's.

A huge truck rattled past, startling Tara and shaking her violently out of her reverie. The car rocked in the truck's draft. She had to move on. She had promised to meet Winfield before seven a.m. She glanced at the clock. She had twenty-three minutes to make her appointment. After that, Winfield might not talk with her. She reached forward, set the car into gear and pressed the accelerator. The car leapt forward, onto the pavement, and in seconds she was racing on again, cruising at sixty five miles an hour.

As she drove, concentrating on the road ahead of her, she was amused more than shocked by her imaginary journeys with raven. Odd, she thought, what the human mind was capable of doing. Certainly there was nothing wrong with amusing herself this way, flying off with raven to explore different perspectives. Wasn't that, after all, what poets and novelists did? All dreamers knew this other world, though most assuredly it was completely fabricated, a world made of legends and myths whose meanings were more symbolic than tangible.

In ancient times, prior to the development of scientific disciplines, primitive people protected themselves and their sacred sites by fabricating powerful myths. The primitive mind, researchers had shown, did not distinguish between reality and fantasy. That single fact, she speculated, might account for why ancient civilizations, based on intuitive principles, had fallen to the Europeans with their more pragmatic and exploitive mentality. The primitives' weapons of fear and superstition, so effective with their own people, were no match for the spears and gunpowder of the empirical forces--the Spaniards, the English and the French who invaded their borders.

Centuries ago--in the late 1500s and after, Spanish missionaries and adventurers had come to this area, drawn by stories about the Seven Cities of Cibola. They believed the legends they'd heard of these mythical cities of gold, discounting as mere delusions the grim tales of fearsome retribution that were said to befall anyone who dared desecrate these sacred sites. Though early conquests turned up none of the legendary caches of gold, the stories of their existence never died. From time to time new grave sites were discovered, and all too soon were pillaged by opportunists driven by selfish gain.

True, the Conquistadors had not found what they'd come for but had nevertheless pillaged the cities they discovered, stealing whatever treasures they could find and leaving a bloody wake behind them. The legends of fear that had protected the sacred lands and artifacts for centuries had been no match for the bloodthirsty, gold-yearning Spaniards. Or had they? History showed some power remained in those ancient tales, for the fall of the Spanish empire was not long in coming.

Tara pulled her mind back into the present. Speeding across the desert, she spotted an object in the middle of the highway. She slowed immediately, peering forward to try to make out what it might be. As she drew closer, two dark objects rose into the sky, circling above the carrion that lay plastered almost flat against the pavement. A rabbit, she guessed, as she passed it. "Ravens," she said aloud, looking up, surprised to discover that the dark birds who feasted on the putrid flesh were not vultures. "My life is being invaded by ravens!"

Her foot shot to the brake pedal again. There, not a hundred feet past where the ravens had been feeding she saw the turnoff to the Winfield ranch. Had she not slowed in deference to the birds, she might have sped by. "Thanks, my shadowy friends," she said aloud, amused by the coincidence.

The road to Winfield's ranch was marked only by a single mailbox, the usual dome-topped metal box on a post, with its familiar metal arm and red flag. It was bent and weathered, with the hand-lettered name half gone. Tara turned in, surveying with some caution the narrow road ahead. It was rutty and littered with rocks. The sight of the road made her wish she'd rented a 4-wheel drive vehicle, or at least one with more ground clearance than the Camaro she drove. She now understood something Chocko had told her about Winfield after he got off the phone last night. Chocko had said Winfield would be in the barn replacing a broken axle on his truck. It all made sense, now. A road as bad as this one would certainly take its toll on the best machinery.

As she navigated through the endless ruts and rocks that defined the road, Tara thought about what she'd ask Winfield. She wondered if he actually believed in these UFO's he claimed to have seen, and if he did, how much of his information would actually help her in finding Drake. Her own belief was that Winfield had seen something but not something from outer space. Rather, it was the product of human engineering; perhaps it was a closely guarded experiment. And somehow, Drake had gotten himself in trouble by sticking his nose into something that was none of his business. For the first time, it occurred to her that Guy Perry's operation might be a cover up for something more momentous.

Winfield's road took her over a mile from the main highway. As she turned behind a promontory of rock, she spied several buildings a few hundred yards away. A large corrugated metal garage over a strip of new concrete held a shiny Cadillac. Behind it there was a modular home which Tara guessed could not be more than two years old, judging by the fact that the paint had not yet been faded by the sun. The Cadillac seemed oddly out of place. Perhaps it belonged to house guests, to a wealthy brother from Albuquerque or Santa Fe or to some other visitor. Beyond the house another hundred yards or so was a large metal building with a horse corral that stretched out to either side and beyond it. At one end of the building, through two large doors, she saw a man bent over the left front wheel of a truck.

She drove past the house and parked a few feet back from the corral. The man turned his head and watched as she got out of her car and approached. He made no gesture of greeting.

"Mr. Winfield?"

"Yes, Ma'am."

"I'm Chocko's friend. I believe he called you."

"Yeah. I figured."

Winfield sat on a wooden box and leaned his right shoulder against the rusty front fender of the truck. Rather than looking at her, he poked at the axle with the end of his wrench. Tara said nothing. For a long time he just studied the ground. When he finally looked up his mouth was twisted and tight on one side, as if part of it wanted to speak, the other to remain silent.

"I don't like talking about them...what you've come to ask about. Some people already think I'm crazy, or a liar."

"I wouldn't have come here if I'd thought you were either," Tara assured him. "I believe my father saw the same things you saw the day he disappeared. You're the only lead I've got."

"Maybe we were wrong, you know? Sometimes the desert light plays tricks on you."

"That's what I'm inclined to believe."

"It was raining real hard."

"But in the newspaper you said you saw it clearly. Chocko showed me the interview they did with you."

"The papers! No matter what you tell them it comes out completely cockeyed."

"Then you didn't see what it said you did?"

"It ain't that. Lots of times you see the lights around here, like I said." He sat back for a moment and waved his wrench toward the sky. "Most people have seen them. When you see the lights, the others usually show up."

"You mean the saucers, what you believe are UFO's?"

"I know what I saw, and they were not from this world."

"Chocko says the FAA reported there weren't any aircraft in the area that day. No helicopters, no experimental planes. Nothing. So maybe what you saw was a light, someone playing tricks on you."

Winfield pressed his thumb against his lips for a moment, as if pondering what she'd said, weighing his words before he spoke: "Here's the way it is," he said. "Any time there's been a report like this, the *gover'ment* comes out here and talks to the papers. They've got it all figured. They've got a whole detail that does nothing but that, deciding how they're going to handle these things. They make you out like a fool. They interview you, then tell the papers their own story, and they make it sound like you made the whole thing up. They make you look bad... stupid, or crazy, or drunk...or some kind of back country bumpkin. I'm none of those, I can assure you. Like our mutual friend Chocko, I had a very different life before I came out here."

He paused, perhaps questioning how much he should tell her about this other life of his, Tara reasoned. Then, apparently deciding to abandon that subject, he went on with his story of the sighting.

"They purposely cast doubt on your story, and attack your character. You see what I'm saying? No matter what, they make you out something you're not. They couldn't care less about you and your family. They just put it across that it all just came out of your own head. I'm not one to play the fool, Miss Fairfield. But these guys, they ruin you. They just ruin you."

"You said there were three strange lights at first?"

"Yeah. Three of them. "

Winfield had shifted his attention back to the axle. Tara stared at the ground under the truck. The jack had sunk a few inches into the dirt. She caught herself wondering if it was going to sink any further, and if it was a danger to Winfield.

"People believe whatever they want to believe about me," Winfield said. "Can't do anything about that."

"Listen, I'm sorry. I really am. I don't think it's a coincidence that my father called me and left a message on the same day you spotted the UFO."

"He's seen them, too?"

"I don't know. I know he's been down here several times looking for them."

"I'm not one of those UFO fanatics, let me tell you that."

"I don't think my father is, either. He's a...a sort of researcher. I think he'd really like to find some good evidence, one way or another..."

"They're real, Miss. Take it from me, they're real."

Winfield swiveled around on the wooden box and leaned his back against the fender. He picked up a wrench and began slapping it gently against his palm. "You think your father could have been...what do you call it?"

"Abducted." The word sounded strange on her lips. She almost laughed out loud.

"Look, Miss, I'm not a delusional old man. I know what I saw and I was not having a pipe dream."

"I'm on your side, Mr. Winfield."

"Where have I heard that before!"

"Have other people interviewed you?"

"Yeah. Other people have interviewed me. Several others. None of them have done me any favors, either. I told our friend Chocko I'd talk to you because he said you weren't a reporter, you weren't from the *government*, and you weren't a UFO-nik. But I promised my wife I'd never talk to nobody else. You're the last one, and she's got a red ass about that, too."

"I'm sorry. I didn't mean to cause any trouble."

"No? Well, this whole damn thing is trouble. But I'll make you a deal. I'll tell you the whole story. Then you go away and don't ever bother us again. Don't ever come back and don't ever call, even though you are a friend of Chocko's. That will be the end of it. After that, it's as if none of it ever happened. No more talk. It's out of my life."

"Can you really just dismiss it like that?"

"I guess you didn't hear me."

"But I don't see..."

"Miss, let me say it one more time. I will tell you the story. But that's the end of it. No more talk about it. No more calls."

Tara nodded.

Satisfied at last, Winfield stared at the ground between his feet and probed the earth with his wrench. "Like the paper said, we were running down some sheep that got broke away from the main flock. I rent some grazing rights back in the canyons there. You'd be surprised at the vegetation back in that spot. You'd never guess it from the road.

"It was me and John Baler that day. Up on Spider Mesa. It's high up, you know? You can see for miles from there. It was around two or three in the afternoon. The lights came along first, just these balls of light. They're not like anything you've ever seen. Nothing I've ever seen. John Baler said the same thing."

"How close were you?"

"Oh, pretty close. Maybe a quarter mile. The lights flew right along the ridge there, actually below us. We were looking down at the time, and there they were."

"Was there a sense that anything piloted the lights, controlled them in any way, you know, like a beacon of some kind?"

Winfield shook his head. "Like I said, they weren't anything like I've ever seen before. John said they acted like they were radio controlled, you know, like those model planes kids have these days. I figure they were scouting the territory, making sure it was safe."

"Do you think they saw you, detected your presence somehow?"

"Now how would I know that! They didn't shoot at us or anything, if that's what you mean. They didn't try to scare us off. Like we both said in the papers, we saw this bright light coming in from the southeast. And then the bigger one showed. At first there was this darkness, this really incredible blackness in the sky, not like a cloud or anything man-made. Then the ship come up like the sun shining through the clouds, you know, like something bursting out of that blackness. It moved toward us pretty fast, too. First we figured it was some kind of aircraft. We've seen that Stealth bomber out here. A lot of people saw that. And it's like nothing you've ever seen. But this wasn't a Stealth.

"The light kept getting brighter, like a huge spotlight or maybe a cluster of halogen landing lights like some airplanes have these days. We watched it while it got closer, then the light changed. It shaped itself into a diamond, a sort of four-cornered, stretched out rectangle, like this." With the end of his wrench he drew a diamond shape in the dirt between his feet.

"It was maybe twenty feet thick and maybe sixty, seventy feet in diameter. The light wasn't anything ordinary. I'd never seen anything that bright and...dense. A dense light, you know what I mean? But the light was cold, not hot like you'd expect it to be. Even when you looked right into it, it didn't hurt your eyes. Anything else that bright would have scorched out your eyeballs."

Winfield became silent. He got up from his box and knelt down in front of the broken axle. Then he placed his wrench over a greasy nut somewhere under the fender and tugged away at it. The truck rocked precariously on the jack. The nut finally gave way and Winfield lurched backwards, cursing. In a second he withdrew his hand. The first two knuckles were bleeding profusely, mingling with the black grease that covered his hands. He wiped the blood away with a greasy red rag from the back pocket of his coveralls.

Winfield ignored the bloodied knuckles. He leaned back under the truck and retrieved his wrench, placing it on the same nut again. It went easier this time, and in a moment the entire front axle assembly dropped to the ground. Only then did he turn back to Tara.

"It's funny. After staring at that light, my eyes got better. I can see better now than I have in years. I used to wear glasses to read the paper but I don't anymore. They just got better right that day. When I got home that night I could read the paper with no trouble at all."

Winfield walked over to his workbench and dipped his hands in a pan of greasy gasoline. When he removed them he wiped each finger with a clean rag. The bleeding knuckles of his right hand dripped onto the ground at his feet. But he didn't seem concerned about his wound.

He sat back down on the box and leaned against the side of the truck. "This UFO came out of the center of the light. I know this much for sure--it was metal, real shiny metal. Wafer-shaped, maybe like two giant soup bowls placed face to face."

He stopped and cupped his hands together, gesturing to show how it had moved. "It came toward us, hovered overhead and tipped from side to side, like pilots do to say hello to someone on the ground. As it got closer, there was no noise whatsoever. That was peculiar. I figured it was something from a very advanced sort of world, not like our own. No sound. In fact, it seemed to soak up all sound and any sense of movement around there. It was peaceful for a while, you know? I never in my life experienced anything like that, and sometimes I wish I could again. Just a real peacefulness.

"As it came through the clouds, the light shrinks, like it's getting focused. Pretty soon it's just this slit in the sky, spread out maybe three-quarters of a mile. You understand? The saucer came out of the center of the light, and then the light was closing behind it, like a door sliding closed in the sky.

"Once the light closed like that, the saucer moved to a flat area west of us. It moved slowly, like a pilot was scouting for just the right landing place. Like maybe there was this special place already marked out. Finally, it descended and as it came down it raised a lot of dust devils all around it. The dust was odd because the desert floor was all wet, even muddy. It had been raining four days. I figure the spacecraft was drying out the desert floor, causing the dust.

"John Baler's truck was pretty tore up. Looked like somebody had taken to it with a ballpeen hammer. Fenders all dinged up, headlamps knocked out, windows shattered. The insurance company is saying John did something just to collect the insurance. Hell, that doesn't make any sense at all. But what are you going to tell an insurance company cop, you know? Well, it was caused by space aliens... What are they going to say to that back at the main office?"

"Wait," Tara interrupted. "What damaged the truck?"

"It was like chunks of the desert floor. It's all rock out there on the mesa. You go out there, the ground's burned. The saucer come in there, cooked the ground and it all chipped away, fried it, sort of."

"Fried it?"

"It wasn't like rocks any more. Whatever it was fried the rocks and left nothing but these little round cinders, hard as diamonds. I kept a handful of them but my wife made me throw them away, said they were bad luck. She's superstitious about those things."

"Superstitious in what way?"

"It comes from her people. She's a Hopi woman, part Hopi anyway. She thinks they're the Katchinas coming in from other planets. They believe this, you know, that the Katchinas are reincarnated souls who now live on other planets. They come in to teach us their religion. Her family tells these stories about ships from the sky. Her grandfather saw them, just like me, about seventy-five years ago, and he died within the year. She's afraid I'm going to die now. She won't look me in the eye, says she sees death in me."

"I'm sure you'll be all right."

"You are, eh! You obviously don't know this country, do you?"

"Are you saying you think you're going to die?"

"I ain't saying one way or another. But John Baler, he doesn't believe in any of that sort of thing and he's come awful close. This here axle, you see this? It's broke off right at the knuckle there. If I'd been on some of these roads back here when it went, I'd be down in the bottom of a canyon now, feeding the vultures. You think that's an accident?"

"I don't know. You said this man who was with you..."

"John, yeah. Between you and me? John's been a good friend but I'm not telling secrets out of school when I say he's had his problems with liquor. After the incident up there on the mesa, he went back to it. He'd been a good friend and a good dependable worker for nearly two years. I've hired him off and on, a day or two here and there. It's a damn shame. I liked John."

"Meaning you don't anymore? I don't understand."

"Meaning he drove off the road into a tree two days ago."

"He's dead?"

Winfield shook his head. "Not dead but might as well be. His truck's gone. It's all he had. He's gone back to hanging around the reservation. People feed him, maybe give him a place to sleep. They'll leave him alone, tolerate him. But it's tough being a white man on the reservation like that, beholden to people like he is."

"I'm sorry."

"Something like this either drives you crazy or drives you to God."

"And which has it been for you?"

"I have my own ways of dealing with it."

"Which are?"

"My wife and her folks believe we've been visited like this for a long time. It's not religious the way you might think. There are things we can't explain. There are things the old people know, from the past. There are even things that happen today that can't be explained. The shamans know. These beings, my wife says, they take over our minds, sort of block our memories and teach us what they know."

"Block our memories? I don't understand."

"Take us over, invade our minds. Just listen to this. Every three years the Indians hold a ceremony out east of here a few miles. No white man has ever gone there. My wife and me was married maybe eight years before she ever told me about it. She doesn't follow the old ways but it sticks in your way of thinking, you know? In fact, it's not just whites that can't go out there. There are only a half-dozen or so Indian men who can go, because they were brought up with it since they were children. They say it's another world. They enter it, who knows how? It's not a place I'd go if I got the chance. They say people from these UFOs go up there for a little pow wow every year.

"There's a whole world there--sun, moon, even stars in the sky. Maybe if all this is so, I'm okay. You know? I saw something that's been going on for thousands of years. Maybe I'm in some way chosen special to see at least part of it, and that means I'm not crazy."

Winfield turned back to the work he was doing on the truck. He looked over his shoulder and smiled. "You think that sounds pretty crazy, don't you?"

"Where is this place you're talking about?"

"You're not allowed out there. It's sacred land. I wouldn't risk it if I did know exactly where it is."

"Does your wife know? Could I talk with her?"

"She's not around. She's with her mother at Indian market."

Tara was silent for a moment, her mind racing. She knew Winfield was lying about one thing, at least: his wife's whereabouts. Indian market was in August, not October. "Do you believe this UFO you saw was going to this place you're talking about?"

"That's what the old people are saying. They're the only ones who don't think I'm crazy."

"Could you draw me a map?"

Winfield shook his head. "The old ones say it is east of here, and south. But there are ceremonies for getting there. Without them, you'll never find the place. And even if you did, you'd never come back."

"And that's it, that's all you can tell me?"

"You promised if I told you, you'd go away and stop bothering me. That's the bargain."

This was clearly the end of their conversation. Like the man of his word that he was, he turned his full attention to the repair of his truck. He leaned under the fender, tugging at a long metal rod while the truck rocked precariously on the jack.

"Thank you," she mumbled, disappointed with what she'd learned. Windfield was silent. She turned and walked back to her car. As she opened the door, she heard a gentle tapping of metal against metal, a curse, then a sigh of relief. Winfield pulled loose the broken front axle and dragged it out from under the truck. That done, he stood up beside the fender, wiped his brow on the back of his wrist and watched Tara as she backed out of the driveway and turned toward the highway again. Tara waved. Winfield nodded, then stooped over and went back to work. ~

Spirit Circle

Pursued

As Tara approached the highway she spotted a black car parked at the junction. Drawing nearer, she saw a yellow sticker on the windshield and thought it was the same car she'd seen at the party store, and later at the compound where she'd been confronted by Guy Perry and the two nervous young soldiers. Two men sat in the front seat of this car. It was on the shoulder of the highway, pointing in the direction Tara planned to go, back to Zuni. As she slowed, then stopped, the black car's occupants continued to stare impassively forward, showing no apparent interest in her. Even so, their presence hardly put her at ease. Tara tried to see if the driver was Guy Perry, but as near as she could tell it wasn't. Both the driver and his passenger wore dark glasses even though it was a cloudy day. She studied the two men for a moment, wondered what they could possibly want.

Tara remembered the polished white tank inside the building back at the military compound near Coyote Mesa. Did the man...the creature inside have anything to do with the story Winfield had just related? Maybe the Roswell story, claiming that the government had actually captured and was holding a space alien was true. Unlikely. Highly unlikely! But even if it was true, why would anyone care that she was poking around, asking questions? Unless...unless there was a tie-in between them and Drake's disappearance.

She turned onto the highway and accelerated to 60, then 75 miles per hour. The black car stayed behind. Then, a mile up the road Tara checked her rear view mirror. The black car was moving up swiftly behind her. Her eyes dropped to her speedometer. She was doing 80, already twenty-five miles over the posted speed limit. The black car closed in, tailgating and giving no indication that it wanted to pass though the road ahead was clear.

For a mile, then two, then three, then twelve, it followed her, following too close, whether she sped up or slowed. Obviously they wanted her to know they were following her. But why? If they had business with her why didn't they pull her over? With government license plates, they presumably could exercise that right.

Though they were close enough for her to make out the general features of the occupants' faces, they were not close enough for her to identify them if she met them on the street. The one in the passenger's seat, however, was bald headed. Even from that distance, and through their tinted windshield she could see his shiny dome, like a fleshy globe. The driver was dark-skinned, with a full head of very black hair, a light colored African-American possibly, but more likely of Indian descent.

Tara reached for her cell phone, switched it on, pressed it to her ear and started to dial Chocko's number. In the mirror she saw what appeared to be a phone pressed to the ear of the passenger in the black car. It could be a coincidence but she didn't think so. More likely they had tuned in to her cell phone channel and were ready to listen in on her conversations. She switched off her own phone and placed it back in the bracket on the console. When she looked up, the man in the car behind her was no longer holding the phone to his ear.

Clearly, they were trying to intimidate her. But they were doing it in a way that was difficult to pin down. She thought about stopping in Zuni, at the most populous spot she could find, perhaps at the convenience store or in front of the museum on the north end of town. She'd get out, and as other people hopefully looked on she'd confront her pursuers. The idea that two men were harassing a single woman kindled her sense of outrage. She'd read them the riot act. She might be a single woman but they wouldn't be the first men who'd backed down from one of her tirades against male bullying.

They drove for ten minutes or more, with Tara constantly glancing up to watch the black car. Always it kept the same distance. Up ahead she caught her first glimpse of the rooftops of Zuni, still a few miles away. She reached for the phone again but hesitated. She had an idea. She pressed the phone to her ear and watched in the rear view mirror. The bald man in the car behind her also pressed his phone to his ear. Now, she held the phone in front of her so that the people in the black car would be sure to see. Then she pretended to dial it. Without turning it on she waited a second and pressed the instrument to her ear. Making a big show of it, she pretended to be carrying on an animated conversation. In the rear view mirror she saw the bald man shaking his phone, pressing different buttons, and obviously getting quite irritated. She continued to talk to her make-believe caller a moment then set the phone down again.

Once more she pretended to dial the phone for another number. Again the man in the car behind her picked up his phone and started pressing buttons and tapping his phone against the dashboard. Her trick had worked! The bald headed man tossed his phone into the back seat and became very animated, talking to the driver.

Now Tara lowered the phone, pretending to hang it up. Meanwhile she held it in her lap, making a great effort to appear as if she was staring straight ahead. She dialed Chocko's number and turned up the volume of her phone as high as it would go.

"Hello?" She barely heard Chocko's voice, but it would have to do.

"This is Tara," she shouted, holding the phone at chest level, trying her best to disguise her movements. "Meet me at the convenience store in three minutes. It's an emergency. I'm being followed."

"I'll be there!"

Tara eased the phone back onto the clip on the console. Meanwhile, the black car pulled up beside her. The passenger rolled down his window and held out an opened wallet containing a badge. He waved it in the window with his right hand, gesturing with his left for Tara to pull over. She squinted back at the badge and shook her head. The man gestured even more vociferously back at her. Instead, she pressed the accelerator to the floor and pulled in front of their car just as they passed the sign announcing they were entering Zuni, where the speed limit was 25 miles per hour. She glanced down at the speedometer. The needle floated near 70!

Tara wondered if she had unwittingly violated some rule of conduct. Was the car legitimately patrolling reservation property? If so, she was in for some real trouble. The reservation police were not known for their compassion for outsiders who violated their traffic laws. She nervously ran through a mental checklist, trying to recall if there was something she'd done. She slowed, eased toward the shoulder, and the wheels on the right side of the car pulled hard in the loose dirt. For a second she wrestled with the steering wheel, and in that instant a vivid picture came into her mind of the man in the Jeep, back toward Fence Lake, grappling with his steering wheel at maybe fifty miles an hour, losing it, and then plunging into the canyon. For an instant she knew what that man must have felt, the moment of clammy fear, followed by the moment when he was certain everything was going to be okay, and then the fear again as the car left the road and there was nothing under him but air. Then the crash, steel pounding sickeningly against rock and then a buzzing in his ears, in his brain, and then nothing.

How did she know this? A new kind of terror spread over her. Generally, her imagination did not carry her into other people's minds like this. She was not particularly known for her sensitivity to other people's thoughts and feelings, unless it happened to be those of her daughter or a current lover. Suddenly she became aware of her hands, clammy and cold on the steering wheel. Something told her not to stop. She pressed the accelerator to the floor. Her car fishtailed onto the blacktop again, straightened out and raced forward. She was approaching the residential section of the town now and she relaxed slightly, scanning the road ahead for Chocko's truck. Nothing.

The image of the Jeep sailing over the edge of the road filled her mind again, and she questioned why she so closely empathized with the driver in the crash. Somewhere she'd seen the Jeep before, not just on the road up at Coyote Mesa but in some totally different context. She'd seen two Jeeps that day with the same color, except that one had a hardtop, the other only a canvas roof. Two entirely different models.

The black car had dropped in behind her, keeping its distance, as they moved toward the center of town. Tara felt relieved. Maybe it would be all right. Her thoughts returned to the mystery of the Jeeps. She could not quite grasp why it had suddenly become such an issue for her, except that she suspected the black car might have been involved in the crash. And then the image of the Jeep popped into her mind. Tom! Tom had a Jeep like that. She'd seen it in a photograph he'd sent to Maya more than a year ago. It was a good quality color photo and Tara was certain the Jeep's color was exactly the same as the others she'd seen. She'd been shocked to see the photo because the vehicle was brand new and Tom had complained for over a year about not having much money. His child support payment had been late three months in a row.

The horror of Tom being the driver of the Jeep that went over the cliff struck her hard. Her mind spun with a turmoil of thoughts. If it was him, what was he doing on that road? He'd sworn to her that he knew nothing about Coyote Mesa. And if that Jeep was his, it meant that he was the one who'd scraped the side of her car that night. And if he was the driver of that Jeep, he was also the person who dug in the garden at Charla's that night. It did not seem likely. And yet, something about it all fit together. Why? Why did it fit together? She couldn't get the question out of her mind. She was certain the man who'd dug in the garden, and who carried away what might have been a treasure, was dark-skinned. So, it could not have been Tom. But the cop at the crash site had said nothing about the deceased driver's race.

Maybe she was trying too hard to make a link. The only possible link was that there were three Jeeps, all painted with the same custom color. Why would Tom have one of these Jeeps? The coincidence of the color and the locale where they'd shown up was too implausible. There had to be a connection. How were the three related?

She spotted the convenience store off to her left, a block up the road. She glanced down at the speedometer. She was doing 40, the black car still on her tail. Where was Chocko's truck? It wasn't on the gravel apron in front of the store, nor did she see it on the opposite side of the road. Without warning, her mind took a quantum leap, completely abandoning all concern for her own safety. Ancient treasures and shiny new Jeeps--the two came together in her consciousness. She remembered Tom's effort to steal the ancient gold treasure he'd dug up in the archaeological dig where they'd worked down in Peru. And she recalled his paper proposing that the ancient cities of Cibola had actually existed, but in caves the Spaniards had missed during their invasion of this area in the Middle Ages. The gold! The lure of gold...

Chocko's truck shot out of a side street and cut across in front of her. In the back, seated in the bed of the truck, were five very burly looking gentlemen in work clothes. They waved at her, grinning, and she waved back. She turned left and pulled in to the right of them, directly in front of the convenience store. She pulled on the emergency brake and shut off the engine just as the black car pulled in to the right of her. She flipped the little switch on the console that automatically locked both doors.

Tara watched as the driver of the black car and his bald-headed passenger got out and strode toward her. The driver kept on his dark glasses and posted himself at her passenger door while the bald headed one removed his glasses and came around to the other side. He tapped at her window and she rolled it down a couple inches, just enough to hear what he might have to say.

"Yes sir?" she asked.

The man reached to the inside pocket of his jacket and drew out his wallet again and as he did she spotted the shoulder holster pressed neatly under his left arm. It was a small, automatic weapon and the leather holster looked well worn. Tara stared at the badge as he pressed it to the glass, her vision blurring, making it impossible to read the etched name of the department he was associated with.

Over the man's shoulder she noticed the workmen slipping down over the tailgate of Chocko's truck and easing around along the narrow space between their vehicle and her car. One man pressed around behind the man with the badge, winking to Tara as he did. This one posted himself at her left front fender, leaning against it casually. He held a shovel in his hand, the spade pointing up toward the sky. She watched as two others walked around the front and then stationed themselves at her right, leaning boldly against the side of the black car. One of them carried a double-headed ax that looked quite lethal, though he rested it casually enough over his left shoulder. His companion, a tall Indian with a long pigtail, grinned ominously, standing uncomfortably close to the driver of the black car.

Before the bald headed man with the badge had a chance to speak to Tara, Chocko appeared at the front of her car. He strode easily over to the man with the badge.

"Any trouble here?" he asked, directing his question to no one in particular.

"Armed Forces Special Services," the man with the badge said, producing the wallet again.

"Yeah?" Chocko said. He reached for the man's wallet, held it firmly, then actually pulled it out of its owner's hand. "Anybody seen any foreign invaders around here?" He glanced around from one of his friends to another. In unison, they all looked down at the ground and shook their heads.

"We're checking on some leads," the owner of the badge said, still reaching out as Chocko rummaged through the contents of his wallet. "It's classified business."

"Really!" Chocko said. "But I'm afraid you've overstepped your authority. This is Indian territory here. You understand that, don't you? You're violating Indian sovereignty. In fact, you're in considerable trouble right now." He carelessly tossed the man's wallet onto the center of Tara's hood. The man started to reach for it, then drew back.

"It's just an inquiry," the bald headed man said, scratching nervously at the beginning of stubble on his chin.

"You clear it with the Council?"

"The Tribal Council? No, sir. It's unofficial, you might say."

"Uh huh," Chocko said. "It looks to me like it might be *very* unofficial. Is this man harassing you, Ma'am?" He looked in Tara's direction, giving no indication that he knew her, his face cold and impassive.

Tara nodded. "They've been following me for several miles."

"I can contact the reservation police if you'd like," Chocko told her, looking very somber but obviously enjoying himself.

"That won't be necessary," the bald headed man said.

"I don't believe that's your decision to make." Chocko moved in closer and Tara rolled down her window. "Do you wish to press charges?" he asked her.

"Not if they promise to leave me alone," she said. "But I'd like to know why they are following me."

Chocko nodded so that both the men from the black car could see him. "The lady wants answers," he said.

"It isn't personal. Look, we can file the necessary papers. It's no problem..."

"You understand this young lady is our guest, and you two are definitely harassing her," Chocko said. "I suggest you pack up and get the hell out of here. The Army isn't welcome here. You haven't been welcome here for three hundred years, and it doesn't look to me you're any more popular now than you were back then."

"I've got no problems with you," the bald headed man said.

"Oh, I wouldn't say that," Chocko said. He glanced from one of his friends to another. "I think we'd better show these men the quickest way out of Indian country." He stepped back and allowed the bald headed man to retrieve his wallet from the hood of Tara's car. Then he waited as the two men got back in the black car and started the engine.

Without a word, the man with the ax, the others with shovels and picks, climbed into the back of Chocko's truck. As the black car backed up, Chocko started the engine of his own truck and pulled in behind them. Slowly, the procession moved forward, heading in the direction of the junction to Gallup where the property line for the Zuni nation ended. Tara leaned her forehead against the top of the steering wheel and let out a long sigh of gratitude and relief.

*　　*　　*

She drove back to Chocko's trailer park, shaken and wondering what the two men in the black car really wanted. Something did not make sense. Actually, a lot of things didn't make sense. Winfield had spoken of government investigators who'd belittled his story and did a very cunning job of covering it up by reporting it first to the tabloids. The men in the black car might have been watching his place. But what would they have wanted of her?

The more she thought about it, the more other pieces of what she'd been told did not correspond with what she'd observed. At the wreck back toward Coyote Mesa, the cop had taken her name and as much as told her she was under suspicion. He also seemed to know that Charla's house was boarded up. But if that was so, Charla and Drake were gone at least a day before Tara even arrived in New Mexico. If the dates in Drake's diary were correct, this was the same period of time that Drake and Charla would have been probing around the ruins.

Tara remembered the black and white photo Drake had sent her, along with the two color snapshots. The black and white print was obviously the work of a professional photographer, probably Jack Milford, the man in the breezy, judging from the elevation it depicted. The two color prints were of a very different quality, however. They had obviously been taken by an amateur. So there were two photographers involved, each with obviously different purposes in mind for their handiwork.

Drake's own notes said he had returned to Charla's house each night after his expeditions into the ruins. Even on those days when Charla was angry with him, Drake reported her being there in the house, smoldering over his activities but nevertheless still there, still in his life. There could be no mistake about it; Drake had definitely been at Charla's house during the time he sent Tara the envelope.

But there was another possibility: Drake's notes said he'd returned "home," and that Charla was there. But what if there was another place he called home in the area, or even a motel or inn where they'd been staying. Still, that didn't explain how the diskette with all this information would have gotten back to the boarded up house at Coyote Mesa. And if the second local house theory were true, why had her father and Charla left all their things behind. The easy explanation was that they had duplicates of everything, that they didn't need the personal items they'd left behind. No, Tara decided, none of this seemed right. Obviously, both Drake and Charla had left in a hurry. The reason why had yet to be discovered.

As she turned into the trailer park, another thought popped into her head. The link between Winfield's statement about the government's going to the tabloids with his story, and Drake's presence in the same area, also seemed an odd coincidence. Drake was the one who was usually contacted by these papers early on, whenever they got a lead. If he'd been reachable the editors would have surely contacted him! He would have been the one to send out for interviews, photos of the area, talk with other eyewitnesses. He would have been working on the story less than a week before he contacted Tara. Surely, if that were the case, he would have been near a functioning phone where he could call in his story to his editor! And she felt certain if he'd stumbled upon this story he would have contacted Tara and told her about it. It also seemed reasonable that there would have been some mention of it in his diary. However, that might not have been the case. His story of the UFO sighting could have been on that part of the computer diskette which Chocko had been unable to retrieve. Once again, the pieces to this puzzle did not fit. Why?

She turned right, up the narrow dirt road to Chocko's mobile home. As she did so she noticed a vehicle parked directly across the street from his place. It was a Jeep, of the same color as the one that had gone over the cliff. She pressed her foot on the brake pedal, slowing the car, her heart racing. It could be another coincidence. Maybe it was somebody visiting the place across the street. And maybe what she had believed to be a custom paint job wasn't that at all; maybe it was a special color sold only in the Southwest. She realized that she was certainly not an expert on vehicle colors.

Her hands trembled on the steering wheel. She thought about turning around and going back in search of Chocko. Then, even as she was having these thoughts his truck appeared behind her. Three of the men who'd been with him at the convenience store were still in the back. Melvin the dog had his head out the right hand window, tongue hanging out, looking truly ecstatic. Chocko pulled up beside her and leaned across the seat, pushing the dog aside.

"You okay?" Chocko asked.

"I'm fine. Thanks for rescuing me."

"I don't think they would have given you much trouble. They've been poking around here since the UFO sightings. Sorry I didn't warn you. They're idiots."

Tara pointed at the Jeep. "Do you see that?"

"Yeah," Chocko said. "He's a friend of yours. He was by earlier today."

Tara shrugged, looked back at Chocko quizzically.

"Tom!" Chocko said. "It's Tom, your *ex*. Said he had to make a trip out to Gallup and decided to hunt you down. He called just after you left this morning."

"I see."

"You don't look all that happy about it." A big grin spread across Chocko's face. "You want I should run him out?"

Tara shook her head. "No. I'll talk to him. It's just odd."

"Look, I've got to deliver our friends back to town. I'll be back in a couple hours."

Tara glanced into the back of the truck and smiled at the three men sitting there. "Thanks, you guys," she said. "You're my saviors."

"No problem," one of them said. "It was our pleasure!" The three of them laughed, speaking amongst themselves in a language that she thought was half Spanish and half something else.

Chocko pulled away and Tara pressed her foot gently on the accelerator and moved forward.

*   *   *

"Chocko tells me you've had quite an adventure down here," Tom said. "I tried to get your cell phone but there hasn't been any response for three days now."

They had sat down at the picnic table on Chocko's deck, him on one side, her on the other.

"I've got a lot to tell you, Tom, and a lot of questions. I hope you don't mind."

"Sure. I got some information about Coyote Mesa. There's a dig going on about forty miles south of there. The theory is that it was a temporary camp of the Acoma people, on their way to Sky City. But it's not a very significant dig, as I said before."

"Dad said it was east of Coyote Mesa, not south."

Tom shook his head. "Nothing out there. I mean nothing. Plain, stark desert. I can assure you, that's a wild goose chase."

"It's hard for me to believe that he'd make a mistake like that. He was so clear about it. There's something out there, I know it. I spoke with this woman at a convenience store just south of the mesa turnoff. She told me about her uncle who lives out there."

"Might be a farm or two. It's pretty piss poor land, though. I think it's a false lead, Tara, I really do."

Tara was silent for a long time. The familiar presence of her ex-husband was comforting in a way, in another way troubling. She stared into his eyes for a moment and found something she hadn't seen or felt for a long time. It wasn't passion, exactly. At the moment she wasn't certain what had happened to that lusty, adventurous part of her, the part that had run off to the Andes with him. Today what she felt was the comfort of a man who'd known her for a very long time and who cared about her. She glanced away, then focused on his face again, his mouth, his finely sculpted features. But not his eyes. She avoided his eyes now.

"What brought you down here?" she asked.

"I needed to talk with you."

"About Maya?" Her thoughts whirled back to their last conversation and she remembered that she was still angry with him for not making a commitment about seeing his daughter for Christmas. At the same time, just saying Maya's name filled Tara with a sense of loneliness and longing.

Tom shook his head slowly, then dropped his eyes to the table. He dug at the weathered varnish with his thumbnail. "It's about you and me," he said. He looked up, eyes creased at the corners in an expression she knew from past experience mirrored his fear.

"You're a married man, Tom. It's been over between us for..."

Tom interrupted, shaking his head. "It hasn't been going well with Margarette and me. We're in the middle of a trial separation."

"But you came to my hotel together..."

"I talked her into it. I didn't want you to know. Pride, I guess. You always said I never could admit when I was wrong."

"Which is the reason you didn't want to make plans with Maya and me..."

Tom nodded. "I called her yesterday."

"You called Maya?"

"We talked a long time. I told her I'd make reservations for a cabin in Taos for the Christmas holidays. There's a place I know about. It'll be great."

"A cabin?"

"It's a wonderful place just out of town. Belongs to a friend of mine. He rents it out to friends. You'll both love it."

"A *romantic getaway?* Tom, please..."

"Don't say anything. Give it some thought."

"I don't know. This is bad timing. I'm sorry."

"Like I say, give it some time." He reached across the table and gently took her hand, caressing it. She shook her head but did not draw her hand away.

"Am I to blame for this?" she asked.

Tom shook his head. "Margarette says I'm too ambitious, that I don't care about her."

"And?"

"It's not ambition. Lately, I've thrown myself into my work as an escape. I started seeing a counselor about a year ago. This is hard to say. I've discovered certain things about myself, that I've used Margarette in a way."

"Tom, you don't have to go into it."

"No, I need to. I've been thinking about it ever since you arrived. It's about you and me, Tara. I didn't leave you for Margarette. I went to Margarette because you scared me half to death."

"I don't understand."

"I didn't want to feel that intensely about anyone. And it only got stronger after Maya was born. You never picked up on that?"

"That...that wasn't my perception...I..." Tara stammered, I'm not sure I like where this conversation is going."

"We need to take it slow."

"You think we should be together again..."

"If you're willing, Tara. I can't go on with my life the way it's been."

"This is not a good time for me."

"I understand."

"There's something crazy about all this. I think Dad has lost it, Tom. I think he's delusional. I'm afraid something has happened to Charla and he's wandering around on the desert with his delusions...I've got to find him."

"What delusions?"

"Maybe not delusions."

Tom suddenly let go of her hand and stood up. "Talk with me, Tara. What delusions?"

Tara stared at him blankly. "Why are you so upset?"

"I'm not. I'm just concerned."

"Oh, really! I don't recall any love lost between you and Dad."

Tom came over and put his hand on her shoulder, then moved it up to her neck and massaged her gently. "What bothers me is the way you obsess about him."

"Obsess?"

"You've always done that. You worry yourself sick about him. *Where is he? What's happened to him now? Is he in danger? How will he ever get out?* He always comes first. It's why things didn't work between us. I never had a chance."

"Never had a chance!" She pulled away from Tom, his hand falling to his side. She made no effort to disguise her fury.

"Tara, I'm sorry. That just spilled out..."

"You aren't out here for my sake. Ever since I've known you, you've had a hidden agenda. You're never straight with me. You're a liar, you know that? You're a very dishonest person, or maybe you're just out of touch..."

"Bullshit! I came out here to tell you I still love you. You're the mother of my child, for god sake. That's nothing I could lie about."

"Tell me something, Tom. Who bought that new Jeep for you? For three months before you got it you begged poor with me. You couldn't pay your child support on time. Now you show up with a fancy new Jeep. I don't like it."

"I haven't missed a payment to you in months. You know that."

"Which is what worries me. You and Margarette are breaking up and suddenly you've got a brand new Jeep and money to burn."

"I can see this isn't a good time to talk."

"You're hiding something. Are you dealing artifacts? I can't imagine where else you'd come up with all this money suddenly. I know the university doesn't pay enough."

"Same old Tara," Tom said. "Here we go with all the accusations, when you don't know anything about anything."

"Just get out, Tom." Tara stood up and started into the house. Her knees trembled and when she got to the door she had to steady herself.

"You're with him, aren't you?" Tom bellowed.

"What?" She half turned, looking over her shoulder at Tom. He stood with his fists jammed down into his pockets, his face belligerent, mean.

"Do you mean what I think you mean?"

"I'm no fool. I saw your stuff in there."

"You bastard!"

"Listen to me, would you? I don't want to fight with you..."

"It's a little late for that."

Tara stepped inside and slammed the door behind her. She slipped the bolt in place and moved toward the bathroom. As she did Tom pounded on the side of the house with his fist. She stepped into the bathroom, closed and locked the door. She dropped down on her knees and stared into the toilet bowl. Her belly knotted up and she clamped her eyes shut as waves of nausea swept violently over her, bitter and sordid as the meager contents of her stomach spewed into the clear water. ~

 Spirit Circle

Betrayal

By mid-afternoon Chocko had still not returned. Tara was not concerned since she guessed he was working at the community garden. In the meantime, she showered, put on fresh clothes and took a short walk on the desert out Chocko's back door. The walk was good, calming her. With a new sense of clarity, a plan began taking shape in her mind. She'd start by cleaning up the mess with Tom. Perhaps she'd been hasty. Not that his behavior had been any great model of virtue! But she also knew she'd over-reacted to his visit. The events of the past five days had put her on edge, to say the least. Tom's backhanded proposal had been ill-timed, bumbling and probably deceitful, well-deserving of her rejection. But she still had to contend with Tom, and leaving things where they were was going to cause problems down the line.

No matter what she thought of Tom, he was still Maya's father. Tara couldn't deny that, and couldn't turn her back on the fact that he was important to Maya. To have this terrible tension in their lives would not be good for anyone. Besides, if Margarette and Tom really were breaking up, Tom could very well be hurting. His actions could have been motivated by pain and anger rather than his better judgment. Who could say? Maybe with a little patience and diplomacy something good could come from the blowup. Maybe. But no matter what, she had to come to some sort of peace with him.

As for her father, there was no doubt he was in some kind of trouble but she suspected it was more in his own scrambled mind than in the real world. She had no label for what might be going on but common sense told her it wasn't good. This wasn't like in the past when he'd taken off for parts unknown, with his typically sardonic enthusiasm for a preposterous new story. His cynicism and determination to enjoy the adventure of his infamous profession had been almost healthy in the past. But with this story of traveling into a different reality, there could be little doubt that he'd snapped, gone over the edge. He'd started believing his own fabrications and half-truths. But why? What veil of sanity had been stripped away? Tara thought of Alzheimer's, of brain tumors and even of a head trauma that he might have suffered climbing around at the ruins he talked about on the disk. How ironical, Tara reflected, that his malady, whatever it was, had ushered him into the ersatz dreamworld of the tabloid! It would have been funny if the wellbeing of a real person wasn't at stake.

As Tara wandered around Chocko's house she found a new printout made from her father's diskette, laying next to the computer. Chocko had scrawled a note to her at the top: "Got this off the disk early this a.m. Sound familiar? Remember the guy I told you about?"

She glanced over the words printed out on the paper, her father's words: "...found the wreckage tucked into a cavern in the side of the mountain about a quarter mile away...bones picked clean and scattered...poor guy hit with a terrible impact, the hand still there, what's left of it, nothing but shattered bones now impaled in the soft shale...camera gear and other paraphernalia battered by the crash and the weather...return to his widow if I can..." That was all.

Tara remembered the story Chocko told her about the "breezy," the ultra light aircraft that the man--Jack Milford--had used to take photographs of remote parts of the desert. It was quite clear that Drake had found the wreck, finally explaining Milford's mysterious disappearance, though not the reason for the crash.

Tara thought about the photos Drake had mailed to her. She wondered if they had come from the cameras Drake described. But as she reread his fragmented notes it was impossible to be certain that he had recovered a camera. He spoke only of "camera gear and other paraphernalia." That didn't necessarily mean he'd found an intact camera or film that could be developed. Furthermore, it wasn't clear when he'd found the wreck. Was it before he found the ruins or afterwards? There was always the possibility that having found the camera and other belongings he had taken the film to be developed and the result--the pictures she now had in her possession--had provided him with the clue he needed to find the ruins. However, it could have happened the other way around; Drake's search for the ruins could have led him to the crash site.

It was going on five when Chocko returned, sweaty and dirty. Melvin the dog trotted into the house with him, raced across the living room and jumped happily up on the couch beside Tara, tail wagging, pushing his wet nose into her face and licking her cheek in greeting. Chocko grabbed the dog by the nape of his neck and dragged him off the couch. The penitent animal looked up at Tara, seeking sympathy, then sighed and curled up at her feet.

"You don't look much the worse for wear," Chocko said. "Any news from your dad?"

Tara shook her head. "I see you got a little more off the disk. I have something I want to show you." She handed Chocko the envelope of photos her father had sent to her lab back in California.

Chocko drew out the pictures, nodding as he did. He held the color photos toward the light and squinted at the details, noting that they depicted the same scene Drake had described on the disk. Then he turned his attention to the black and white photo.

"What do you think?" Tara asked.

"We might be able to find this place." Chocko tucked the photos under his arm and headed for the kitchen. "You want a beer?"

"Thanks, no. I've got to drive up to Gallup."

She heard Chocko open the refrigerator door, the jingle of glass as he selected a bottle of beer, and then the characteristic pop as he removed a cap. When he returned to the living room he'd kicked off his shoes. He sat down at the opposite end of the couch from her.

"I've got to settle something with Tom. We got into a bit of a fracas. Did he happen to tell you where he was staying?"

Chocko thought for a moment, then nodded. "The Desert Light. He left a number. I wrote it down on an envelope by the phone."

Tara got up from the couch and went into the kitchen, the dog following at her heels. She came back, holding the envelope. "You're a life saver! For the second time today."

Chocko shrugged. "The boys had fun. They hate those government guys poking around here, especially the Army special services jerks. Is sheer ineptitude one of the prerequisites for their job, I wonder? I mean, maybe it's deliberate. Maybe their real job is just to go around and irritate the citizenry."

"I should get going," Tara said, absently.

"You want to call first?"

"Nah! If Tom hears my voice he'll probably hang up on me."

Chocko studied her face for a moment. "Drake never liked him much, did he?" he said.

Tara shook her head vaguely. For a second she stared distractedly at Chocko. "Is it okay if I stay here tonight?"

"By all means. I've got a meeting tonight at the Council. But you know where to find the key."

"Thanks. This means a lot to me."

Chocko nodded.

"You said the photos might help you figure out where Dad was poking around," Tara said.

"Maybe. But you're sure not going to get anybody's permission to go in there."

"Because it's sacred ground..."

"Yeah. You know how the Indians feel about that."

"I'm not familiar with the Zuni's policies, no."

"Not Zunis."

"Who then?"

Chocko shrugged and looked down at the floor.

She did not have to probe any further. Besides, it would be futile. She'd seen this same gesture many times before, working with native peoples. What surprised her was who it was coming from this time. She'd always considered Chocko a modern man, above superstitions and secrets that could not be shared with whites. His silence meant that she had stepped over a boundary. To probe further would most likely produce nothing more than a cold, stubborn silence.

In spite of her skepticism, visions of the secret society of shamans filled her head. In the past, working in the Dakotas, she'd found the people protected their knowledge of secret societies of healers and holy people who lived beyond their immediate boundaries. Sometimes, they had no names for these people, in strict confidence admitting that they were not sure they existed in the physical form that Tara studied.

"What's the risk of going up there?" Tara asked. "What's the worst that could happen?"

"The worst that could happen, that's what could happen."

Tara fidgeted with the envelope, noting Chocko's hasty writing as if it contained a code. "Do you think that's what's happened to Dad?"

Chocko leaned forward and scratched Melvin's ears, not so much to comfort the dog, Tara concluded, as to hide his eyes from her.

"Drake and I have shared a lot of history," he said. "I think he went too far this time."

"Can we try to find the place?" she asked, shakily. "I have to know...you can understand that."

Chocko raised his head. Rubbing his eyes, he answered with a grunt which Tara took as a reluctant affirmation.

* * *

As Tara stepped outside an eagle circled in the sky, high over the desert west of the trailer park. The sun was already low and through the dark clouds it looked more like a distant planet. The eagle rose higher and higher, its silently spiraling circle taking it nearer and nearer the cloud banks whose presence threatened yet another new storm. Melvin the dog had followed her out onto the deck and he looked up expectantly. For a moment she wondered why the dog had decided to adopt her as a friend, what it was he'd apparently found in her. She didn't particularly like dogs, had never had a pet of her own, and really didn't understand the attachment so many people enjoyed with their animals. In spite of these sentiments, she caught herself feeling critical of how roughly Chocko treated the animal.

"You stay!" she said, stepping down from the deck and heading for her car. Melvin cocked his head and sat down on the step, watching as she backed away. Then he sighed and lay down resignedly, his nose resting on one paw.

The drive to Gallup was uneventful. She stopped for gas, filled the tank at the first station she came to, then turned left on the frontage road and drove west.

The Desert Light motel was tucked back off the road, a single row of clean looking units, each with its own narrow front porch with metal chairs painted in bright colors. She spotted Tom's Jeep parked directly in front of unit 7 and pulled into the parking slot next to it. As she shut off the engine of her car the porch light came on. That was an encouraging sign! But as she got out of the car she noticed that all the porch lights were on. Apparently they'd tripped on from an electric timer.

She glanced into the front seat of the Jeep. There was little doubt in her mind that it belonged to Tom. She saw several topo maps on the passenger's seat. One of them was unfolded and had slipped down onto the floor. It had been marked up with a pink highlighter pen. She craned her neck to see if she could identify the area that had been indicated.

At that moment a thin, middle-aged woman wearing a colorful Mexican serape came out of the office at the front of the complex and shouted across the parking lot to Tara. A great cascade of snow white hair flowed down over her shoulders. "Can I help you, Senora?"

Startled, and suddenly self-conscious as she recognized the fact that the woman had been watching her from the moment she drove in, Tara shouted back: "Tom Pushkin. I was looking for Mr. Pushkin."

The woman crossed the lot in long strides and stood at the rear of Tom's Jeep. "He's not here," she said. "He left with somebody a couple hours ago."

Ignoring this, Tara stepped up on the porch and knocked on the door. There were no lights on inside, however. Apparently, the woman was telling the truth.

"If you're a guest, you have to sign in," the woman said.

Tara turned and stepped down off the porch. "I'm not staying. I am just dropping by to say hello."

"I don't want no scenes around here. If you got trouble with him, you take it somewhere else. Not in my place!"

"There won't be any trouble."

The woman looked skeptical. "Maybe you keep it outside, okay? My guests are very particular. Maybe I call the police."

Tara smiled, hoping to be reassuring. "I'll go to dinner and come back in an hour or so."

"Okay. But no problems."

Tara climbed into her car and backed out of the parking place. The woman stood at the rear bumper of Tom's Jeep, looking protective and determined. Tara watched her in the rear-view mirror, amused by the woman's over protectiveness.

For the next hour or so she cruised up and down the frontage road, watching for any signs of Tom. At a little after seven-thirty she stopped at a fast food restaurant and bought some French fries and a cup of coffee. Gobbling down the French fries she was reminded that she hadn't eaten since early that morning. The fact is, she could not remember when she last had an actual sit down and relax meal. It had to have been in the restaurant where the young man warned her about going to Coyote Mesa. For a moment she felt almost nostalgic about that evening, recalling the comfort and warmth, the protection from the storm she'd enjoyed. Though she was not hungry, she considered stopping in again. It would be good to touch down in a familiar place, to spend a moment in a place where somebody might recognize her. Not that there were any guarantees about that. The boy and his mother had probably served a couple hundred people since the night she stopped off. Still, they might recognize her.

She slowed as she approached the restaurant but then saw the sign on the window: "Sorry. Closed." She drove on. At the Desert Light again she made a U-turn and headed back. An empty used car lot just north of the motel caught her attention and she pulled in. From the center of the lot, overgrown with weeds, she could keep an eye on the motel driveway. She switched off the headlights but before turning off the ignition she reached for the cell phone.

As she punched in the most familiar phone number in her repertoire, Tara thought of how much she missed Maya and Viveka. Her heart ached with the poignant reminiscence of the best times at home. And once again she acknowledged that she envied Viveka her life. Leisure days at home with Maya, no pressures other than the normal pressures of daily living, seemed such a luxury from her present vantage point. For a moment she dared dream that Tom and she might one day reconcile, that there would be a time when she could spend whole weeks on end with Maya, time filled with the luxury of unrushed hours to enjoy each other's company.

"It's me," Tara said when she heard Maya's voice came on the line.

"I knew it was going to be you! I told Viveka it was you, Mommy! I really did."

"Hi Sweety. I miss you."

"Are you still in Mexico?"

"In *New* Mexico," Tara corrected. "I'm still here."

"Did you find grandpa?"

"Not yet. But I will very soon. You talked with your daddy, I hear."

"You said you would talk to him."

"I did."

"What did he say?"

"What do you mean, *what did he say?*"

"No, you said...you said... Mommy, you're mixing me up."

"Honey, didn't your daddy call you?"

There was a long pause on the line, then: "No." Her answer sounded more like a question.

"You didn't talk to your dad?"

"A long time ago."

"Listen to me carefully, sweetheart. Did you talk to your daddy yesterday?"

"No."

"The day before that?"

"No."

For a moment Tara was speechless. She was certain Tom had said he'd spoken with Maya in the last couple days, that they had made plans for going to Taos for Christmas. He'd even rented a cottage. "Sweetheart, is Viveka right there? Could I talk to her?"

"What in the world did you say to Maya?" Viveka admonished. "She looks like she just lost her best friend."

"I'm sorry, Viveka. I need to ask you, did Tom call?"

"No. I'm sure he didn't."

At that moment a green utility vehicle pulled up in front of the motel. Parked in the shadows, the driver's face was invisible to Tara. But there were two people in the front seat. The right front door opened slightly and the interior light went on. The passenger put one foot on the ground, as if preparing to get out. But then he stopped. Now there was a heated conversation between driver and passenger.

Watching the action carefully, Tara lowered her voice and spoke into the phone. "You're certain Tom didn't call. You're certain of that?"

"I'm positive." Tara could hear Viveka talking to Maya, and then Maya was crying. Out of the corner of Tara's eye, she saw the passenger in the green utility vehicle move into the light. It was Tom! No doubt about it.

"Listen, Viveka," Tara said. "I need to hang up now. I'll call back tonight, okay?"

Tara watched as Tom stepped from the green car and stood at the curb. He was still holding the door open, talking to the driver with the dome light illuminating his face.

Tara tossed the phone on the passenger's seat and opened the door of her own car.

"Tom! It's me, Tara," she shouted.

Tom whirled to face her. There was an instant's recognition and he yelled something to the driver and lifted one leg to get in. With tires shrieking the green car suddenly accelerated and rocketed away, the door flapping in the breeze like a broken wing. Tom leapt back, stumbled against the curb and fell. In an instant he was on his feet, limping up the driveway toward his motel room.

Tara moved quickly, crossing the lot and jumping a low stone divider marking the edge of the motel property. She fell in beside Tom and followed along beside him as they made their way up to the steps of his unit.

"I'm sorry about this afternoon," Tara said. "I was pretty rude."

"What are you doing here, spying on me?"

"*Spying* on you? Tom, I came to apologize!"

"Sure you did." He stepped up on the tiny porch and shoved his key into the front door lock. "I'd invite you in but it's getting late."

"Tom. Will you cut it out!"

He turned. "What do you want me to say?"

"I just want to talk. I don't want to fight with you. For your daughter's sake, let's try to get along."

"For my daughter's sake...that's what this visit is about."

"Not just that. I don't see why there has to be this tension. We're two reasonable human beings. We've shared a lot..."

"If you still love me, go to bed with me."

"Shit!" Tara slipped in beside him and shoved open the door. As the light from the porch spilled into the room, it fell over the curves of several, large earthen pots resting in a neat row on the floor. She let out a gasp, then felt his hand around her forearm as he dragged her roughly outside and slammed the door.

"You're poking your nose in business that has nothing to do with you," he snarled. "Stay out of this, Tara. For godsake, stay out of this."

"So that's it!" She didn't have to ask, and he didn't have to lie. It was quite clear what was going on, that he was selling artifacts, possibly artifacts stolen from the university. Or perhaps these pots were from one of the collections he was purportedly assessing for the different Indian cultures in the area. All this explained what he'd meant about her spying on him.

"Tom, you can go to jail for this."

"Stay out of it," he said. "You may think you understand what's going on here, but you don't. Believe me, you don't. Just go back home, Tara!"

She turned back to the door, twisted the handle. Locked. She turned around again just as Tom bolted toward his Jeep, unlocked the driver's door and slammed it shut. For a moment he struggled with the ignition keys, giving Tara time to race to the side of the vehicle. The engine roared into action. Tara grabbed the side view mirror and clung to it as Tom jammed the transmission into reverse. The Jeep lurched backwards and Tara felt her arms nearly yanked from the sockets. Tom slammed on the brakes and she was flung to the ground, screaming. She had rolled and her ankle was now wedged under the rear wheel. She pulled but it wouldn't come loose.

"Tom, for Chrissake!"

For an instant he opened the door a crack, leaned out and looked down at her. There was fear and anger in his eyes. She heard the engine roar again. Miraculously the wheel rolled back for just an instant and she pulled her foot free. Then the rear tires spun, grinding into the pavement.

Tara lay in the middle of the parking lot, watching helplessly while Tom's tail lights bounced over the curb at the street, turned right and disappeared into the night. She lifted herself to her knees just as the woman from the office came flying out.

"I told you no trouble," the woman screeched. "I'll call the police! You get out of here and don't come back."

"I'm not the one you should be worried about," Tara muttered.

"You're a bad woman! You get out of here now!"

Tara lifted herself to her feet. Sharp pain enveloped her left ankle and rose up through her leg. She cursed under her breath as the woman, her long white hair like a bizarre halo swirling around her head, hovered nearby, screaming, threatening to call the police.

Limping with her injured ankle, Tara dragged herself back to her car. She sat down on the edge of the seat, removed her shoe and just held her foot for a long time. The idea of chasing after Tom was not only a painful prospect, it also seemed ludicrous. By now he'd be ten miles away on god-knows-what back road. Besides, he'd return for the artifacts. And then...what? If she reported him, he would be sure to come up with a million excuses for having such artifacts in his possession. He was an anthropologist after all. He handled treasures such as these all the time. He could say he was doing research at the university. Clearly, he already realized that Tara knew better, or else he wouldn't have run. When she got back to California she could explore what to do. Not the least of her questions at this point was whether or not she wanted the father of her child sent to prison, or for that matter exposed in his profession for plundering ancient sites for his own profit.

A thousand questions spiraled around in her mind. Where had Tom gotten these artifacts? Though she'd only caught a glimpse of them in dim light, she'd seen enough to know they were perfect, at least four ritual jars, judging by their size and elaborate decorations. And she couldn't be certain but it was possible that the painted designs in the fired clay had been embellished with gold for even in the dim light there had been a metallic reflection off their surface. If that were the case, Tom had possession of some extremely valuable objects.

The questions didn't stop there, of course. Who was the driver of the green car? Why did he or she race off like that? What was Tom's business with him? What had he said or done that caused that driver's hasty retreat? Tara tossed her shoe onto the seat beside her and pulled the door shut. It was indeed strange that all of this was happening along with Drake's disappearance. Was that mere coincidence?

As she settled into the seat, a strange whistling sound came from inside the car. For a moment she panicked, thinking of car bombs, but brushed the thought aside. The cell phone! That was it. She had forgotten to switch it off. She picked up the instrument, shut it off, then back on, and pressed the redial button. In an instant Viveka's voice came on the line.

"I'm sorry," Tara said. "There was a little...uh...traffic problem here." She did not want to explain to Viveka what had just happened.

"Maya is very upset. She's gone up to her room. I don't know what you told her."

"I'm sorry, Viveka." Tara felt scolded, rebuked by her child's own Nanny. Under ordinary circumstances, she might have been amused. But now she found herself fighting an impulse to defend herself.

"Why in heavens name are you being so mysterious? I don't like that kind of behavior."

In spite of herself, Tara grinned. She felt like a small child disciplined by her mother. "It can't be helped. Please tell Maya I love her very much and I think about her every minute."

"When are you coming back?"

"I can't say yet. You'll tell Maya for me?"

"Yes, Ma'am. I'll tell Maya."

"And Viveka, if anyone else calls for me or Maya, please contact me immediately. You have my cell phone number."

"A lot of good the number does us! We've called you several times and get nothing but a no-connection signal."

"I know. But do try to call, will you, if you hear from my father or Tom? The cell phone service out here is bad. But keep trying."

"Anything else?" Viveka was making no effort to hide her irritation.

"No. That's all. Thank you. When I get home I'll explain the whole thing."

"Yes, Ma'am. Goodnight now."

As Tara set the cell phone back into its bracket on the car's console, the image of the green utility vehicle flashed into her mind again. And with it came the name: Charla Mather. She couldn't be certain but the vehicle could have been a Land Rover, and Charla's Land Rover had definitely been green.

Tara reached forward, turned the key and the engine caught immediately, its confident rumble a source of security and strength. Turning south, back toward the junction to Zuni, she longed for the asylum of her own home, of Maya's tender innocence and the solidity of Viveka's firm resolve. Chocko's home beckoned, promising some of that. But what he offered wasn't the same. *Home.* The comfort of that word inspired her forward. Even her housekeeper's tongue-lashing would be welcome after this evening's events. She would never complain about domestic life again!

As she stared into the twin pillars of light cast into the desert night by the bright beams of her headlights, she felt frightened and lonely. It was an old feeling and only too familiar, but never before had she felt it quite so profoundly, quite so deeply. It clawed at her heart, like some great animal desperately trying to escape. In the beginning it was little more than an image in her mind, an image that went along with a thousand conflicting emotions. As she stared into the night, at the seemingly endless ribbon of blacktop, the pain of anxiety and betrayal spread through her body.

At last she cried out, wailing against the anguish, and the long strip of road illuminated by her headlights became a dim blur. Then, without warning, the wheels dropped over the edge of the pavement onto the loose gravel shoulder and for a moment the highway spun away from her. The car careened sideways, tires shrieking as they left the pavement, then plunged violently across a narrow ditch.

Sage brush, rocks and dust ricocheted off the hood and windshield. Tara took her foot off the accelerator, as Drake had taught her long ago. If she didn't slam on the brakes, the tires would stay on top of the loose ground and chances were good that she wouldn't get stuck or lose control and roll the car. She continued rolling across the desert, a hundred feet from the road, then stopped. Tara stared straight ahead, grateful this hadn't happened on a steep mountain road. Her fate could have been the same as the man in the Jeep back toward Coyote Mesa. She shoved the gear shift into the Park position, released her seat belt and swung open the door.

As she stood up, she heard coyotes howling in the distance. Her heart pounded. She felt a sudden wave of nausea, her stomach churning. She dropped to her knees and leaned against the left front fender. Her entire being convulsed, spewing forth her grief, confusion and anger. She coughed, the bitter bile of her stomach spilling out onto the ground, the sickly sweet-acrid smell of vomit filling her nostrils. Twice more her stomach wretched. Then a sudden calm came over her.

She got to her feet, leaned into the car and grabbed a bottle of water which she'd jammed into the space between the seat and the console. After rinsing her mouth she walked around to the rear of the car and sat down on the desert floor, pressing her back against the rear bumper. Above her was a brilliant sky. Coyotes howled in the distance. In spite of everything, there was magic in this moment. Tom was lost. How or why he had turned against her, cruelly, insanely, she could not say. Explanations no longer mattered. There would never be any way to repair what had occurred. Perhaps she could one day forgive him but she knew she would never trust him again. With that realization, a dream had died. It was a dream she had held at a distance, denying to herself since the day he left, that one day he might change and return to her. He was gone. That was the end of it. There was closure and grief and many questions to be answered, but her bond with him was broken forever.

And Drake? Had he ever really been in her life at all? Did he ever truly exist for her, except in her dreams, in her fantasies of what she wanted him to be for her? She could count on one hand the number of times he had even come close to being what she wanted. Was it ever any other way, for anybody? And was she any better at mothering Maya than Drake had been at fathering her? How did one ever learn not to hurt the people they loved?

Doubt and sadness flooded into Tara's consciousness, drowning out everything they touched. There was nothing to be done but yield. At that moment she wanted more than anything she had ever wanted in her life, to just let go of it all, all her dreams, all her aspirations, everything that was responsible for this inner affliction.

Slowly, coming from some secret place behind her grief, she began to feel a new sense of confidence, something so solid and incontestable she almost stood up and shouted. It came so unexpectedly, she simply sat with it for a long, long time, basking in it, drinking it in. Somewhere in all the pain was the key to her freedom, liberation from dreams once meant to bring comfort but which now only brought pain.

Loneliness, solitude...these had a power all their own, which she would cherish forever. And greater than that was the beauty of the dark night, the infinite sky, the chorus of coyotes whose songs surrounded her. There was mystery here, an unknown source so much greater than anything or anybody she'd ever known. Here, for a fleeting moment, she felt herself enfolded by an inexplicable peace, something she'd been seeking, without knowing it, forever.

As she gazed into the darkness, her back pressed against the bumper of the car, she wondered if it was possible to hold this feeling of release, this feeling of freedom and rapture, for the rest of her life. But she knew it was not possible. Life didn't work that way. Some great inner taskmaster would get her to her feet and thrust her back behind the steering wheel and into the cold realities of everyday life. Then a part of her would erase the larger truth she had discovered and doubt would draw her back to the struggle. ~

 Spirit Circle

Revelations

The dim glow of the shaman's smudge stick floated magically in the night air as he swept the smoldering bundle of dried herbs back and forth over his head and around his body. Tara caught the movement out of the corner of her eye just as she came around the side of Chocko's house from the driveway. She smelled the burning sage drifting toward her, driven by a gentle breeze that breathed tenderly over the face of the desert.

The two of them, Chocko and the shaman, sat on the ground a few hundred feet from the rear deck, their profiles silhouetted against a star lit horizon. As Tara limped onto the rear deck, Chocko spotted her, rose to his feet and called out. She waved back, acknowledging him but proceeded to move toward the front door.

"Come join us," Chocko called. "I want you to sit with us."

She turned and walked gingerly past the cleared area of his yard, then out into the open desert. Halfway to the two men she stopped again. "I need to go inside," she said. "I've had a very upsetting night."

"We can talk about it later. This is important," Chocko urged.

She drew closer. In the light of the star lit sky she saw that the shaman had cleared a circle about six feet in diameter. He had established the perimeter of his circle with a line of tiny pebbles, the radius so perfect she wondered if its maker had used a compass. Medicine wheel! But why would he make it out here at night? And why would Chocko think it so important for her to attend?

Tara glanced back at the house, wondering what the other residents at the trailer park would think of three grown people sitting out on the desert like this at night. If anyone was interested there was certainly no indication of it. Most windows were dark. The characteristic pallor of television sets glowed in a couple. Apparently holding ceremony in the middle of the desert at night, out amidst the tumble-weed and crawling creatures, held less interest for probing eyes than sleep and late night TV talk shows or videos.

"This is Tony Fox," Chocko said in a hoarse whisper.

The shaman leaned over and set his smudge stick in a small bowl on the ground. He looked up, grinning, welcoming her, almost as if he'd been expecting her. He sat down, took up a hand drum about two feet in diameter, and began rubbing his palm around the rawhide face, smoothing it, caressing it, mumbling prayers as he did. His left hand held the webbing in the back of the drum, which Tara now saw was decorated with black feathers, bones, seashells, and all matter of small objects. Chocko sat down at the Western quadrant of the medicine wheel, directly opposite the shaman.

Tony Fox was in his late sixties or early seventies, Tara guessed. He wore his traditional dress, a woven blanket draped over his shoulders, his feet bare. Raven hair, streaked with gray, was parted at the center, drawn back in two braids that hung down over his shoulders. His hair looked as if it had been recently brushed and meticulously braided, seemingly with not a single hair out of place, and so shiny that it picked up the light from the stars, producing a thin, eery aura over his head and down around his shoulders.

While both men's demeanor was casual and inviting, there was an air about them that was unmistakably reverent. She felt that she was being welcomed into a space, an event, that was very special, something that both of them held in the very highest favor. Moving toward them, contemplating whether or not to accept their invitation, she felt honored that she'd been asked to be with them.

Chocko had a blanket pulled around himself. The desert air was cold and Tara shivered, wishing she'd brought her jacket and contemplating whether or not to go into the house for one. She decided against it, not wanting to interrupt the ceremony.

As she joined the men at the circle, Chocko handed Tara the small clay pot with the burning smudge stick inside, a long, cigar-shaped bundle of dried sage and cedar. Then he put a large fan made of feathers into her hand. She found herself taking it automatically, as if she knew exactly what to do with it. Her lips moved as she softly whispered words of a language she did not understand. Holding the smudge pot close to her solar plexus, she fanned the rising, pungent smoke down over her body, particularly around her heart, head and pelvis. Closing her eyes, she lightly inhaled the smoke, feeling strangely energized yet relaxed. The events of the past few hours faded from her mind and she felt deeply comforted, the smoke lifting away the dark energy of her encounter with Tom.

"Sit at the South. Close your eyes," the shaman told her. He took up the long willow stick that he used to beat the drum and proceeded to lay down a slow, steady rhythm.

The drum's cadence filled her body. She bowed her head and began to sob. Neither Chocko or the shaman looked at her, immersed in their own thoughts. She had come to the circle feeling alone, defeated, but now she felt oddly contained in her grief and confusion, strong and strangely confident. As she settled into the drumming, her mind became increasingly clear. Anger played at the corners of her consciousness, anger at Tom, then anger at Drake, then anger at the mystery that had lured her to this place. Old feelings of loneliness and abandonment--dark, empty, as gray as slate--filled her heart for a split second, then moved through.

She felt herself buoyed up by the ritual, her confidence in the strange little man, Tony Fox, building with each throbbing beat of the drum. She had heard it said many times that wherever a medicine wheel ceremony was held by those who had been tutored in its power, it brought out the greatest wisdom of all who took part. And as that wisdom came together and was contained by the wheel, it brought in a higher wisdom, the wisdom of the natural world and the wisdom of the ancients who went before. She felt herself settling into the ritual, remembering her dreams of the night in the cave and now finding comfort in being here, at this wonderfully peaceful place.

As the reverberations of the shaman's drum drove away the weight of her darkest feelings, she became increasingly aware of the rage she felt inside her but as the drumming continued those feelings no longer seemed foreign or dark but an important part of her, belonging there, solid and focused, as essential to her existence as her bones. She opened her eyes and looked up. The men sat impassively, their eyes wide open but not focused on the outside; their awareness of the darkness around them was eclipsed by a more commanding inner vision.

The drumming continued, even and steady. The shaman's hand seemingly detached from his body as he beat the drum, the long willow stick with its sheepskin tip taking on an energy of its own, moving the shaman's hand rather than being moved by it. And then the drumming stopped. Chocko shifted around, changing the position of his legs. He leaned toward Tara, took her hand and squeezed it, smiling.

"You okay?"

She looked into the softness of his eyes, finding an openness she'd never seen before. His smile was filled with the innocence and warmth of a young child, and as their eyes met she was magically filled with the same feeling within herself. She felt a bond with these two men, as if she had known them her entire life. Had the drum-ming and the circle generated this emotion, or was it the formal feeling that often comes after shattering experiences?

She turned her attention to the shaman who had taken up a large leather bundle he'd been holding at his left side. He placed it in the center of the circle, lifted away the leather wrapping and smoothed it out on the ground. Resting on the leather wrapping was an earthen pot about eight inches high and slightly larger in diameter. In the dim light of the star lit sky, Tara gazed at the out-side of the pot, coated with turquoise dust, crushed coral and white chips of unknown origin. The pot possessed the worn, smooth surfaces, of an ancient artifact, hundreds of years old, passed down through a long lineage of shamans who had been its custodian during their lives. The presence of the ancient ones was palpable, filling Tara with a sense of awe and mystery.

For several seconds, her rational self intruded, cataloging and judging what she saw--a pot housing animal fetishes for special healing and divination ceremonies. Anthropologists referred to them as *fetish jars*. She had handled them many times in museums but had never seen them in the hands of a shaman, nor had she ever thought about such practices still prevailing in modern times. Her rational self slipped away and she was immersed in the medicine wheel ceremony again. What she saw at the center of the wheel now connected her with a truth that far exceeded anything she'd ever learned in her formal studies.

For a moment Tony Fox knelt over the fetish jar, mumbling prayers in a language she did not understand. She picked up one word she'd read once before: *Pa-u-ti-wa*, the name for monster birds which legend described as being twelve feet tall. She heard another word which sounded close to one she thought she knew: *K'ia-ma-k'ia-kwin*. This referred to an ancient place, one never confirmed by anthropologists, that lay south of Zuniland and was known as the place of the Snail People. The rest of the words the shaman used were not in a tongue of the local tribes. From time to time there were words with familiar sounds but it was as if they were being pronounced in reverse, or uttered with a kind of shamanic *pig Latin* to disguise them. Tara felt moved within her heart to honor the sanctity of this moment with her full attention.

Tony reached into his pocket and sprinkled something onto the deer skin. He made four distinct piles of blue corn meal, offerings to the Four Sacred Directions, North, South, East and West. Then the shaman rose to his feet and tossed a small amount of the same meal into the air, then sang prayers in a language Tara did not know. That done, he knelt down and dug away a handful of earth, placing corn meal in that hole and smoothing it over, sealing it with more prayers. Instantly, the earth in that same spot moved, as if a small burrowing animal had been disturbed--or perhaps lured to that place by the shaman's gift.

As if by some unseen cue from Tony, Chocko relit the smudge stick, using a cigarette lighter with a silver case. He blew on the coals until they glowed bright red, and handed the smoldering stick to the shaman. Tony took it, blew on it himself so that sparks scattered over the top of the pot in the center of the circle. Then he reached down inside the pot and drew something out, an object about four inches long with feathers protruding from one end. He held it in the smoke of the smudge stick, then pressed it to his lips, breathing noisily in and out. Tara recognized what he was doing. This was an animal fetish, a small stone carving decorated with feathers, the latter identifying it as a particularly sacred object. When the shaman breathed against it, it was believed that he was exchanging breath with the animal spirit that fetish evoked, the gesture giving it life in this circle, just as a Christian prayer brought the spirit of Christ into the minds of parishioners.

Tony Fox placed the first fetish at the Northern quadrant of the medicine wheel, took a pinch of the corn meal he'd placed there before, and sprinkled it over the figure. Tara gazed at the long, narrow body of a mountain lion fetish, decorated with feathers and a saddle of turquoise and coral. For a moment, she felt the ripple of muscle in her own body, transported into the lithe motions of that animal.

Carved of stone from the region, Mountain Lion was known as the Master Hunter. As Guardian of the North he stood for ancient wisdom, a link with natural forces that were a mystery to most humans.

Except for small details, the shaman's Mountain Lion fetish was very much like the carving Tara had admired in the *Indian Trader* tabloid she'd read in the Mexican restaurant days before. She'd been drawn to the Mountain Lion fetish. It was filled with importance for her. The shaman's fetish was different from the one she'd seen in the tabloid; his was decorated with soft white feathers. She knew that the fetishes sold to tourists were never decorated that way since the feathers meant the fetish had been sanctified by a high priest of a clan dedicated to healing, hunting...or witchcraft.

Tara glanced at Chocko, as if for some signal of reassurance. For a second, she felt rigid and distant, pulling herself back from this strange desert ritual. *But this is pure superstition! Witchcraft.* The thought that she might be participating in such a ritual sent a shiver of aversion throughout her body. Then she remembered the prayer stick she'd seen at Charla Mather's abandoned home, back at Coyote Mesa. It had been decorated with beads fashioned of bone, a taboo practice among those who honored the ancient ways. And as she stared at the fetish jar she tried to remember what she'd seen carried away by the man who'd appeared at Charla's. There could be no doubt about it. Fully wrapped in its deerskin sheath, this fetish jar was approximately the dimensions of the object the thief had taken that night. Could it have been the same object? This was indeed a long shot, with repercussions she preferred not to entertain. There had to be hundreds of pots this same size, though not all would be fetish jars.

Something shifted again within her consciousness. She remembered the fantasies she'd had in the cave, of merging with the dream body of a young Indian woman as she placed an eagle feather on the mound. Suddenly, she knew the purpose of that gesture, knew it not in the analytical way of a scholar and academic, but from an ancient, instinctual place deep within her heart. And then she knew that she had a purpose here at this circle, a purpose that she could not define with words, nor did she feel compelled to try. This quest was not for her father but for a different reality that for now seemed far beyond her reach. She had a sense of belonging that she had never felt before.

The shaman reached into the pot again. This time he quickly smudged the object, raised it to his mouth and pressed his lips firmly against it, breathing noisily. Suddenly he thrust the fetish toward the sky and made a loud crowing sound, the cry of a raven. Then he placed the fetish on the ground directly in front of Tara. As he sprinkled corn meal over it, she saw an object that filled her with disgust. It was the shrunken body of a baby raven, ancient, desiccated and stiff, preserved perhaps decades before. The center of its body was wrapped in a wide belt of dark leather, to which had been sewn white beads, bits of seashells ground into perfect globes.

The mummified bodies of birds had been known to be used in rare ceremonies, and even in the costumes of certain Katchinas. But she knew little about them except for the aversion she felt deep inside whenever she saw one of these objects. As she stared at them, however, her aversion faded and became a very different feeling, one of reverence and trust.

Instantly, she felt herself withdraw. What was happening to her? It was not at all like her to participate in rituals such as this. She had always sat back as a dispassionate witness, maintaining the safety of the rational observer. She'd always seen herself as a silent recorder. She'd prided herself in her ability to report what she'd seen with objectivity and reason.

As the shaman reached into the fetish jar again, Tara repressed an impulse to leave the circle. She was afraid. She'd return to her car and race back to Gallup, or even Albuquerque, to a world she understood. She felt a puzzling horror rising within her. It had less to do with the ceremony than with the realization that as an anthropologist she'd taken great pride in her knowledge of the indigenous peoples of the Americas. But now, sitting at this circle, she suddenly realized she had viewed such practices only from the safety of her profession. In truth, she did not know the ways of these people at all! But she felt moved by them in ways she would never have imagined. She felt drawn into them, a part of her connecting this ancient ritual as an intimate part of her. Even so, the proud, disciplined anthropologist in her fought against a part of her that was entirely at peace sitting at this circle with two men from a world very different from her own.

The shaman was now smudging an object about the size of a baby's fist. It was carved of a substance she guessed might be bone or antler. She recognized it as a bear fetish, decorated with brown feathers, bright crimson beads and coarse twine. The shaman made a growling sound, deep in his throat, as he exchanged breath with this fetish. He ritually fed it and placed it in front of him at the western coordinate.

Continuing with his liturgies, the shaman brought forward a fourth object, this time a wolf fetish, carved from a shiny white stone, its body worn smooth with age. Of all the objects she'd seen thus far, this was the most beautiful. Its carver had rendered the body and head with obvious love, and had added a saddle of brightly-colored beads--coral to represent a strong heart and turquoise to represent a strong spirit. There was also a *point*--an arrowhead carved of flint--attached to the uppermost top of its back. The wolf had eyes of black beads whose shiny surfaces caught the reflections of the stars as the shaman breathed into its nostrils, then pressed the chest of the animal against his lips in what Tara thought might have been a kiss. This fetish was placed at the eastern coordinate, in front of Chocko.

Now the shaman rose to his feet, leaned over and reached into the fetish jar once more. He held something high in the air, something that oozed and dripped viscous fluids from his hand. Then the shaman made a piercing cry which cut through the desert silence. Still holding the dripping thing high in the air, he made the cry three more times. Suddenly, Tara heard a rush of wings. A huge bird, with a wingspan of at least four feet, swooped down from the sky and snatched the object from the shaman's hand. The bird appeared and disappeared in seconds.

Chocko reached over and touched Tara's forearm. In that moment she realized she'd been transfixed by the appearance of the bird, not out of horror but out of reverance.

"An owl," she said, whispering, needing the confirmation of a word to name what she had seen.

"She sometimes comes, sometimes not," Tony Fox said. "You never know. Maybe she's an owl, maybe not."

The shaman once again reached into the fetish jar. This time he drew out a live animal, a small furry creature, a rodent that he held lovingly in the palm of his hand, speaking to it in a language Tara could not identify. The small creature lay calmly in his palm as he spoke to it. Then he fed it a pinch of corn meal, which it lapped up hungrily. Taking it by the scruff of its neck he pressed its snout to his lips and exchanged breaths, just as he'd done with the other fetishes. When he was done, he set the animal on the ground at his right side. It immediately began burrowing into the earth, and in an instant had disappeared beneath the surface. Tara did not know quite what to make of this. Clearly this was some kind of magic, but it was almost as if the whole thing was happening in a dream.

These things completed, Tony took up his drum again. The slow, steady rhythm he had followed before was now replaced with a cadence that was almost melodic. The shaman sang. His voice rose and fell in a flowing series of consonants and guttural groans. Tara watched his face, his rocking movements as he drummed, observed how his hand seemed to be moved by the willow branch with which he beat the drum. The song he sang soaring out into the night, at times melodic and soothing, at other times sharp and stern, as if calling to a stubborn child.

Tara found herself drifting, floating as if in endless space, and in spite of herself her eyes closed and she eased herself to the ground. She lay curled in a fetal position around the raven fetish, one arm reaching toward Chocko and the white wolf fetish, her knees pointing toward Tony Fox and the bear fetish. Exhausted, hypnotized by the drumming and the shaman's song, she felt herself rising. Time and space became a jumble of illusions she no longer understood. One moment she was in her infancy, the next here in the present, the next in a strange, indescribable place as ancient as the desert itself. There were voices, people talking to her, addressing her by name, but she could not awaken herself enough to respond. Or did she awaken? She was sobbing, calling Tom's name. Somebody was holding her--Tom, Drake, another man? Perhaps it was her mother, dead now but somehow returned for this moment, to hold her, comfort her. But that could not be!

From what seemed a great distance, she saw her own physical

form moving through the night, slipping soundlessly across the desert to what destination she did not know. Curiously, she did not feel afraid, only a little giddy and light-headed as she effortlessly climbed to the top of a great cliff of red rock. She stopped and looked down into a brightly lit canyon, her eyes following a narrow creek cut into the rock at the bottom. Then, to the north of the creek she saw lines drawn in the valley floor. The lines stretched out for several hundred feet north and south, a hundred feet or so east and west.

"Kokopeli," she said, believing she had uttered the name aloud. But nobody responded and she sensed that she was alone again. In her dreams Kokopeli, the hump-backed flute player, rose out of the terraglyph and took form as a person, a changeling, smaller than others who gathered around him. She saw him leading his people to the different worlds in all four directions. Time had dissolved and she was watching a long movie that documented the passing ages. The warm, soothing sounds of the hump-back's flute drew them along on their difficult journeys to new worlds. Upon reaching their destination Kokopeli reached into the hump on his back and scattered seeds, bringing prosperity and happiness to his devoted sojourners.

Now Tara found herself sitting on a ledge, high in the mountains. As she opened her eyes wider she saw that she was sitting at the southern quadrant of a large circle. But she was not alone. Directly across from her sat James Dean. He was dressed differently, nothing like the images of him that she held in her mind. Over his shoulders he'd draped a colorful, handwoven blanket. He wrapped it around him, as if to protect himself from the cold. Then she saw that he had something attached to the back of his head. It was a huge eagle feather, the white shaft standing a good foot and a half above his head. In spite of herself she began to snigger.

"You look like Little Beaver," she said. "Do you remember, in the Red Ryder comics?"

A large grin lit up James Dean's handsome face. Then, as Tara watched, his face dissolved, rearranged itself, and before her eyes he was transformed into a wizened old woman. Toothless and wrinkled, her dark skin was so profoundly creased and furrowed that the terrain of her face resembled a desert landscape seen from afar.

Tara felt a presence at her left side and turned her head. Chocko sat there, calm and composed, his face impassive, expressionless. She felt a presence at her right. Turning her head she saw that it was the shaman, Tony Fox, who now sat silently, as if deep in a trance.

She heard a rustle of wings and looked up. Six ravens circled restlessly above her head. She was reminded of the ravens in the tree on the road to Coyote Mesa and the teachings of the ancient shaman. The message was clear. The ravens were there to give her new vision, a way of shifting her perception of reality. But what reality? This bizarre imagery, these animals and birds and witches, these characters straight out of a child's fairy tale, could surely not be taken seriously!

"Be still!"

The words seemed to come from nowhere. It wasn't Chocko's voice, nor the shaman's. And it certainly didn't sound like an old woman's voice. Tara stared across the circle at the old one, wrapped in a blanket. As she did, first one raven and then another dropped slowly down and rested gently upon the old one's timeless form. Two birds rested on each shoulder, one on her head, and one settled before her on the ground. Each bird stared across the circle at Tara, focusing its attention only on her, as if the others at the circle mattered not at all.

"Your head is filled with questions," the old woman said.

"Why should I listen to you?" Tara asked.

"Two hundred years before the New People came, the old ones knew it would happen and that the world would change. The old ones saw even further into the future, saying the New People would bring animals and would move across the desert not on foot but on horseback, and then, further in the future, they would travel in boxes that moved by unknown forces. They predicted what they called *great silver eagles* that would carry people through the sky. They said that one day we would send voices and even pictures over invisible filaments in the air. And they said that the New People would find a way to travel to the stars and moon."

"All those prophesies were proven to be a hoax," Tara argued. "I can show you documentation from the university. Those so-called oracles were written in modern times as a way to manipulate your people."

The ravens roosting on the old woman suddenly rose in the air, swirled around the others at the medicine wheel, then came down again, taking up different positions on the old one's shoulders, head, and at her feet.

"Look at our earth home today," the old woman said. "When we sent a man to the moon, we brought darkness to our world. We were not meant to disturb the stars and the moon. The air is poisoned. The water is undrinkable. Living creatures within the soil are destroyed by chemicals. Forests, animals, and plants that could be used in healing are being destroyed. We are surrounded by disasters--wars, famines, earthquakes, floods, great storms and angry eruptions from within the earth. Violence is all around us. But worst of all, it is within ourselves."

"These are technological advances," Tara protested. "You can't just write off the whole thing as the product of human degradation!"

"You came to me for what I know," the old woman continued. "This is what I know. These things have been taught for many generations. They were first spoken by my great grandfather. He taught them to me. He learned them from his grandfather, and he from his grandfather before him."

"I won't accept the idea that everything we have accomplished for the past five-hundred years is the result of our violent inner nature!" Tara's face tightened into a mask of indignation.

"Listen to her," Chocko told Tara. "I brought you here to listen, not argue."

"I didn't ask to come."

"Listen, listen, listen!" The old woman's voice grew harsh and demanding. "You're a messenger. You have no choice."

"I have a choice about telling the truth," Tara said. "And I won't propagate lies."

"Lies, lies, lies," the shaman chanted.

Once more the ravens flew into the air, the muffled sound of their wings eerie and mysterious. They circled high above, and Tara watched them, rising higher and higher above the medicine wheel. Slowly they began to drift back to earth, toward the circle and the four people sitting there. As they came down Tara saw that the old woman was no longer across the wheel from her. In her place was James Dean. The ravens settled down on the ground, to his left and right. She smiled. He returned her smile, as if enjoying the irony. He looked funny, this handsome young Anglo, with his single, tall, eagle feather standing atop his head. At last, a sense of sanity was restored to the circle, Tara thought.

"Whether you want to accept this or not," the young man said. "You were brought here for a reason."

"Yes. To find my father."

The young man shrugged. "Listen. What the old woman told you is not a lie. It's part of the truth you will carry back. The ancient ones prophesied today's world and all the disasters that would befall Mother Earth's people and her creatures. They saw beneath the surface, beyond the present, into invisible worlds that still elude those who are so steeped in the deceptions of modern technology and science."

As Tara listened, a thousand memories rushed into her brain. She remembered the strange movies from her childhood, movies that in her innocence she had not understood. Each time they appeared in her mind she lost all sense of time. It was as if she was transported to a secret place where she was being educated to a very different reality than what she experienced in everyday life. She remembered odd-looking creatures, bearing only a remote resemblance to humans, sometimes dressed in strange, elaborate costumes, at other times gray and dimensionless. No matter in which form they came to her, they possessed powers of thought beyond anything known in the world she understood. They projected their thoughts not through language but through invisible powers that were not even telepathic but beyond that. They were able, moreover, to change forms, to vanish and reappear as the most everyday-looking humans, or as animals, or in bizarre shapes like the Katchinas of the Southwestern Indians, or simply as rays of light or energy that had no visible form.

These beings had appeared first in what she had thought were movies. But were they actually that? Perhaps they were not memories of films at all! In the world she remembered she was liberated from the limitations of the flesh. Time was no longer an impediment to space travel. One moved between worlds with ease, transcending time and space. In that life magic was reversed; the physical laws which seemed so absolute and immutable in our everyday world proved to be the illusion. Sorcery carried us beyond that hallucination into a reality of a different kind.

Science and technology said it was impossible to do the things she'd dreamed about over the years, and part of her accepted the fact that they must be right. She reasoned that in her entire life she'd never found any concrete evidence for any of these dreams, these fanciful visions of other realities. But then, neither did people in horse and buggy days dream that one day the skies would be filled with silver birds, transporting people billions of miles each year.

"You will understand all this in a little while," the young James Dean was saying.

Once more, the ravens rose and lifted high into the air. As Tara watched they appeared to dissolve into the sky itself.

* * *

The starter motor of a car or truck groaned and whined, then its engine burst to life in a great cacophony of popping backfires that built to a startling roar that cut through her dream-world. After a moment, the engine, apparently that of a neighbor's truck, evened out and moved away, into the distance. Sunlight streamed into the space where Tara lay. But she was no longer on the desert floor. She lay on the bed in the room Chocko had assigned her in his home. Fully clothed, except for her shoes, she vaguely remembered some- one drawing a blanket over her the night before. Opening her eyes, she stared at the ceiling for a long time, trying to make sense of the sounds she heard around her. Her senses were jumbled, in a way she'd never experienced before. Sounds were distorted, and the light streaming in through the interstices of the Venetian blinds seemed far more intense than it should have been.

Once again she'd experienced a loss of time. But now, with crystal clarity, she realized that she was not losing her mind but that something very different was taking place. None of these lapses were empty, as she'd once thought. On the contrary, they had a purpose and meaning. Each time, she was pulled out of the mundane routine of her everyday life into...into what? She'd read somewhere that shamans in ancient times slipped into other realities where they received what legends called a "secret education." She'd always passed off such descriptions as day dreams, fantasies that primitive peoples simply didn't understand. They couldn't separate fantasy from reality and so it was only logical that they would describe these lapses as visitations to another world. But now that it was happening to her she was certain it was much more than a daydream.

She tried to sort out what she'd experienced in the hours before--the violent confrontation with Tom, the strange interlude with the shaman, the rantings of the old woman. She was certain the episode with Tom was real. There were bruises and scrapes on her arms and knees to prove it, and her muscles ached. And what about the medicine wheel on the desert behind Chocko's home? Was that real? The smell of burning sage lingering on her clothes told her that this had not been a dream. Tony Fox was real.

She swung her legs over the edge of the bed, and winced as she put weight on her feet. She remembered now; she'd twisted her ankle in the fracas with Tom. She sat back on the bed, lifted her leg and felt her swollen ankle. Amazingly, someone had wrapped it in an elastic bandage for her. She could not remember that but assumed her attendant must have been Chocko. She would have to thank him.

She touched her feet to the carpeted floor again. Though painful she found she could walk. She limped toward the door, touched the knob and listened for a moment. A radio was playing in another part of the house, a modern rock song about eagles and hope and empowerment. Though never a lover of popular music the song seemed familiar and she loved the sense of fulfillment and confidence it invoked. It was an old song, probably twenty years old, but she now realized she was hearing it for the first time.

Turning the knob she swung the door open and limped out into the hallway. From the kitchen she heard the occasional tapping of a computer keyboard and headed in that direction. Chocko turned and looked up from the computer as she entered the room.

"Hi. You feeling any better?"

"Yeah, I think so." Tara shrugged. "I need some coffee."

Chocko pointed to a chair at the breakfast table and she sat down. He poured her a cup of coffee from a pot on the stove and set it down in front of her. She lifted the cup to her lips and sipped. The hot, bitter liquid brought her back to her senses, put her back into her body.

"Do you want to talk about it any more?" Chocko asked.

"About what?"

"You said Tom tried to kill you."

"Oh, Jeziz! Chocko, I can't deal with all this! Tom is the father of my child. The father of my child tried to run me down. What do you do with that?"

"You protect yourself and your daughter."

Tara let out a little cry and her coffee cup went crashing to the table, then bounced to the floor, shattering all over the linoleum and spraying coffee halfway across the room. "I'm sorry," she moaned, immediately jumping up and dashing to the sink for a sponge to mop up the mess.

"Stop. The cup's not important. Let's talk this out." Chocko stood up, took her by the hand and led her firmly into the living room. They sat down together on the couch. He hugged her, clumsily and stiffly, but in spite of his obvious discomfort with the role of supporter he was doing a decent job of it. She reflexively leaned into his shoulder.

"He wouldn't hurt Maya. He loves her," she said, wanting with all her heart to believe it.

"He loved you once, too."

"But why would he hurt us?"

"I'm not the one to answer that."

"Chocko, my life is coming apart. My father has disappeared into another world, a reality I can't even allow myself to accept. The man I once loved, the father of my child has gone berserk. I can't trust anything or anyone any more. I can't even trust my own vision of what this life is about."

"You trusted your dream from last night. That's enough for now."

Tara drew away from him. He slid back, withdrawing his arm and turning to face her more directly. His body language told her he was wanting to distance himself. From what, she wondered. Her grief? Her hysteria? Her fear? Perhaps all of it. Men were like that. She could hardly blame them. These were not emotions to which she was accustomed. How could she ask another person, particularly a man, to take them on? They were not a part of the neat world she'd created for herself.

"There's more than one way to protect yourself," Chocko said. "Tony would know."

"Tony! He's a *brujo*, isn't he, a witch?"

Chocko shrugged.

"I don't know..."

"He knows things about the passage between worlds. He's our only hope."

"Our only hope, you said *our.*"

"I've given it a lot of thought. I'm caught between worlds, just like you, like Drake, in a way. It's not the path I'd like to take, using Tony's powers I mean. But Drake is a friend. I can't leave him out there. There isn't any choice for me, or for you."

"We can go to the people, the clan or whatever, the people who know about this place where my father has disappeared."

Chocko shook his head. "No. They take a vow of secrecy that can never be broken. Tony is different. He transits between worlds, not restricted by any of the values that would give you or me second thoughts."

"You're going to bank your life on a man like that? And maybe my father's, and mine, too?"

"He's already told me where to find the opening."

Tara was silent. For a long time she just stared at him. "You believe this...opening...really exists.

Chocko shrugged and Tara already knew he would not answer. He got up and crossed the room, resuming his place at the computer keyboard resting on the kitchen table. He typed in a few commands and in a moment the printer began to buzz, printing out what he'd been working on. "I got a little more off your father's disk," he said. "It's not much, something about a long trail up from the bottom of a canyon and a terraglyph..."

"I know. I saw it last night, in a dream," Tara said. "I'm telling you, it's all coming together now. I'm sure of it. I can't believe I'm saying this but the way the dream came to me...I saw it all so clearly. I can't deny this other reality any longer, can I? I was there, Chocko. I know if I see the spot again I can show you every rock, every tree, every turn in the path. I don't know how I know it but I do. Yet, there's a part of me that says no. It can't be!"

"It has taken me years to accept this other world," Chocko confessed. "You're not alone."

"And what you found today on his disk, what does it tell us?"

"I know the general region. We can go there." ~

 Spirit Circle

Blood Treasure

Their destination was a small box canyon, seven miles east, out over a desert road that began less than a mile from that desolate spot where Tara had watched the tow truck haul the savagely demolished Jeep back up onto the road. Seen from three miles away, the region Chocko identified rose out of the center of the earth, looking more like the towering spires of a great castle than a mountain. It stood alone, like Australia's Ayer's Rock, for the aborigines a monument to the gods, full of mystery, a riveting specter whose rich earthen reds and golds stood in sharp contrast to an infinitely blue sky.

The road, two tire ruts worn into the earth, circled the base of this natural monument. Chocko pulled off the trail and into a wooded area nestled between two towering precipices. Leaving his truck hidden in the brush they set out on foot, taking only basic supplies-- water, some snack food, and an extra sweater, should they be stuck on the high desert that night. A quarter mile from where he'd parked the truck, on a trail Tara could barely discern, Chocko held up his hand. Just before them stood three tall, narrow spires of red rock, rising ten stories into the air. Like three sentries, they appeared to be guarding a vague trail that rambled from the base of the cliffs high into the mountains above them.

"Look!" Chocko pointed to a spot high on the cliff. Pressing her binoculars to her eyes, Tara focused the lens on the spot he indicated, a good three hundred feet above them, at the very top of a narrow ridge. There, a tiny bit of white fabric, no larger than a man's handkerchief, fluttered in the breeze. It was so small she had trouble picking it out even with the help of the binoculars. Melvin the dog panted at her side, eager for them to move on up the path.

"How did you know it was here?" Tara asked. She did not have to say what it was. They both understood.

"The photos I told you about, plus ones you showed me from your father, plus some of the things Drake described on the disk."

Chocko slid his backpack from his shoulders and dropped it to the ground at his feet. He squatted down and zipped it open. From inside, he withdrew a large envelope that had been torn open at the top. He pulled out three black and white photographs, then a topo map of the area. He spread the map out on the ground and weighted down the four corners with small stones. Then he selected the first photo, one that had obviously been shot from a great elevation, showing only the general mountain range. The dog forced his muzzle into the backpack and Chocko shoved him aside roughly. The animal hung his head, dejected, pressing his shoulder into Tara's leg.

"This could be anywhere," Tara said, taking the photo in her hand and studying it. "I don't see what you could tell from it."

"It's like the one the search parties used. There's a reason they didn't find this place." Chocko pointed to the bottom left corner of the photo. Then he reached into his pocket and removed a compass with a built-in magnifying glass, which he also handed to her. "What do you read there?"

She took the magnifying glass and focused on the tiny lettering at the lower left corner of the photo. "There's some marks. I can't tell what they are. They could be numbers with the tops cut off..."

"It's a date. I noticed it a couple days ago. All of Jack Milford's photos are that way. They were shot with one of those cameras that imprints the date automatically."

"I see now. These marks are the bottoms of some numbers but they are also reversed. Which means..."

"...that the photo itself is reversed, and that's why they couldn't identify this place in the original search. They were looking for a place that matched the photo but this is a mirror image of the real thing. They couldn't find it because the terrain pictured here doesn't exist!"

"Unless you reverse it back."

Chocko nodded. "Last night I checked it out in the bathroom mirror. Then I marked out the area I saw right here." He pointed to some marks he'd made with a blue pencil on the topo map.

"I don't get it. Why did Jack reverse it?"

"I'm pretty sure he was trying to disguise what he'd found. A number of his photos were both reversed and undated. He'd processed them that way, apparently because he felt he was onto something that should be protected.

"I think he was afraid of what he'd found and hadn't decided what he was going to do about it, whether he'd tell others or keep it a secret. Take a look at the map."

Chocko set the last photo from the envelope beside the topo map and pointed out three landmarks. Each of them showed up on the map as a series of tiny circles, one inside the other, very close together. Given the scale of the map, these three circled areas stood for three tall spires of rock, just like the ones Tara could see in the reversed photo.

Tara reached into her own pack and withdrew a postcard her father had sent her. A tiny, printed ad on the back told her it had been printed by a personalized mail-in photo service in Albuquerque, one that specialized in making picture postcards and posters from shots taken by amateur photographers. Over the years Drake had sent her many such postcards, showing places he'd been. She set this one on top of Chocko's photo. "It's the same place," she said.

"Notice the angle of Drake's picture," Chocko said. "Try to locate where the photographer was standing when he shot it."

"Right here. At least, not far from here. So maybe Dad knew whatever it was your photographer friend knew."

Chocko nodded. "Drake and I discussed it last time he visited. We only had the reversed print at the time. He could have figured it out on his own, I mean, that they'd been reversed. He'd be likely to notice that, wouldn't he? He's worked with photos all his life."

"But why didn't he tell you?"

Chocko shrugged. "Who knows? Maybe he hadn't discovered it yet. With an aerial view like this, it would be pretty hard to determine. Maybe he was studying topo maps and just stumbled upon it, noticed the reversal. I can't say."

"What we're seeing up there, all jammed under the ledge, that could be what Dad described on the disk."

"Most probably. And if my theory works out, we'll find something else up there, something that may have led to the crash."

"Meaning?"

"Meaning, wait and see."

*   *   *

The trek to the crash site was arduous and with each step Tara cringed from the pain of her throbbing ankle. Halfway to the top, the path changed. It was no longer a single rut worn into the land but narrow steps carved into rock. Even so, Chocko hardly altered his pace as he came to them, instead taking them completely in his stride, his feet as familiar with each step as Tara was familiar with the steps in her own home. Chocko even navigated easily around steps that were missing, as if he knew the alternative trail. Tara's ankle throbbed with pain, each step another reminder of her confrontation with Tom the night before.

She had seen similar steps at other archaeological digs, cleverly carved to accomodate only a single, small foot. Climbing them forced her to turn her foot sideways, straining the bruised and torn muscle in her ankle. She gritted her teeth against the pain, all too aware that if she gave into the pain she could easily loose her footing and tumble hundreds of feet down. If her ankle collapsed, she'd surely fall.

Besides the short length of the steps, they were paltry in width as well. One theory Tara had heard was that the steps led to sacred ceremonial places. Being exceedingly steep, it was impossible for two people to pass, discouraging anyone from climbing them without very good cause. This was strictly a one-way trail, and then only for those practiced in the climb. Tara noticed, uncomfortably, that these steps had an extra hazard built in; each tread sloped downhill. That slope, on the slippery rock, was hazardous enough going up. It would make the trip down suicidal.

Different anthropologists theorized that such steps, in steep mountainous terrain, were carefully engineered to discourage penetration by the uninitiated. They led to sites that were considered to have great power, where the ceremonies conducted were often carried out by a select few members of the tribe, usually no more than five or six people. The odd thing was that sites such as this were found in virtually every part of the world. In many of these places, some of them separated by oceans and continents, archaeologists had noted the same number of steps, with the same design--narrow, and sloping downhill. It was almost as if those who ascended these steps never returned, or at least returned by a different route. A safe alternative route down the side of the mountain, however, had never been discovered in any of these places. That meant the participants in these ceremonies had hidden routes down or were highly trained in scaling these perilous stairways, or...

Following along behind Chocko, Tara was surprised at how easily he negotiated the steps. He walked on tiptoes with an ease and grace that made Tara wonder if it came from practice. Had he been up these steps before or was there something akin to a racial memory, a genetic imprinting that made it so easy for him?

As they approached their destination, Chocko stopped and pointed off into the distance. A good five miles away a spiral of dust rose in the air, stirred up by a vehicle traveling at a high rate of speed in their direction. For a moment, as she looked down, Tara felt dizzy. She realized that one small error of judgment on the narrow trail could result in her suddenly plummeting downward to her death. Leaning against a wall of rock to steady herself, she pressed the binoculars to her eyes and focused on the approaching vehicle.

"Anybody you know?" Chocko asked.

"It's a Jeep, some kind of utility vehicle. It could be anyone."

"Well, they're definitely heading in our direction. There's only a single road into this place. So it can't be a mistake. Whoever it is, they're not just passing through. Do you want to go on?"

"Why do you ask?"

"We're not exactly welcome here."

"I can't even think about it, Chocko. I've got to go on."

The remaining climb to the top of the ridge became increasingly dizzying and hazardous. In places where the trail narrowed, Tara found herself looking down two hundred feet or more into the desolate rocky canyon. She fought back vertigo, terrified by the prospect of losing her footing. All the while, the approaching vehicle drew nearer.

"Don't move!" Chocko's voice, a hoarse whisper, stopped her. Heart pounding, she looked forward, seeing only his broad back. His jeans jacket and dusty denims formed a wall, beyond which she could not see. He was holding Melvin by his collar and the animal clawed the ground, desperately trying to escape.

Chocko held up his hand, warning her to stop, and pointing toward the base of the cliff. She turned and watched the approaching Jeep. It seemed to be heading directly toward the canyon where they'd begun their climb. Then, at the last moment, it veered off and disappeared behind a wall of rock to the south.

"Do you think he saw us?" Tara asked.

Without answering, Chocko pushed on. They moved to the East, climbed another fifty feet in elevation, and soon were on the top of a sharp ridge of barren rock. The ridge itself ran north and south for a quarter mile or so. From the air, Tara imagined, it must have looked like the tail of a giant iguana, its body stretching out further to the north for another mile.

Breathless, she stood by Chocko and gazed down into the valley to the east. In contrast with the western terrain, this land was thick with vegetation. Pine trees, sage, and green buffalo grasses filled the bottom of the canyon and stretched up a long draw into the higher elevations.

"It's beautiful," Tara said. "What makes this valley so different? It's so lush, almost as if it had been cultivated."

"Maybe there was a time when it was," Chocko replied distractedly. He had turned his back and was gazing at a rock formation fifty feet above them. Tara followed his gaze up the side of the mountain to a rugged ledge. That's when she spotted it.

The wreckage of the *breezy* was little more than a crumpled bundle of metal. To Tara it looked more like a pile of ruined deck chairs than something that had once carried a man aloft. It was crushed back under a stony ledge, the debris all but hidden from view, as if the mountain had suddenly produced a mouth that swallowed up aircraft and pilot. Now the crumbs of this grisly meal spilled out over its lip, in the form of a few twisted strips of darkened metal.

"You can see why they couldn't find it from the air," Chocko said. "I doubt you could see anything from directly above." He began climbing toward the wreck. "Are you coming?"

After a ten minute climb they reached the ledge which formed the lower lip of the cave. Chocko scrambled up first, then lay down flat on the ground and gave Tara a hand up the last few feet.

As Tara sat massaging her sore ankle, which was now more numb than painful, she gazed into the distance. The view was magnificent. A lofty, high desert terrain stretched out before her in every direction. The sun, high overhead, bleached out the shadows made by the deep crevasses along the side of the mountain, so that the sculptural ledges and spires, in myriad shades of deep red, looked for all the world as if they'd been carved into the landscape by ancient gods.

"You may not want to see this."

Tara turned in the direction of Chocko's voice. He knelt down on the rocky ledge, probing a broken propeller attached to a crude-looking engine. Scattered around it were the remains of the pilot, the bones startlingly white, picked clean by desert scavengers and baked by the sun. The skull rested in a slight indentation in the ground, the lower jaw gone and a large piece missing from the cranium, extending from the right eye socket to the lower cheek. The evidence indicated that death had come quickly to the pilot. Chocko probed the broken skull, then picked it up gingerly, almost lovingly in his hands. At digs where she had worked, Tara had noticed that Indians usually avoided any direct contact with the bones.

Tara had seen many skeletons at archaeological digs but they had been the last remains of people who'd lived hundreds of years before. She had never connected them with incidents directly related to her own life. Now she did. These bones most likely belonged to a man who had not only lived in her own lifetime but was in pursuit of something she herself was even now pursuing. Furthermore, Chocko had known this man as a friend, had spoken with him less than a year before. She had held his photos in her hands, knew his story, and had admired his handiwork. Seeing his bones filled her with a deep melancholy.

"Do you think it's Jack Milford?" she asked.

"I'm pretty sure." He pointed to the eye teeth. "Capped in gold," he said. "I remember that." He turned the skull and pointed to a hole in the back, an inch or two behind where the left ear would have been.

"A bullet hole," Tara said, her voice flat, full of dread.

"And a pretty large caliber. I did the computers for a big forensics lab up in L.A.," Chocko said. "I saw a lot of gunshot evidence. The entry hole is always pretty small unless it's from a hollow point bullet. Then the bullet spreads and where it comes out it really does a lot of damage."

"That explains the big hole around the right eye. That's the exit hole."

Chocko set the skull down where he'd found it, touching it respectfully as he did. He turned, gazed deeper into the mouth of the cave which held the wreck. He pointed to an indentation in the rock wall inside the cave. Tara dropped down on all fours and moved in closer to inspect Chocko's find. Unmistakably, these were the crushed bones of what had once been a man's hand and forearm, pressed into a crevice in the rock. They told the story of their owner's last desperate effort to reach out, to ward off the deadly impact with the rocky wall. Here was evidence that in spite of his mortal wound he was somehow still aware of his own death approaching, that he had known a moment of horror, and the second or two of sheer dread that comes in the face of imminent disaster.

As Tara reconstructed the incident in her mind, the pilot must have spotted his killer and in trying to elude him had flown too close to the rocks. Perhaps he'd known he was going to crash at the same instant that he'd heard the rifle shot with the bullet that penetrated his head, churning through his gray matter. Or maybe he'd even made an ill-advised effort to crash land the plane in the cave, seeing this option as a last-ditch effort to avoid being shot out of the air.

But then an even more horrifying scenario came to mind. What if Jack Milford was shot after he crashed? The bones embedded in the rock wall attested to the fact that the pilot might have already been injured when he was shot. Tara shuddered as she imagined the injured Milford crouching in the cave as a final bullet finished him off. What kind of person would it take to level a gun at an injured man's head and squeeze the trigger?

Chocko made a sweeping gesture of the area. "No cameras. No camera equipment," he said.

"But it could have scattered. It could be down the side of the mountain somewhere."

"I don't think so. The crash site is a pocket in the mountain. Look at the way the other junk is scattered, all jammed up against the inner wall. My guess is that everything attached to the plane was thrown against the wall, with the same impact that his arm hit. Somebody was up here. I want you to notice something else, too. Most of the fabric has been stripped from the wings."

Chocko pointed to the edge of the frames where, indeed, it appeared that someone had carefully cut the fabric from the wings with a very sharp knife. The remnant they'd spotted from below was not cloth from the plane itself, as it turned out, but a piece of what perhaps had been a T-shirt snagged on a protruding rock.

"Someone definitely didn't want the wreck to be spotted. They went to a lot of trouble to make certain it wasn't."

"And the other equipment was stolen because somebody knew what the pilot had found," Tara speculated.

"Somebody picked over the wreck, developed the photos that maybe were still in the camera, or cameras, and saw something important..."

"My Dad!"

"If it was him, wouldn't he have sent these photos to you, like he did the others?"

"Maybe he did," Tara said. "Most of the photos he sent me were shot by an amateur, yet there was that single black and white enlargement, shot from a higher elevation, maybe by the pilot way before the wreck. Maybe whoever found the wreck just took the equipment. Maybe that was the motive. The stuff must have been pretty valuable..."

"Or someone wanted the photos bad enough to kill for them."

"Dad was...is not a violent man."

"Except maybe in self-defense," Chocko said. "I think even that would be hard for him."

As if suddenly recalling an important detail, Chocko turned away, dropped down on all fours and crept to the outer edge of the ledge. "Come here. Look at this!"

She joined him at the edge. Far below them, scratched out on the ground, barely visible through the trees and underbrush, was a huge terraglyph of Kokopeli. Because of the angle of the trees and the artful way the figure had been carved into the rocky floor of the canyon, it would have been nearly impossible to spot this gigantic drawing from the air. Only from this ledge would it have been clear. With this picture, another piece of the puzzle fell into place. This was perhaps the picture the pilot-photographer had been shooting when he confronted his assassin and crashed into the rocks. And this was the picture that had so intrigued Drake. This was the hunchbacked flute player he'd described in his first message to Tara. It was also the crude drawing he'd made on the postcard to her.

"We're there," Tara said. "That's pretty clear, isn't it?"

"The thing that troubles me is that we're not the only ones who know. Whoever picked up Milford's cameras may know."

"What difference does it make?"

"A lot. We know this is sacred land, for one. We're trespassing. If we're discovered we might be...how did they say it down in South America? We might be *disappeared*. The other possibility is treasure hunters. If they've found this place, and they discovered something of value here, they're not likely to welcome us with open arms."

"And if it's Dad?" Tara waited but for a long time Chocko was silent. It was clear that he didn't hold out much hope for that.

"I'm sorry," Chocko said at last. "But the truth is, you've got to prepare for whatever we find."

"Look over to the left." Tara used the binoculars to survey a further extension of the trail. She saw impossibly narrow steps, some only a foot or two wide, sculpted into the mountain. Her ankle throbbed and pain shot up her leg, just thinking about the climb. Without handholds, the course would indeed be precarious.

The trail zigzagged to the top of the mountain. Even from a great distance, she could see the outline of a manmade wall, apparently the destination of this tortuous trek. Tara pressed the binoculars to her eyes. There was no doubt about it now. It was a wall, eight to ten feet wide and six feet high, with a narrow window opening at the center. It seemed to mark what was left of an ancient ruins, constructed hundreds, maybe even thousands of years before.

As she stared at the scene her heart raced. All the evidence she had thus far pointed to the very real possibility that this quest for her father had ironically led to the site of what very well might be the home of the secret society of shamans.

As she peered through the glasses, she saw that the trail started at the base of the mountain, though a second trail, higher up, broke away and turned north. This second trail brought the climber toward the ledge where Tara and Chocko now crouched. She handed the binoculars to Chocko and pointed all this out to him.

"It's a whole complex," he said, studying the trails. "There's another trail going south. The trails might have gone to the six sacred directions..." He suddenly stopped talking, handed her the glasses and pointed.

She again pressed the glasses to her eyes, directing them to the place where Chocko pointed. A single figure was making his way up the side of the mountain. He...and she was certain it was a man...wore a green and tan camouflaged parka which blended in amongst the trees, making him nearly invisible.

Tara moved her gaze down the trail to the floor of the canyon.

The Jeep they'd seen earlier was parked there. The tailgate was down and two large boxes rested upon it, half opened. She knew exactly what the boxes were since she'd seen similar ones at many archaeological digs. They were used for storing precious objects. They contained packing materials and partitions to keep each object separated and safe. She abruptly shifted her sight up the trail again, focusing on the man's back as he climbed.

"It's Tom!"

"You said he didn't know anything about this area."

"He lied to me."

"You might have guessed that."

Tara nodded. "I've got to stop him."

"I wouldn't recommend that."

"I can't let him get away with it."

"Just remember he's bigger than you."

She was silent for a moment, then: "I can't just..."

"I'd let the authorities worry about it."

"That means jail. He'd lose his academic standing. God, Chocko, he's my kid's dad!"

Chocko stared back at her, impassively. "He lied to you, was abusive to you...he's a thief. What more do you have to know? Face up to it!"

"You want to know the truth? I'd like to kill him with my bare hands."

"Good. Check out his right hip. What do you see?"

Tara pressed the binoculars to her face again. "A gun! Lots of people carry guns out on the desert."

"We're not."

"But you don't think..."

"What he's hauling out could be worth tens of thousands of dollars to the right collectors, even hundreds of thousands if he's found what I think he has. Most of us will never even come close to that kind of money. What are you worth to him?"

She studied Chocko's face as if she might find the answer there. He stared back at her, waiting for her reply. "That's so cold!" she said.

"It's your call, Tara, I'll back you up."

"You know my answer."

His nod was nearly imperceptible.

*   *   *

She called his name from behind the embankment where she had hidden to watch him. For ten minutes or more she had watched him, down on all fours, crouched in the shallow excavation, carefully brushing away dirt from an object she could not see. Unlike the shadowy figure she had seen digging in Charla's gardens days before, Tom worked cautiously, in the way they'd been taught by the archaeologists in Peru more than seven years before.

"Tom..." Her voice was low, almost gentle, as if she did not want to frighten him, as if she had a special message, intended only for his ears. It was intimate, not threatening or confrontive, begging patience.

For a long, tense moment he barely moved. All motion, even the birds in the sky, seemed to freeze. Tara stood, partially hidden by the rock, her left arm resting against it, feeling its stability and impenetrability. In the split seconds that seemed like hours, her heart pounded, so loud in her own ears that she was certain Tom could hear it. She almost wished he would, for then he might understand what she was going through. Maybe he would see the pain his actions caused. Maybe he would care.

For that last split second of clinging to a lie she could live with, one she would not have to do anything about, she blocked the movement of time, preventing the inevitable truth from turning to reveal itself.

Tom rose from the hole slowly, like a man rising from his own grave. He was holding something in his hands. As he turned, the object, too, moved out of the shadow of his body and glittered in the sun. For one brief moment she thought he was offering it to her and from a very childish, hopeful place in her mind she thought of shiny jewelry and glittering crowns once worn by royalty. *Why is he offering this? A peace offering? A bribe?*

Dreams of her childhood tumbled into her mind, impossible dreams that she suddenly and savagely discovered she'd held too long. It was not a crown he was offering. Not a gift at all. The sun's reflection had deceived her, now sparkling from the polished metallic surface of a revolver so large she at first took it to be a joke. Tom wasn't smiling.

"I tried to warn you, Tara. You're so goddamned stubborn! Why couldn't you just stay out of this?"

"Where's my father? If I thought for one minute..."

"Shut up! You never should have come here, never."

"The dig, down in the hole. It's gold, isn't it? You found the gold. You were right about the Seven Cities then. Isn't that enough, Tom?"

"Nobody would listen. They all called it a hoax. Do you know what I went through? Do you have any idea?"

"So this is your vindication?"

Tom laughed scornfully, his laughter cold, maniacal. "You don't have any idea what this is about, do you? I couldn't care less what they think about my theories. Not now. It really doesn't matter. But you should know what it's about. Do you know what's down there? What I found is worth millions. Millions! Don't you get it? Are you so fucking dense you can't get that? I've barely scratched the surface and I've already stashed away enough stuff to pay off the national debt. I'm telling you..."

"You're telling me nothing, Tom. All I'm hearing is more of your lies, to yourself and everyone else in your life." Her voice was calm, yet she trembled inside.

"Let me show you something!" Tom jumped down into the hole where he'd been working and leapt out of it again dragging a canvas bag weighted down with objects. Still holding his gun in his hand, he reached inside and pulled out a huge bowl. He rubbed the surface against his shirt and turned that side around for her to see.

"That's gold you're looking at. Solid gold, Tara. And this is only the beginning. There are rooms full of this stuff!"

She had never been tempted by riches. Tom should have known that. She walked over closer to the hole he was working. He backed away, moving to the opposite side of the opening, maintaining his distance. She peered down into the dig. It was much deeper than she had imagined. It appeared that they were standing on what must once have been the roof of one kiva, looking down through a hole into a second. In the area Tom had been working, in the first kiva, there were mounds in the shape of various artifacts. She saw a huge life sized eagle laying in the dirt where Tom had apparently been cleaning it. He had brushed away some of the mud caked around it but even through the heavy patina of the ore itself she could see that it, too, was gold.

The sight of so many precious artifacts, in one place and apparently in perfect condition was dazzling and for a moment she found herself sharing his avarice. She glanced at Tom, then back at the excavation. She felt *his* greed, *his* covetousness, and for the first time in her life knew what had driven him, what had eaten away at him all these years. He was a treasure hunter, not an anthropologist! He was driven by greed, not a reverence for the past.

In spite of herself she imagined what it could mean in her own life to silently walk away with even a single one of these treasures. The part of her that in the past had so easily pushed back thoughts of self-gain had succumbed to temptation at last. She'd struggled with these demons long ago, at her first dig at a site down in Mexico, and had won out over them. But never before had her resolve been tested as it now was.

"Tell me where my Dad is and I'll walk away from here," she said, doing her best to beat back a nagging inner voice telling her that if she hoped to survive she would have to cooperate with Tom, to share his find with him, to play along with him, like a partner.

"You're not ever going to walk away from here."

"Don't be melodramatic. Where is my father, Tom?"

He shrugged. His face hardened as he stared back at Tara.

"If you tell me where he is, I'll keep silent about this."

"You'd never keep your mouth shut."

"You wouldn't harm him. I know you wouldn't." Tara prayed she was right. "The photographer...Jack Milford...what's left of him at the wreck back there..."

"It's not what you think, Tara. I found him like that. He'd crashed. He was badly injured. He'd been there for two or three days. He would have been dead by the time I'd gotten help to him."

"And you were afraid the rescue crew would see all this."

"I couldn't chance it."

"So you..." She could not bear to say what she knew was true. For a long time she was silent. "God, Tom. What's happened to you?" She stopped. An image of the twisted wreckage of the Jeep she'd seen just days before filled her mind. "The man down at Coyote Mesa, the one who went over the cliff, who was he?"

"I have no idea what you're talking about."

"I think you do. He knew about this, didn't he?" She glanced down into the hole. The treasures, all that wealth, endless riches, it was all worthless, all of it. There weren't enough material riches in all the world to justify what he'd done, what he'd become.

A thousand thoughts raced through her mind, all scrambled together with the love she'd once felt for Tom, and for what was going to happen to Maya if Tom carried out his threats. Only one thing was certain in her life at this moment--she did not want to die, not like this, not at the hand of a man she'd once loved. What a bitter, bitter revelation.

She could imagine Tom somehow getting away with it, burying her body, then murdering and burying Chocko, and then getting Maya's custody. He could actually accomplish that since he would be his daughter's only living relative. The idea that this man might actually carry through with his threat, with Maya ending up being raised by her mother's murderer, was too much to bear. Yet, she was powerless. Tom was much stronger than her. She was no match for him. Besides, he had the gun and judging by the shrewd determination she saw in his face he had every intention of using it.

Out of the corner of her eye Tara detected movement. She turned her head ever so slightly. It was Melvin the dog! Alerted by her change of expression, Tom whirled and fired off two shots in rapid succession. The whine and whistle of the spent bullets ricocheting off rock confirmed that he'd missed both times. Tucking his tail between his legs, Melvin raced off and disappeared down the trail.

"Goddamn mongrel!" Tom growled. "He some friend of yours?"

"Please think about this, Tom. You can't go through with this! I'm your child's mother, for god sake."

"Yeah, and you'd deprive her of all this wealth. You would, wouldn't you? You're so goddamn proper, so fucking virtuous!"

"Say I did go along with you..."

"Oh, so now you're willing to bargain. Too late, Tara. You know way too much. I could never trust you. I have never been able to trust you with any of my secrets."

"And Margarette? Does she go along with your ideas?"

He shrugged. "Margarette's not your problem. She's nobody's problem any more."

His words chilled her. She stared at the gun in his hand. It was easy to imagine him killing not just once but twice. But why? Maybe Margarette had discovered what he was doing and threatened to go to the authorities.

Once again she noticed movement out of the corner of her eye, but this time she did not telegraph the fact to Tom. It was Chocko she saw this time, not Melvin. He moved silently, disturbing not a single pebble as he crept forward. One minute he wasn't there, the next moment he was, appearing as if out of nowhere. He held something in his right hand, a rock about the size of a softball. It wasn't difficult to anticipate his intent.

When he was within three or four feet of Tom, Chocko stopped. Tara looked down. Chocko had walked all that way in his bare feet in order to cover the perilous distance without attracting attention. Startled by a sound or a sense of movement, Tom whirled around, fired once, then a second time as the rock in Chocko's hand came down hard on the wrist that held the gun. Tom screamed as his second shot echoed over the countryside, and in the next moment both men were down on all fours scrambling for the gun which had fallen away. For a moment Chocko had the gun in his hand, then they were wrestling for it. Again a loud report echoed over the land and Chocko fell away. Instantly, Tom was on his feet. He winced with pain as he tried to level the gun at Chocko's head, his right hand crippled by the rock with which Chocko had hit him seconds before. Unable to hold the gun in that hand, he shifted it to his left.

Without thinking, Tara leapt forward, drove her head deep into Tom's mid-back and felt the impact shudder through her own body as she struck him squarely in the center of his spine. A long cry of rage reverberated from his body and he tumbled to the ground.

Grabbing him around the waist, Tara clung to his torso, pushing, scrambling crabwise to force them both toward the excavation, away from Chocko. And then, desperately clutching Tom's waist, she heard Chocko calling a warning and then she was falling, her arms locked around Tom. A sudden jarring spun them both around, and they were falling again. With a sickening thump they came to a final, shuddering stop, locked in a lover's embrace, Tara's head now resting against Tom's shoulder.

They had fallen nearly thirty feet. For what seemed like an eternity she lay dazed and trembling in Tom's arms, her mind grappling with it all, trying to make sense of everything that had happened. She heard Chocko calling her name from above and she tried to call back but only a weak, trembling sound came from her throat. For a split second she felt almost euphoric, in a state of shock. She felt like a young girl again, that twenty-two-year old who'd run off with her handsome young man for adventures in Peru. Tom had been at the top of his class. He had been the fulfillment of her childhood dream, the talented, caring man, the man who would love her forever, who promised to quiet the restless longing that had ruled her life.

Cautiously, she lifted her head away from Tom's still form. In the darkness of this cavern she saw shadowy corridors leading to other rooms, circular passageways to other kivas. Her right arm was caught under Tom's back. As she pulled away from him, his shoulder rolled to the right and a dull rasping sound came from his throat. His head tilted limply away, settling at an oblique angle that she knew wasn't right.

It took Tara a moment to size up what had happened. When they fell, Tom landed under her, cushioning her fall, a distance of about eight feet to the floor of the first kiva. They'd fallen near the center of the hole that Tom had made into the second kiva, and he had struck his head as they fell through. It all came back to her now, a cruel memory that she could not push to the quiet recesses of her mind. She'd heard the sharp thud of his head when it hit, and then the sickening, unmistakable snap of his neck.

She instantly thought of the gun. It lay under him, in his left hand. He was still clutching it in his fingers. She reached for it reflexively, expecting to wrestle it from his grip. Instead, his limp fingers yielded the weapon without the trace of a struggle.

Tara leaned over Tom and pressed her fingers to his neck, feeling for a pulse. But she already knew the truth. His flesh felt shockingly cold. Tara had been with her mother when she died, and the unmistakable dispersion of energy that comes with death had come here, too, and was gone. Tara trembled uncontrollably. She knelt beside Tom's body, and felt a terrible urge to lift his head and cradle him in her arms in spite of what he'd done. Enemy or not, she had loved him. Enemy or not, he was Maya's father. The enmity she'd felt moments before dissolved, and tears came, flooding her eyes.

"Oh, my god!" she groaned, as the finality of this moment sank in. Between wrenching sobs, she whispered Tom's name, staring down at him, shaking her head in disbelief. She moved away from his body and wiped her tears across her dirty forearm. A great smear of red dirt appeared on her cheek and across her mouth, and for a moment she looked for all the world like a warrior beginning to apply war paint.

Slowly coming to her senses, she looked around her. It seemed they were in the middle of a storeroom dug into the rock. Like the kiva above them it held artifacts such as large bowls, figures of animals, and small human effigies whose features were still caked with dirt. She turned her gaze back to Tom's still form, wondering if, in that instant before he died, he'd had a moment to reflect on what he'd done, on what his life had come to. Her compassion for him suddenly slipped away, replaced by anger.

She looked up. Thirty feet above her, outlined against a blue sky, Melvin the dog stood trembling, leaning toward her, panting, sniffing the air, looking for all the world as if he might jump down into her arms any second. She looked down at Tom's face. His eyes stared straight up toward Melvin, his face oddly peaceful and benign. A little cry escaped from her throat. She leaned over him, touched her fingers to his eyelids, almost as if to caress his face, then gently closed his eyes. She wondered what to do with him, how to get him out of the hole. She could not leave him there. But he was a big man. She'd need help to pull him out.

Chocko, she thought. Chocko! She'd almost forgotten him. She listened. Except for Melvin sniffing the ground above her, and her own breathing, there was not a single sound. I have to get out of here! She studied the walls of the hole. She spied the crude rope ladder Tom had used to climb in and out. It was nothing but a single strand of half-inch nylon line with loops for footholds knotted every fifteen inches or so. As she stepped into the first loop, the rope pulled away from her, swinging wildly to the left. She held on, waited for it to stabilize, then took her first steps, lifting herself upward, a foot at a time.

At the top of the hole the dog licked her face, turned and ran a few steps to Chocko's still form lying a few feet away. She dug her fingers into the earth and pulled herself onto solid ground. Chocko sat back several feet from the hole, clutching his forearm. Blood covered his fingers and had soaked the waistband of his jeans. "It's not as bad as it looks," he said. "It's my forearm, maybe a broken bone. I'll be okay."

"Tom's dead. He's dead, Chocko." She spoke in a dull monotone, not wanting to believe her own words.

Chocko nodded.

Through tears Tara managed to fashion a bandage and splint from a bundle of dry pine branches and torn strips of fabric from a parka she'd stowed in her backpack. She could feel the shattered bone as she did what she could to stabilize the arm, but except for a bit of cursing Chocko didn't complain. As she worked on him, tenderly, fearful of hurting him further, she was amazed at his ability to handle pain. His tolerance for it seemed extraordinary, and she wondered what magic allowed him to detach himself from his affliction, treating it as coolly as if it were only a small bruise or cut finger.

For a long time they just sat there, side by side, their backs against the rock. Tara sobbed. There were no words to discharge what she was feeling. Tears. Grief. The horror of having the man she'd once loved die in her arms, the man who'd fathered her daughter, was more than she could bear.

Melvin the dog lay at their feet, curiously studying the landscape, as if in search of some form of amusement, something to pass the time. It was odd, Tara thought, how animals accepted death, how trauma and tragedy rolled off them, even the tragedy of their own demise. Her thoughts turned back in time, recalling the death of a cat. The animal had died in Tara's arms, so gently, so smooth in its transition that she had barely noticed its passing. She did not know why she remembered this now but somehow there was comfort in the memory.

Chocko got to his feet, turned to the north and pointed with his good hand. Further up the mountain, another hundred yards or so, he indicated a mesa, covering no more than a half acre. Once again, a narrow row of steps zigzagged back and forth, climbing steeply to the top. With his left hand, Chocko pointed to what was obviously a man-made wall near the center of the mesa. The wall was no more than forty feet wide and about six feet tall. In its center, facing out onto the rugged mountainous landscape beyond, was a single, narrow window opening, a couple of feet square.

Suddenly, even as Chocko was still pointing, Melvin began to howl. He ran ahead, up the trail leading to the top of the mesa. Chocko and Tara watched in amazement as the dog ran, barking and howling wildly and mournfully as he scrambled up the path, his passage following the lightning zig-zag pattern of the path, lacing its way up the side of the mountain. As they watched spellbound, the dog stopped at the wall, then paced back and forth, whining and jumping up to rest his front paws on the weather-worn sill at the center of the structure. He scratched at the adobe wall frantically, then ran back down the trail toward Tara and Chocko, who were now gingerly making their way up the steep, narrow steps.

"Melvin, down!" Chocko bellowed, trying to silence the animal. But the dog raced back up the trail, howling.

"Probably a damn jack rabbit!" Chocko wheezed. He stopped for a moment to catch his breath, grinning from ear to ear as he turned to Tara, amused by the animal's antics. Again the dog ran down the trail, quivering all over, as if he could not get his master to move fast enough, to join him in this exciting chase. Chocko patted the animal's head. "Take it easy boy. Don't give yourself a coronary."

Once again the animal howled, turned suddenly and raced to the top of the hill. Melvin stopped at the window, paced back and forth, then sniffed the air frenetically. He turned back to the two people on the trail, barked twice, then ran around to the opposite side of the wall, momentarily disappearing from view. Again Tara and Chocko heard his howling, more frantic and mournful than before. Chocko stopped. He turned to Tara, his brow knit with concern.

As they watched, Melvin circled the wall, running around it, nose to the ground, as if chasing an invisible rabbit, leaping forward, leaning as he turned, scrambling for footing in his haste. He disappeared behind the wall, yelping, disconsolate, then appeared once again, suddenly, tormented. He raced down the hill, jumped up on first Chocko and then Tara, whined, licking their faces, then raced back up the hill to repeat his crazed dance around the wall.

As they came within fifty feet of their destination, Chocko and Tara stopped once more to catch their breath. The wall itself stood at the very top of the mesa, where the hard rock of the mountain had been flattened either by human labor or nature. Stretching toward them from the single portion of adobe wall was a perfectly circular formation, what was left of a once proud architectural creation. Tara could almost recreate in her mind how the structure must have looked in its heyday. The wall had been at least eighteen inches thick, forming a room fifty feet in diameter. Judging by the remaining piece of wall, the ceiling had been six or seven feet high. Tara had seen artist's renderings of similar buildings, based on anthropologists' speculations. This one had probably boasted a conical roof of stripped lodge-poles, fashioned of pine, cedar, or even willow, transported from forests ten or twenty miles north. The poles would then have been spanned with stripped saplings and thatched over to carry off the rains. At the center, the highest portion of the building, the ceiling would have been at least twelve feet high.

"I've been here before," Tara said. "But it can't be. I'm sure that I've never..."

"It's the ruins of an old round house, like in your Dad's journal. That's probably what you remember."

Tara nodded slowly. "I can imagine him standing in this place and making the whole thing up." She pointed to the window opening in the remaining section of wall. "It's pretty much as he described it. You've got to give him that much, he's a hell of a writer."

"Look at this." Chocko knelt down and picked something up, examining it carefully. He handed it to Tara.

It was a dark blue plastic object, one side faded by the sun. It was the top of a ballpoint pen.

"It could be Dad's. But then, it could be anyone's."

Melvin the dog ran up to Tara, licked her face frantically and turned toward the window. He looked back over his shoulder, whimpering as if he wanted her to follow. Then he yelped and took off running. As Chocko and Tara watched, Melvin leapt at the window opening. This time, as he jumped toward it, then passed through the opening, the space into which he hurled himself was suddenly transformed. It was like looking at a holographic picture from a child's story book, one whose image changed depending on the angle you looked at it.

At one moment Tara saw the dog jumping into the air, the mountainous skyscape behind him. At the next moment, the skyscape disappeared and for just an instant she thought she saw the rooftops of an ancient pueblo. The dog appeared to be caught in the air, suspended as if by some invisible force. Tara and Chocko watched helplessly as Melvin swam in the air, his legs pumping for traction.

Suddenly his body appeared to elongate, becoming a caricature of itself. It stretched out against the sky, looking more like a gigantic lizard than a dog now, extending into space. The poor animal appeared to move in slow motion and at a very high rate of speed simultaneously. Even as Melvin shot out into space, like a rocket racing through the void, he also appeared to be just inching forward. And indeed, his posture and the slow side to side movement of his head indicated that the bizarrely elongated Melvin was enjoying a slow crawl through an ocean of dimensionlessness. Further on, the dog's body seemed to gather itself up. For a split second it returned to normal size. And then a slit formed in the sky; it opened up and the dog slid through.

Now the entire scene beyond the wall changed, from a mountain range with blue-gray sky at one moment to something quite different the next. Tara and Chocko momentarily saw an ancient village, a pueblo of as many as a hundred dwellings carved into the side of a cliff. Hovering over it were billowy white clouds suspended in a turquoise-blue sky. The reddish adobe walls of the village were brand new, Tara noted, though the architecture was clearly of a style that was hundreds of years old.

Stunned by the beauty and mystery of this event, Tara walked toward the window, then turned away and walked around behind it. She stood at the opening and looked back through at Chocko. It was a normal opening, a window in the center of a narrow wall, looking out onto a normal landscape on either side of it.

"This is impossible!" Tara said, leaning on the sill and staring at Chocko, who had knelt down on the ground a few feet back.

"You'd better come back here and sit down," Chocko said.

Detecting the gravity in his voice, she did as he said, taking her place on the ground beside him. They sat at what would have been the center of the roundhouse, staring in awe at the window.

"It is some kind of trick, isn't it?"

Chocko shook his head. "Have you ever heard of this thing the astronomers talk about--*black holes?*"

"Of course. Einstein and other physicists speculated they might exist in deep space."

"What if it's something like that? After all, aren't we floating around in deep space? We are not outside looking in because there is no such thing as outside and inside, not really. Do you see what I mean? It is all the same. There is only one world, all of this, the stars, the moon, the sun, our own planet. Think about it this way--that we are standing in the center of it because no matter where you stand it is the center. If I follow what the physicists are saying these days, it really couldn't be any other way because the universe is infinite. People have invented space and time. My shaman friends tell me that it's only in the little-ness of our minds that we create the finite. Maybe they're right, maybe the universe doesn't know the finite. Do you follow what I'm trying to say? It is like your father said in his notes. And if the center is wherever you stand, we are all, at any given moment, standing in all-time and all-dimension.

"I read somewhere that our ability to focus on everyday reality is what separates us from other beings, particularly plants and lower animals. The old people in my community say that when we are dying we are like plants. We start coming into this other world, and for a moment we look back and see the illusions we've been living. Maybe the black holes are passages into other realities but we know little about them except that it's where time and space curve back into themselves."

"And my father's in there, that's what you believe, isn't it?"

"*We* are all in there!"

"Black holes are theoretical. Nobody has actually proved they are there. It's all speculation and games. Besides, black holes are huge, the size of our entire solar system."

"This place, this window," Chocko continued. "My people have been aware of it for hundreds of years. Maybe thousands! It has been in our mythology for centuries. I never knew if these stories were spiritual lessons, teaching metaphors, or if they were real. The old story-tellers tell about this window. They say that it goes to the *pueblo of the unseen*, which they believe is the underworld governing everything that happens in our own world."

Tara thought about what she'd seen back in the vaults where Tom had died and she knew that all of this was part of a reality that she had always fought to deny. There had to be reasonable, scientific explanations for what seemed to be extraordinary events. But if she had ever entertained the real possibility of a metaphysical reality that defied all of science's truths, it was now. Throughout the fields of anthropology and archaeology, there were legends as wild as those told by the indigenous peoples, of workers at sacred digs who had gone crazy, committed suicide, or simply disappeared soon after violating a sacred site. The society of shamans! Was this it? Could it be that Tom had uncovered evidence for the North American Oracle that she herself had sought for so many years?

But ancient legends also warned of deadly repercussions for those who dared violate the sanctity of such sites. She had heard rumors about a place in Peru, not far from the dig where she and Tom had worked. There'd been a cave-in at a tunnel. Three native workers had lost their lives. Then, within a year, Professors Victor Cardoza and Norma Wainwright had died in a plane crash returning to Mexico City. Two months later, an assistant from the University of California, who'd been with Dr. Wainwright, died instantly when his bicycle was struck by a hit and run driver.

Efforts were made to debunk any rumors that these deaths were anything more than sheer coincidence. Then, two more people who'd worked on the dig died, one of them a young student from Mexico, who succumbed to pneumonia. Another, a resident of Cuszco, had his throat slit during a senseless fight in a local tavern.

Tara did not know what legends or superstitions guarded this site but with Tom dead, Drake unaccounted for, and two others known to be dead--murdered!--she could not deny the possibility that she had been plunged into something far beyond her experience or belief. Fear and the lure of the unknown, along with a dark fascination with the possibility that she had stumbled upon the society of shamans, spurred her on. Though she had denied it, even to herself, she now realized that a sense of intrigue concerning the unknowable had never been far beneath the surface as she probed ancient cultures for clues that might tell her about worlds where all modern knowledge was challenged. Besides, she knew that a part of her was familiar with this place, knew it as well as she knew the streets of her own home town. But how could that be? She had no Indian blood, of that she was quite certain. Something beyond a genetic magnetism drew her to this place. Perhaps it resembled other places. Maybe she had seen photos.

"Is it yes?" Chocko asked.

She stared at Chocko, dumbly. What was he asking? Yes to what? Why yes? But she was nodding and there was something electrifying about saying yes. It was a declaration and affirmation of a deep yearning that had ached to be recognized her whole life, that had fought her denial and finally won.

How could he have known what to say, what she was feeling? How could he have known she needed, longed to go forward into this unknown reality? There was something about saying *yes*, that declared her belief to herself and the world, just as the words "I do" declared a marriage bond.

She was grateful, just terribly grateful. She felt her entire chest opening up. She could not walk away from this moment. She could not. She could not leave without knowing what she might discover beyond the window. ~

Magical Passage

Chocko and Tara stood for a long time beside the window, the last remnant of the ancient ruin. Tara walked around it, looking back through it, first one side and then the other. There was nothing there to explain what she'd seen with her own eyes. Unless some genius lighting engineer had projected a perfect hologram into the air from miles away, the vision they'd shared as Melvin flew through this space into the ancient village beyond it was real.

They sat down on the ground and leaned against the hard adobe wall. Tara's thoughts returned to the dig and to Tom's body lying at the bottom of the hole. A part of her was filled with the remorse and horror of what had happened, while another part felt free, liberated in a way she had never felt before. She could not explain it. How could the anguish of Tom's violent death possibly set her free? *Free from what? Surely, there was nothing to celebrate in the dark truth of Tom's life, or in his life slipping away in her arms.*

Abandoning what it could not accept, her attention turned to the artifacts that lay buried in the dig. It was an extraordinary find, not only because of the great wealth that lay buried there but because here at last was proof for the legendary Seven Cities of Cibola that drew the Spanish conquistadors to the southwest in 1536. There was no telling what further probing of the site would reveal. Instinctively, she knew there was a link between this place and the society of shamans that she'd been seeking.

"What will happen to the artifacts at the dig?" Tara asked.

"According to the ancient teachers, they will just disappear. We could leave now, come back tomorrow, and never find any of them again."

"And Tom?"

Chocko turned his hands palms up and shrugged.

"So, if something happened to my father and Charla...if they're down there..."

Chocko was silent. "Drake talked about the roundhouse, not the gold. That's what interested him."

"Surely, if he found the window, he would have seen the dig."

"You and I could have missed it if we'd followed the trail from the breezy up to the mesa. We spotted Tom first. We were watching to see where he'd go."

There was a long lull in their conversation. Staring through the empty space of the window, Tara asked, "How do you go through?"

Chocko studied her face. "Are you certain of this? There are risks."

"Dad went through and came back."

"We don't know that for certain." Chocko sighed, then distractedly scratched with his forefinger in the dirt by his side. "There are seven openings. Animals see them but ordinarily we humans don't."

"But we saw Melvin go through!"

"As I say, animals can see the openings."

"So how would Dad have known?"

"He either stumbled on it or someone guided him."

"The man at Charla Mather's house...White Crow. Maybe him."

"Haera. His name is Jose Haera. He calls himself White Crow. But nobody around here acknowledges him as one of theirs. People say he came from Brazil or Peru."

"Haera is White Crow? But he went to prison for looting. Charla Mather and him were named in a suit the Navajo people brought against him."

"He never went to prison. Jumped bail. Went across the border."

"My father knew about him and about Charla's involvement with him."

Tara shut her eyes, hugging her knees as she let this thought sink in. Hatred for this man Haera welled up in her. He represented the darkest of all forces in life--greed, deceit, the destruction of valuable sites. He was disdainful of everything beautiful and nurturing and loving--driven only by selfish gain. Sometimes she could feel those forces in her own life, a desire to be better, richer, more famous than anyone in her field. Sometimes, too, like Tom, she had been tempted by the treasures uncovered at ancient digs, though she'd never fallen to that temptation. Perhaps it was not Haera she hated but what he made her see, things about herself that she wrestled with in her own heart, impulses that she hid in the darkest recesses of her own mind.

The worst horror of all was how Haera might have influenced her own father. She wanted assurance that Drake would not be tempted by Haera's evil inducements. But when she reviewed

Drake's life in her mind, the risks he'd taken, the sacrifices he'd made to get the big story, she suddenly realized that he lacked an inner strength that she knew she possessed--the ability to resist sinking into the darkness of the soul that Haera and his kind represented.

Shame, fear, her hope that her gravest doubts about her father weren't true, prevented her from saying these things aloud. She could not accept that Drake would stoop so low, would use this loathsome creature, Haera, for his own selfish gain. Yet, she could not help but recall how he'd once used the mass murderer, Gary Steve Honnig, to get a big story. He'd actually befriended this monster, had even shared his earnings with him. Where would Drake draw the line? A part of her wanted to annihilate all the Haeras in the world. Even so, a part of her knew this was impossible, that there would always be Haeras. They would be born again and again until every man, woman and child in the universe could free themselves from the greed, deceit, and fear in their own hearts. The Haeras of the world only mirrored what others harbored in their own souls.

"Your doubt is driving you crazy, isn't it?" Chocko spoke slowly, weighing his words. "You're going to have to go through to prove something to yourself--that your dad is not who you are afraid he might be."

Tara dropped her eyes, not daring to look at him.

Chocko pointed with his good hand. "There's a spot in the center of the roundhouse." He stood up, oriented himself, then walked toward what he'd calculated to be the radius point of the roundhouse floor. He kicked in the dirt with the toe of his boots, then moved a few inches back and repeated the action. This time he knelt down and brushed away the dirt from a perfectly domed rock about a foot in diameter. It protruded a few inches above the ground, and as she inspected it Tara could see that it had not been naturally formed. It had been carved and ground into a perfect sphere, mostly buried, and it was of a hard, black substance she had never seen before.

"You sit here," Chocko instructed. "From this place at night you may be able to see the openings, maybe one, maybe more, like narrow slits of light. That's all."

"I simply walk through?"

"Purify yourself first."

Tara looked puzzled.

"We'll collect some sage before dark and you'll smudge yourself. Then there are prayers and songs, telling of your desire to go through. The words will come to you. And then the spaces will open up."

"Who told you these things?"

"Tony Fox."

In spite of her skepticism, Tara had to admit that Tony's magic had been extraordinary so far. It might be true what Chocko said about him. She would do as he suggested. There was no alternative in any case.

Late in the afternoon Tara gathered sage, following Chocko's instructions. They found feathers preened from wings of different birds and he showed her how to fashion a crude fan from them for smudging. With Chocko coaching her she scooped handfuls of loose rock and shaped them into a little mound, with a crater in the middle. This would serve as their smudge pot. When it got to be time, they'd burn dry twigs in the little crater. When these had burned down to glowing coals they'd add the green sage. It would smolder nicely and Tara could then smudge herself as Chocko instructed.

Preparations complete, they sat cross legged at the edge of the mesa, facing west, and dug into the meager supply of food they'd brought with them in their backpacks. Their meal consisted of trail mix, water, and a can of sardines that Chocko had tossed into his pack at the last minute.

"Have you thought of what happens if you don't come back through?" Chocko asked. "What about your daughter?"

"I'll come back through. I just will. I have to." She could not afford to think about Maya now. She would not let herself.

"Drake was right about you, you know. You're a very stubborn young woman."

"He said that?"

"He said a lot of things about you."

"I never knew he talked with his friends about me. He's always so wrapped up in his work."

"A man works to hide his grief, like a dog lying down in the dust to lick his wounds after tangling with a badger. Work takes some of the pain out of your life, lets you think maybe you weren't such a fool as you know damn well you are. Gives you a chance to feel like maybe your time here matters. That's why I came back. That's why I started the garden with the others." He turned to her, flashing a self-conscious grin."

"What's Drake's grief? What did you mean by that?"

"Losing his family, losing you when you were still very small." He said this with no hesitation.

"He didn't lose me, Chocko. He abandoned me."

Chocko nodded. "I'm not his lawyer, you know. I'm not defending him. But I've known him longer than you have. He's a kind of thrill junky, you know? He can't help that. It's his path. He had to make a difficult choice a long time ago, when he was still a very young man. At twenty-two a man hasn't got enough wisdom to make a decision like that. He's only got his passion. Choices made from passion come at a high price. So it took your dad twenty years to discover his mistake, and another ten to admit it. By the time he let the heartache catch up with him, he maybe thought he was too old to do anything about it. And what makes you think you should expect any more than that from him?"

"Because he's my father. That's a good enough reason."

"But before he's your father he's human. Stop acting as if you're in charge of the world."

He said it matter-of-factly but it stirred something up in Tara. She felt angry, then defensive. She wanted to say, "Don't you understand that all I ever wanted from him was to have him put his arms around me..." But she could not. She could not admit even to herself that this was what she had wanted, that perhaps this single obsession was what had drawn her here. She was a grown woman, beyond such petty needs. *Am I really?* she asked, startled by the question she'd never asked herself before, startled by what she'd felt in Tom's arms. *But that was because of the fall. I was in shock.* It wasn't that. It was more. Then, what could his death release for me?

"My father is a grown man. Why can't he..." Her voice broke and she sobbed. "Goddamn it!"

Chocko turned, swiveling around to face her just as the tears came. But he did not extend his arms. Nor did he offer solace. He simply watched, holding the moment for her to cry. When at last she stopped she wiped her eyes with her sleeve. A muddy streak stained her left cheek.

"I'm frightened," she said, "very frightened."

The desert below them turned from red to brown. Then for a moment the horizon blazed with orange light. All along the western horizon, for as far as they could see, a thin ribbon of pure white light marked the line between earth and sky. As day transformed into night, Tara watched the land below her, stretching out for thousands of miles, slipping into the shadows. An orange western sky turned deep crimson. For the briefest moment the ribbon of white light danced over the land, then flashed green, and then was suddenly extinguished.

Overhead, and for as far as she could see in every direction, the dense night sky filled with tiny pinpoints of light. Infinity. A dull glow of light in the eastern sky reminded her that just three hours distant was Albuquerque, the modern world where time and distance were measured and predictable, where ancient villages didn't just suddenly appear out of nowhere. *How could it be that in the space of less than two hundred miles, one could slip into such a different reality?*

"I'm ready," she said, not knowing exactly what signaled her that it was time, though her decision was firm.

They got up and walked slowly to the round rock at the center of the ruins. Chocko knelt and struck a match to the mound of dry twigs he'd laid for smudging. As the flames flared up, Tara thought she saw a brief glow of light around the window in the ruins, but then it faded and died. As moments slipped away the flames in the smudge pot gradually reddened, glowing eerily.

Chocko took Tara by the hand and told her to kneel down close to the smudge pot, her back toward the window. He added sprigs of sage to the glowing embers and the smoke rose around her, as if drawn by a draft from the window behind her. Chocko knelt opposite her, took the feathered fan and fanned the glowing embers, directing the smoke toward himself, closing his eyes serenely and gently inhaling the spicy scent of the smoldering green sage and sweet grass.

He chanted something under his breath, a prayer, Tara assumed, then fanned the smudge again, directing the smoke to her left and right. That done, he dropped the fan at his side and allowed the smudge to die down. In a few moments there was only the light of the stars. Tara found herself wondering why there was no moon tonight, why the night seemed so still. Usually there was the rustle of night birds' wings, faraway coyotes howling, dogs barking, the swish and groan of distant traffic. But tonight, in this place, there was no sound.

Chocko began slapping his thigh, using his body as a drum, setting a slow, heartbeat rhythm, holding the beat even and steady, so that soon Tara felt herself moving into the beat, her own heartbeat gradually becoming synchronized with it. In her mind's eye she saw night dancers, Katchinas like the ones she'd seen one fall night in Zuni. Images of their huge colorful masks flashed through her mind, costumes of bright colors, some with their feet wrapped in straw, some in buckskin, some with anklets of brass bells. She heard their feet caress the earth as they moved mysteriously through the village in the darkness. The Night Dances. But these were not the Night Dances she saw in her mind! Perhaps, she decided, her mind had distorted what she recalled.

Slipping deeper and deeper into a comforting dreamlike state, bordering on sleep, her heart filled with gratitude for Chocko's presence, his body close enough that she could reach out and touch him. She felt overwhelming gratitude for the night air and the infinite sheltering sky of the desert. She smelled the still smoldering sage and felt exalted by its purifying scent, pungent and earthy.

Suddenly she realized that she was not only thinking these things; she was singing them. She was singing her song aloud, just as Chocko had said she would! Softly, her song mingled with the rhythmic slapping sound Chocko made with his hand against his thigh. Chocko chanted with her song, the deep, almost guttural resonance of his voice supportive and empowering. Then the song stopped. It no longer came through her. She fell silent.

She imagined herself walking barefoot along a narrow path, her shuffling footsteps echoing off a high adobe wall that curved around to her right. Her body ached with the weight of mourning. But mourning what? She was recalling something. It seemed so long ago. She was still carrying Maya in her womb. The thought came to her, now my child will be suckled with the heaviness of my mourning. It will be a child of importance. The words *child of importance* were not something to celebrate but,to be dreaded, an affliction that she would not wish upon her baby. But why? Children of importance grew up to be leaders, warriors, men and women with causes, with missions. A mother did not wish such burdens on her children.

She heard footsteps approaching. For a moment she opened her eyes. Where were the footsteps--in her mind? In this other reality? Or did they belong to someone approaching the mesa? As her eyes opened she was comforted to find Chocko sitting across from her, his eyes closed, still holding the gentle, heartbeat-like rhythm.

"Keep going," he said.

She was back once again inside her vision, her journey. As she closed her eyes she thought she saw distant lightning. But no thunder came. She moved forward, a young woman with child, along a path that seemed both strange and familiar to her. The sound of the approaching footsteps grew stronger, and with it her fear. She turned a corner on the path and then the man, a stranger, was standing there before her, his eyes like the eyes of a startled buck on a forest trail. His eyes were glazed with fear and he smelled of terror. *Fear smells,* Tara thought. It was something she'd never noticed before. Perhaps this heightened awareness came with the altered state of Chocko's spell.

"Dad!" she said aloud. "It's my father."

"Keep going," Chocko urged.

A million thoughts and sensations raced through her mind, filling her with feelings of urgency, of caring, knowing what she must do. She felt comfort in her feelings, though she knew there was danger in acting on them, too.

"You should not be here," she heard herself tell him. And then, sounds she did not recognize began coming from her mouth, a different language. Deep in the vision she took her father's hand and raced with him back along the path she'd been following. One thought filled her mind: He should not be here. He is in the wrong time! If they find him he will be captured and become one of us...them... Filled with confusion she moved on, racing along the walled path.

She sank deep into memories of how the warm flesh of her father's hand had felt, holding hers so long ago...a million years ago, it now seemed. *But why do I cling to that?* she asked herself. Her heart filled with love for him, the love that she felt only when she was with those who were like beads on the long familiar threads of a mother's bond. These words startled her. They were not her language! Where did she learn these things?

"Does he recognize me?" she asked, aloud.

"Not now."

Was it Chocko's voice she heard? Where did the vision start and the reality she shared with Chocko begin? She could no longer answer this. And where was the reality beyond the window, beyond this space in time? *Nobody can answer that, not from this space,* Tara told herself. She could not remember her passage through the light. Something was wrong! It was not at all as Chock had described it to her.

She felt the child stirring in her body, and felt the heaviness of her mourning. But it was not for this man who raced with her along the narrow path of her village...*my village,* she thought. *Yes, I have to allow myself that. There is something I need to complete here.* The man's grip tightened and she stopped, turned to face him, and as their eyes met he gasped, shook his head, disbelieving. She jerked his hand as she might jerk the halter of a stubborn animal to urge it ahead.

Running again, she saw the opening, then they were upon it. He seemed to recognize what it was. She tried to speak to him, explain it to him, how he might be injured as he fell back to his own time. But he must go. He must not be caught! If he was caught he would become one of them and the web of life would be tangled, bending back in on itself.

The Web of Life! These words seemed familiar, yet unfamiliar. Tara recalled a story...who told her, how she knew it, was a mystery to her. Spider Woman, the story taught, had woven the filaments of life so that they all connected in a spiral web, like the beautiful silvery webs that caught the morning light at the corners of windows during hot summer months. The filaments of the web all seeped from the woman's body. All women served in the weaving of the web. All women, even those who bore no children of their own, spun the filaments and knew how they stretched through time. And now, just as the stories of Spider Woman said, this journey was carrying Tara back along the furthest strands of the web.

The man took her in his arms and pressing her palms to his firm back muscles she held him close. *Drake? Father? Who was this?* His eyes shone with gratitude now. For a moment he held her. She felt his heart beating against her breast, racing, pounding with fear and the exertion of their run. The beat of his heart matched hers, their rhythmic pulsing connecting them forever through time. Tears suddenly spilled from her eyes, filling her with this mystery, imagined or not, that seemed to have no beginning or end.

"Go now," she said, pushing him away. He disappeared into the darkness, back through the tunnel to his own time.

Something was drawing her back over the path she'd just traveled, but this time to a kiva at the center of the village. She ran, feeling a sense of urgency. Tara wondered, why is Drake a stranger to this woman if I am her? And then she tried to remember why she was running. What was drawing her? Others would want her there, she knew. But where was this place where she was wanted? Running, she felt the movement of life in her body and caught herself wondering, will the spirit of this man come back through my child? The question startled her so that she briefly opened her eyes.

Chocko was gone! She was sitting in the night all alone. She called out to Chocko. She heard only her own voice and felt completely disoriented. She was hemmed in by great walls of adobe, like the central walls of a great labyrinth covering the mesa and perhaps an immeasurable space beyond it. There was no way out. She was inside. She had slipped through time, into that other reality which she had always denied.

It's a real place, she thought. It is not a space within my dreams. It is as real as the dirt under my feet.

She stood at the entrance of the kiva. The shaman priests were waiting for her. At the door she smelled burning sage and felt the drums joining the heartbeats of those already inside. She hesitated, emptying her own heart, allowing it to slow and connect with the others, the path to this special joining guided by the drums. When she entered, she moved into the circle, feeling the heat and moisture of the bodies that completed the medicine wheel, her rhythms synchronized with the rhythms in the room.

The chanting began, the songs catching and carrying her spirit. A death was being mourned, but whose death? A deep sob erupted from her throat. She tried to stifle it but could not. She cried out, wailing, but the drumming continued, the chanting continued, and she felt comforted, assured that her tears would be honored here.

And then the horror of it struck her. It was her own father who had died! She felt his death inside her, the violent severing of a filament that connected her to the others. Where was her mother? She was gone, dead for many years. Where were other members of her family? They were gone, all of them, mother, father, sisters, brothers. *They are gone.* The dawning realization that this mourning and this loneliness stretched far into the future, and far into the past, filled her with a strange mixture of grief and excitement. Grief that loved ones were gone from this life. Excitement that the wheel of life continued to turn, always returning what she felt she had lost. Life was not just what was contained in her own body, or their bodies. It was an eternal force without boundaries, without limits of any kind.

She felt so shallow, so ignorant of all these things. How could she know so much about this ancient spiritual community she had mysteriously entered, yet know so little! She looked around her, at the dirt floor of the kiva, trampled down as hard and smooth as concrete by perhaps centuries of dancers and celebrants. She felt the woven clothes that adorned her body, and felt her own body, younger, firmer, more resilient than it had ever been. A tougher body, connected to a mind she barely recognized. She was not Tara. She did not even know her own name. This woman who sat in the kiva, in the midst of the drumming and chanting, was a woman whose life seemed to span all time. Yet, Tara's entire being was immersed in this person, merging with her...different times, different spaces, yet all the same.

Then perhaps it was not her father who was dead but others, other fathers, grandfathers, great grandfathers, distant ancestors. But I have no Indian blood, she caught herself thinking. What is the connection that binds us like this? Even as the drumming continued and great sobs shook the body she was momentarily inhabiting, Tara remembered Drake's escape back along the narrow path, and she recalled the blazing shock of recognition as their eyes met. Her father had been confused, totally disoriented. Had he recognized her? What did he see in my face? Who is this woman I have become? Who was it that he encountered? What did he understand about this place?

The chanting reverberated through the walls, the roof, the floor of the kiva, rising in song. The voices around the circle, the wheel of participants, rose higher and higher, turning the wheel, the eternal wheel of life. The voices came together in wondrous harmony, moving through the room like the wind, caressing and encompassing

Tara. Tonight the wheel was turning, spinning, filling the space, lacing together all the threads of time.

Where was her father? Where was he now? Which father, in which lifetime would she love? Which would she mourn? It came to her at that moment that there were endless fathers. They came down to her over many lifetimes, and so if she mourned one she must mourn them all, and celebrate them all. Yet, there was only a single mother, one mother who bound them all, even all the fathers. Out of the single mother came all of life, in every nation, in every color, in the good and the evil who came...a single mother. And so, this was why the mother was not mourned, why her power endured, eternally.

The songs ended abruptly. The chanting and the drumming ended. People were filing out of the kiva. Someone had ignited tallow lamps in the room. Tara smelled the burning animal fat that gave them their fire. A whole wall flickered with the light from at least a dozen tallow lamps glowing inside indentations carved into the stone walls.

She heard the voices of people outside in the street, no longer harmonious and joined as they had been at the medicine wheel but chattering away, easing into the world outside the kiva, outside the sacred space they had created. Yet Tara continued to sit in the same position she'd held at the wheel. *Close to the center.* Eyes closed, she listened to the night sounds. *Close to the center of all things.* Voices faded and the people who'd been in the kiva were returning to their families.

She was not alone. She felt a presence but saw only a vague, shadowy figure through the gloom. She was expecting Chocko. But it wasn't him. As her eyes adjusted to the darkness, she saw that this man across the room from her was dark-skinned, very thin, a wiry body and gaunt, sunken cheeks. He sat several feet away, his knees up, resting his elbows on them, gazing across the room with a bemused expression. He wore an elaborate necklace of turquoise and white beads, several strands of them. Unlike the other people who'd been there moments before, this man wore modern clothes--khaki pants, sneakers, a white cotton shirt, and a dirty red bandanna around his head. On the pinky finger of his right hand he wore a gold ring of modern design, with a large fire opal peering out at her, catching and reflecting back the flickering light of the tallow lamps. Tara noticed an expensive watch on his right wrist and another ring, a gold wedding band, on that hand. He was from the world she'd left behind.

As she gazed in his direction she began to see his face more clearly. There was something familiar about his eyes but she could not place what it was. For a long time he simply sat, apparently quite comfortable with the silence. His head was tipped back slightly, thin lips clamped tight, eyes closed. For what seemed an interminably long period, he was silent. At last he opened his eyes, looked across the room, nodded peremptorily, reached into his breast pocket and produced a cheroot. From the same pocket he retrieved a single match, struck it with his thumbnail and lit up. He lightly inhaled the smoke, then let it drift out of his mouth as he spoke. Tara was shocked. One did not smoke in this sacred space. Only the smoke of the sage and sweetgrass and pinon and tallow was allowed here.

"You comfortable?" the man asked, in a voice that betrayed no hint of an accent. Clearly, he was not from an exotic otherworldly place. He spoke and looked like a thousand other men from her own world, her own reality.

"I'm okay," Tara replied guardedly.

"You've been here before but you wouldn't remember."

In spite of his offensive manner, Tara felt free to speak with this man, and she heard her voice speaking the modern language. "I remember movies," she said. "Spaceships. UFO's." She did not know exactly why she said this except that if she had ever traveled to other realities it would have had to be through childhood dreams and fantasies, not in her physical body. As a child, movies and television shows, especially ones about traveling to other dimensions, had mesmerized her, even though they filled her sleep with terror.

The man laughed, a kind of cackling laugh that Tara thought made him sound like a fool. "Whatever it takes to get you here," he said.

"I don't understand."

"Your imagination is a wonderful thing. It can take any form, carry you anywhere."

"But this is real. It's not a dream. I know the difference." As soon as she spoke she wondered why she was arguing with this man.

He began to laugh again, and as he did Tara became indignant. Whether out of respect for her discomfort or because he had more important things to convey, he stopped. "My name is Angwusi. It means crow. My other name is Tony Fox."

"Yes, I remember."

She was not at all pleased to find the shaman here. Out on the desert in front of Chocko's trailer home the night before, it had been different. He seemed to fit there somehow, a broken down Indian with his feathers and beads, drumming for his friend at the trailer park. But this was different. This wasn't a trailer park. It was an ancient site, perhaps a holy site. What right did he have to impose himself on this place, on these people, in this sacred setting! She hadn't recognized him at first because in her estimation he did not belong here. He wasn't worthy! Except for the fact that his hair was covered and he didn't have a blanket draped around his shoulders, she might have recognized him. But he was the last person she would have expected to meet in this place.

Tony Fox smiled, took a light drag from his cheroot and let the smoke curl out around his nose as he spoke.

"My name, it's kind of a joke. Do you know why?"

"No."

"Because foxes eat crows." He grinned and Tara saw that he had no teeth in his upper jaw. "Eat crow, do you get it?" When she did not laugh he suddenly sobered. "Do you know why you're here?" He squinted through the smoke.

"To find my father."

"But you sent him away," Fox said. "Don't you remember?"

He obviously found this amusing; Tara didn't.

"Then he's okay?" she asked.

Tony shrugged. "Don't know much about where he went after this. Him and that woman were having quite a squabble, though. I don't think they're very good for each other. Not a good match. You ought to tell them that. If my wife and me fought like that, all our gifts would be taken from us."

After what Tara had been through, after how far she'd come, she had no tolerance for Fox's mundane observations about her father's love life. Here, in this otherworldly place, she somehow expected more. This man was coarse in his manner, crude and off-putting. *How did he make his way into this place? He was way too common to be here!*

"Don't you ever wonder about yourself?" he asked her. "Doesn't it ever occur to ask why you of all people would be marked a child of importance?"

There was that phrase again...child of importance. The burden of leadership, all that went with it...there was nothing in her life to indicate that this was so. How could he know these things?

"I think you're mistaken," Tara argued.

"Others have seen it, even those from your world."

"I don't think so."

"Tom. He saw it. Don't you remember this? He said you were ambitious. Of course, he had it wrong. It wasn't ambition he saw. But it drove him pretty crazy, in any case. He missed it, missed what you were about. It drove him into the darkness."

"You're blaming me for what..."

"No, no, no! He made his choices."

"Then you know what happened?"

"Fell in with a bad crowd, suffered for it dearly. Don't we all know that one?"

Tara could not tell if Tony Fox was mocking her or not. Apparently he did not know about the confrontation at the ruins, the gun, and Tom's fall through the roof of the kiva. The more the old shaman spoke, the more his language changed, his words and his level of sophistication no longer that of a broken, uneducated man but of something very different. His observations were those of an educated man, a man as wise as he was articulate.

"How do you know about Tom? Were you a friend of his?"

"Never mind that. Think about it. He knew ambition, a dark ambition, and because he didn't know any other kind he saw himself in you. He...ah, to hell with it. Don't bother with it. It's not important."

"But it is important! Tom is dead..."

Fox gazed at her sternly. "Don't take it on. It's no fault of yours and there's nothing, absolutely nothing you can do about it now. Move on. We got business here that's far more important."

"I only came here to find my father."

"Well, I can't tell you much beyond what you already know. But I do want to tell you some other things. It's your mission to take something back with you."

"Take what back? Who are you, anyway?"

"Told you that..."

"Yeah, Tony Fox. But that's just a name."

"Here's the thing. You don't need to know anything about me, where I came from, which reality I am from, none of that, okay? You're sitting there trying to sort all this out, trying to figure which reality is which, how to label your cubby holes and what to shove into them. All that kind of crap, give it a rest! Don't worry about what belongs where, which reality you're in. It'll just give you an ulcer.

"Look here, we have only two choices: either we take everything we hear and see as real, or we don't. And if we choose the latter, we're in real trouble. Because there will be some who will choose this and some who'll choose that. Then whose side are you going to take? Whose side? You'll start arguing this is more real than this and that is more real than that. You'll create moral laws and punish those who don't follow them, all in the name of *rightness*, of proving that you are right and the rest of the world is wrong. Pretty soon you gotta start killing those people who don't agree with you, just so as you can have some agreement in the world. Choose that and your whole life is going to end up with you trying to dominate others or them you...and that's what you're here to carry back."

He leaned forward, peering across the short distance between them, a fierce glint in his eyes. To Tara he looked like some strange wild animal, yet he was articulate and clear, very verbal. His thoughts were coherent and reasonable, not the chatter of a mad man, at least not exactly.

"There's someone I want you to meet," Tony said. "She will be here any minute. She has lived in your world and speaks your language. For that matter, she has lived in many worlds and speaks many languages. So you'll be able to talk freely with her."

"I want to know about my father."

"Mission accomplished! Stick around long enough and he might even wander back in here and get his bony ass run out." Tony laughed, then added: "Or you might find he's not what you are seeking after all."

Tara heard a rustling of skirts at the kiva entrance. Turning in that direction she saw a figure so outlandish that she nearly burst out laughing. It was that of a very old woman, draped in a cape made of fluffy, brown and white feathers. Her bare feet, spindly ankles, gnarled and twisted toes, looked for all the world like the claws of a giant bird. Her face was hidden by a mask, not like those of the Katchinas but far more realistic, depicting a being that was part owl and part old woman.

Tony Fox rose to his feet, his demeanor changing from sardonic to reverent. From under the bird woman's costume came two long, spindly arms, with claw-like hands that clutched the edges of her feathered cape and spread it out around her as she slowly took a seat. Tony Fox waited as she settled down, then resumed his own position, giving her his full attention.

The bird woman took a few moments to get herself comfortable, her feet tucked under her in a semi-lotus posture. Apparently satisfied, she looked across the room at Tara.

"I am Mongwa," the woman said. "To put you at ease we've brought a friend of yours across." When she spoke, her voice was not at all what Tara had expected. It was a young woman's voice, with all the inflections of a person who'd indeed lived in the modern world. She spoke with the authority of a person who'd accomplished a great deal in the world, a woman of many achievements. Mongwa turned her head and nodded toward the entrance.

The familiar figure strode unceremoniously into the room. *Chocko!* Somehow Tara was not exactly surprised. But she did not greet him with open arms. With his entrance, she grew suspicious, certain that all this was staged, that somehow she'd been tricked and this *other reality* was nothing more than a manipulation of her senses and her fragile emotional state.

Chocko took a seat next to Tara, so close she felt the heat of his body. She glanced at his face, distrustful and irritated, growing increasingly impatient. "Why am I here?"

"Because you asked," Mongwa said. "Think back over your life's journey. You were once excited by the mystery, by the awe and wonder of life itself."

"It was long ago," Tara answered, sadly.

"And then the closer you came to what you thought you wanted, the further you withdrew from the truth."

"I don't understand."

"Obviously!" Tony Fox exclaimed, rudely, smoke from his cheroot entirely encircling his head. "Listen to her, listen!"

Tara's thoughts spun back over the past. She remembered the crone back at Teotehuacan. She remembered the owl with the old woman, and then an old memory rose in her mind. There was a word--*mongua* or *mongwa*--maybe Hopi or Navajo in origin. It meant owl!

This Mongwa held up her hand for silence, demanding Tara's attention and clearly not pleased with Tony's outburst. "The path you've taken," Mongwa continued, directing her words to Tara, "has been a path to power. But you've been deceived. You sought power in education, in motherhood, and finally in the anger you feel for your father. But all of these have failed you."

"They haven't failed," Tara protested. "I love my life. I love being a mother, my profession..."

"And men of the wrong world?"

"I don't understand." Tara glared at Mongwa's eyes. They were large, round. Mongwa peered at Tara without blinking, more owl-like than human. The light from the tallow lamps flickered deep inside them, unearthly and mysterious.

"These men you love are seduced by the powers of the third world. You are of the fifth. You must separate yourself. We'll teach you to do that."

The third world, the world of domination, of power over others, the world of coercion and force. Tara glanced at Chocko. He had once mentioned these to her. But she also knew about them from her studies at the university.

Legend had it that there were worlds within worlds. Each represented a different level of moral, ethical and spiritual evolution. Those in the third world were bound by an absolute belief in good and evil, and everything this implied. The third world was demonstrated in the Crusades, when Christians, driven by a vision of dominating the world, slaughtering everyone in their path who disagreed with them. This, the third world, was about human greed, moral coercion and economic dictatorship. That world has nearly destroyed itself, proving once again that those who live by the sword die by the sword.

There were many who had lived by the edicts of the third world--the Hitlers, the U.S. Government, the Ku Klux Klanners, White Supremacists, Black Supremacists, Skinheads, many others. Theirs was a cruel, wrathful world, an unforgiving world, a world devoid of tenderness, with no understanding of the power that lies in caring for others, for all that lives, and for nurturing the natural world. Theirs was a compassionless world where *good deeds* were measured against rules laid out by despots. One dared not disagree with those who held the greatest physical power; one did so only at the risk of death.

The ancient teachings said that while everyone alive today was born into the fourth world, each still had connections with the third. This connection shows up as intolerance for those unlike ourselves, who look different, think different, hold different beliefs, or whose emotional lives are different. There is at least a small part in all of us that in moments of conflict wants to destroy or beat into submission anyone who disagrees with us, convinced that our only security lies in worldwide conformity, where everyone thinks and feels alike. It is the part that clings rigidly to order and control, disavowing the human heart.

"Most recently," Mongwa continued, "the power of the fourth world is expressed through new capacities for controlling nature, the power to harness nature's rivers to generate electricity, to mine ore and process it into steel to build cars and trains and planes that race across the Earth's surface, cheating time and distance, to fly into outer space, to harness the atom and create a source of power great enough to destroy all that we know, including our home planet. All these exercises of power have thrown the world out of balance. This is where we now stand, in a world out of control. In seeking control through domination, we have lost control completely. It could be no other way. If we are to move to the fifth world, we must learn to let go, to lose control and discover what lies beyond."

"These different worlds," Chocko added, "were given to teach us to know the limits of human will, that we might learn about the twin paths of power--the power of domination and force and the power of co-operation, creativity, and love." Mongwa nodded in agreement.

"As the fourth world turns in on itself," Mongwa said, "we will move back into balance and move toward the fifth. The power coming into us now is the final power you will struggle with. It is the power of self-mastery, power over yourself. You will not find it by embracing or controlling other humans but only by embracing the darkness and the gift each person brings into this life. You will find it by embracing the Mystery."

"But we're not there yet," Tony Fox interrupted. "We're a hell of a long ways from that!"

Mongwa turned coldly toward Tony and quieted him with a piercing look. He chewed nervously on the cheroot, whose fire had gone out. As Mongwa continued to stare at him, his face changed, shifting into a new shape, his features no longer Indian but the smoother, paler face of James Dean. He smiled back at her from across the room, suddenly a very different man from the shaman, Tony Fox.

The light from the tallow lamps flickered, dimmed, and Tara felt rather than heard a deep rumbling. Vibration like the beginning of a great earthquake shook the kiva, and in a moment a dark shape appeared to glide down from above, moving through the roof as if the timbers and rafters didn't exist. She looked up. The disk-like shape looked familiar. She'd seen it in her dreams. But it was not nearly as large as she'd always perceived it to be. At the most it was twelve or fifteen feet across. It glowed in the dim light but there was no doubt in her mind that it was made of gold. *Had it been in the room all along, somehow suspended there in the ceiling,* she wondered, *or did it enter through a space she had not noticed?* She remembered Drake's description of a similar disk in the notes he'd left on the computer diskette.

The outer edges of the disk began to glow, emitting a light that grew in intensity until it was the color of molten metal. The colors changed from a molten red glow to white-hot, the light vibrating now, brighter than a thousand moons. Yet even as it grew in intensity, the disk gave off no heat. In the next few moments, the glow expanded out into a beautiful rainbow of color that lit up the room. The disk groaned as the glow spread to every wall of the room, the walls themselves becoming mere extensions of the light. At last Tara clasped her hands over her eyes, protecting them from a glare as great as the sun. And then, just as suddenly and mysteriously as it had first appeared, the light dimmed. Cautiously, Tara removed her hands from her face and looked up. The disk was still there, hovering overhead. It wobbled slightly from side to side, but gave no sign of going away.

Mongwa rose. She was chanting words Tara could not understand. They were of a different language, spoken with rhythms and cadences like nothing she'd ever heard before.

Chocko nudged Tara, signaling her to stand. Immediately, a bizarre male figure leapt into the center of the room from somewhere behind Tara. He was at least eight feet tall, with massive legs, like the legs of a powerful beast. His dark mask was splotched with irregular white spots. Naked except for a breechcloth of reeds that rustled as he moved, his entire body was painted ashen gray. Around his waist, suspended from a woven sash of many colors, were small pieces of petrified wood polished to a high sheen. As he danced, racing around the center of the circle, his huge bare feet, twice the size of her own, slapped the hard earth noisily, coming within a fraction of an inch of Tara's legs. The petrified wood pieces dangling from his belt made a delightful tinkling sound, reminding her of icicles hitting together. Yet, his presence was terrifying, this giant creature like no human she'd ever seen. If he was indeed a man, he was like no other.

Mongwa continued to chant as the Katchina danced his wild dance. Suddenly the figure leapt from the center of the room, sailed over Tara's head and was swallowed up in the darkest shadows of the kiva. Tara turned, stared into the darkness, but she could see no sign of him, anywhere. In the momentary silence, something, a small animal, made a strange squeaking sound and scuttled over the floor, hidden in the shadows.

Completely unnerved by the Katchinas' entrance, and by the fact that he was still somewhere in the room, but now unseen, Tara sat down, suddenly frozen to the spot, virtually paralyzed. What kind of world was this, where people appeared out of nowhere and where faces could be transformed before her very eyes!

A pinpoint of light appeared at the center of the circle. It grew in intensity. Suddenly the ground under it burst into flame and the flame climbed to the roof of the kiva. It made a crackling sound. Out of the flame stepped a second Katchina, a frightening figure with a black mask. Immediately the flame was extinguished. The mask of this Katchina consisted of two huge yellow eyes with black pupils, and a rectangular mouth with thin red lips and bared teeth. From the mouth dangled a long red tongue, flopping down nearly to its chest. This was a female Katchina, and like the first dancer she was huge, at least seven feet tall. Her hair consisted of grasses dyed a bright red, hanging down over her shoulders on one side, tied up in a swirl on the other. She wore a black dress, woven of heavy wool, secured at the waist with a bright red sash. Over her right shoulder she carried a buckskin quiver full of arrows, and in her left hand a ceremonial bow.

This Katchina glided around the circle three times, then approached Tara, stopped in front of her and let out a blood-curdling cry, shaking her bow threateningly while holding an arrow up straight in the opposite hand. At the end of the arrow was a lethal-looking triangular point made of sharpened flint, while at the other end of the shaft were the white feathers of an eagle. The Katchina stepped effortlessly over Tara, as if she wasn't even there. Tara felt the heat of the giant's body and the musky stink of her sweat.

Tara turned, watching carefully as the Katchina slipped into the shadows at the southern wall of the kiva. But this Katchina did not vanish like the first. She sat less than a dozen feet directly behind Tara, as if guarding her back.

Now, other dark figures danced in the room, back in the shadows where, in the dim light, Tara could barely make out their shapes and colors. She became aware of their breathing, all of them inhaling and exhaling in unison, machine-like in their precision. One, sitting directly opposite Tara on the floor, had a huge round face, as big around as a modern stop sign. The face was painted a light blue, illuminated by the reflection of the flickering lamps at Tara's back. This Katchina had long slits for eyes and a tiny, almost sweet-looking mouth painted on with coral-colored paint. It wore a pointed hat of a design Tara had seen on Tibetan priests. It seemed really out of place here. *But if we have truly entered a timeless space,* she reflected, *virtually anything is possible!* Theoretically, there could be representatives from every space and time, perhaps even from worlds beyond our own solar system.

"Today you end your connections with the third world," Mongwa announced. "You will sever yourself from that place in the web. These Katchinas are here to help you in your passage. They come from far away, a long, long way, from neighboring stars, constellations too distant to be seen, from spirit worlds you have yet to enter. They come as helpers and guides, if you will learn to seek their help. They each have their own lessons to teach for they have all lived through the third and fourth worlds, into the fifth."

"I don't understand," Tara said. "They are deities, gods and goddesses..."

"No. They have lived as you have lived, as mortal beings, but through many more lives and deaths and rebirths than you have yet known. They are intermediaries, messengers, bringing the wisdom they have gathered in their own journeys, reminding us to respect the spirits that give us all life. They remind us that we are each bound to the past, to the future, and to dimensions beyond what we've come to know as time and space, galaxies and worlds beyond our power to see. Invisible filaments of energy tie us one to another, making us who we are.

"We know, because they tell us, that the fourth world is decaying, dying, as it must. In its death throes, the struggles of that world are becoming increasingly violent and dangerous. It gnaws at itself like the mink or the fox who will gnaw through his own leg to escape the trap. Your tasks are elsewhere. You and others like you, who have honored the spirits of light, will sever yourself from this world so that you may go on to the fifth and help guide others along that path. You will accomplish this by disconnecting yourself from your last enemy."

"And who is my last enemy?"

Mongwa turned, looked past Tara, and nodded in the direction of the kiva's entrance.

There, framed by the luminous night sky beyond the kiva, stood none other than White Crow, the man she now knew was Jose Haera! He nodded to Tara and strode across the room to sit opposite her at the medicine wheel. Tara could not believe her eyes. Up until that moment she had believed this man had been killed in the wrecked jeep outside Coyote Mesa. All her rage at this man, her hatred of his deceits and everything his life stood for welled up in her. She glared at Mongwa, incensed that this wise woman would bring such a despicable creature into this place.

"Why are you allowing this man here?" she demanded.

"At the medicine wheel that has been prepared for you, everyone is equal," Mongwa explained. "Be humble before the forces of our different worlds. We are all of one spirit, no matter how it might seem to you. In the fifth world we sit opposite our enemies and so find larger truths. Though we may see more than they see, we are still equals here. At the medicine wheel, each of us mirrors to the other the truths about our lives that we do not want to see. Some of us serve the Dark Mother who suckles the forces of death and destruction. Others serve the light that makes all life possible. Each of us must choose how we work with these forces in our lives. Which of these forces will you bring into your life? Will you fight them, make peace with them? We must each come to know both the darkness and the light within us. And we can make these choices only by gazing into the eyes of both the best and the worst of what we bring to this spot."

"But that man stands for everything I despise!" Tara pointed her finger accusingly at White Crow, who gazed back at her impassively, smirking as if to belittle her every thought. She saw the murderous look in his eyes, could easily imagine his intentions. It was the gold he wanted, nothing else mattered to him, and he would surely even commit murder to have his way.

"Be patient. As it is," Mongwa said. "He has his own mission at this wheel which at this moment is a mystery. As the mystery unfolds, you will find the medicine he brings you."

"My medicine!" Tara leaned forward, her face burning with the hatred she felt for this man. "My medicine would be to see this man die before he brings anymore grief into this world."

"If that is to be, your hatred will continue to feed him," Mongwa said. "Your malice is his life's blood."

White Crow began to laugh, staring across the medicine wheel at Tara, mocking her.

Before Tara could gather her thoughts, an old woman hobbled out of the shadows and stood in the middle of the circle. She leaned on a cane, which was nothing more than a stick cut from a tree branch. Her clothes were so torn and filthy that Tara could not even determine their color, and her entire demeanor was so wretched that she looked like little more than a pile of rags herself. If White Crow was the very embodiment of the basest of human motives, this creature, leaning on her cane, was the embodiment of death. *Why were they invited into this circle?* Tara asked herself. *What role could they possibly take in this sacred council?*

Once again Mongwa began chanting, and from the shadows the drumming started up, a deep reverberation, slow, steady, unhurried. The old woman, Death's sister, bowed her head and leaned on her cane. She hobbled around and around the crude stick in a tight circle at the middle of the medicine wheel, spiraling around her cane as if it were the axle of the wheel itself. She joined in the chanting but while Mongwa's voice was resonant and youthful, the old woman's was raspy and feeble. The only sounds Tara heard from the crone's mouth were "la, la, la, la..." on and on, incessantly, as if she did not know the real words of the chant or had lost all capacity for exact speech. Suddenly the drumming, the chanting, and the puny sounds from the old woman stopped.

The old woman continued her circling shuffle around the cane for a moment, then stopped. She lifted her head enough for Tara to stare into her eyes. It was a face Tara remembered from many years before. But where had she seen it? *In another country...so far away. So many years ago, a lifetime.* And then, "Teotehuacan!" Tara said. "That's where I saw you, in Teotehuacan!"

The old woman stared back at her, her eyes hollow and care-worn. She did not speak or make any gesture to acknowledge Tara's guess. She hobbled over next to Tara and slowly sank down, groaning, clinging to her cane as she settled on the ground next to her. The old woman reeked of disease, the repulsive stench of decaying flesh and stale, urine-soaked clothes.

Above the wretched crone, Tara heard a rustling of wings and looking up saw a large owl settling in the rafters above the old woman. "You dare to look at death," Mongwa said. "Dare to ask her name, to look into her eyes. That, too, sits with us at this medicine wheel."

"*No tengo cuidado...*" the crone said, leaning over and whispering into Tara's ear. Then she laughed, a cackling, spine-tingling chortle that convinced Tara she was crazy. The old woman's breath against Tara's ear was cold, sending shivers up her back. *No tengo cuidado. Not to worry. Nothing to worry about. What could this possibly mean, coming from the lips of the lowest of the low? Was the old woman not aware how the shadow of death hovered over her?*

"Why have you brought this poor old woman here?" Tara asked.

"Until you know her face, until you dance with her, your mind and your heart are veiled," Mongwa replied. "Ask her name."

"I don't understand," Tara complained. Again she asked, "Veiled from what?"

"From your own life. Push her away and you push away your greatest joys, your most powerful medicine. I say again, ask her name."

"Death is hardly my medicine," Tara exclaimed, argumentatively.

"Treat her as your enemy and you'll regret it," White Crow crooned from across the room. Hearing his voice, Tara was inflamed, yet she felt paralyzed by the thought of responding to him. The loathing she felt for this man swelled in her throat like a lethal venom; along with it was an inner voice that told her to hold her tongue, that if she engaged him in battle he would outwit her. She knew from past experience that such men were masters in the weapons of adversity. She would never win.

"Once more, ask her name," Mongwa said.

Broodingly, Tara turned to the old woman, nearly gagging as she inhaled the air around her. "What is your name?"

"*Usted, senora.*"

"I asked your name," Tara repeated, thinking the crone had not heard her.

"That is her answer," Chocko replied gently. "Her name is *you.*"

Shaken by the answer, Tara averted her face from the old woman. For a terrible moment, she sank into her own anguish. Only three years before, she'd watched her own mother die and in the last moments Tara recognized her own mortality for the first time. Death stalked her, just as this dark sister stalked her mother and stalks everyone else, and there was no escape. No escape.

"And now, who is missing?" Mongwa asked, her voice ringing out, startling Tara out of her reverie. "Whoever they are, let their spirits be with us, even if they cannot join us in the physical body."

With these words, Tara looked around the room, fully expecting her father to miraculously materialize, as some of the others had done. That, after all, was the only reason she had come, to find some assurance that he was safe...and if not safe, she wanted some assurance that he was dead. She could seek him no longer.

But no one entered. Even so, she felt Drake's presence, just as she had always felt it, however insufficient in her life. His presence was like an uncertain wish that she held within her heart, knowing all along that these dreams, these childish hopes, were a sham.

"Let it be as it is," Mongwa said. And then, when Tara did not respond, she repeated, "Understand me, let it be as it is. Your father's presence, as it is! You cannot make it more than this nor less. This is how he sits at the wheel." Mongwa spread out her arms in an all-embracing gesture, and said to Tara, "This is your life. This is how you connect with your own power, with all the powers that offer themselves to you. You are seeing your wheel as it is."

For a moment, Tara felt panicked. What was Mongwa trying to tell her? What was she intending to demonstrate? It seemed so incomplete, this wheel. How could an emptiness connect her with her own power? How could death and the most contemptible of dark motives reveal her power? What did these spirits, these Katchinas from another galaxy, beings who she feared, possibly offer her? How could they represent the wheel of her life, her strength, her power, her medicine? Mongwa mumbled comments that made no sense at all. Tara wanted to ask, Why can't you speak like ordinary people? Is my father dead? Where are you keeping him? If you know, release him now. But she could not bring herself to ask her father's fate or demand his return. And the longer she sat here at this circle, the more hopeless she grew.

"You are listening only to the words," Mongwa said. "You are pushing away the greatest powers of your life because of fears and superstitions your world has instilled in you. Reach into the treasures of your own gifts. Listen for the message beyond all words."

The deep heartbeat of a huge mother drum began, a drum so huge that as the head vibrated it sent shockwaves throughout the room. *Thumb-pa, thumb-pa, thumb-pa,* it went, a slow, throbbing, uncompromising beat. *Thumb-pa, thumb-pa, thumb-pa.* Tara closed her eyes, leaned back her head, and in spite of her suspicions and horror she sought strength in the sounds, letting herself float on the resonance, drift with it.

Suddenly, amidst the steady beat of the drums, a man's booming voice cried a warning. A woman shrieked, her long, drawn out howl of horror and pain pierced the air. Tara opened her eyes. Why did these rituals need to be so terrifying and dark? Why the war cries and false drama? Then she noticed a dark figure standing over Mongwa, screaming profanities at her, some in a language Tara could not make out, though the intent was somehow very clear. The candles cast their flickering light over the faces of Mongwa and the second person, who Tara now recognized as White Crow. White Crow had something in his hand. A knife! In a flash, Tara was scrambling forward, flying toward Mongwa's aid. The shiny steel blade of the knife caught the light and as it flickered across the room a cry of utter despair and anguish cut through the night. White Crow leapt back into the darkness.

Mongwa still sat alone, just as before, except that now she wore a crimson necklace. Blood poured from a huge gaping flap of skin under her chin. A croaking sound came from her throat but whatever words Mongwa had intended turned into an unintelligible gurgle.

Tara grabbed Mongwa, embracing her tightly, as if by sheer affection she might hold her life within her. The bird woman fell limp in Tara's arms. In spite of her horror, Tara sighed, a long, grievous sob that echoed the terrible despair of every murdered soul since time began. Slowly, Tara eased Mongwa's lifeless form down onto the floor. The drumming paused and across the room, the old crone had begun her monotonous lilt once again: "*No tengo cuidado! No tengo cuidado!*"

The drums resumed as Tara stared in horror at the blood soaked form of Mongwa. Tara turned. White Crow crouched in the shadows holding the long blade that with one hateful swipe had taken Mongwa's life. *Why were the drums starting? Didn't they see what had happened?* All the hatred Tara had been holding for White Crow welled up inside her. *This man must die!* She glanced around the room, looking for a weapon, wishing she'd brought Tom's gun with her. But it was too late for that.

Two dark Katchinas emerged from the shadows. To Tara's utter consternation they began dancing in the center of the circle, their crouching, bobbing, whirling forms spinning chaos in the room. Why was nobody doing anything? Why were they sitting passively or dancing as if nothing had happened? A lifetime of frustration and anger exploded within her and Tara sprang toward White Crow, screaming, grasping for his face. As she raced toward him, his arm lifted, the blade once again catching the dim light. Colliding with this target of her hatred, the two of them crashed to the floor of the kiva. She tore at his eyes, her fingernails boring deep into soft flesh. She heard his cry, then felt the sting of the sharp blade as he drove it down between her shoulder blades.

Then she was sailing across the room. In a cry of rage and anguish, White Crow had flung her away from him. Her body smashed against the hard, adobe wall. Down on all fours, she tried to lift herself upright. She screamed in agony as the wounded muscle in her back spasmed and stung. Shadows moved around her, closing in. White Crow leaped at her, bellowing insanely with rage. She waited for the cold steel blade of the knife, imagining it slipping across her exposed throat, slicing through the soft flesh as it had done with Mongwa.

Was it the drumming she heard, increasing in intensity, or the last terrified pounding of her own heart? The dancers whirled around her, closing in. *But where was White Crow?* Tara pushed herself up to a sitting position, her back supported by the wall. White Crow lay crumpled in a heap, not a yard behind her. He moaned. Something or someone had struck him. The knife lay on the ground, only inches from his right hand. For what seemed an eternity, she just stared at the weapon, measuring her chances of getting to it before he came to his senses.

She inched herself forward, sharp spasms of pain constricting her whole body. She sobbed, reaching for the weapon. White Crow turned, looked into her eyes, did not appear to comprehend what was happening. Her fingers closed around the handle of the knife. And then someone was kneeling at her side. *Chocko!* His fingers closed around hers for a moment and he eased the knife from her grip. She watched as Chocko moved toward the dazed, sightless White Crow.

"No!" Tara cried, her voice clear, resonant and purposeful. She had to stop Chocko. There'd been too much bloodshed already. Another life would never even the score. It never had. It never would. Chocko hovered over White Crow's still form. He seemed to be embracing him, holding him close, like a lover, but the words coming from his mouth were filled with rage.

The dancers, the dark Katchinas, closed their circle around Tara. She struggled to call out to Chocko again but no words came from her mouth. The wound in her back stung, muscles cramping up around it like a steel trap. She cried out in torment, howling like a tortured animal. She felt herself being lifted...or was she falling? Suddenly she could not tell because she had lost all sense of direction. *Dizzy. Where are the lights?*

They were chanting louder now, and the violence spiraled around her in an ever-narrowing circle. Death! The old woman leaning on her cane was shouting to her. *No tengo cuidado!* Her feeble voice rose to a fever pitch, screaming in Tara's ears, filling her mind like a siren pressing in upon her. She heard the rustle of wings. The owl hunted in the darkness, circling overhead. ~

Transformation

Tara moved her head cautiously, peering into the darkness, attempting to determine where she was. The effort was futile. She wondered if she had lost her sight.

Something prickly cushioned her body, protecting her from the cold, hard ground. When she moved, it made a crackling sound. Her fingers explored the soft blanket covering her. It was finely woven, probably of cotton, she guessed, since the surfaces were smooth and comforting.

She remembered dark figures, strong and assertive, their faces hidden behind masks. She remembered unusual scents. Metallic, like after a storm, she thought, a rainstorm electrically charged by the lightning.

Time had evaporated. Hours, days, weeks? How could she know? None of it made sense. Attendants coming and going, small female figures, gentle and reassuring. Faceless. Voiceless. Who were they? What were they doing? Why am I here?

Tara lay quietly, listening. If she could not see, perhaps the sounds would give her a clue of her whereabouts. Even the tiniest sounds echoed back to her. From far in the distance came a voice, maybe two voices. Maybe it was the wind. Slowly she became aware of her body. This was reassuring. At least she was alive! Whatever it was she was lying on rustled when she moved, a bed of grasses and supple leaves, aromatic and smooth, leaves that someone had gathered for her and placed...where? Charla's, I'm back at Charla's, she told herself. She thought about her father's notes on the computer disk. He'd escaped from the village and the other reality through a tunnel in the side of the mountain. That had to be what happened to her too. It had to be. A dim circle of light. What was it? The mouth of the cave...the opening into the outside world!

"Hello!" she called. "Is anybody out there?"

Her voice echoed back to her from the walls of the cave. She felt a familiarity about this place. But how could that be? Somehow that familiarity was comforting. She was certain she could get up any minute and walk out onto the ledge where she could look down at Charla's boarded up house. Maybe her father and Charla would be back by now. The entire mystery would turn out to have been just a bad dream.

But that wasn't right! Things had changed. Someone had added the comfortable pallet of aromatic leaves. And a faint scent of sulfur wafting up from the invisible caverns behind her suggested she might be near hot springs. Like the pallet, that was new. She hadn't smelled that before. Then, this place wasn't familiar after all. She was not in a place she knew.

The medicine wheel! Now she recalled the medicine wheel with Mongwa and the others, and slowly the pieces of her recent past began to come together. Had that wheel been prepared for her? She remembered somebody telling her that. Judging from what she could recall of what happened, there couldn't be any doubt of that! The focus had been on her quest for her father and where that quest had taken her...but it had become more than that, a quest for her own power, her own medicine.

Memory was slowly returning, some of it painful and frightening. She was not at all sure she wanted to return to reality, to the world outside her dream. The face of Tony Fox rose up in her mind. Why had he been called to her circle? Chocko was convinced Tony was a powerful shaman. More likely he was the town fool, a two-bit con man whose parlor tricks had convinced Chocko he had magical powers. But there he had sat, across the wheel from her, Tony Fox in all his glory. If it was true that the wheel had been prepared for her, Tony's presence there could not have been a mistake. But what did he have to do with her medicine, her power?

Her mind drifted back to her studies at the university. That whole world seemed so distant now, another time and space...except for her own private work on the society of shaman. There could be no doubt that she had been taken to the very center of what she'd only theorized could be. But what *proof* did she have? How could she be certain all this hadn't been staged, created as a kind of bizarre joke? As she turned that thought over in her mind, Tara realized that the thought itself was ridiculous...unless it was Drake's doing. No, that couldn't be. He could never have gotten so many people to participate in such a hoax. No, she decided she must herself be half-delusional to even imagine such a thing.

She turned her attention back to Tony Fox. Who, or what, was he? Could she take this man seriously? She knew from her own research that in the ancient indigenous cultures that prevailed before the rise of science, people like Tony, fools or not, were often seen as tricksters, not merely the players of practical jokes but more than that. Even in his most mundane form, the trickster was a most important archetype, a teacher like no other, one whose lessons reminded us of our own human limitations, of our vanity and pride, of our capacity for rationalization and fantasy designed to mask the truth.

But what was being masked here? What wasn't! Everything on this long journey had been more than it seemed...and less. How had this search for her father taken such an odd turn? Disoriented, all the events around Tara had spun out of control, beyond her ability to explain. This tornado of experience threatened to rob her of her own sanity and maybe even her life.

Her thoughts turned to Tom. Dead. Tom was dead. It seemed impossible. Tears welled up in her eyes, not just from grief--though she felt this intensely, regardless of what he had done to her--so much as from the realization that for so long she had hidden the truth about him from herself. Not that she hadn't known about his corrupt side. She'd certainly been acutely aware of this part of him. But she had not recognized the depth of his corruption. Now his mask was completely stripped away...and she saw, at last, how deeply his soul had been tainted, that he was willing to commit murder for his own selfish gain...even the murder of his own daughter's mother!

As Tara's mind filled with images of Tom's death, of lying in his motionless arms for that horror-stricken moment in the dig where they had fallen, she tried once again to deny the evil that had been revealed to her. But she could not. The truth was merciless, without pity or tenderness. Like death it rose to the surface again and again. The fool, the trickster's mind, could veil it for a time but never conceal the steadfast eyes staring out from behind the mask. From across the medicine wheel Tony Fox had mocked her...mirrored her...that was it! He reviled her for masking the truth about Tom until it had come to this. And now what? Now, nothing...he was dead.

In her mind's eye Tara saw the old woman. Death's sister, she had called her. Death's sister! But why not Death herself? What did being a sister to Death have to do with anything? Tara remembered looking into the old woman's face. The hollow eyes had revealed nothing, nothing at all, no more than the glazed, lifeless eyes of a corpse. What did Tara see except the fact that this poor wretch was dead, already dead and void except that she tottered around on her cane.

Death in the guise of a human being could have but one purpose and one only, to remind the living of their own mortality. But who or what was Death's *sister?* This was the second time she had appeared in Tara's life, the first being in Mexico with Tom, long ago. He had denied her presence...and maybe that was the point. He could not accept his own mortality.

Like a grim oracle, the squalid creature had leaned on her cane, turning in a circle with no beginning and no end. She shuffled along in the dirt, her feet barely raising dust as she slid first one foot and then the other along the ground. What ritual was this that she did not lift the cane but tramped around that narrow circle as if she were tethered and there was no end to her dance?

Tara remembered that first encounter with Death's sister in Mexico, the old woman sitting in the ruined room, the fluttering of wings above her head, and the huge owl climbing toward the sky through the ruined roof.

"No more. Let Death's sister dance with it!" Was this the message of that dark crone's presence at the medicine wheel? In her monotonous circular dance she spun a web, an invisible cocoon around the past, encasing it like a worm that might one day emerge as a butterfly. Teachers of the ancient traditions said that in the medicine wheel we confront our own fate, that here we find the lives we have lived in the past, and that what we see here can project our lives into the future. *The future is mirrored in the past.* But what was to happen with the cocoon Death's sister wove in this place?

Tara imagined Mongwa's voice, and for a moment she peered into the shadows, wondering if the wise one was near her now. But there was no movement in the cave. Mongwa's voice continued, however, somewhere in her mind, more like a memory than a voice which she heard with her ears: "If you can see the image in the mirror clearly, you can interrupt the flow of fate and change the future. That's the importance of the wheel. It is clarity. Let your own best intentions, not the past, be the lens through which your future is projected."

Voices in her head! Her heart pounded. Was she going mad, talking to the shadows? But no, she was not crazy. She could rationally review everything she'd experienced in the past week or so. Rationally! Well, maybe not rationally, for some of the events she'd witnessed were far beyond the rational. If she tried to explain them to the uninitiated, there was a good chance somebody would lock her up and throw away the key.

She had to remember everyone at the medicine wheel: Mongwa, Chocko, Tony Fox, Death's sister...who was missing? White Crow! Haera, her dark nemesis, her rival. His spirit hung over her life like a cloud that not even the darkness of a moonless night could hide. Maybe that was the secret of his name--White Crow, the impossible bird who swallowed shadows. She remembered the story of the crow who pecked at his shadow until it turned and swallowed him up. What it meant, she couldn't say. Was she herself like that bird? But how? It didn't make sense. Why was there so much darkness at her wheel? What medicine could be found here, in the very darkest of the dark? For the life of her, Tara could not imagine how anything good could ever come from dwelling on these sordid and unwelcome intruders, from having to stare across her own medicine wheel at them.

And then there was the presence that was not a presence...the hard fact of Drake's absence. It was true, as Mongwa had implied, that his absence itself was palpable, holding a truth that she could no longer ignore. "Let it be as it is," Mongwa had instructed. It was easy for Mongwa to deliver such edicts. She hadn't wrestled with Drake's erratic comings and goings. She hadn't spent her childhood wondering why she was so different than other children in that quiet, conventional, academic community where she'd grown up, where fathers returned home every night. Mongwa hadn't longed for Drake's presence, wondering, in her child's mind, what she might have done to drive him away, burning with guilt over the mystery.

Let it be as it is! Tara wondered if she would ever learn to do that. For a while, at the medicine wheel, she felt peace in letting it be as it is. She saw her father as he really was, not as she wanted him to be, and surprisingly her heart flooded with love for him. She saw him in some distant city, alone, sitting in a forty dollar a night motel, pounding away on his laptop computer, writing up a story of...of what? It did not matter. The story could be anything, half-real, half made-up, a blending of fiction, partial-truths and a great deal of imagination.

For that fleeting moment in time, she felt his excitement, his boundless hope, his willing and dynamic imagination. But what else? She felt something sad, something desperately lonely, a longing so poignant and melancholy that she thought she'd cry. She knew this longing herself. It was a longing she'd always associated with her own singular existence. But was it?

Maybe the longing she felt was not her longing for Drake but for a connection across the miles with her father's loneliness, his sense of separation, loss, a kind of reaching out that was simultaneously a pushing away. But now she had a clear insight about her father that she'd never had before, that his reaching out was and always had been futile. It was futile because he never let himself see how he was pushing away from those he loved and who loved him. And it was futile because he had never identified what he was reaching for! In fact, what he thought he must pursue--the big story, the story of a lifetime--achieved only one thing, a selfish pride in the spoils of a private battle where there were no winners. The real source of his longing might forever elude him.

Why was it, she wondered, that she still felt responsible for his absence from her life? She tried to tell herself that her thinking was wrong, neurotic, that she must cling to reason, to the fact that the innocent child she'd once been could never possess the kind of power she imagined, but that didn't matter. The tiny, lonely child in her would not let go of old illusions. Why? she asked herself. Why does the child cling to old fears and self-recriminations? Maybe self-blame was a kind of mask, too, a way of holding onto a lie. Suddenly Mongwa's command took on a whole new meaning: *Let it be as it is!* She didn't mean leave it alone. She meant lift the mask. Let yourself see what's really there. Let it be as it is!

For a moment Tara did exactly that. She let herself see Drake without the mask that she had created for him. He was not the man, the father she wanted him to be. He would never be, never. But by not letting him be as he is she robbed herself of his presence. She was the one who created the empty mask of her longing! At the medicine wheel she had felt that she'd come to terms with this cold fact. But now it was clearer than ever. She saw him with all his human weaknesses and foibles, and it was okay. It was this person, and only this person, that she would love, because that was all there was. That was Drake.

"How are you feeling?"

Startled, Tara rolled to her side, rose halfway to her knees and peered through the darkness toward the sound of the voice. "Who's there? I can't see you," she called, her own voice cracking, betraying her fear.

A ghostly figure stood in the mouth of the cave, outlined by a dark sky in the distance. There was something familiar about his outline. She'd seen it before. It was the young man from her dreams, the young man who had comforted her before, the one she called James Dean.

"Come outside with me," he said.

"But who are you?"

"I've been in your life since the beginning."

She was standing now. Her legs felt weak and her muscles ached but that was all. She felt as if she had slept for a very long time. In spite of her lethargy from her deep sleep, her body felt younger, lighter than it had in many years.

"You've been in my dreams," she said. "You're not real."

"But dreams *are* real!" James Dean smiled, amused by this little game of psychological cat and mouse.

"Dreams are dreams," Tara said. "It's been well-established that they are created in our own minds, as sublimations for our fears and desires."

Laughter. He was laughing at her--that gentle but cutting James Dean laugh. It was not unkind laughter but Tara was annoyed. Everyone knew that dreams were not real. What did he find so amusing? She stepped closer to the mouth of the cave. She could see him clearly enough, but there appeared to be a gauzy curtain between them, a thin membrane which made her wonder if something had happened to her eyes. She wasn't focusing properly.

"I apologize," James Dean said. "I've used your dreams to make contact with you since you were very young. It has been important to have contact."

"You were a father figure, that's what you meant to me. But now...you're so young!"

"Mongwa is waiting for us," he said.

"But Mongwa is dead. I saw her murdered with my own eyes."

"Yes and no," James Dean said. "Mongwa moves between the worlds. Her death, all that was revealed at the wheel, is your medicine. It is the lens through which you view the world. Unless you see your lens with all its flaws, its black holes, its nuances of night and fog, its color and light, you can see nothing. Your power will forever be a paltry illusion that you impose on your life and those around you. You cannot know your true power without knowing Death. That's the lesson Mongwa offers."

As Tara approached the figure, he stepped away from the mouth of the cave, and vanished from sight. Cautiously, she stepped outside the cave and into full sunlight! But how could that be? When she looked out beyond the door of the cave, only moments before, it had been pitch dark. She had expected to see the back of Charla Mather's house and the little garden containing the medicine wheel. When was that, the night before, two days before, a week in the past? She had no sense of how much time had passed. Moreover, she was not behind Charla's house. Instead, she was standing on a stony ledge, looking down upon a mountain village.

All around her was a serene blue sky, a sky so ethereal and clear she knew she must be at a very high elevation. But where was this place? Where was the place she'd sat at the medicine wheel? Had that been here, at a kiva in this village? As she stood there in the sunlight Tara felt warm, comfortable, and safe. The air she breathed was fresh and fragrant, rich with oxygen and a sweet perfume that emanated from acres and acres of cultivated fields.

For a moment it occurred to her that she had lost all semblance of reason, that some great trauma had robbed her of her sanity.

What she saw before her was a delusion, nothing more, and at any moment she would come to her senses and everything would be clear again. She would see that none of this was real, that none of it mattered at all. She would see, with great relief, that none of it had anything to do with her real life.

Then, in her mind's eye she began reliving the macabre encounter in the kiva, the brutal attack on Mongwa, and then the blow of the knife as White Crow drove it into Tara's back. She remembered reaching for the knife as White Crow lay momentarily stunned, then Chocko taking the knife from her hand and moving toward White Crow...and then her own cry, her scream, "No!" No more bloodshed.

She had not seen what happened in the kiva after that. Nor had she been able to see Chocko or White Crow or the knife. She recalled that her body had been lifted and carried away to this place. She felt like a warrior, a hero in an event she did not understand, an event in which she played an important part that she had not willfully chosen. These people had taken her in as their fallen hero...or perhaps their sacrifice. Ridiculous! The whole thing was absolutely ridiculous.

She glanced up at the sky, searching for the sun. It was directly overhead. But it was not like any sun she'd ever seen. It opalesced in the sky, and swirling all around it was a whirlwind of energy and color. As Tara stared into this vortex, she thought how much it resembled a beautiful rainbow condensed into a sensational globe of color and light, hypnotic, constantly changing. And oddly, that opalescent globe hanging in the sky seemed the very essence of this world into which she had moved, a world of energy in motion, energy that moved freely, fluidly, slipping silently through space. Maybe it was not a sun at all but a huge lens projecting this strange and beautiful world onto the earth's surface.

Tara suddenly recognized that she was not seeing with the physical eyes of her body. Yet, her perceptions were sharper than ever. The sight, sound, touch, taste and smell of things was more intense than ever but came to her intuitively. She no longer needed her earthly sense organs! There was another way of comprehending the world around her, a way that resembled dreaming but was far more vivid and intense than any dream she'd ever had.

Her newfound sight was very different than anything she'd ever experienced. At one and the same time she had the capacity for telescopic and microscopic sight. Objects far in the distance appeared as sharp and clear as those just ten feet away. And if she looked at a leaf on a tree a mile away she could see the veins and structure of the leaf backlit by the sun. This was impossible! But it was real. She could actually see with an unlimited field of vision, with no need to focus or move closer or further away to see objects more clearly.

"It's beautiful! Where are we? What is this place?"

Lost in her own preoccupations, she'd almost forgotten about James Dean. He had promised they'd see Mongwa. Where was he now? Looking around, she saw him casually leaning against a rocky wall. He looked exactly like the picture she'd always had in her mind, the movie actor who resembled her father as a young man.

"Go ahead," James Dean said. "Explore this world. That's what it's for. That's why you're here."

He knew! He was talking about her new sight and the wonderful landscape that spread out before her. Was all this a mere fantasy? What she saw and felt was like make believe but not like make believe. Unlike what she experienced when she imagined something, she now exercised the strength of her own will. She could direct her own movements, make choices about where she was directing her attention. James Dean leaning against the rock was real enough. She could choose to talk with him or not. She could will to turn her eyes toward him or not. In her dreams, it wasn't like that. She was merely a witness, watching a kind of internal movie where she booed villains and spurred on heroes who never knew she was there. Here, in this super-reality, she was a full participant, able to move her hands, her feet, direct her movements, say what she wanted to say. No longer a witness, she was right down deep inside herself.

Tara had read about ancient spiritual leaders who claimed that human consciousness was not confined to the physical body, as was the general assumption. Instead, it had unlimited boundaries, stretching out into infinite space.

Looking out over this world she now realized that she had developed omnipresence, an ability to be in any and all places at once. Even as she gazed into the opalescent globe above her, she had left the ledge outside the cave, had left James Dean behind and was hovering over beautifully cultivated fields, terraces and tiers arranged along the side of the mountain. Some of these fields had been recently tilled, and the newly turned soil was dark and rich with humus. She could smell and nearly taste the rich soil. For the first time in her life she became aware that here, in the soil itself, were whole worlds, bugs and micro-organisms, an alchemy that was as vital to life as the greatest oceans. There were fresh crops growing here as well. Lush vegetation swayed in the slight breeze moving up from the distant valley floor. Tara could not identify the crops growing in this place but she felt a kinship with them that she did not understand.

Tara watched a woman carrying a large basket of what appeared to be tiny colorful potatoes. The woman wore loose-fitting clothes woven of vibrant colors and had a colorful woven disk pressed into her hair. She walked slowly, though with the grace and fluidity of youth. Each footstep touched the earth in a peculiar way, as if to feel the ground was a sensual delight in itself. Now the woman stopped, knelt, clasped her hands in prayer for a brief moment, then plunged them into the freshly tilled earth and lifted out several handfuls of dirt, making a hole several inches deep.

The woman reached into her basket and removed one of the potatoes. The tuber was small, shiny and dark purple. In Tara's consciousness, the potato seemed to speak to her, not with words but with a voice and a coherence that startled her. She became aware for the first time of how all things--animals, vegetables, even rocks--possessed consciousnesses themselves.

The planter woman held the seed potato in her hand and pressed it into the hole she'd made for it in the soil, moving her hand back and forth in a boring motion until she had reached the appropriate depth. Then, removing her hand, she patted the earth back into place and paused for a moment, surveying her work.

As Tara watched this planter of potatoes she saw what she estimated to be at least a hundred acres of terraces working their way back and forth down the mountainside. A half-dozen people, mostly women, dotted the countryside, some planting like the woman Tara had watched, others stooping over to weed the crops that were already flourishing. Some picked what appeared to be long, bright yellow beans that they placed in woven baskets slung over their arms.

There was a beauty and grace to what Tara saw here, a connection from the earth that she knew she herself did not have. This society, long separated from the modern world, still appreciated the miracle of the earth's bounty and treated it as the gift it was. *How separated we've become from this great source,* Tara thought. Was it possible to reclaim this connection with the vast riches, the *bounty* these people enjoyed? To Tara they seemed the richest of the rich.

There was something familiar to Tara about this mountain society. She felt she'd been here before but much had changed since her last visit. Then she put the pictures together in her mind. This was the mountain Chocko and she had climbed to the site where they'd found Tom, where the ruined wall with the window had stood, atop the mesa! When was that? Yesterday? Last week? But this world had to be thousands of years old. This was a world of an entirely different epoch. It wasn't possible! She had moved back in time, far back, maybe hundreds of years. But that was impossible. It had to be an hallucination! There could be no other explanation.

"We need to go soon. Mongwa will be waiting."

At first Tara could not figure out who had said this, then remembered James Dean, standing to one side of her cave. In an instant, she was back at that place, in her body once again and he was there beside her. He pointed to a trail further up the mountain and moved toward it, leading her along.

The trail was narrow and steep, snaking back and forth along the side of the cliff. As with the trail Chocko and she had originally followed to the mesa, steps had been carved into the rock. But these steps had been recently cut and the trail was well-maintained.

Tara and her guide climbed for twenty minutes or more, resting several times along the way. They finally reached the top of the ridge, then began descending. They came around a bend in the steep trail and James Dean held up his hand and stopped. There, a hundred feet below them, nestled at the bottom of a canyon, was a rich meadow as green and fecund as any she'd ever seen. The rich vegetation convinced her the area must be fed by copious springs.

The meadow was not much larger than a football field and exactly in the center was a huge stone formation poking up out of the earth. It was about the size of a car, the stone as dense and black as obsidian. It appeared to have been formed by an ancient sculptor, since it possessed a number of geometric planes, or facets. With the sunlight directly overhead, this magnificent stone fairly glowed, casting a deep purple radiance around it.

James Dean pointed toward the north wall of the canyon. "Look there," he said.

Tara turned her head in that direction. The red, striated rock, as formidable as it was beautiful, shone brilliantly in the late afternoon light. Her escort pointed to a spot about a hundred feet above the canyon floor. It was a narrow ledge carved into the great wall. In the center of the ledge was a tiny structure made of stone. From the distance it looked to be a dome-shaped sweat lodge, barely large enough, Tara estimated, for more than a single person. Perched near the lodge sat a giant bird, its head nearly as high as the roof of the lodge itself.

Tara saw a trail part of the way up the cliff, consisting of a series of steps like the ones James Dean had been following. Below the ledge was a series of three ladders, each approximately twenty feet tall, affixed to the rock. The ladders were extremely narrow, no more than a foot wide, made of two weathered saplings with rungs every foot or so. The ladders were lashed together with vines that had long since dried in the sun.

Tara's escort signaled her to move forward and they started

down the trail toward the meadow. Tara fell in behind him. At the bottom of the climb they crossed the meadow, soft and damp under foot. At last they stood at the beginning of the steps to the tiny hogan. On the left side of the steps, at chest height, a tiny alcove had been carved into the rock. Inside was a red clay bowl filled with scented oil in which there floated a long cotton wick. The end of the wick held a flame that flickered slightly, protected in the shelter of its rocky nook.

James Dean went up to the little alcove, dipped his fingers into a second, smaller bowl and sprinkled something over the flame. The flame flared up for a moment, died down, and a beautifully scented smoke puffed out from the wall. James Dean stepped back away from the lamp and gestured for Tara to follow suit. When she repeated what she'd seen her escort do, the scented smoke puffed back in her face and chest, covering her with a scent of sweet grass and cedar.

"Go on up," James Dean said.

The first and second rows of steps were similar to those they'd already traversed on the other side of the ridge. But when Tara came to the first of the three ladders, she balked. The ladders pointed almost straight up, each one reaching twenty feet into the air. At last she placed her right foot on the first rung and lifted herself up. The ladder shuddered under her weight but otherwise seemed stable. Shortly, she'd climbed up to the very top. On her hands and knees she crawled over another ledge to the second ladder and started up.

In the middle of the second ladder she looked down. James Dean was gone. He was nowhere to be seen! Clinging to the rung in front of her she leaned out away from the wall. Nothing! He was gone. Nobody was out on the meadow nor on the trail up the opposite wall of the canyon. She was on her own! This wasn't fair to abandon her like this. She looked up. The third and final ladder was only a half dozen rungs above her now. She had to go on. But why? she asked herself. There was nothing at the top but the bird and the little hogan.

There was no answer, except perhaps that it had obviously been James Dean's mission to bring her here. She moved on, exhausted as she lifted herself over the top of the third ladder and crawled to the center of the ledge holding the tiny structure. She rose to her feet, terrified of looking down. She looked across the ledge toward the little house. Beyond it, the giant bird barely stirred. She watched its feathers, ruffled by the wind. She stepped closer. The bird turned its head, its huge round eyes full upon her. It appeared to study her for a moment, then it stepped out to the edge of the ledge and teetered over. Tara gasped. Thirty feet down the great bird spread its wings, dropped for a moment, then rose as it caught an updraft. It glided gracefully down again, flapped its wings a few feet from the canyon floor and settled in, perching atop the black rock formation at the center of the meadow.

Tara was now alone on the ledge, a few feet from the door of the dome-like structure. She stepped forward. Inches from the threshold to the little building, she heard a movement inside. She approached the door and peered in. For a moment she saw only darkness, but as her eyes adjusted a figure appeared. Mongwa sat on the floor inside, staring with huge unblinking eyes straight at Tara! Without waiting to be asked, Tara ducked her head and joined Mongwa inside, sitting down opposite her. The space inside was larger than she'd anticipated, but even so she was sitting so close to Mongwa that she could have reached out and touched her. The little hogan was windowless and the flame from a single tallow lamp provided the only light.

Mongwa said: "Don't doubt what you have seen and heard these past few days. All that you experienced at the medicine wheel was real. All that you see now is also real. Let it all be as it is. Let it all be."

Bewildered, unable to accept either what had happened in the past or what was happening now, Tara's mind went blank. She became aware of her own mouth tightening into a smile, her shoulders turning to stone. She wanted to return to her own world, one that made sense to her.

"I want to go home," Tara said. "I don't understand any of what's going on here. I don't know why I'm here at all."

"Listen," Mongwa said. "Listen and watch." ~

 Spirit Circle

Emergence

Mongwa reached behind her and drew out a large clay bowl. Something glowed inside it, a small bed of hot coals. Mongwa set it down in front of her, then sprinkled something into it from her hand. Fire flared up and instantly died down in the bowl as sparks rose toward the roof of the little hogan. Smoke circled up from the coals now, along with the pungent scent of burning sage.

Mongwa took up a fan made of feathers. Holding the bowl in one hand, she fanned the smoke over her own body, smudging herself from head to foot. Then she handed the bowl and feathered fan to Tara, indicating she should do the same.

When Tara was done, she handed the smudge pot and fan back to Mongwa, who set them down beside her again. Mongwa leaned toward Tara and touched the tip of her right finger to a spot in the middle of the younger woman's forehead. The sensation Tara felt was electric.

"Come here," Mongwa said. She held out her arms invitingly, beckoning for Tara to come closer. "Move slowly. Don't be afraid."

Tara did as she was told, expecting the woman to embrace her. Instead, as Tara drew close she felt a pull of energy, like the invisible tug of a magnetic field. She heard a loud pop in her ears, like what happened in an airplane.

One moment she was outside, staring in disbelief at Mongwa's face, at the strange owlish mask that perhaps was no mask at all. Then she noticed a sudden shift, and like a small bird snatched from the sky, felt herself suddenly thrust into a tiny space, a bony, fleshy place, a terribly confining cage. Disoriented and fearful she no longer had any sense of her own body.

As preposterous as it seemed, Tara had slipped into Mongwa's world, into her mind, sharing her very existence! At first Tara felt uneasy, like a timid child in a stranger's home. But uneasiness quickly faded as her own presence penetrated bone and muscle, then the very fingers, feet and belly of this wonderful being.

"Here our lives have merged as one." These thoughts came to Tara as her own, yet she knew they were Mongwa's thoughts, gentle and reassuring. "Here you share my vision and my power. Here you and I are bonded, where we will serve as one mind forever. You will be able to see all that you now see whenever you wish."

Instantly, Tara caught glimpses of events back at the big kiva, where they had sat together at the medicine wheel. She felt Chocko's presence, Tony Fox', Death's sister's, and...White Crow's. But somehow she now saw White Crow in a very different way than before, a way that puzzled and agitated her. Didn't Mongwa recognize that this man was dangerous? Didn't she see his fundamental evil, the fact that he was her executioner? No, Mongwa did not appear to see this at all!

There was a wonderful lightness about Mongwa's life. Tara felt comfort and safety in this strange, bird-like body. Though it was clearly not her own body, Tara felt a deep welcoming and love here. Within Mongwa she became aware of a powerful sense of both total involvement and total detachment from the events of the past few days. There was humor here too, a kind of playfulness of spirit, a freedom from confusion and anger and fear, along with deep compassion and totally unconditional love.

Allowing herself to relax into Mongwa's being, Tara felt filled with joy, a joy that extended even to her own tumultuous emotions and apprehension about her fate. The words, *let it be as it is* suddenly took on a new meaning for her. Mongwa embodied this perception totally. Here was a person who embraced all of life's experiences, covering the full spectrum from ecstasy to grief, from tranquility to rage. She rejected nothing.

Tara felt a new sense of power here as well, a kind she'd never known before, a kind she had never even imagined. It was somehow linked with Mongwa's humor, an alchemy of detachment that simultaneously produced complete involvement with life. This all-embracing capacity which Mongwa embodied drew sustenance and strength from every thought, every feeling, even fear. Tara felt whole here, complete and vibrant.

Mongwa was moving now. Tara felt this woman's body as her own, ducking her head as she crossed the hogan's threshold into the light again. They stood on the ledge looking down into the meadow. Tara felt the energy of the earth here, the life of the rich green grasses rising skyward. She saw the huge bird, the owl, roosting on the great rock formation, and out toward the edge of the meadow saw the long expanses of desert to the east.

Tara looked out through Mongwa's eyes at a world completely

unexpected. All around her, substance and form, everything Tara associated with the material world, faded into clear, perfect light. Far in the distance she saw buttes rising from the earth like great stone platforms. Yet it was not rock she saw. In fact, there was no matter in it at all! It was all light, light of varying colors, denser colors--purples, deep reds, and deep, vibrant greens--vibrating within solid areas where Tara expected to see rock. Here was a universe without seams, without edges, where all blended together as pure light. If there were boundaries, they were defined only by color, only as one color merged into another. This was a universe where infinite molecules danced, a constantly changing ballet with no beginning or end.

It is important for you to know this, to see it very clearly and take it back into your world. Mongwa's thoughts were Tara's thoughts now as well.

Little crescent shapes of light passed in front of her eyes, running from left to right. They looked like tiny suns just beginning to rise over the eastern horizon. Tiny crescent windows flashed before her eyes, endlessly, and she heard an inner voice telling her, *This is important. This is the secret. This is the beginning of all form, all life. Watch!*

Tara watched, awed by the sight as light streamed through the little crescents, radiating in infinite directions all at once, a billion stars glistening through what had been nothingness. Then the clear light turned to color, endless colors--reds, blues, greens, deep purples, yellows, turquoise, earthen tans and sanguine tones, endless colors--vibrant, fierce, calming, erotic, tranquil, tender, filled with mystery. There were no words to describe it all! There would never be words for it.

This is the birth of all form, the inner voice told her. *Take this knowledge with you. Remember it always. It is the wisdom that will allow you to see beyond all illusions, beyond all self deception and fallacy and invention. This light is your true source, beyond the limits of the finite form you know as your body.*

As she studied this wondrous display of light and color, she noticed something else. Microscopic bands of light shot through everything she beheld. They were barely visible at first. The bands were the thinnest of the thin, fragile strands of a spider web projected throughout space and time. Spider web, Spider Woman. It was as Mongwa had said, exactly as she said. Spider Woman's web isn't a myth. It actually exists! The web crisscrossed everything, extending in all directions for as far as Tara could see.

"Imagine the circle," Mongwa said. "It is all-spirit, touching all, touching everything."

With a little effort, Tara brought back her own memory of the medicine wheel, seeing for the first time that she still had her own thoughts, her own memories, separate from Mongwa's. Even as her memories of the wheel came into focus in her mind, Tara's vision extended beyond the kiva, beyond normal geographic boundaries. It was as if she could see the entire world except that it floated in space, etheric as in a dream, a gigantic hologram. Here, space itself was the single defining form.

Tara could see any part of it in microscopic detail. She saw her daughter Maya, far in the distance, and seeing her Tara wept. The little girl was sleeping, at home in her bed, peaceful, tender and composed. Tara saw Drake, moving away from her on a darkened city street. She saw only his back but there was no doubt in her mind that it was him. She saw Tom's lifeless body, now lying under thirty feet of dirt. Something had happened to the dig where she had struggled with him. The place where he discovered the treasure had now become his grave. Earth covered him, the walls of the kivas having crumbled in around his flesh. Then she saw White Crow, Chocko, and others whose faces she did not recognize.

All of these figures floated in the dream-like space of her mind's eye--but this dream was different. Laser-thin bands of light criss-crossed each of the figures and Tara noticed that some of these long bands either intersected with her own body or shot past her, passing within fractions of an inch. This was a very different medicine wheel, revealing the web of true interconnectedness that Mongwa had described.

"There are many lessons to be learned from the web," Mongwa said. "That is your mission now, to weave these lessons into the life around you, into your own world. As you learn to see the filaments with your inner eye, you will also find people whose journeys are truly connected with yours, and you'll see how they are connected, making the spirit circle complete. There is so much to be learned from the filaments! Notice that you and your daughter have many filaments connecting you--at your heart, your throat, your crowns, and your navels. The navel connection is your common birthright but the other connections are not. Parents do not usually share all these intersections. Notice how very bright these filaments are, as bright as the rays of the sun, the emblems you both share as children of importance."

In Tara's heart she felt a chill at the mention of the term "child of importance." She experienced great pride, knowing a child of hers was assigned such a role; but she also felt grief, conscious of the sacrifices that inevitably accompanied such laurels.

"You are both pathfinders. But you are not alone. There are

millions like you, sharing this mission. In the third world you would be warriors or politicians who might sacrifice your lives for your people. In the fourth world you might be great inventors, wizards of matter, sorcerers in the alchemy of the physical universe. In the fifth world your purpose is to hold a truth that is yet to be fully recognized on this planet, a truth that carries us beyond the goals of the third and fourth worlds, beyond the powers of domination and beyond the mastery of nature.

"I cannot instruct you fully in your journey, or your child's journey. But there are signs to watch for, and these will help to guide you. Look around your medicine wheel and you will see that the filaments coming to and from your body are much brighter than most. The most important are those that illuminate your heart, brighten your voice, and highlight your crown. Notice that there are people at your circle who do not have filaments at all these points. Your father's filaments, for example, are strong of voice but barely visible for the heart and the crown. White Crow's filaments are brightest in the pelvis, for he is a man of the third world, struggling with power over others and the domination of the physical world. He will never evolve beyond being a witch. His fate is a sad and violent one, sacrificed to a plan that neither you nor I can ever know. We can only trust that, like the night or the seasons, there is a purpose for the darkness he serves."

Despite Mongwa's words, Tara's hatred for White Crow again rose in her heart, and for a moment she caught a glimpse of her connection with him. Filaments of light spread out from her own heart, surrounding him, intersecting haphazardly with his limbs and torso. The filaments were dim, but they were definitely there, connecting their two lives.

"As much as you might fear and despise this man," Mongwa said, "You must be grateful for his lessons. Without them your own wisdom would be narrow and weak. Without them you would not ever come to know the darkness you hold within you."

"Darkness?"

"Your capacity for murder. It is the ultimate form of domination, and the most primitive of all powers, sealed in the alchemy of the physical world. You encountered it in the kiva with the man who was once your lover and husband, but it takes many forms."

"But I stopped. I did not want to kill even him."

Mongwa continued. "I said that you know the darkness. In knowing it, you no longer find others to carry it for you. That is part of what makes you a child of importance."

"I want to go back to my daughter, to my own life..."

"It is too soon. She will teach you tenderness. You will teach her to bring strength to her tenderness. Beyond that, you cannot know the future for her, nor do I know it. I can only tell you this, that both your paths will be lit at all times by wide filaments beneath your feet, ones that will be brighter than any others you will see. There are many people at your wheel, and there will be many more. All have lessons that will be important to you but be cautious of what you ask or expect of them. All of them have their own paths, some like your own, but they will be few. You will learn from them but ultimately you are their teacher, not the other way around. Sometimes the greatest lessons you can offer will be transmitted in your silence and your patience. As a child of importance, solitude will be your greatest companion, your sorrow and your joy."

"Meaning that we will be alone," Tara muttered. "That's what you're saying, isn't it?"

"You will not be satisfied by what pleases others."

"And you? Has this been your path?"

"I live in a world very different from yours."

"But our filaments intersect," Tara said. "I can see them." Indeed, as she focused on the filaments she saw a thousand tiny beams of light emanating from Mongwa's body. The old woman radiated filaments of light in every direction, like the opalescent globe Tara had seen hovering over the terraced village back near the cave.

"I will be with you always, from this day forward," Mongwa said. "I will come to you in dreams but you can call me forward, into your consciousness, by simply thinking of me. Turn to me when you wish to find the center of the circle."

"This is pure fantasy," Tara complained. "It can't be real!"

Mongwa appeared to not hear Tara's complaint, or if she heard she preferred not to respond. Instead, the consciousness Tara was sharing suddenly shifted. Tara no longer saw or felt, smelled or tasted anything. The light was gone. Darkness was gone. Even the filaments were gone. *Nothingness! Death.* Tara slipped back and forth between nothingness and light, unable to comprehend.

Mongwa's words entered once again, filling this infinite space. *Now you know your true identity,* Mongwa told her. *This is death but here you see that there is no death. Here you see that death is a creation of the mind that for a time lives within the body. What we know when we come into form, into a physical body, are the fears of the body itself.*

Tara felt these fears, these overwhelming fears of death, and she wanted more than anything to escape them. The sense of vulnerability and exposure Mongwa described seemed to have literally burst into her consciousness.

"This is the most terrifying insight of the human experience,"

Mongwa said. "It is the horror that each of us never quite conquers as long as we are in physical form. Because in physical form we are vulnerable. We learn danger and we learn the experience of being separate and alone."

It took Tara a moment to realize that she was no longer inside Mongwa's consciousness. She was outside it now, standing beside the older woman, the two of them looking down over the meadow. Tara was not certain when the transition occurred from Mongwa's body to her own, but it had been sudden and unannounced. For a moment, a sense of grief and loss filled her heart, matching the feelings Mongwa described.

"But why?" Tara heard herself ask, her voice shrill, frightened and unsure, coming from her own body.

"Why the lesson? The purpose is to feel the strength that comes of knowing death as nothingness, that in the larger reality beyond the limits of our bodies, death does not exist!"

The hard-edged image of Mongwa standing before her frightened Tara, though moments before, within her body, she had felt completely at ease, even joyful.

Tara studied the beautiful meadow below. Her eyes came to rest on the rock formation towering twenty feet above the ground. But something had changed! It was the bird. Gone. Tara searched the skies. High above the meadow, hundreds of feet above them, she spotted it. But beside the bird was a shape, a huge globe that caught the rays of the sun and radiated deep purple light in every direction. She'd seen this shape before, back in the kiva when the Katchinas appeared, danced their dances and receded into the shadows around the medicine wheel.

Tara's attention moved back to the meadow. She stared at the great rock, this dense, imposing chunk of matter like nothing she'd ever seen. Words came to her mind, reflecting on the source of this object: Ageless, something from a time long before the Earth was born, a dense mass...pure intelligence...not a machine. Created by...whom or what? Not created...not created. How could it be not created? Reason, Mongwa says, is an invention of the physical form, and so this is beyond that, beyond reason. But how does one even begin to comprehend?

"Let it be as it is," Mongwa said, quietly, gently. "Just know that it is here, where it will stay for eternity, a beacon and a passageway beyond a life of separation. It is not time for you to know any more than this."

A harsh wind had come up from the north, sweeping down through the canyon. But it wasn't the cool breeze over her skin that caused Tara to tremble. Strange, she thought, that here, bathed in the light of a truth much greater than my own existence, steeped in the macrocosm, it is affection for those nearest me that fills my heart. Her thoughts turned again to her young daughter and Viveka. Caught in a world so distant from theirs, Tara was filled with sadness. She missed them both, but mostly she missed Maya, ached to reach out and touch her, to take her into her arms and hug her, hold her. How would she ever escape from this space, this strange and unfamiliar world, and get back to the life she'd known before Drake's mysterious phone calls! How did one cross such distances? How did one even measure time or distance here?

Mongwa touched Tara on the shoulder and Tara turned tearfully to face her. For a long time Mongwa did not speak, her face hidden by her long, salt and pepper hair, blown helter skelter in the wind.

"You were brought here to witness the most basic of all forces in the universe," Mongwa said. "You can touch this place any time you wish, and you can know this power through what you call love, not the sentiment of love, not the love you have for yourself, for others or for your worldly possessions, but the love you know when you empty your mind and stand in the presence of death...at the outer boundaries of the circle."

Tara let out a gasp. Death felt all too close in this place, the horror of it hovering so near she could nearly smell it. She remembered her mother's death--the deep loss, the grief, the stark finality of separation that filled her with such sadness. What could Mongwa possibly mean by the love you feel when you empty your mind and stand in the presence of death!

"...because it is here we encounter the edge between the illusion of the physical world and the invisible reality that is the source of all that you now know and all that you will ever know. Those from other galaxies may know what I describe in the rush of infinite wisdom that comes when thoughts of your collective minds merge, focusing on the One."

"Wait," Tara interrupted. "What are these other galaxies?"

"Those who visit in your dreams. Those who you find in the Katchinas, in the dances...those you call extraterrestrial. They have been your guides since you were born, but you have denied them, pushed them away."

Tara knew the Indian legends, of course, of how the Katchinas were evolved souls from Earth, now living in far distant galaxies not even known to our astronomers. She knew that the Katchinas traveled through the universe from time to time to instruct others still bound to this world. But those beings were religious artifacts, not actual entities with minds and physical presences of their own, ethereal or not! It was difficult to think of them as real, as part of the modern world.

"All these populate the invisible world," Mongwa explained. "All that you have seen here is of this world. Those, like you, children of importance, come to know this world of formlessness as others know the world of the five senses. It is through this knowledge that your power comes. Those who know the invisible world have nothing to fear of the visible one. You have a mission, to live in the light of the invisible and to bring it into its fullest manifestation. When you can do this, you have nothing to fear of the other, the physical world. Most do not see the invisible, and not knowing it they live in a shriveled reality, bound by their own fantasies, their own distortions of what is and what is not."

"But I don't..."

"Shh!" Mongwa placed her finger to her lips. She pointed across the meadow. Down the same trail that Tara had traveled with James Dean there came several shadowy figures. Tara counted seven. They walked in single file along the narrow trail, each of them covered by a gray cloak.

Tara turned back to Mongwa. "Who are they?"

"Our friends from other galaxies, places you will never visit in this lifetime. They come as teachers to remind us of how poorly our own thoughts can guide us if we do not listen and heed the warnings of higher truths."

The group came down the canyon trail and across to the great rock formation that marked the center of the meadow, where they sat down on the ground to wait.

"Let yourself be with them," Mongwa said.

Closing her eyes, Tara imagined herself in their presence. She felt herself sink back into the openness and peace she'd experienced within Mongwa's consciousness. And as she did, she felt strong emotions coming from the Katchinas.

They spoke all at once. It was very odd...a cacophony of voices. She could not hear what any one of them was saying. Then slowly, like a radio being fine-tuned, the cacophony became a single voice. This voice was not carried by vibrations to her ear but was transmitted directly to her brain, waves more subtle than sound stimulating her visual and verbal centers.

In her mind's eye Tara saw a single figure standing in front of her. It was a grayish creature with huge, gold-colored eyes that shimmered like sunlight on a placid, crystal-clear pond. These were not ordinary eyes, not like any she'd ever seen. There were no pupils at all, only a fluid quietude that gave little sign of recognition. The being had a tiny mouth, much like the sucking mouth of certain bottom-feeding fish, and its face seemed as if cast in plastic, with none of the muscles of expression that humans possess. Yet, the creature radiated a grace and affability that immediately put Tara at ease.

We have known each other since the day of your birth, the creature communicated to her. *I've waited for the time when you could join us in this way.*

"I don't understand," Tara complained. "I've never seen you before. What do you want of me?"

Even as she stared into the face of the gray creature, it changed before her eyes. Suddenly she saw the face of her father as a young man. Her heart leapt at the specter of young Drake Fairfield, triggering old memories that Tara thought she'd buried long ago. For a fleeting moment she was an infant again, gazing with awe into the loving, amazed eyes of a young father. But even as she stared into these eyes, the face changed, becoming the young man who'd escorted her from the cave. Now it was James Dean who smiled at her, and she calmed down, sliding into teenage fantasies that had once brought her so much comfort. But even this comfort slipped from her as James Dean's face faded and transmuted back into the face of the gray. Whoever or whatever this being was, he had the ability to change forms, to switch his image at will.

"The Katchinas offer you their wisdom," the creature said. "For centuries we have been guides. You need to know, there are many half-truths told about us. You are now seeing the truth. We are from a world where form and substance are mere illusions. We can take any form and we do this to move beyond your fears. But how do we reach those who have cut themselves off from the invisible reality of their lives? With certain ancient peoples who have kept the portals open we are angels, Katchinas, mythic beings, power animals. But in your world we are..."

"ETs," Tara said aloud, thinking, movie magic, creations of Hollywood, television characters...

The gray creature laughed, finding great humor in Tara's thoughts. "James Dean! You see? Your mythology is lost. You have shriveled your world, trying to fill your souls with wishes and fears attached only to your physical bodies. Your deep longing can never be appeased in this way.

"You are a child of importance," the gray said. "Your life's journey takes you into the fifth world. We have at times helped you keep your focus so that you would not be tempted to slip back, to step back into the filaments of the third and fourth worlds. Now that you are aware of us you can call upon us any time you have doubts about where you stand within the web, whether in the third, fourth or fifth worlds. Sometimes it will not be easy to see where you stand in the web. But we are your guides. Call upon us when you have doubts.

"The worlds are changing. Those of the third world must go their way, following the filaments of deceit, domination, struggles for control over others. Those of the fourth world must go their way, as well, following the filaments of confusion, seeking answers in the world of material, though touching into the truths of the fifth world."

"And my father?"

"He will find his way as he must, wandering back and forth along the filaments he understands."

"But those are the filaments of the third and fourth worlds," Tara said. "If that's true, he will never..." She stopped. Suddenly she realized the truth of what Mongwa had been trying to teach her, that her father could not or would not ever meet Tara on her own ground. He perhaps wandered into the fifth world from time to time. But it was not a world he knew or trusted. Not only Mongwa but Chocko had been right, then. Tara had to let go of her illusions, relinquish hopes she'd harbored since she was a very small child.

"Is he dead?" she asked.

The gray creature smiled. "No. He will come and go from your life for many years. That is his way. Let it be as it is."

Tara shifted restlessly on the ledge beside Mongwa. She opened her eyes, letting her attention focus once again on the older woman who was her teacher.

"Are you a Katchina?" Tara asked Mongwa.

For a moment, it seemed, she saw James Dean standing there with them. He and Mongwa exchanged thoughts Tara did not understand, but she had the distinct feeling they were amused by her question.

"Mongwa is a shaman," James Dean said. "She is what they call a Shapeshifter, able to play with the illusions of what you know as the physical world. And in this play you find the truth, that your world is not at all as you have imagined it to be. For hundreds of years now you have reversed the truth. In the third and fourth worlds you have learned how you project your hopes and fears to others around you, that you make the world into your own image and likeness, just as you make movies of James Dean and ET and all the rest. Your great cities, your arts, your religions, your science...all that you have created has come from that place within you that lives in terror of your separation. You misuse what you call your imagination. You defile what you label creativity. In the fifth world you discover that you are not the makers, that you are projections of the nameless..."

"No more can be said," Mongwa interrupted. "You and others come into self-power now, into the spirit circle. Life initiates you.

Out of the storm of your search comes an answer that you didn't expect. But it is not the answer you sought because you could not have known it was here. Had you known, the journey would not have been required. You would not have felt the need to pursue the quest that brought you here.

"Wherever you stand you must make choices between staying in the fifth world, moving deeper into it, or moving back. You make your life, as all of us do, in the web of Spider Woman. Remember that. The pictures of the filaments that you presently hold in your mind will guide you. Like the web of a spider, the filaments upon which you travel can be broken. Like the web of a spider our cosmic web is constantly being damaged, repaired and expanded. The filaments of the fifth world are still new but they are strong and can be trusted. Their strength will support all the rest. Carry that trust with you, and do not forget where you stand within the web."

"Expand your vision beyond your Earthly home," James Dean interjected. "You are not alone in this universe. The filaments that join us all extend far beyond anything your scientists yet know of the cosmos. Don't deny the existence of realities beyond your solar system. We have come from such a place. We have been living among you for thousands of years. We will continue to guide you as long as you welcome us in."

With heart pounding, Tara stared at the young man before her, knowing his true identity now, beyond his James Dean visage, or his appearance in her imagination as an extraterrestrial, or as her father when he was young. She reached out her hand, wanting to touch him but knowing that such contact was probably impossible. Yet, for just an instant their fingers touched and the moment of their touching was electric. When they drew away, Tara felt a profound sadness but also profound love. She did not want to be separated this way. Tears welled up in her eyes, expressing what she felt in her heart, that something quite magical had happened here, something she could not understand.

"You will find me in others," the young man said. "These feelings we have experienced together exist in many forms. With your eyes now opened you will find all that you know and all that you truly seek. Make space for it. Let it be as it is."

"Let it be as it is," Tara echoed, smiling. Even as she said these words she knew that her life was changed forever. She could never go back to her old way of thinking. The shift in perception seemed so small, yet so great and far-reaching.

In the next few seconds the image of James Dean faded from Tara's mind. As it did, Mongwa reached toward the thick collar of her shirt, drew back the fabric and curled her fingers around a string suspended from her neck. Mongwa bowed her head slightly as she removed the object, revealing a worn, silver medallion dangling from a thin rawhide cord. She held the medallion in the palm of her hand for Tara to see. It was round and flat like a coin but on its face the artisan had fashioned a medicine wheel. The outer perimeter of the wheel was represented by the placement of sixteen irregular-shaped circles, like the rocks that were laid on the ground at the circles Tara had attended with Mongwa and Tony Fox. Each of the four coordinates--North, South, East and West--were marked by double rocks. At the center of the larger circle was a second circle of five rocks.

"This is the wheel of the fifth world," Mongwa explained, pointing to the center of the medallion." She turned the object over in her palm. On the opposite side was a magnificent impression of an owl in flight. Mongwa continued her explanation: "By this talisman you will make yourself known to others on the path of the fifth world. And they will be known to you by the talismans they wear. You will also be known by the way you greet one another: Let it be as it is."

Mongwa held out the cord of the talisman and Tara bowed her head to receive it.

"I can't take it," Tara said.

For a long moment Mongwa stared at her, waiting, watching for any change of expression that might indicate a shift of thought. But it was not to be. The old woman reached out and took Tara's left hand, clenched tightly into a fist. Mongwa's touch relaxed Tara's fingers and when she opened her hand Mongwa pressed the medallion into her palm, then closed her fingers back around it.

"There will come a time," Mongwa said.

The two women hugged, sealing the bond between them forever. Then Tara took the silver medallion in her fingers and felt its surface, worn smooth from the many years it had been in Mongwa's possession. The talisman felt warm, in her hand, still holding the energy of the old woman's body. Reflexively, Tara pressed the talisman to her lips and kissed it as Mongwa watched, smiling.

Now Mongwa pointed toward the sky. The great bird, the owl, appeared, as if to guide in the silvery object that had been hovering overhead. The object descended into the canyon, an irregularly-shaped globe spinning at a high rate of speed, glowing brighter and brighter the closer it came to the ground. Then, without warning, a profound silence fell over the canyon. A dark, bluish glow filled the landscape, swallowing up everything else. In Tara's mind, all color, all sound, all sense of being ended, and was consumed by this event. Then, just as suddenly as it began, this veil of nothingness lifted.

When she looked out onto the meadow again, she saw only a normal landscape. A bird circled, perhaps hunting for small animals hiding in the lush grasses below. The sun was setting over the top of the western ridge. And the great rock protruding from the center of the canyon floor now seemed a simple marker, nothing more.

Mongwa nodded and gestured for Tara to follow her. They descended from the ledge, Mongwa navigating the narrow ladders and the precarious steps carved into the rock with ease. The older woman's agility gave Tara courage as she followed her mentor down to a path around the edge of the meadow. They continued along the path to the eastern edge of the desert, where Mongwa invited Tara to sit down with her. Mongwa pointed toward the east, and suddenly they were just two women of the world enjoying the beauty of the Southwestern landscape together. The desert spread out before them, a great ocean of space that filled Tara with delight and awe.

"I can go back now, can't I," Tara said. She felt exhausted, drained. But it was clear to her that this was the end, a completion and also a beginning. "I have more questions than I know how to ask."

Mongwa nodded. "That's why I'm here. New questions will come up for you as you move through your journey. You cannot anticipate them all from where you now stand. But I know the way. Turn to me. I will always be available to counsel you, if you are willing to go deep within yourself and listen."

"Mostly, I'm afraid."

"Yes, of course. Trust your fear. But don't let it stop you."

The first thing that came to Tara's mind was that she could never tell her father what had happened to her, least of all him. For him it would be nothing more than another adventure, a spectacle to be exploited for its story, put into the same category as an interview with a mass murderer or the saga of a two-headed space baby. Tara smiled, amused by this observation, revealing so much about how she would conduct her friendship with her father--how she would love him--from this day forward.

"I want you to know something about White Crow," Mongwa said. "He is alive and well. He moves in your world, coming and going in many forms. His journey weaves through the filaments of the third and fourth worlds. You will encounter him again but no longer fear him. The filaments of your worlds intersect but he can never control your consciousness so long as you hold to what you have learned here."

A dog barked in the distance and Mongwa grinned, as if she knew some great joke.

"Why are you smiling?" Tara asked.

"Ask your friend Chocko," the old woman said.

* * *

"...and every time in history when humans believed they understood and believed they knew how to make life better, they made it
worse. Only humility will correct these errors."

"What?" Tara asked.

"Weren't you listening?" Chocko shook his head, staring down at
the earth and the cold ashes in their makeshift smudge pot.

"I'm sorry," Tara said. "Where are the others? Where is
Mongwa?"

"You remember then?"

"Of course I remember!" She looked around. Behind Chocko's
back was the ruined wall and the single window, framing a dark,
brooding sky. They were sitting, once again, on the deserted mesa
where it all began, where she had found the passage of light into the
reality beyond the ruined wall.

"You told me I had to find the openings, the little shafts of light
to go through," Tara said.

Chocko shrugged. "A little magic never hurts." He paused. "Can
you keep a secret?"

Tara stared at him suspiciously. "Meaning?"

"Watch." Chocko stood up, turned around and put two fingers
to his lips. Blowing across his teeth, he produced a long, harsh,
ear-splitting whistle.

A rasping bark sounded in the distance, and as Tara stared into
the window in the ruins she once again saw the tiny crescents of
pure, white light far in the distance. Light radiated out from these
crescents, reaching far into the universe, surrounding and embracing
the worlds on both sides of the window, the light they radiated
turning into brilliant bands of color--reds, blues, greens, deep
purples, yellows, turquoise, earthen tans and sanguine tones, endless
colors--fragile strands of the legendary spider web projected
throughout space and time.

As Tara stared at the window, Melvin the dog came sailing
through, looking for a moment like a fly caught in a spider web, ears
plastered back against his skull, eyes squinting as he broke through
the veil between the two worlds. When he hit the ground Melvin
tumbled head over heels. Then he yelped and howled, recklessly
racing up to Chocko, barely able to keep his feet under him, then
kneeling down, cowering, excited but using all his dog-will to not
jump up.

Chocko knelt down, grabbed the back of the dog's neck and
scratched his head roughly. As if released from its obligation to its
master, Melvin leapt up on Tara, knocking her down, and proceeded

to lick her face in great slobbering ecstasy. Chocko grabbed the nape of the animal's neck and dragged him off.

Laughing, Tara got to her feet, brushed herself off and turned away from the window. Melvin the dog raced in bumbling circles around her and Chocko, yelping, celebrating their reunion. Suddenly, a sobering thought crossed Tara's mind and she turned back to Chocko, her face drawn in anguish. Something she'd hoped would be there, below them, was gone.

"The dig," she said, her voice hoarse, a mere whisper.

Chocko shook his head, then pointed toward the sky. "It's time to go back. A storm is coming in."

Tara stared down at her closed left hand. She opened it slowly. There in the center of her palm lay the silver medallion Mongwa had given her. Slowly, carefully, she lifted the leather cord and placed it gently around her neck. When she looked up again Chocko was watching her, smiling. He knew. ~

Epilogue: Shaman's Vision
(The author's reflections)

I have always been intrigued by the role of the storyteller in ancient societies. In times long past, reason was not the dominant
mode of operating in the world. More important was the mode
known as "dreamtime." Shamans and spiritual leaders understood the
relationship between the invisible world of our dreams and our
physical activities in the world of the senses. They knew that
disharmonies and conflicts born in this invisible world carried over
into our physical reality. They also knew that we could not find
peace or strength or power in the physical world without
acknowledging our dependence on *that which cannot be seen.* Issues
were resolved, strength and peace were found not through linear
thinking, that keeps us isolated in the physical realm, but through
dreaming, through speaking with guides or dream entities from the
unseen.

The novel comes from a long shamanic tradition wherein the
shaman-storyteller himself is transformed, no longer storyteller but a
character, an animal, a god, a goddess, or a natural force that is not
his everyday identity. And these moments, when the characters
come alive and the author disappears, take us into another world.
They allow us to tap into what C.G. Jung once called the "collective
consciousness."

Shamans take us deep into the mysterious realm that lies beyond
the five senses so that we can step outside the highly individualized
concerns of our everyday lives. We can discover truths that exist
outside time, outside the finite boundaries of our singular lives. Here
we encounter *universal wisdom,* which one of my teachers defined
as, "that which applies to all equally." Bathed in universal wisdom, if
only for brief periods, we often see beyond our own conflicts and
passions. As important as our preoccupations with our personal lives
may be, the power of universal wisdom emboldens us to transcend
self involvement.

Seen in the light of these considerations, Tara's adventures in *Spirit Circle* become not so much a search for her father as a manifestation of the ancient dance between faith in the rational mind and the tug of those powers of the unseen world that lie beyond it. In this dance, the players in the story become entities who populate our inner world. Some are very dark, such as the figure who calls himself White Crow (Jose Haera), who ritually murders Mongwa. Some are comic, such as Tony Fox, the cheroot-smoking shaman who is part wise man, part fool. But each and every one of the characters has her or his special part to play in our quest for a larger truth, a journey that perhaps can take us beyond both the rational and the intuitive.

In my writing of this story, Tara at first seemed to be little more than a foil for her father's foolhardy pursuit of another reality. But she fooled me. Very early on she encountered the invisible world. In her hotel room, just after arriving in Albuquerque, she had a vision of James Dean. Slowly, this screen idol, who had been a childhood fantasy for her, eased his way back into her adult life. As an anthropologist Tara was stubbornly dedicated to *scientific* thinking, yet now she allowed herself this luxury of the imagination. Like so many of us, she had adopted a popular media hero to fill a hole in her life. James Dean embodied a special kind of longing she had for her father--or for maleness within herself. It is a longing that says, "I want you in my life but I can do it all alone. I don't need anyone." Though James Dean might have started out as a celluloid fantasy, he came alive within the field of her consciousness and ultimately led her through the veil that separates the world of the five senses from the invisible world that lies beyond.

When I started this book I had no idea that James Dean would become so important. In fact, I had not planned on his appearance in the book at all. Several times I wrote him out of the manuscript, but he kept coming back, manifesting out of Tara's consciousness again and again. I literally could not keep him out of the story and, like Tara, I ultimately surrendered to his presence.

In the cave scene, where Tara first ventures across the boundary between the two worlds, I actually stopped writing the story, went into a deep meditation, and asked James Dean what he was doing in my story. I wanted him out. Why did he keep reappearing? Like a spirit who comes into the shaman's dreams, this character told me that I did not understand him, that I needed to be patient and let him be. He was a guide from "the other side," he claimed, meaning from the world beyond the senses. He said that guides like him often use our adolescent fantasies, characters and situations gleaned from the popular culture to get us to listen to them. That is the role he was playing with Tara. He was her teacher, her spirit guide, speaking with the *mask* of James Dean. This was the only way she would let herself sneak a look into the world beyond the senses. And so, I decided to stop fighting him. James Dean could stay in the story.

I learn from my characters because they seem to reach into a world which I, being of corporeal existence, cannot. They serve as mediators between the world I'm most familiar with and the less familiar world of dreamtime. But within the shamanic tradition, fictional characters become ways of focusing our attention. As they become more and more real, they open our eyes to concepts that we might otherwise overlook. The shaman's stories remind us to look and listen through the eyes and ears of other people--or characters. That's how the story functions in *Spirit Circle* as well.

When I focus my attention on Tara, for example, by simply sitting quietly and thinking about her with an open mind, I become increasingly aware of my own resistance to the *invisible reality*. That is, after all, a central part of her character. Tara pushed away the truth about both her father and Tom, through her own need to make them something they were not. And I think about how, as she let herself see who they really were, her resistance dissipated and the invisible reality opened up to her. In the process of my reliving her story, a little window of insight opens up to me as well; I catch a brief glimpse of my own resistance to what lies beyond the physical world, and to Tara's eventual breakthrough that came as a result of her willingness to entertain that possibility. Through this insight I see a different sort of reality that impacts me at least as much as does the physical world. It's the reality of dream, emotion and the universal truths that live from generation to generation, over the millennia, as steadfast and eternal as the wind. I can't touch this other world with my five senses--thus the term "invisible reality"--and so it constantly eludes me. I need the shamanic story to remind me that so much of what's important to us is invisible. Love, fear, self-esteem, our sense of awe with the life force, the emotional bonds we experience with our families--all these are invisible but essential to who we are.

Like Tara, I confess that I prefer the safety of the rational, that which can be boxed in and studied under a microscope, as it were. The mystery of life itself, the mystery of love, of the purpose of the cycles of life, death and rebirth...these and more, challenge me. But when I think about Tara and allow myself to again experience her story, an interesting thing begins to happen. She magically draws to me lessons I need in my life in order to move beyond my own limiting perceptions.

It is not, of course, only fictional characters who open our eyes to realities we could not previously see on our own. We might hear a friend tell a story about an emotional insight or spiritual breakthrough they had and we then become aware of possibilities we hadn't been aware of before. Or we hear a lecture or read a book that expands how we think about the world or how we experience it. Or maybe we buy a new car with a special paint job and suddenly become aware of every other car on the road with the same color.

One of the great lessons of the medicine wheel, which is the structure upon which the book is based, is that it takes a collective of people to see the larger truth. Standing alone, there is no single one of us who has that capacity. Each of us has one narrow slice of the truth. Sitting together we share one another's perspectives and create a larger picture than any single one of us would otherwise ever see.

Each character in *Spirit Circle* offers perceptions that actually go beyond my own. They inspire me to look through new windows: Chocko becomes the gateway between the rational and mystical worlds, between the ancient and the modern. Tony Fox becomes the wise man, part fool, who dabbles constantly with practices that he only partially understands. Drake is like that piece of our everyday lives that the Buddhists call "Monkey Mind," constantly pulling us this way and that through the excitement of current trends, our own self-distractions, and sensational events. The old woman, Death's sister, who dances endlessly around her cane, is a constant reminder that we must all come to terms with the finite nature of our existence, with aging and death. And Mongwa evokes thoughts of that power greater than ourselves that we cannot possibly know or understand as long as we limit ourselves to the rational. It is through Mongwa that we dare to--as she herself says--"Let it be as it is." Recognize the mystery, then let it be. Let myself dance with the mystery rather than struggling to *solve* it. It takes courage to do that. We somehow feel more secure when we can tie up the unknown in a neat little bundle. Mongwa reminds us of the vanity in that.

We all have these inner beings who send us messages--doubt and fear, but also encouragement, goodness and strength. Maybe we still carry around memories of a special person who was supportive and loving when we were children. We think about them fondly when we need a mental boost. We recall how we felt when in their presence, and they come alive in our minds. We carry on imaginary conversations with them, and we recreate the self-trust they once inspired through their belief in us.

Most of us also carry around in our minds characters that we've drawn from the popular culture or from books, plays or movies we've seen. Or we have a favorite hero from history who inspires us. When

James Dean's movie, *Rebel Without a Cause* came out, hundreds of thousands of teenagers copied his style. They wore their hair like him, bought leather jackets like his, and affected many of his mannerisms. If you talked with those people today they might still have pictures of James Dean in their minds. Some might even admit that, like Tara, they think about him when they feel alone, or when they are confronted with issues around authority figures--since this was the key to his character in that movie.

Many teenagers growing up with the James Dean mythology learned to see through their hero's eyes. By getting inside his mind, which the movie allowed them to do, a new perspective was offered them. He gave them a different way of dealing with the conflicts his generation had with authority figures. His heroics in *Rebel* supported them in the belief that their own judgment had value and that sometimes the wisest thing to do was to challenge authority. Furthermore, through identifying with the James Dean character they were able to see that they could--and must--create a more caring and compassionate world. If Dean's character was the epitome of the lonely rebel, he also embodied a caring sensitivity that young people were hungry to experience. He taught not by preaching but by our experiencing and assimilating what it was like to be him, to see with his eyes, hear with his ears, think with his mind and feel with his heart.

I am reminded of a story a friend told me about the writer Napoleon Hill. Hill had his own version of the medicine wheel, a circle of historical figures who he assembled in his mind. Each night before going to sleep he brought these historical heroes into consciousness. He imagined them all together with him at a conference table. Since he had read a great deal about them in books they came alive as individuals in his mind. He was able to ask them questions and fantasize how they might answer. And answer they did, providing him with much of the information he published in his now-famous book, *Think and Grow Rich.*

In a very real way, *Spirit Circle* offers us characters and situations that open our minds to a new way of looking at the world, just as Napoleon Hill's historic figures did for him, or as James Dean did for the generation that grew up with *Rebel.* There are characters in *Spirit Circle* with whom we can identify, characters whose experiences offer a perspective we might otherwise never have known. The book itself is like a medicine wheel that offers us a new way of looking at the world. *Spirit Circle* is like the story told by the shaman as we sit with her or him at the circle. It is a teaching story, if you will, that allows us to actually experience the invisible reality. Its magic is the magic of the human consciousness itself, our ability

to create new visions of what our lives can be.

Taking my lead from *Spirit Circle,* I now sit with Tara and the others at my own medicine wheel. The model I use appears in chapter sixteen, when Tara joins Chocko and Tony Fox at the medicine wheel ceremony behind Chocko's house. I imagine myself standing at a distance, watching as Tony Fox chews on his cheroot and traces a circle about eight feet in diameter in the dry earth. He lays out a series of stones, about the size of baseballs, around the outside of his circle so that I see it quite clearly. Then he marks the four cardinal directions, North, South, East and West, with extra rocks.

Now the shaman invites me to sit at the edge of the circle, pointing to a place for me to sit. He explains to me why he is seating me where he does. "You need to be more introspective," he says, seating me in the west. Or, "You need to focus on a new beginning," he says, seating me to the east. As often as not, Tony himself sits in the northern quadrant, telling me that is the direction of knowledge and wisdom. He points out, however, that he is facing the south, the place of basic human drives, the direction of the raw life force, the ego and the survival instincts, which he says contain much power.

At the medicine wheel I might bring in my own group of friends, imaginary or not. I sometimes imagine my best friends at the circle, or my parents, a favorite teacher or a hero from literature or the movies. I select them as I might select dinner guests or a meeting of the minds to help me with a problem in my everyday life.

To begin, I might have one of the characters state the purpose for the meeting, or I state that purpose myself. If I am having trouble with a book I am writing, I might state that my purpose is to get some new insights about why the book isn't working as I wished and what I might do to correct the problem. Then I might offer a dedication or a prayer. A Cherokee prayer I like goes something like this:

> *Help me to speak my truth quietly,*
> *To listen with an open mind when others speak,*
> *And to remember the peace that comes with silence.*

Having offered these preambles I might then imagine Tony conducting one or more rituals. For example, he might burn some sage and even walk around the circle with his smudge bowl of smoldering sage, purifying the space. I like this part of the medicine wheel ritual. Sometimes, to make it more real in my mind, I actually burn sage in my room at home. I keep either bundles of sage or incense in stock for just this purpose.

At last I imagine Tony beginning to drum. Usually, he drums with a slow, steady, almost monotonous beat, about the same speed as my heartbeat. There are times when I augment my imagination with an audio tape of Native American or Celtic drumming, such tapes being readily available at good bookstores, particularly those that specialize in metaphysical books and supplies.

Once the stage is set I might even forget that Tony Fox is there. Instead, I imagine myself describing a problem or challenge I am facing. I imagine my associates at the medicine wheel listening to me intently. And then I ask each one of them for *feedback*. What would they do in a situation like mine? What advice do they have to offer? What thoughts or feelings come from their unique perspective?

It takes time to make the wheel "turn," that is, to imagine all the characters taking turns talking to me. But with practice it does happen. What's most important is to be patient, stilling the mind so that there is mental space and a new receptiveness, allowing information from my characters to come in.

Spirit Circle characters can be extremely important in this process. You have, after all, entered their minds in the process of sharing their adventures with them. I bring whoever I wish to my medicine wheel, and sometimes there are one or two more who come in uninvited. Any ritual you imagine or perform creates a kind of bridge, a separation between everyday reality and this special inner world experience that is unfolding.

As the circle becomes more and more real in your mind, ask questions. You might ask about something puzzling or troubling you. Soon, to your surprise and delight, those at the wheel will begin to *speak* to you. You won't necessarily hear a voice. As often as not you'll just get a feeling, the kind of feeling you sometimes have staring at an old photograph of people you may have known. At other times, however, your experience will be like a dream in which people speak and interact with you in convincing ways. The only difference is that in the more conscious state you are able to make more deliberate and intentional choices than you seem able to do in sleeping dreams.

Address important issues in your everyday life and ask your companions at the imaginary medicine wheel for each of their perspectives. What issues do they see in what you're struggling with? What experience have they had in that area? What new insights will they offer? They teach and you listen; in time, you'll get beyond your own resistance and doubt and truly take in what your partners at the medicine wheel have to say. The reward will be new information, a deeper understanding, a greater sense of peace, or a greater sense of self-acceptance and love.

Beyond the Known and Predictable

Even as I was writing *Spirit Circle* it became my medicine wheel, taking me beyond what I consciously know. I remember how Mongwa emerged from the shadows in the kiva. I had not imagined her before the moment she appeared and I do not know why she came into my consciousness. Her appearance was a surprise. I had not expected the old woman, Death's little sister, to appear, either, and certainly hadn't expected her to dance and speak. And I had not expected to find White Crow there. After all, I reasoned, White Crow belonged in that *other reality,* the physical reality Tara had left behind in order to be in this different world of the shaman. When he attacked Mongwa I thought I'd completely lost control of the scene. His act did not appear in my carefully considered story outlines. As I write these words I am reminded of something C.G. Jung, the famous psychologist, said in his book *Memories, Dreams, Reflections:* "There are things in the psyche which I do not produce, but which produce themselves and have their own life."

Now, as I sit at the medicine wheel which is *Spirit Circle,* I realize that our culture has lost touch with the deeper purpose of storytelling, when the shaman's tales carried us into worlds beyond our own life experiences, thus broadening our own self-centered perspectives. Through shamanic storytelling around the medicine wheel we create bridges between our individual consciousnesses, dissolving the illusions of separation that we ourselves have created. Through storytelling we can perhaps touch those truths that allow us to move beyond the reality of our five senses. It is only here, beyond the veil of the physical world, that we encounter the mystery and learn how to dance with it. Basking in the mystery, we discover that love, not carbon, is the most universal of elements, the vital ingredient that animates all that we know and all that we seek to know.

My hope would be that readers might begin exploring in their own lives the same techniques and principles that Tara discovered. We all engage in what the human consciousness experts call "self-talk;" we chastise ourselves for making mistakes ("That was stupid of me! I know better than that,") or we congratulate ourselves for an achievement ("Great! I finally got it,") or we express relief following an escape from danger ("Whew, that was a close call!") And, of course, there are those times when we think of all the things we should have said but didn't, ("Joe, may I remind you that you are the one who insisted we do it this way!")

The practice of imagining and talking to characters we've created in our minds is perhaps as old as language itself. Ancient parts of our brains come alive by imagining a medicine wheel and populating it with imaginary beings. While most of us are familiar with negative self-talk, such as we do when we've just done something stupid, the medicine wheel creates positive self-talk. It is a more deliberate and constructive use of self-talk, and mental visualization. It is a way of tapping into information that we perhaps did not even know we had. Sometimes this is simply information we knew but forgot. At other times it seems to be information that comes from a source outside our life experiences, a source far greater than ourselves.

Spirit Circle lives on in my consciousness. The characters reach out to me, urging me to pay attention, to pursue the mysteries of life more deeply. I would hope that they might do the same for readers because I am convinced that through the ancient tools introduced here we can improve the quality of our lives, of *all life* everywhere, since we are truly One. Perhaps even more important, it is through these powerful spiritual tools that we can restore our relationship with the spiritual realm that we have all but lost in the busy-ness of the modern world. ~

The Lessons of Spirit Circle

1. Millions of *children of importance* are now here and are continuing to be born. They are evolving into the fifth world, where a worldview of a common spiritual bond with all of life is replacing the third and fourth worldviews based on physical identity, separation and alienation.

2. The teachings of the fifth world are Earth-centered, affirming a relationship to our planet, and to each other, of love and co-operation rather than exploitation and domination.

3. It is important for those moving into the fifth world to recognize their responsibility as guides, and not become enmeshed with those of the third and fourth worlds, whose evolutionary task it has been to explore the meaning of life in our present physical form.

4. Children of importance are finding new sources of wisdom, along with tools, to help develop the view of the fifth world and usher in this next level of consciousness. They are drawing from many different sources, ranging from the traditional teachings of ancient intuitive-based cultures to spirit-helpers from other realities.

5. At times children of importance will meet with great resistance, both from within themselves and from the outside world, since the fifth world teachings are very different from those of the third and fourth worlds. The fifth world reality will become increasingly known and trusted as first-hand experience dissolves doubt.

6. Central to the fifth world teachings is the unfolding recognition of love as the universal chemistry, seamlessly binding all to all.

7. As we let go of our need to dominate and control, we will discover in ourselves senses beyond the normal five which will allow us to experience other worlds and other realities, previously unimaginable, which have existed alongside and within our own world since long before life began.

8. With the emergence of the fifth world entirely new human perceptions will unfold, allowing us to stay connected with the Spiritual Source out of which we all have come, no longer masking love, fearing death, or allowing ourselves to be alienated from other living beings for any reason. ~

The Bonds Between Children of Importance

When meeting, children of importance acknowledge each other with a simple thought held in the mind: "Let it be as it is." Whether spoken aloud or experienced at a deep intuitive level, this thought acknowledges a specific way of looking at the world, with heartfelt dedication to certain values:

1. A deep sense of connection with a power and a community larger than themselves, with longing, sadness and feelings of dissatisfaction and emptiness when this connection is missing.

2. A strong belief that nature is sacred, with a drive to help create an environment that is balanced, harmonious and sustainable.

3. A desire for simplicity, rejecting material objects and technologies that don't serve to actually improve the quality of the inner life.

4. A strong focus on situations that are nurturing and supportive, embracing the values of altruism, equality, nourishing relationships and making a contribution to a cause larger than themselves.

5. An intuitive understanding of the links between creativity, self-discovery, self-actualization and action that helps to create a better world.

6. An interest in the spiritual mysteries, belief in a higher power and a hunger for involvement with mental and spiritual disciplines and activities such as meditation, dedication to a spiritual belief system, and an evolving self-awareness. ~

 Spirit Circle

The Medicine Wheel

Respecting Tradition and
Your Own Life Experience

Every ancient Earth-centered spiritual tradition the world over has some variation of the medicine wheel. Each one also has different explantions and teachings associated with the four cardinal directions and the regions above and below. In general, though, they all draw from their observations of nature and experiences with the world around them.

As you work with the medicine wheel you may develop your own meanings and explanations, perhaps integrating them with ancient teachings. You'll come to respect it as a valuable way of looking at your life and the world around you. So feel free to blend your own knowledge and life lessons with the Spirits of the Directions.

Your Place at The Wheel

Sit at the location where you feel most strongly drawn. Then address the spirits of that direction. Do this by meditating on the values described for that area (see "Spirits of the Six Directions, below) or ask for help as if an inner voice or feeling were there to inform you. Then wait for answers to come through.

For example, if you were working on family issues you might start by addressing the Spirits of the East, since that is the direction of family and community values in this medicine wheel. If you are going through a healing, either emotional or physical, you might want to address the Spirits of the South since it is here that we begin to get in touch with the life force itself, without which no healing can occur.

To sit in the southern quadrant can mean that you need the spiritual powers of that place or that you are offering your own healing powers to others sitting at the wheel or who are absent but requesting your help.

You may, of course, sit anywhere you wish at the wheel, each position having its own unique set of values, insights and powers. In addition to noting the meaning of where you sit, note that you can observe every other positioin on the wheel and always have access to all that is brought to the wheel.

When you are working with several other people at the wheel, you may not be able to choose exactly where you sit. Nevertheless, explore the meaning of the place you do take, aware of the posibility that you have been guided to this place by a force greater than your own mind and ego. Very often this *accidental* placement will turn out to be more beneficial than your original choice.

Spirits of the Six Directions

Upper Regions--From the Upper Regions, the Sky, the Sun, the Moon and the myriad of planets and stars, comes the Spirit of the Great Mystery, which we can neither name nor fully know but which is the Source of All and Everything.

North--From the North comes the Spirit of Ancient Wisdom, the universal knowledge, steeped in the human experience of love, compassion, pity, pride, and a vision of the common bond shared by all that lives and has its being in our world.

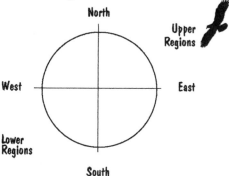

South--From the South comes the Spirit of the Life Force itself, the part within each of us tht holds all life precious and sacred, the part within us that seeks health and physical safety for ourselves, our loved ones and all that shares the planet.

East--From the East comes the Spirit of New Beginnings, the place of New Light, new ideas, new life, and renewed bonds of love. This is also the place of community values, of nurturing and teaching our young, of doing our best to make this world a better, more comfortable place to live.

West--From the West comes the Spirit of Endings and closure, the place where the Sun disappears at the end of the day. It is a reminder that change and renewal is constant. And it is the place of introspection, self-knowledge and inner reflection, where we discover how best to give back to the world.

Lower Regions--From the Lower Regions, under our feet, comes the Spirit of the Earth herself, the alchemy of this wondrous planet that nurtures and supports us all. From this spirit we learn the values of gratitude for all that is given to us through Nature.

About the Author

Born in Detroit in 1936, Hal grew up in rural Michigan, in Great Lakes country. In his teen years, he contracted a rare disease, tuloremia, or rabbit fever, and fell into a coma which lasted for several days. During this period of unconsiousness he felt himself separating from his body and becoming aware of a very different world--what spiritual teachers often refer to as the "invisible reality." This experience initiated him into an often challenging spiritual quest that has now spanned four and a half decades.

This book draws from a lifetime of experiences "shapeshifted into a spiritual odyssey," as one reviewer put it.

Hal is the author of more than 25 successful books. *Spirit Circle* is his second novel in three years. His bestselling book *Zuni Fetishes* was his first effort to bring ancient teachings of the Southwest into a modern context, while his book *Lens of Perception* passes along the wisdom of shamanic teachings about perception and projection that he has received over the past 25 years.

Other books he has authored include the bestselling *Well Body Book*, with Mike Samuels, MD, *Follow Your Bliss* as well as *Spirit Guides*, with Susan J. Sparrow, and finally *Write From the Heart*.

With his wife, Susan J. Sparrow, Hal teaches seminars on creativity and spiritual development, in California, New Mexico, the East Coast, and the Great Lakes area.

For information about Hal's workshops, other books, and lectures, please call:

1-800-738-6721

Special Patron Acknowledgements

We wish to thank our wonderful patrons who made the publication of a special limited first edition of this book possible. Your participation not only supports our efforts as independent author-publishers but also pays homage to an old, honored and important tradition in publishing.

Mari Anoran
Tom & Linda Baker
Mary J. Bates
Rosemarie Bell
Christy Bennett
Gabriel Patrick Duff Bennett
Paul & Marge Bennett
Maridel Bowes
Sandy Breckenridge
Dawn Callan
Caitlin "Kate" Chaom Hanach
Becky Coleman
Raymond Davi
Darlene Baker DeMille
Faith Doonan
Marty Eppler
Joseph Felser
Frances Fowler
Shakti Gawain
Ric Giardina
Patty & Michael Gold
Trudy Green, Ph.D.
Helen Hazlett
Toby Heathcotte
Mary L. Hill
Jane Hogan
Gail Lois Jaffe
Cindy Jarrett
Ellen June
Ellen Kaminsky
Philip & Nancy Kavanaugh
Joyce Kennedy
Dharma & Kirti Khalsa
Chuck Laurenson

Lynnaea Lumbard
Sarah Malone
Cydria Manette
Louise H. Mann
Peggy Mansfield
Dorothy May
Judith Mogilka
Maria Nemeth & Rita
Pat Olcott
Sally O'Neil
Adrienne L. Pearlman
Rich Pinto
Stan Politi
Joan Porter
Aminah Raheem
Metece Riccio
Gabrielle Roth
Pati Rouzer
Paul Sibcy
Susan St. Thomas
Linda Salazar
Barth Satuloff
Diana Sebek, Rn
Carole Shaver
Sid & Naomi Simon
Kelly Sorensen
Alice Spencer
Kalinda & James Stevenson
Kirk VandenBerghe
Bud Volberding
Danielle Williams
Randy Wolferding
Christine Word
Fortune Zuckerman

Special thanks to Don Gerrard of *The Bookworks*, one of the true geniuses of publishing, for his tireless support as editor and friend.